Tell Me

M JANE COLETTE

mischief

This novel is entirely a work of fiction.
The names, characters and incidents portrayed in it are the work
of the author's imagination. Any resemblance to actual persons,
living or dead, events or localities is entirely coincidental.

Mischief
An imprint of HarperCollins*Publishers*
1 London Bridge Street
London SE1 9GF

www.mischiefbooks.com

This paperback edition 2016
1

First published in Great Britain in ebook format

by HarperCollins*Publishers* 2015

A catalogue record for this book

is available from the British Library

ISBN-13: 978-0-00-816278-8

Find out more about HarperCollins and the environment at
www.harpercollins.co.uk/green

CAST OF CHARACTERS

Jane: protagonist-narrator. 38. Married. Four children. Works from home erratically as a financial analyst. Analytical, realistic, rational, almost detached . . . until she gets *that* text from Matt.

Matt: hero/anti-hero in one. 41. Married. Childless. A lover from Jane's past who re-enters her life and shakes its foundations.

Marie: Jane's best friend. 39. Married. Two children. As emotional and volatile in her expressions and search for passion and romance as Jane is controlled and restrained. Actively and constantly searching for affairs; failing to consummate any of them.

Alex: Jane's husband. 40. Lawyer. Workaholic. Good father. Affectionate but perhaps unexciting. Except to his young associate, whose texts he reads in the bathroom . . .

Lacey: Jane's next-door neighbour. 53. Gorgeous, sexy, confident and loving. The only person Jane comes close to confiding in. In a twelve-year-long, on-again-off-again relationship with Clint.

Clint: Lacey's lover and father of her ten-year-old son. Player. Engaged to Lacey, but still involved sexually with the mother of his other son, who becomes pregnant (by him? Or her other lover?) while Clint is wedding planning with Lacey.

Nicola: Marie and Jane's friend. 40. Two children. In the middle of an acrimonious divorce from Paul, her husband of twelve years. Angry, resentful. But also . . . hungry.

Jesse: Jane and Nicola's personal trainer. 26. Eye candy. Not very bright. Taken for granted by Jane. Coveted by Nicola.

Jane's mother and father: In their 60s, spry and attractive. The tensions in their 43-year-old relationship, a defining feature of Jane's childhood, reach a breaking point as Jane begins her mindfuck with Matt.

JP: Marie's husband. 45. Lawyer. Works with Alex. 'King of foreplay', but otherwise thoroughly unsatisfactory.

Paul: Nicola's husband. Referred to by Nicola and her friends as cheating rat-fuck bastard so often, Jane forgets what his name is . . . until he starts sexting with Marie.

Colleen: Nicola's best friend. Long divorced. Appears intermittently in role of 'Greek chorus' to offer unconditional support to Nicola and vent against all cheating spouses.

Melanie-Susan-Shelley: Alex's associate, whose name Jane refuses to remember. 28. Has a huge crush on Alex. Not sure how to deal with the fact he has a wife and children.

Craig: Married. 45. Attractive, restless. Minor character who enters Jane's life and is passed on to Marie.

Alex's mother, father and assorted stepmothers: Alex's mother was 'the first wife', and she's still not quite over the divorce. Neither is the second wife. The third wife wants to have a baby. His son desperately wishes he didn't have any of his genes.

Before

2001

Recovered from the exertions of your wedding night, lover? And the honeymoon?
—Fuck off.
Of course. Tell me next time you're in Montreal.
—I will.
Good.

2002

Jane, what the fuck happened? What did I do? Tell me.
—Nothing. It's not you. I have to be done.
Clarify.
—I can't do this. I can't be – his. Yours. And now the other. I can't. I have to be done.
I don't understand. But you know I won't chase. I'm gone.
—Go. I'll miss you. But please go.
Gone.

2002

Congratulations.

2004

Lover. Are you all right?
—I'm alive. Don't fucking call me that.

2008

More new baby pics have made it my way.
Congratulations, lover. You look happy.
—A) Don't call me that. B) I am. C) Still an evolutionary dead end?
Is that an indirect way of telling me to fuck off?
—Yes.
Gone. I am happy for you. Truly.

2010

Love the new look. Hot.
—Yup.
Knowing you're hot – also hot.
—Not for you.
Ouch.

2011

—Happy birthday and all that.
Thank you. Lover. How are you?
—Fine.
Will you come see me next time you're in Montreal?
—I have four children. I don't jet-set very much these days. Are you ever in YYC?
Rarely. But sometimes. Is that an invitation?

2012

I have a new client who will have me flying into YYC now and then. If that happens – will you see me?
—Maybe.

Maybe. That's how it begins.

Day 1 – Maybe

Fuck. I close my eyes. Turn this way, that. Open them. 5.01 a.m. Well. This is productive. I get up – give the alarm clock a resentful stare. Go downstairs. Ponder making coffee – making that first pot is a sign of surrender to the morning, an admission that I will not go back to bed.

I make the coffee. Sullenly at first, then with just the slightest tinge of happiness as the grinder whirrs the beans. I breathe in its scent. And I listen to the quiet of the house – everyone's still sleeping upstairs. I am awake and I am alone. I let go of the 'why did I get up so early when I didn't have to?' resentment and relish the feeling of being. Awake. Alone.

Eight minutes later, I'm on the couch, curled up with a cup of coffee and my laptop. Check email . . . Seven minutes later, when Alex comes down the stairs, I'm working.

'What are you doing up so early?' we say simultaneously. Laugh.

'One of my idiot partners in Toronto scheduled a conference call for eight a.m.,' Alex says, stretching. 'Eastern. I've got to be in the office in forty-five minutes. You?'

'Just couldn't sleep,' I say. 'As it turns out, some idiot in Toronto is having a panic attack and desperately needs me to review this business study. For nine a.m. Eastern. So you know – the insomnia was fortunate.'

He laughs. Kisses my forehead, grabs a cup of coffee, heads back up to shower. I read, think, type. I have three – less than

3

three, really – hours until the little people start making their way down the stairs and claiming my attention. Focused. Fast.

Alex is back down the stairs in twenty minutes. 'Bye, love,' he calls as he rounds past me to the front door.

'Bye, love you,' I call back, without a break in the typing. 'Going to be home in time for dinner tonight?'

'Unless some idiot in Toronto screws it up,' he says as he slips into his coat. 'Will text you.'

Of course.

By the time I've made my way through most of the second pot of coffee, the kids are coming down. Cassandra, my ten-year-old, first – shocked to see me up and awake before her. And then as appreciative of the silence around us as I am. She curls up on the couch beside me, with a bowl of cereal and a book.

The peace and silence end when the boys stampede down. Henry's seven. Eddie's six. Together, they sound like a platoon of baboons. Even at 7.15 in the morning. Cereal. *Avatar: The Last Airbender* on Netflix. Annie, the four-year-old, bum-slides down the stairs at 7.45, and my day's work is done – parenting begins as Annie starts her day by cuddling in my lap for half an hour.

You cannot be cuddled by a four-year-old and be as brutal as my clients need me to be. I hold her. Drink coffee. Check Facebook. New messages.

'What are our plans for the day?' Cassandra asks. 'This is a weird school day, right?'

'You've got that pioneer Christmas thing at the Farm, and then we're watching Marie's kids in the afternoon,' I tell her. She whoops in delight and races upstairs to get dressed. Annie follows her. I have to holler at the boys to do likewise.

The first message is from Marie.

We still on for this afternoon? I'll see you at the Farm, right?

4

The second.

*Maybe. Never was a word so full of potential. I'm glad
you wrote me back, I was worried there for a while.
For a decade.*

My lips curl into an involuntary smile. I won't write back.
Not yet. I'll just enjoy knowing he's in my inbox.

'Mom! Eddie's wearing my favourite shirt!'

'Am not!'

'Mom! I have no socks!'

I climb the stairs slowly, cooling coffee cup still in hand.
Mondays. Really, not that much different from Sundays.

'And you're of course welcome to participate if you like,' the
Laura Ingalls Wilder lookalike who checks us in at the Farm
tells me. 'Parents welcome!' I look at her in horror. The thought
of spending the morning churning butter, milking cows, making
candles, splitting wood or whatever it is the pioneers did to
prepare for Christmas is an experience I'm willing to forgo.
Happily. If the four-year-old lets me . . . but she's already gone,
holding on to her sister's hand. 'We get to make candles!' she
calls out to me over her shoulder. I give her a thumbs-up. The
boys have already found their friends. I beat a retreat to the
cafeteria.

Marie's already there, two coffee cups in hand.

'I got your mocha for you,' she says. 'An advance thank you
for this afternoon.' I accept. 'Thank God you're here too – I
was having an I'm-the-worst-mom-ever moment,' she continues.
'Look at all those women crowding around the gingerbread
table. For Christ's sake, don't they do enough of that at home?'

'Have you ever made gingerbread at home?' I ask Marie.

'No one likes gingerbread at my house, thank God,' she
says. 'I've made chocolate chip cookies. You've even eaten
them, bitch. Stop ragging me. Drink.'

That's Marie-speak for 'I need to talk'. I look at her and wait.

She makes an extravagant gesture with her hands, but before she says a word, she is interrupted. A chattering herd of women, mothers of our children's friends and classmates, enters the cafeteria. We're an incestuous community. They know us. We know them. Our kids go to the same alternative 'private' school. Too many of our husbands work together – for each other – against each other. For all its urban pretensions, this is a painfully small town. A subgroup of them meanders to our table. We exchange meaningless pleasantries.

The conversation flows down well-trodden tracks. Christmas. Field trips. Anyone doing the Christmas at Heritage Park day? No? Why not? Shopping. Someone's got the flu. Someone else is just recovering. Someone else is getting divorced, have you heard? Another revealed affair. A sense of ennui, almost overpowering, envelops me. I've had this same conversation . . . last week. And the week before.

I pull out my phone. Email. Panicked client. Another emergency. Ah, not going to happen today. Maybe for tomorrow. Not acceptable. This is a real emergency. Please. Double my fee. Anything. Fine. Your inbox, tomorrow a.m. Ecstatic client. How I'm going to accomplish that, I'm not sure . . .

The women's voices around me rise and fall. Marie and I exchange looks – 'Later', hers says – but she falls into the conversation enthusiastically. I haven't the desire.

Ennui.

Maybe. Never was a word so full of potential.

I check Facebook. I'll write back. Maybe.

There's a new message. From him.

Breaking news. In town December 14/15. Would love to see you. Can we make that happen?

Oh.

The air around me vibrates and it has nothing to do with the speed at which my heart is beating. My pulse is not elevated and my breathing is not changed. Yes, I'm smiling. Fuck that, of course I am. Old friend. Oldest of friends. It's been years. Pleasurable anticipation.

I lift my eyes from the face of the phone briefly, and realise that the mood of the conversation has now changed. Its topic is no longer kids, teachers, enrichment programmes and who's reading what or buying what for whom. It is now Nicola's rat-fuck bastard of a husband and their gong-show of a divorce. Or is it still a separation? Nicola's talking in a slightly hysterical voice about their current fight over the line of credit, what to do with the mortgage, and his lack of co-operation on the co-parenting plan. 'Step one is taking the Parenting After Divorce Seminar, how hard is it to just take a weekend and do it, God knows he doesn't take the kids every weekend!' she wails. Colleen, her own gong-show of a divorce story almost four years old now, is leading the offers of unconditional support. Everyone else is murmuring in assent, saying, 'What an asshat' or 'Rat-fuck bastard' every once in a while.

I take a moment to be, once again, astounded that Nicola's rat-fuck bastard of a husband managed to be, first, attractive to Nicola, and then, attractive enough to his mildly skanky intern to get pursued, seduced, played. Proof there's someone out there for everyone.

And I turn back to the phone. And type.

—Breaking news indeed. Message me when your
schedule nails down. Coffee? Wine? Jägermeister?

There. Friendly, but not eager.

My pulse has not quickened. My lips are curling into that stupid smile, but that's what he's always done to me. But. There's nothing wrong with smiling.

7

Ping. Fucking Facebook. Immediate response. He's on.

I vote Jäger shots.

I don't have to respond. I look up from the phone at the women around me. 'So there we are, on our first family holiday in two years, we're about to go to Disneyland, fucking Disneyland! And he's in the bathroom, sexting with the girl-friend!' Nicola's voice rises. 'Sending her pictures of his erect cock, for fuck's sake!'

'What a bastard,' Colleen says and shakes her head. The voices of the others rumble in the background, a continuing Greek chorus of indignation and support.

I'm perverse. And I've heard this story about six times in the last month.

I text Matt back immediately.

—Nice. I have almost two weeks to work up some level of resistance to Jäger. Where? Are we bringing our significant others, or living dangerously?

I vote danger.

I let the lips do as they will. Type a smiley face. Delete it. Disclose the deletion. Type:

—(I'm looking for the right emoticon)
I'm looking for the elevated heart rate emoticon.

Fuck. Matt. No.

I should stop typing. Engaging. Turn off the fucking phone. Instead:

—I can't find the right one. Jesus. How many years has it been? I hope we won't be disappointed.

8

You couldn't disappoint me if you tried.
—I won't try. See you on the 14th.
I very much look forward to it.

I wish this was the kind of phone you could snap shut. That's what I want to do: I want to terminate the conversation with Matt, because where he draws me, where he's always drawn me, I am reluctant to go. Reluctant sometimes, anyway. Reluctant for the past ten years and still reluctant now, today, in this precise moment.

I turn off the phone – not nearly as satisfying as the sound made by clicking it shut would be – and turn my attention to the continued crucifixion of Nicola's rat-fuck bastard of a husband and his clichéd affair, conducted primarily via texts on an un-password-protected phone he'd just leave lying around the house. 'Who does that? How does a man with a fucking Master's degree from MIT do that?' Nicola asks, and I'm uncertain if she's talking about the carelessness or the betrayal.

'At least it was easy to track, and you found out about it as quickly as you did,' Colleen counsels her. 'My ex was screwing around on me for years.'

Marie looks at me and taps her phone. She starts texting.

Fine. He'll be gone by now anyway. I turn the phone back on. Marie's text is short and to the point. 'OMFG pls tell me you this bores you as much as it does me.' I look at her and bite my lips.

Ping.

Did you find the emoticon that captures your feelings?

I don't have to respond. But. I do.

—No. Maybe there isn't one. I'll have to express my emotions live.

Or we could go old school. Use adjectives. I'll start.
Hopeful.

'Jane?' It's Nicola. 'What do you think?'

I have no fucking clue what she's talking about. It's possible my pulse rate is elevated and my breathing jagged. Fuck. And my eyes glassy. Marie jumps in.

'Don't bother her,' she says. 'She's dealing with some client emergency.' Nicola feels slighted, but I am saved. And grateful for my bizarre work-from-home job, so esoteric and complicated that no one really understands what I do – and, in this circle of stay-at-home-moms and ladies-who-lunch at least, I'm treated with cautious respect as a result.

When they're not thinking I neglect my children and my husband's career, that is.

'Clients,' I say. 'And with these phones, we're always on call.'

Fucking liar.

I type.

—Nervous.
Really? Pulse pounding.
—Not an adjective.
Hard.

I have to cover my mouth with my hand. Oh, my fucking God, Matt. Really? From hopeful to hard in two adjectives? Some things never change, I think. And I type:

—Some things never change.
Like your effect on me.
—Things slow at work today, are they?
Not at all. Give me an adjective.
—Titillated.
Hungry.

10

—Anticipating. (Is that an adjective?)
I'll allow it.
Throbbing.
What will you wear?
—Clothes.
Not for long.
—Public place
Good.
—Overselling?
Ha.

'Jane?' It's Marie. 'Cassandra, waving at you madly.'

I drop the phone into my purse and leave the cafeteria. Behind me, Nicola is passing around her iPhone, showing screenshots of the rat-fuck bastard's texts . . . and naked photos of the girlfriend. I choose not to think about what was involved in transferring these from his phone to hers – oh, fuck, I thought it: did he forward them during their brief 'we must be open and honest about this if we are to save our marriage' phase? Did she forward them to herself during the following, and still ongoing, 'I must gather evidence if I am to skin his hide' period? Why am I thinking about this? – and go to find out what's up with my children.

Nothing much, as it turns out, but the candle-making isn't as horridly uninteresting as I thought it might be, and the metal-ornamenting is actually really cool, and Henry and Eddie really want me to go with them to see the cows, so I stay with them for the rest of pioneer Christmas. And then back into our minivan. And home, with Marie and her crew of two on our heels.

Marie's anxious.

'Are you sure this is OK?' she asks for the umpteenth time as she follows her kids into the house.

'Jeezus, woman, if it wasn't, I'd have said so when you asked me,' I chastise. 'Besides, four kids, six kids, not much

11

difference. How much louder or messier can they be? I'm going to run them up the hill, get them to sled, and if I decide I want to kill them, I'll make them watch Minecraft videos on YouTube. It's all good. Go.'

'Let me just get their lunch things into the kitchen,' she says. She follows me into the kitchen, puts down the bag on the table.

Sits down.

Marie is my first, and sometimes I think only, adult female friend. Those other women – the ones from the school, the neighbourhood, the ones from Alex's work – I socialise with. Sometimes just endure. Alex says I don't like women very much, and perhaps he's right. Still. Motherhood has thrust me fully into a community of women. Playgroups, playdates, play-schools. Mom's nights out. Gymnastics classes, book clubs. Goddamned pioneer Christmas field trips.

They would all be, I think, barely tolerable without Marie. And I have come to love Marie in all her facets, even her most annoying ones. One of these facets, so very, I think, feminine, and the one I enjoy the least, is that she confides in me. Constantly. She tells me of the rough patches in her marriage, the on-again-off-again online flirtation with her old flames, her secret hope – or fear – that one day this flirtation, or another, might become something else, something bigger, her immense guilt over those feelings when her marriage survives its rough patches and moves into harmony.

Because she confides – constantly, constantly, constantly – I know more about the intimacies of her marriage than I really want to. I know that when JP 'wants to get laid' (that's how Marie always puts it), he turns on the charm and has even been known to unload the dishwasher. I know that, in contrast to his rather unpleasant living-room demeanour, in the bedroom he is a considerate and gentle lover – 'the king of foreplay'. I know that he prefers to be on top – or sideways – and thinks doggie-style's undignified. I know he gets a great deal of satisfaction from taking Marie from orgasm to orgasm. I know he doesn't really like to give oral, his overall love of foreplay notwithstanding. In fact, he fakes it – 'with wet fingers and slurping noises,' Marie reports. How he thinks any woman can't tell the difference between a finger and a tongue, I don't know. Marie, apparently, has never called him on it. He spends a great deal of time on her boobs, and wanted her to get a boob-tightening job after she weaned their youngest to 'get them back the way they're supposed to be'.

I also know he prefers straight missionary vaginal sex to the best blowjob, and long stretches of abstinence followed by mara-fuck-athons to seize-the-moment quickies.

I also know, although Marie's never put it like this, the major problem with JP and Marie's marriage is that JP is a wanker and treats her like shit on a daily basis.

And I also know that Marie thinks they don't fuck enough. Whether JP's satisfied with the situation as it is, I don't know – I go out of my way to not talk to him, or to be in the same physical space with him. But Marie . . . oh, Marie wants to fuck more.

She tells me this all the time.

I suppose that's the other reason – surely, the first must be that JP is a wanker and treats her like shit – behind her obsession with and pursuit of *faux* affairs.

About which she tells me all as well.

I accept Marie's confidences as a sign of our friendship; sometimes I even enjoy them, because she tells a good story. She does not look to me for advice or any kind of commentary. She just wants someone to listen to her.

I can do that.

And I can tell, right now, that she needs to tell me something.

'Tell me,' I say. 'What is it?'

'I'm not going Christmas shopping,' she says, after casting her eyes right and left to make sure the children are out of earshot. 'I'm going for lunch, and I don't know, maybe more, with, you know. Zoltan.'

Zoltan. Probably *not* his real name, but who's being particular? Marie's latest attempt at an affair. This one's a stranger, someone she met online for the explicit purpose of having a hook-up. These days, I think of each of her flirtations as her latest attempt to sabotage the marriage she wants to end. But maybe not. Next week, maybe staying married, whatever the cost, may be the most important thing.

I arrange my face to look – supportive. I listen as Marie lambasts JP. Segues into lambasting the self-righteousness of 'those women' – Nicola, Colleen, the Greek chorus. 'Do they not have feelings? Hormones? Desires? Are they all in denial? They're all our age! Where the fuck are their hormones?'

She looks at me expectantly. Expecting what? Acquiescence, confirmation, confession?

Hard.
—Some things never change.
Like your effect on me.

I could. I could tell her. But I am a bad friend. I do not betray her confidences, never. But I never reciprocate either.

It's not a conscious choice, exactly. It's just . . . not me. I don't tell. Plus, what do I have to reciprocate with? Sure, Alex annoys me from time to time. He has no sense of time, and will text me at 8.15 p.m. to tell me he should be home before 7 p.m. His relationship with his mother is co-dependent, and his relationship with his father and stepmothers is fucked up. I've given up trying to get him to put his shoes on the boot mat, and his idea of helping clean the house is to suggest the cleaners come in more often. But. He's a great dad. And he's been known to load the dishwasher. Well, supervise the kids as they load the dishwasher. More importantly: he gets hard the second he sees me naked. Now. And always. When

14

I had a belly swollen with six-months'-worth of baby in it. When it was flabby and stretchy six months after the fourth baby.

Yeah, he gets cranky. Annoying. Distant. So do I. But at our worst, I do not wish to leave our marriage – nor do I secretly hope, as Marie sometimes does, that he leaves, so that I would be . . . what? Free but blameless. I'm . . . what am I? Perhaps less deluded? Alex and I, we are what we are, and it's usually good, and it has downs, but it's all about the long play. It's about forever: not fairy-tale forever, just . . . nuclear-family forever.

A child of parents who will celebrate their forty-third wedding anniversary next year, I buy into that.

Marie calls us a fairy-tale marriage every once in a while, and pauses, and waits for me to say something. And I shrug. Five pregnancies, fourth births. Eleven, almost twelve years of solid monogamy. Of days too full of children and quotidian obligations to have much space for even audacious thought crime, much less real crime.

This thought intrudes: the last time I saw Matt, I had just found out I was pregnant with Cassandra.

And I did what I had to do, what had to be done.

This thought comes, too: a little more time and space for thought crime these days. My work ensures I get taken out to lunch and dinner by powerful and occasionally attractive men. Occasionally, after, I commit thought crime with them while fucking Alex.

But.

Why would I tell Marie that? To what end?

And – my fingers find the phone in my purse – she does not know anything about this part of me. This past part of me.

—See you . . . on the 14th.
I very much look forward to it.

15

'What if he thinks I'm a skank?' Marie asks me. 'He knows I'm married. With children. And there I am . . . Do you think I'm a skank?' She turns to me suddenly, sharply. I take a step back, creating space between us again.

'Jesus, Marie, what do you think I am?' I ask. 'Your friend. Who's looking after your kids so you can do whatever you need to do this afternoon. You don't need to justify anything to me.'

'I'd just feel better if you and Alex didn't have this fairy-tale marriage,' Marie says. There she goes again. 'The prince and the princess. And I know JP's more than ten years older than Alex. But Alex still looks so good, and young, and in shape – and the two of you together. You're so . . . perfect.'

I love her and I do not want her to feel judged.

I could tell her.

'I don't want you to judge me,' Marie says. 'And I know you never say anything. But how can you not judge me when you're so fucking happily married and faithful and . . .'

I could do this. I could. I could open the Facebook app on my phone, and go into messages. Hand the phone to Marie.

She would read. She would say, 'Oh, my God,' and I would I hear a *thunk* – me, falling off the pedestal.

'Never think I'm judging you,' I would say as she read.

'Who is this?' she would ask.

And this is where it ends. Where I know I won't tell. I can't tell. Because . . . because I don't. Mine. Only mine to know and bear and carry.

So. I don't show, I don't share. Instead:

'I never judge you,' I say. 'He won't think you're a skank. OK, well, he might. But he wants you to be a skank. Right? That's what this whole thing is about.'

It's almost the right thing to say. Marie smiles.

''K,' she says. ''K. It will be OK. I'll be fine. I look good, right?' I nod. 'See you in three or so hours.'

'Be safe.' I send her on her way. To her lunch. Or a parking-lot fuck.

I hope she's packed a condom.

I spend a joyous but exhausting day with the kids. I don't text. I don't think about Matt. Really. I think about work – the bizarre financial case study I promised to review for a client for tomorrow morning, which clearly I'm not doing as I sled with the kids. Oh, fuck. What time will Alex be home? As Marie comes back – hair and makeup intact and overall mood light and neither angst-ridden nor post-coitally joyous, making me infer she only lunched and transgressed not much (we can't talk with the kids around) – he texts to say he won't be back until 8, maybe later – 'fucking clients,' he writes, the excuse for everything, always – and that won't get him home in time to do bedtime . . . and, since I've been up since 5 a.m., I'll be useless post-bedtime.

Marie's kids and mine are starting to fight, tired of each other, so despite her half-hearted offer, I decline to send my brood home with her. Maybe I can sell them to my mom in the evening so I can work? I only need an hour, maybe two . . .

And that is why, a few hours later, I'm sitting in my parents' kitchen eating liver and onions (ugh, how can they not know I hate liver and onions after all these years?), listening to four children vie for their grandparents' attention . . . while the grandparents fight.

I have an odd sense of dissonance: I'm there but not there, and I hear my parents in freaky stereo. 'They would have been better,' my mother says of the mashed potatoes, 'but your father insisted on using the new potato masher.' 'Insisted?' my father asks. Voice low. But tired, tense. 'I took what was in the drawer. I didn't realise we had a *right* potato masher and a *wrong* potato masher.' Stupid, stupid exchange. And not the first one I've heard like this – they are like this all the time now. Sometimes it's funny. Often it's sad. And always, after we leave, Alex and I promise ourselves that if we ever get like this, I'll shoot him and then turn the gun on myself.

'Put the pie in the oven to warm it up, Jerry,' my mother

says. Commands. 'Gran bought you guys pie!' she squeals at the kids, and they squeal back. 'Where's the pie?' my father asks. 'Where it always is!' my mother screams and rolls her eyes. No, really. She screams. I stare at her in shock. Appalled. My father doesn't even blink an eye. 'Which is?' he says with an excessive show of patience. My stomach turns and I suddenly very badly need to leave the room.

'I'm going to go work,' I say. 'I don't want any pie anyway. Be good for Gran and Gramps,' I tell the progeny, handing out kisses. I look at Gran and Gramps. 'Be good in front of the kids,' I say. It could be taken as a joke. Or a warning. But it's taken as neither; it's not heard. The pie's coming.

I exit stage right, camp out in one of the spare bedrooms, pull out the laptop.

Start typing. I turn on Facebook as I work. Cause that's how the professionals do it, right? Having your Twitter feed and Facebook and LinkedIn on in the background increases your work efficiency. Well-proven fact. Not.

Confession: I use social media almost exclusively as a procrastination tool.

Still.

I have no ulterior motive.

I am not hoping to see a message from Matt.

No, really. And so I am not the least bit disappointed that there isn't one.

I work. God, who crunched these numbers? Either an idiot or a liar. I identify all the red flags. I get into it. There is a sick kind of satisfaction to it; bringing order to chaos. I work. I am . . . tranquil.

Ping.

Answer the question.
—Working.
Waiting. I want you to dress for the occasion. The occasion being our reunion, after what, 10 years?

Almost eleven. But who's counting? And how many years since we met? I think . . . twenty. Oh, my fucking God, twenty. When did that happen? The first time we met, I was . . . I think I was eighteen. Jesus-fucking-Christ. Grunge ruled. I wore distinctly unsexy jean overalls. I type.

—Overalls have a certain nostalgic value.
Oh, yes. Nostalgic.
And harder.
—Demure.
Sceptical.
Get nostalgic with me, lover. I remember the lingerie store changing room in Bankers Hall.
—Do you?
And you reading me erotica over the phone when I was up North. With John's permission.
Two memories from hundreds.
—I remember stairwells. Too many stairwells.
—The recording booth at the studio.
—The roof of your apartment building . . .
The dark room.
Halloween party. The lawn. Do you remember?
—Oh yes. That might be my favourite . . .
Scandalised populace.
—We had no shame.
What's your adjective right now?
—Disturbed.
Guess mine.
—You've been using one consistently.
The correct answer is lustful. Also acceptable: dirty (the good kind).

I pause. Shudder. I feel . . . yes, I feel. And I type:

—Lusciously pleased.

—God I miss you
—I really didn't think I did.
And I you. Tell me what you want. Be blunt.
—Your tongue in my ear, on my neck
—Other places
Curse these tight jeans.
I miss your mind. And your mouth.
And the serious tone of voice you take when you talk dirty.
—Oh god
—Terrified
Eager.
Demanding.
—Are you?
Dominant.
—Oh really?
Determined.
—On top.
Challenged.
—Tumbling
Pleased.
Hungrier and harder than ever.
—Ecstatic
Sublimely motivated.
Aggressive.
—Sublime
—Lovely word
—Luscious
—Languorous
Throbbing
Pounding.
God. I want to fuck your mind.
Savage your vocabulary.
—Savage?
—I would prefer to be ravaged.

Or ruled? With a firm hand.

—Oh god.

Tell me you're going to make yourself come. Tonight.

—I think I just did.

With a full report upon completion.

—Well that you might need to wait for.

No time like the present.

—Making you wait and anticipate has always been my MO

Making you submit has always been mine. (Or attempt therein)

—Almost disarmed

Pleased

—// almost //

Determined. Now what are you going to wear for me?

—I do have these fuck-me heels that will be perfect.

—So long as I don't have to walk anywhere in them.

Describe.

—Just wait

—Some things just have to be seen

Put them on.

—They're hard to type in

—That's how hot they are

Intrigued.

You won't be on your feet for long.

—Nice. We'll be arrested for indecent exposure.

Hopeful.

Fuck-me heels. Good start.

This has been . . . electrifying. Illuminating. Awoken thoughts I'm glad to be reminded of. I think I'm going to go . . . take care of myself right now.

—Enjoy.

Still at the office.

—Very professional

—Close the door first

21

Tell me where do you want this cum?
—Running down to my belly button
Where do I aim?
—at black lace of the bra I'll be wearing with the
fuck-me shoes.
—Go. See you in 12 days.
I count the hours.
Xx
—oo

I finish the analysis in a stupor. And before hitting *send*, take it to my dad. Ask him to read it to make sure there are no odd adjectives or metaphors in the copy.

He doesn't ask why. Points to 'orgasmic', 'sublime' and a completely extraneous 'pounding'. I delete them. Send the file to the client. Take the kids home, put them to bed.

When Alex finally gets home, close to midnight, I'm still awake and give him the most adventurous night in bed he's had in months. Possibly years.

'Jesus,' he says when it's over. 'What happened to you?'

'Hormones,' I say. 'I think . . . yes, hormones.'

And we sleep.

Day 2 – Did she just?

Alex brings me coffee up to bed before he leaves for the firm. I stumble out of bed and into the shower. The brood's already up, the boys fighting over who gets to play Minecraft first, the girls curled up on the couch with books, one reading, the other carefully, seriously imitating her sister. I look at them intensely. Feel my love for them reverberate in waves, through me, throughout the room.

No one wants to do much of anything in the short hour or two of the morning before I have to bundle the kids into the car to drop them off at school. They just chill. I consider it an ultimate test of character not to check Facebook.

It causes me physical pain.

I drop the elder three at school and Annie at my mom's for the morning, and then head off to the gym. If I was a woman nearing 40 somewhere sexy like New York City, say, I'd probably have a therapist. But I'm a skiing Calgarian so I have a personal trainer. Also a chiropractor and an acupuncturist. And a massage therapist. Winter sports kill the spine . . . and our tendency to drive SUVs and mega-trucks any distances over 0.6 kilometres when we're not on the hills means we need fucking treadmills to get exercise.

There really is no hope for humanity, I think as I careen down one overpass, then another. It's my usual think as I drive to the gym. That if I just went for a (free) bike ride, (free) run or did some real physical work – chopped wood, I don't know,

23

laid some bricks or something – I'd achieve the same result in a less self-centred, narcissistic environment.

I keep on getting distracted from my self-inflicted lecture by imagining Matt's tongue between my thighs.

Fuck. Focus.

I park. Wave to Jesse as I run to the changing room. Jesse. My trainer. The very very very junior fourth partner, as he puts it, in a very clean, very bright, very Zen gym, filled with inspirational quotes and a dizzying array of equipment. The gym runs classes, sells memberships and all that other stuff, but its real draw is the personal training services – or just going to the gym to ogle the trainers. The personal trainers, male and female, look like Greek – in one case, Nubian – gods.

Mine is, not to put too much of a point on it, the prettiest. He was a gift from Alex for my birthday a couple of years ago.

'So I saw Nicola yesterday,' he says as he loads up weights for me. I stare at him blankly. What the fuck is he talking about? Nicola? Nicola! Who is Nicola?

Not important. What's important is how you will look in those fuck-me heels when we meet.
—Go away. Not in my head. Not now.

I know Nicola. Jesse knows Nicola. I introduced Nicola to Jesse, actually. Before the gong-show of a divorce, when her own struggle with careening towards 40 resulted in a fitness-must-lose-weight-and-look-hotter craze. I don't judge: I don't come to Jesse because it's fun or because I enjoy exercise. I too have no desire to be a fat, frumpy middle-aged woman who wears yoga pants because they're more forgiving than jeans. Regardless. Jesus, what is happening in my head? Narcissistic bitch, snap out of it. He's talking about Nicola. I need to listen. 'She told me about, you know, her situation. She said you knew,' Jesse says. He blushes slightly.

24

I nod. I'm fond of Jesse. He's beautiful and has a nice voice, and is ridiculously young. Chronologically, he's 26, and half the time – when he's doing his job and telling me what to do – he's older than his birth age, confident, in control, in charge. And the other half – when he moves on to any other ground – he's so very, very young. And awkward. And so unaware of life.

Sometimes, I think he might be gay – the question's never been asked and answered, because, when I'm with him, he makes me lift heavy shit and I scream and grunt and pant and so there is not much room for conversation. I infer his potential homosexuality purely from the fact that although he is built like an Adonis and eminently fuckable – when Alex introduced me to him, I cooed that other men buy their wives flowers and chocolate and my beloved got me a ripped boy toy – he comes across as very, very . . . safe. He gropes and prods and readjusts me – and his dozens-upon-dozens of other female clients – fairly thoroughly. It never feels inappropriate, or edgy. I sweat with him two or three times a week, and I've committed no thought crime with him, no matter how ardent my mood is otherwise. He's that safe. So safe, I've pondered setting him up with my neighbour's seventeen-year-old daughter . . . except for that he-might-be-gay thing. We've all got to go through our gay lovers – I've had two – but it really sucks if the gay boy's your first one. A little disheartening.

'I'm just so shocked,' Jesse says. I nod and grunt. Lift up. Hold. Drop down. 'Have you met her husband?'

'Y . . . e . . . s,' I exhale. 'Total dork. Even before he became a cheating rat-fuck bastard.'

'Well, I wasn't going to be so . . .' Jesse pauses.

'Offensive?' I offer as I gasp.

'Blunt,' Jesse says. 'But yes. Not exactly a Don Juan. I wouldn't have thought . . . have you seen the pictures of the girlfriend?'

'The naked pictures?' I get out between lifts. 'No. I managed to avoid that. I guess you didn't.'

'Nicola showed me,' Jesse says.

'Skanky?' I ask. Jesse is shocked. His Puritanism and youth come out at the most unexpected times. He's shocked – that I said skank. He's shocked that Nicola and her dorky husband are divorcing because of his torrid affair with a skanky but sufficiently attractive, to Nicola's ex at least ('If you like that type' – that's Nicola's voice providing commentary in the background), intern. He's shocked the dorky husband was fucking the attractive skank. He might be shocked people in their 30s and 40s, and those really old 50-year-olds sweating on the ellipticals over there, have sex. Dirty thoughts.

I'm not quite 40 yet. But it's less than two years away. And Matt . . . is Matt 40 now? He's got to be. Maybe even 41.

'Hey, Jesse,' I ask. 'How old do you think I am?'

He pauses. Yes, it's a test. I asked him how old he was a few months ago. I thought 28 – he was 26. My two-year misjudgement didn't matter. But he really can't win with me, I realise. If he says 40, I'll throw the barbell at him. If he says 36, who gives a crap? What's two years less? I catch the thought and stare it in the face. It's never ever bothered me that I'm now 38. Four kids. Soft, loose breasts, stretched skin on the belly. That's all part of me, of what I am. Am I anxious about my age? Am I having a mid-life crisis? A stupid fucking mid-life crisis that's making me easy fodder for a manipulative fuck like Matt who clearly is having a mid-life crisis of his own, much like Nicola's husband was having when he started fucking the skank? Except, instead of looking for something new, he comes looking for me, because he knows . . .

Fuck.

Selfish, evil bastard.

I am so *not* going to see him on December 14.

'I've never thought about it,' he says. And I think, clever boy, that's the right answer. But he plods on. 'Well,' he says, 'I know your oldest girl is ten. So . . . you must be . . . you

26

must be thirty-something, like at least thirty-two? Maybe even thirty-four?'

I stop listening. I don't really hear. I'm away again. Teeth marks on my neck. My thighs. Oh, fuck. Where was I? What were we talking about?

'But she seems to be coping OK.' Jesse returns to Nicola. 'I mean, she's angry and all that. But I think she'll be OK.'

She'd probably be a hell of a lot better if you sort of accidentally-on-purpose patted her ass after her workout session, I think. Don't say out loud. Slap myself mentally. Feel Matt's breath on the back of my neck . . .

'She's tough,' I say. 'And really . . . well. The only really shocking thing here is that he left *her*. Well, OK, not exactly left her. What he wanted to do was to fuck the skank and to stay married. And she didn't. So she's the one who asked for a divorce. But what I mean is – we all kind of expected her to lose her patience with him somewhere along the line without the illicit sex, you know? Cause he was – you know, a dork.'

Jesse gives me an odd look. My Puritan boy. He does not like it when I swear. I hope he chalks it up to my indignation on my friend's behalf.

'Anyway,' he says, 'exercise helps.'

Oh, Jesse. So cute. So sweet. So dumb.

I like it better when he doesn't talk.

I stay silent for the remainder of the session, and try hard not to think about Matt's cock.

Fail.

My mom seems frazzled when I come to pick up Annie, so I don't stay. Pack up Annie. We run errands – bank, big grocery shop – then pick up her siblings at school. 'Gran was weird,' Annie says at one point. 'Sad.' 'Really?' I murmur, indifferent. My mother's always a bit weird. Groceries, kids in car . . . but I'm reluctant to go home. Restless. I take the kids to the Glenbow Museum's Discovery Room instead. Middle of the week, so it's quiet, empty. The two volunteers fight with each other for the privilege of assisting Annie with her craft.

So of course I sit on the couch. And pull out the phone.

Evil bastard.

Why am I doing this?

Because . . . ah. Yes. There is a message.

Enjoy your evening?

Well. This I can answer.

> —So much. My husband thanks you.
> *Delighted.*
> *I have a perhaps undeserved feeling of accomplishment and pride.*
> *(Inspiring you and lucky Alex.)*
> —That's you. Spreading sweetness and light wherever you go.
> *The Johnny Appleseed of Eros.*

I can stop now. I should stop now. What the fuck am I doing? This:

> —My mind was busy with you last night. And this morning *en route* to my personal trainer.

I am a fucking idiot who should know better.

> *I love to be kept busy. Tell me your thoughts. Paint me a picture.*
> —Electrifying.
> —I was rehearsing our meeting.
> *I am charged.*
> —You've got a lot to live up to.
> *As do you.*

But I'm confident you will work hard to please me.
I'm seducing you subliminally (lick) is it working?
—Not so very subliminally
Tell me what you want most.
—You
I like that answer.
—I'm wondering if your lips feel the way I remember them
I want you in all your darkest ways.
The things you would only ever tell me about.
I want you to scare me.
—How?
I'd like you to try.
—Overwhelmed
—Shivering
—11 days?
Yes.
Demand something. Scare me. Right now.
—Take off your tie, wrap it around my hands
—Restrain me
That's a promise
I will put you to work
—I see us at a table, someplace dark . . . and eyes on us, and someone wondering, 'Did I just see that? Did they just . . . no . . . did they?'
'I think she just stroked his cock through his jeans.'
—'Where are his hands?'
'I'm sure she just pulled her skirt up and her shirt down . . .'
—'Was that her nipple between his fingers?'
'I'm pretty positive she just handed him her panties.'
Scandalous
I have to run to a client meeting now.
I request a picture of you in your fuck-me shoes.
—I think I just came without touching myself.

—Remember that during the boring parts of the meeting.
—xo
That is so unbelievably sexy
Get on that photo
Demanding, I know
11 days xx

'Mom?' I turn my head. 'Look what I made!'

I am a really good mom.

Except I'm not sure really good moms exchange 'Was that her nipple between his fingers?' and *'I'm pretty positive she just handed him her panties'* texts with their ex-lovers while their kids do crafts. In a fucking museum.

Well, Marie probably does.

And she's a good mom.

Ex-lover. Returning lover. Oh, fucking hell. The point here is . . . what is the point? The point is this: am I genuinely planning to fuck Matt when he comes to town?

I drive like a maniac across the downtown, and it's a minor miracle we get home without an accident.

'Ja-ane!'

My neighbour Lacey is pulling into her driveway as I'm stepping out of the car. 'Ja-ane! You have to see this! You won't believe what I've just been dooo-ing!'

Lacey is . . . Lacey is perfection.

I think she's 52 or 53, and I only think this because I've been to her fiftieth birthday party a couple of years ago. You would never say of Lacey, 'Oh, my God, I hope I look like that when I'm fifty.' You would say, 'Fuck, I wish I *was* that when I was twenty.' And then you'd try to get her into bed.

I'm not overselling. Carved out of ebony, voluptuous, curvy, and perfect in every way – the centre of any room into which she saunters. (She doesn't walk; she saunters.) She makes me want to climb into her lap and nibble on her ears.

And she makes me smile, always, when I see her. Not even Marie does that.

Lacey's been my neighbour almost all of my mother-life. She has spent much of this time searching for a soulmate – and almost all of it fucking Clint.

Clint's car pulls up behind Lacey's. She waves at him as she runs over to me.

'You will never believe what Clint and I have been doing!' she whispers. She leans in closer to me, her lips almost touching my ear. (Does she do this on purpose? No. Of course not. It's just me. I think about her ear lobes at the most inappropriate times.) 'We've been ring shopping!'

As she reaches into her purse – to pull out a box? – I'm stunned. Yes, Clint allegedly proposed last summer, after *he* turned 50. Part of *his* mid-life crisis. And Lacey seemed to actually believe it. But ring shopping? Really? Clint?

Lacey whips out her phone. 'Look,' she says. 'I like this one. And this one. And this one. Clint likes this one.'

Just pictures. Not yet the real thing.

That I can believe.

Clint has opened his car door. One long leg is hanging out. The rest of him will stay in the car until I'm gone. That's his MO. Limit contact with women he's not sleeping with – and keep contact with the women he's sleeping with or wants to sleep with to the minimum necessary to sleep with them.

'They're beautiful, Lacey,' I say sincerely.

Lacey smiles, and puts the phone away.

'I think it's actually going to happen,' she says. 'You know, the wedding.'

I flush. My scepticism about the ring, the wedding – the relationship – is justifiable. How many years? How many 'Lacey is single'/'Lacey is in a relationship'/'It's complicated' switchbacks on her Facebook status? But I would not express that to Lacey for anything.

I arrange my lips into what is meant to be a supportive smile. Perhaps it comes out wrong, as Lacey takes a step back.

'You look different,' she says. 'Have you cut your hair?' I shake my head. 'Lost weight?' 'Uhm-no.' 'New dress?' 'No.'

'Well, there's something about you.' She gives me a critical look. 'I like it,' she pronounces. 'Whatever you're doing, keep doing it!' And she saunters into the house.

Lacey claims to be a little bit psychic. Perhaps she is.

As I unbuckle Annie, I see Clint get out of his car. As I lock the van, he's reaching Lacey's front door.

Jesus Christ, was he unbuckling his belt with one hand while reaching for the door knob with the other?

I need to get my mind out of the gutter.

'Mom!' Eddie wails. 'Open the door! It's so cold!'

The kids snack, then disappear into various corners of the house, except for Annie, who sits in my lap as I make pasta. Alex makes it home just as I'm slopping it into bowls on the table; the children squeal with delight, and then fight over who gets to sit next to him. He offers to do bedtime if they stop fighting, and they suppress it, a little.

I do a half-ass job cleaning the kitchen – good mother. A morally ambiguous wife. A horrid housekeeper. And then, to the sound of my husband running our children's bath, I pop open the laptop. And this time I take the initiative.

Because I am clearly insane.

—I've rethought the visuals. I've never seen you in a tie. Use your belt. It'll have to come off anyway.

And of course he's there.

No, the only time I've ever used a tie on you, we borrowed it. Remember?
And leather is more fun.

32

—Indeed.

How long will I have you?

—I guess that depends on when you untie me.

I'll try not to be greedy. // Try // I make no promises.
Now tell me. In detail. What you did last night.

—I don't know how to start.

Begin at the beginning, insatiable you. And take me
through every filthy detail.

—No. I think I'll just tell you Alex had gouge marks all
the way down his back at the end.

Lucky man. Unless he doesn't enjoy the scratches.

—And you? Did you aim at the lace and watch it trickle
down?

I had you tied up (thinking ahead . . . though your
wrists were behind your back), working your mouth,
laced breasts jutting forward from having your wrists
bound. Then when I was ready, I stroked the last few
moments, freeing your mouth. I wanted you to word-
fuck me to the end.
Then I aimed.
A hot beautiful messy sight.

—You were always much better at this than I.

Love making you wet
(presumptive)

—(right)

Hungry

—yes

Ready to devour you

—trembling

Are you ready to be put to work?

—No

No? Wet and trembling sounds ready to me

—still need something

Tell me. What do you need?

—Something to nudge me over the edge

33

—a hand in just the right place, a tongue on just the right spot

a firm handprint on your lovely skin

—perhaps

—just enough pressure

just enough to motivate

an encouraging spank

not being punished.

(yet)

—Fuck. Has it been 10 years since we've seen each other?

More, perhaps

a long interval

—I'm astounded you can still do this to me.

Amazing how fast to rekindle, yes.

—primeval

I've never stopped wanting you.

I always thought we were sexual equals.

—I like that.

We are a twisted pair.

—Twisted?

In the best way – woven together in some primal way. We match.

Tell me you want me.

—So much. You?

I want to feel your hair in my hands as I take you from behind.

I want to unleash you, drive you mad. Fuck you until you lose your words, all your self-restraint.

—Fuck. So primal. I still remember the way you smell, you know. I didn't think I did, but in this moment, it is all around me.

It's what you need to nudge you over the edge.

Now get on your knees.

Open your mouth.

—Oh
Thrust your tongue out so I can fuck your mouth
deeper.
—yes . . .
further
—you're bigger than I remember
I can feel the tip of your tongue on my balls each time
I bury my cock in your face.
—you curve
—where are my hands?
Rubbing your wet pussy
your moans transmit along the shaft of my cock
—vibrating
'Come for me while I use your pretty mouth'
I tighten my grip on your hair to raise the tension.
Raise the stakes. Nudge you over the edge.
—teeth on your cock
I like it
now come.
—teeth and mouth off your cock, my face just pressed
against you while I writhe
I press your face against me, clutching you, almost
smothering you, your hot wet breathing burning into
me.
—I moan. You tell me . . .
'Come for me. Show me how hard you can come.'
—My teeth are clenched and I hiss
—My hands can't keep up any more. I press myself
against your leg, I rub
fucking yourself with my leg like a bitch in heat
your pussy so scorching hot and slippery wet against
me
just when you can't take any more I turn you around,
hard, and slide my spit-covered cock inside your pussy.
One hand never leaving your neck.

35

your fuck-me heels have you at the perfect height. Your
pussy right where I want it.
so wet I can feel you dripping down your thighs, onto
my legs
making the most delicious wet sounds echoing off the
hotel walls.
—Someone pounds on the wall.
'Tell them to fuck off. Loudly.'
SLAP on your ass. 'SAY IT.'
—'Fuck off. We're busy.'
Yes, you are
I want to look at you
'Go sit on the chair. Spread for me.'
—good, I can't support my weight any more, knees
giving out
—I'm shaved
—you like that
I do. I like the thought of you preparing yourself to get
fucked.
Gift-wrapping yourself for me
giving yourself to me utterly
—utterly
I take a long moment to admire and appreciate your
gift of yourself.
I sit on the edge of the bed and drink in the sight of
you. I stroke my curved cock. Is it as you remember it?
—yes
—I want to straddle it, will you let me?
Play with yourself a bit longer. I've missed you.
I want to record this movie into my memory.
—but I want to be touching you
and I want to drive you even more mad
— . . . it's working . . .
now come take this cock inside your pretty pussy
the view of your luscious breasts over me

36

—I sit on your thighs
—rest my head on your shoulder
—bite
mmmmmmM
—bite harder
—I slide over your cock, now that I'm sitting on you, it's
my turn to tease
bitch
—your hands on my ass
—not gentle
—you say . . .
'Show me how you like to ride a cock.'
'Fuck me. Show me how hard you can take it.'
I'm gripping your ass hard enough to mark you.
—I bite you again
—lower
oh you biting little tease
SLAP on your ass
you're so going to get it for that.
—I let you in . . .
—just for a moment
—One stroke, two . . . I slide off
Get that pussy back here.
I grip your ass HARD
right now
you are fucking tight.
—reality obtrudes: I've had four babies, my lover. I
don't know about that.
You are truly erotic. Beats merely tight any day
—my lover
—delicious
My lover. I like the sound of that. You wouldn't say that
to me for a long time . . .
Now I grab your legs. The sight of them on either side
of my neck as I put them over my shoulders my cock

reaching so fucking deep inside you, fuck yes . . .
your heels pointed straight to the hotel room above
—jeezus fucking christ
your clit pounded by the hard bone above my even
harder cock
—you push every button
—I scream
you scream so loudly I shove your pretty lace panties in
your mouth
—you will never be able to stay at this hotel again
you will never be able to wear that lace lingerie again
not without blushing at the things you did in it. Gladly.
—I am so wet there are rivulets streaming down the
inside of my thighs.
I want to see that.
Show me
—I slide off you. Stand up. Push you down on the bed.
My cock is yours
—I climb over you, up your torso. Slither up you. I am
so wet, I leave slick along you where I touch you.
—I straddle your face. I'm up high – you can't reach me
yet. But you see me. And you feel me as I drip. Droplet
by droplet.
Mmmmm the sweet scent of you
I open my mouth to catch your sweet juice
on my chin, on my tongue, on my lips . . . dripping
down the sides of my face
'Play with your pussy. I want you to gush on me.'
—Christ.
Do as you're told. Now.
—My hands: one on my clit, the other hugging my
breasts.
—Yours – on my calves. Just holding them.
No, gripping them tight.
Feel the pressure of my hands?

—Yes . . .

—(can we match this in real life, my lover? Because this conversation is turning into the most erotic chapter of my life . . . And we've set the bar fucking high in the past.)

(Yes, oh, yes, we will. In 11 days.)

—I drop a little lower, just graze you with my pussy

—oh god

—and again

my tongue just barely able to lap at your slit

'Squeeze your breasts fucking HARD. Cum on me.'

my fingers dig into your legs HARD

—I'm not really there. I'm on that front lawn in . . . what neighbourhood was that? Do you remember? My skirt around my waist . . .

—and on your roof, your mouth on my pussy, my breasts

YES

— . . . and in a stairwell . . . which one? Oh god

There were several. All of them fucking hot.

—I scream again, and oh my god, I'm coming all over your face, right now, and every moment in the past all at once

I can see your pussy clench and spasm as your juice pours down on me hot and sweet

—I collapse

you are delicious

—the world spins

And now you're ready to be really fucked. Before you can recover. I'm far from through with you.

Though sadly I have to leave now. To the gym. With my wife. Reality does intrude. But you'll know I'm sweating to look good for you.

And you have a photo to take for me.

—Reality is.

—But. Wow. Thank you, my lover.
Thank YOU. You know what I want to see, don't you?
—yes
Good.
I'll check later.
—xx
xo

I am not going to send him a picture of my pussy. What sort of skank does he think I am?

Day 3 – Fuck Foreplay

I don't sleep. I don't think. I just . . . is feel even the right verb? I'm sick with desire. And generally sick. And resentful. And angry. And so filled with lust, sleep is impossible.

I go downstairs and try to find a make-work project. But it's too early for even Toronto to panic and send me work and I've met all my other deadlines. I work to calm myself by organising family photos. Thanksgiving. Halloween. Random life shots – but all real life. Children. Mother. Not a psychotic skank whore orgasming on command to words on the computer screen.

Mmmm, orgasm.

Fuck. I slap my face. Then, stupid, thoughtless, log into Twitter and Facebook. And read this:

You kept me up all night, lover. I dreamed I was watching you fuck a man like an animal, your eyes locked on mine the whole time. Even when you came. Ten days.

Oh, my fucking God. Real life. Children. Mother. *Wife!* It all recedes into the background. Instead:

—I walk around on edge of orgasm all day and I read this, and I come, instantly, immediately. Silently.

41

And he's in Montréal, so of course, he is already awake, moving, online. And he writes back:

> *10 days. Nine, really.*
> *Love the thought of you on a hair trigger.*
> —I'm still worried the reality will fall short of the build-up.
> *Reality has many things in its favour. Such as the feeling of you wrapped around my cock.*
> —Your tongue on my skin.
> *Enjoy your heightened state, my lover. And get on that photo. My inbox was empty this morning. Disappointed; verging on angry.*
> —Demanding.
> *You have no idea how demanding.*

I slam the laptop lid down as Alex comes down the stairs. 'Up early again? Is this one of the signs of the apocalypse?' he jokes as he kisses me. Running joke in our household – me, the most un-morning of un-morning people. Alex, often up at 6 a.m. on weekends. Freak.

'Possibly,' I say. 'Or peri-menopause. Am I old enough for peri-menopause?'

'Jesus, I hope not,' Alex says, shocked. 'Working?'

'Facebooking,' I say. 'I probably drank all the coffee already. You'll have to make another pot.'

Alex sighs dramatically. I hear the *whirr* of the coffee grinder.

My fingers tickle the top of the laptop. I make myself think about Nicola's rat-fuck bastard of a husband, whose two or three graduate degrees from MIT did not teach him to not sex-text with his intern on the un-password-protected family-plan phone. In the bathroom. At the dinner table. Apparently, in church. ('You guys go to church?' I remember asking Nicola in shock when I heard that story. 'Aren't you atheists?' 'Taoists,' she corrects me. 'But the grandparents . . .' her voice trails off. Grandparents. No need to say more. The things we do for grandparents.)

Alex tramps up past me, upstairs. I hear the shower. I open the laptop.

I'm hoping you disappeared to play with the camera. I am checking my email obsessively. Verging on compulsively. Where is my photo?
—The photo is not going to happen. Disobedient. *Insubordinate. Lucky for you, I feel understanding.*
—More to look forward to.
Agreed. Mostly I just like picturing you being subversive.
—You are incorrigible. Corrupting.
And I believe you love it.
—Do you?
—So presumptive.
Wholeheartedly.
Deductive.
Fuck. Already want to cum. Jeans still done up. Hands only typing. Amazing.
—How was your sweat session? Focused on the task at hand?
I was. The task being to look good for you. You are inspiring. I imagined there was an email waiting for me back in my locker. I even imagined the subject line: come fuck me. I think that inspired 20 per cent heavier weights, minimum.
—I have a picture of you lying down on a bench. And I come in.
Yes.
Continue while I type with my left hand . . .
—Are you sure you want to do this again?
Very.
—And straddle you. You're still holding the weight. But your attention is, um, divided. I say, 'Fuck foreplay.'

43

I want to show you how hard you just made me.
—I just slide off your pants and slip you right in. You drop the bar – it just makes it into the safeties.
Shove my cock.
—I lean forward, feel that angle?
Mmm, yes, so deep. Your clit grinding into me now.
—My hands are on your hips and I hold you down as I lift up. You want to thrust, but I keep on pushing you down.
Hungry bitch. I love it.
(Give me a safe email address. I need to show you.)
—(Fuck. numberslie, at the usual domain)
—I move up and down your shaft. I hold myself up with my hands . . .
—And crush down on you
Check your email.
—Looking. Oh, god. Fuck.
—Jeezus. Flood of memory . . .
Glad you approve.
—you're lovely
Appreciative. Inspired.
—Ashamed, excited, overwrought, distracted . . . I might need to slide off you and lick you a while . . . But first . . .
First?
—First . . .
—I bring my legs up onto the bench – they're resting on your hips – the weight of me presses you into the bench, the pressure of your hip bones bruises me. I change angles a little, feel that? But this is about me, not you. My hands on your shoulders. My pussy slapping down on you.
Use my cock.
—You're at my disposal.
—I arch.
Milk your pleasure from me.

—No, I will milk you later

—Now I just need . . .

—. . . a little more friction

—. . . a little more pressure . . .

—. . . and here I cum.

—(why is it so much dirtier as cum instead of come? what a difference a vowel makes)

—. . . and oh, you're about to as well, so I slide off even as I writhe . . .

Cum on my cock.

—and I touch my lips to your head

—My tongue finds the hole

—Droplets

—I lick

—I caress you with one hand and myself with the other

Your skills impress. Just the sight of your hands working both of us is enough to make my balls tighten, my cock swells even harder . . .

You can taste the salty precum.

—I lap it up

Such a submissive sentence.

—Your effect on me: you turn me from mistress to slave with one taste. I forget that I meant to ride you and pleasure myself selfishly. I worship at your cock.

I want to hear you say you're my fuckslave.

—I can't. My mouth is full of your cock.

The words muffled by my cock. Say it.

—I'm your fuckslave, I whisper, as I take more and more of you down my throat.

Yesss.

My hands gripping your hair as you choke on my cock. Your spit dripping.

—Your hands in my hair, gripping, pulling

—it hurts

—(I look at your picture again)

Take it deep.
Forcing you down.
Thrust out your tongue.
I pull you up for air.
—I'm gasping breathless smeared
Slap your lips with my cock. They swell.
Then it's right back to work.
Get on your hands and knees. On the bench.
Mouth at the perfect height.
—I crawl up . . .
Keep your hands where they are. I want to use your
mouth like a pussy. My cock is crammed into your throat.
—I gag.
I reach over you and slap your ass, just to feel you
moan against my shaft. Take it. SLAP.
—(moan)
Do you want this?
—So much.
Good.
Tell me you're my fuckslave again. I like to see you type
it.
—I whisper, I'm your fuckslave, my head bent down.
—Fuck.
—I can't believe you can still . . . again . . . do this to me.
—No one else does.
—A part of me hates it.
—I. Hate. It.
That's so fucking hot.
Angry hate fucking.
—It's barely consensual what you do to me.
—But so wet . . .
So hard.
Knowing how forced you are.
—Take me.
—Push me onto the floor.

46

No. I will use your mouth even longer because I know
you'd rather be fucked in your pussy.
—oh dear fucking god I am so wet
Rub your clit. I want to feel it in your throat when you
cum
—My hands on my pussy, thumbs on clit, fingers
stretching me, probing, rubbing
—so weak
I enjoy seeing you debase yourself for me.
My cock twitching.
—for you
For me. All for me.
—for you
—selfish bastard
Cum for me.
—Palm of hand on my clit, pressing
Your selfish master.
—I arch up on the floor as I cum
—Your cock slides deeper into my throat
—I couldn't spit out your cum if I wanted to
—It sloshes into me
Drink it.
All of it.
—I have no choice all inside me
—a little dribble at the corner of my mouth
You please me so.
Lick it off. No spilling.

Alex walks into the room, and I raise my glazed eyes from
the screen to look at him, but my fingers remain on the
keyboard:

—Lick (not alone)
—tongue in corner of mouth
I should release you then

47

—yes
—then come fuck me
You please me.
—9 days xx
9 xo

Alex kisses my forehead on his way out the door, and it burns. I have one of those odd moments of gratitude for my faithlessness – my lack of faith in the Christian God or any other nasty vengeful cosmic being – because if I believed, I too would burn. The act of physical transgression totally unnecessary; all the sin sufficient in this act, this thought crime, cyberfuck, mindfuck.

What the fuck is wrong with me?

The kids' school has one of its random days off today, so I drive over to meet Marie and her brood right after breakfast. We meet in the Confederation Park parking lot, and, between us, unload six kids and ten sleds out of our minivans. 'Why do we have more sleds than kids?' Cassandra asks. 'Because we're really clever moms,' I tell her. 'At some point, everyone will want to be on the saucers. And then someone will throw a hissy fit because what he really wants is the steering sleigh. Plus, Marie and I need something under our tooshies.'

'Can I just sit and hang out with you when I get bored?' Cassandra asks.

'Of course,' I say. But the snow is alluring, and in minutes she's running up the hill at full speed along with the boys and Annie.

Marie hands me a mug of hot chocolate.

'You rock,' I say.

'You look like shit,' she says. 'How do I look?'

I look at her. Much as usual. But she clearly wants a different type of answer.

'Ambiguous,' I say. It's a good word. So many potential interpretations. And it pleases Marie.

'That pretty much nails it,' she says. And I know she wants to talk about the lunch, and probably resents me a little for not bringing it up yesterday.

'So?' I say. She shrugs eloquently.

'I don't know,' she says. 'We ate lunch. We held hands. We necked, like high-school kids, in the parkade. And then I came back.'

I wait.

'I sent him a text after, thanks for a great time,' she says. 'And he hasn't written me back.' She bites her lips. 'I think it's over.'

I wait.

'Because if he had had a great time, he'd text me back, right? With plans to do it again? He was clearly disappointed in the whole experience.'

Oh, my Marie.

'Should I text him to find out if he received my text?' she asks, and I see her reaching for the phone.

'Jesus-fucking-Christ, Marie, what are you, twelve?' I snap. And she takes half a step back and stares at me, because I don't snap. Out of character. 'It's what, half a day. Don't fucking chase. Enjoy . . . enjoy the memory.'

'But I'm just not sure I'm really enjoying the memory,' she says wistfully. 'It was, you know, OK. But a little awkward. And the chemistry in person . . . it wasn't . . . it wasn't quite the same as in the texts. And I think maybe he felt that too . . .'

I don't understand women.

'But if you felt that, then why are you so anxious for him to get back to you?' I ask.

'Because!' Marie exclaims. 'I don't want him to be the one to leave! I want to be the one to make the decision that it's over. Jesus, Jane, don't you understand anything?'

Apparently not.

I give Marie a pat on the arm that she morphs into a hug. Again, I think I could tell her. I should tell her. So she doesn't feel alone. So I don't feel alone. We could be the anti-Nicola-and-Colleen. Commiserating, instead of about their cheating husbands, about our fucking lovers.

But I can't.

Because . . .

I just don't.

'You really, really don't look well,' Marie repeats.

Too much cyberfucking, not enough sleep, I'm tempted to say. Except it's of course not just that. Secrets. They exhaust. Moral ambiguity, it exhausts.

And there's a big crash halfway up the hill, and Marie and I race up to disentangle limbs and sleds and to kiss bruises and fix toques and mittens.

Use your mouth even longer because I know you'd
rather be fucked in your pussy
—oh dear fucking god I am so wet
Cum for me.

Oh, Jesus. I really need to work on feeling badly about this. And I need to . . . I don't know what I need. A smack upside my head. A reality check.

The phone rings as I'm unloading the kids at the front door. 'Dad?' I say with surprise. My mother calls me and texts me constantly. Annoying 'What are you doing?' texts, random 'I love you guys!' texts, to-the-point 'Do the kids want anything special for lunch on Tuesday?' texts, passive-aggressive 'I know you don't care about such things, but it really means a lot to Dad and me to have our anniversary acknowledged . . .' my father calls only in real emergencies. As do I.

'What's wrong?' I say. Anxiety mounting.

'Why does something have to be wrong for me to call my only daughter?' my father says. 'I just called to see how you guys are doing. And to tell you I love you.'

Fucking twilight zone.

'OK,' I say. 'We love you too. You sure everything's OK?'

'Fine, fine,' he says. 'You know, it's that time of the year when there's just not much to do at work. So an old man's mind wanders. To the things he loves.'

This is not my father talking.

'Dad?' I ask. 'Are you by any chance recovering from a Christmas lunch that involved too much wine?'

'Jane!' he's appalled. 'You know I never drink at work. With work colleagues. I guess it's just the season to feel, you know, sentimental. And we're having our lunch tomorrow, and I just . . . I wanted to tell you I love you. And how much I'm looking forward to seeing you.'

'OK,' I say. 'Well, we're just fine. And I love you too. You sure nothing's wrong?'

'Everything's fine, fine,' he says again. And rings off.

I'm a little weirded out.

When Alex comes home and I tell him about the phone call – he's also weirded out.

'Maybe he had a prostate exam or a colonoscopy or something and is suddenly aware of his own mortality again,' Alex suggests. 'Remember that time he had to have an MRI? He wouldn't stop hugging me.'

'Maybe,' I agree. The phone blips to announce an 'I love you xoxoxoxoxo love Mom' text from my mother. I type back 'xoxo' without saying anything to Alex. Sigh.

'Is it too much to ask of your parents to be predictable?' I ask.

'Yes!' Cassandra and Henry call in unison from the living room.

'Little ingrates,' I shout back. 'Supper in five!'

I make it through the evening, bedtime and beyond without starting up Facebook, or even picking up my phone.

But I still don't sleep.

51

Day 4 – Fatherhood

This is how I start my mornings now. Waiting for you.
—I'm here. I guess playing coy and hard to get when
you come won't really cut it.
Not anymore. Nor would I want that.
—What do you want?
You. Angry and wet. Dressed to please. A half-willing slave.
—oh my lover
—there is a special place in all hells for people like you
I know it.
What do you want?
—you
—on no terms
—so entwined with me we don't end
—for a few hours
Then I send you home. Bruised and happy.
—not too bruised, not in any too obvious places
Of course.
Perhaps hating me just a little more.
—Of course. Inevitable.
Swear at me. Curse me when I'm fucking you.
Walk in my door. Say 'fuck you.' Then – submit.
—I want to meet you in a public place first.
—Will you let me?
*If you demonstrate your submission in public. By how
you dress*

How you speak.
How you admit you're my whore.
—I want your hands under my clothes, on my skin, in a
place with eyes
My shameless exhibitionist whore.
—(suddenly all of our . . . previous . . . encounters
seem so fucking tame)
(Practice.)
Will you do all that I ask?
—yes
Good answer.
—I've forgotten . . .
—I've forgotten how you fit into the crevices,
indentations of my mind
I very much like reminding you of yourself
—Tell me, what do I do to you?
You feel like a counterpart. A woman me. You spark a
fire deep in me. And you bring to mind how I was
shaped, erotically. You affected me so. Of course we fit.
You impressed me.
—impressed
—imprinted
I still have the bruises
—inside
Deep.
— [deleted]
— [and again – I can't form the words]
Say it
—you're like a disease
—I knew it then
—wanted you so badly, I needed to run away from you
—too much
—it's a hard thing when you understand what someone
is, perfectly.

Footsteps down the stairs and I slam the laptop lid down. I should really just do this on my phone. Less conspicuous. As the thought enters my head, I push it away. I don't like it. I do not like to be . . . deceitful. I lift the laptop lid up.

—Reality calls. Xx
xx

Alex piggybacks Annie down the stairs and into my lap. I enfold her, kiss her, smell her hair. He brushes his lips against my forehead, then hers. 'Running late,' he calls over his shoulder as he runs into the kitchen, grabs coffee, runs back upstairs. 'Want me to get the boys out of bed before I shower?'

'No, there's lots of time for them,' I say to his disappearing back. Stretch on the couch. Don't look at the laptop. Pull my thoughts away from where they inevitably wend and think about what a fantastic, fantastic father Alex is. And how precious what I have here, in my arms at this moment, all around me in this house, in this family, in this life, is to me. And try to wrap myself in that thought. Protect myself with it.

I fail.

What do you want?
—You
—on no terms
—so entwined with me we don't end
—for a few hours
Then I send you home. Bruised and happy.
Perhaps hating me just a little more

Breakfast. Shower. Clothes. Everyone has socks and pants; minor miracle. Into the minivan. I'm so rattled, I almost ram into Clint as he pulls into the driveway to pick up his son Clayton.

'Jeezus, I'm so sorry,' I say through the rolled-down window.

'You OK, Jane?' he asks, peering at me through his. One of the longest sentences he's ever said to me. Of course, I did just almost kill him.

'Fine,' I lie. 'Just late. Be safe.'

'You be safe,' he says, and I can see he's pondering the logistics of driving all my four kids as well as Clayton wherever it is they have to go, because clearly I can't be trusted behind the wheel of a car right now . . . and I smile. My head clears, briefly, and I have one of those sharp insights into why Lacey has loved him for the past nine, ten, eleven years – as he's fucked other women and fathered at least one other child – and why women keep on falling into bed with him even though he makes no pretence of what he is and what he is not.

Cause he's a really, really rockin' dad. His always-pointing-to-the-hottest-target cock notwithstanding.

I've told this to Lacey before, not that she really needs to hear it, for she knows – that he's a great dad. Because it's not something hidden. This is not a new revelation for me either; Clint's commitment to fatherhood has always been there. Not in being Clayton's weekend dad – although he's never, as far as I know, missed a weekend. Not in showering either Clayton or even Lacey with gifts, because he's no Disney dad. In fact, he's kind of . . . cheap, really. Lacey orders herself gifts from Clint and tells him what he got her. Sometimes he reimburses her. Sometimes he conveniently forgets. His presents to his son, birthday and Christmas alike, consist of on-sale clothes, the price tag of which is further driven down by Clint's employee discount. I know this, because Lacey has no secrets, important or otherwise. She shows me Clayton's clothes, tags still on – and she shows me the earrings 'I bought myself from Clint.'

This is how, why Clint is a great father: most days, he stops at Lacey's on the way to his home from work to say hi and bye to Clayton. He does this when he's fucking Lacey, and he does this when she doesn't want to look at him. He does this when they're fighting (and, thanks to Facebook, I know when they're fighting even before Lacey tells me) and he does this when they're reconciled, as Lacey puts it, 'again madly in love.' When he can't come – he calls. And he calls to say goodnight to his boy every single night.

Alex, who is also a great father, does not call to say goodnight when he's not going to be home for bedtime.

Of course, he sleeps in the same house as his children every night. I don't expect it.

I try to recall if I call to say goodnight on those nights when I'm out late. I used to, all the time. These days, now that they're older? Maybe not.

I resolve to start doing so again.

Back to Clint. This must be part of his attraction, to Lacey and others. Can they tell, do they pick up this thread, this power – can they tell this man will make a great father? Not as a beautiful physical specimen only, but in those post-conception essentials? That he will rock your baby to sleep, and teach your toddler to throw a ball, and take your six-year-old to cheesy Disney movies he himself hates?

I think they can. I could – I knew Alex would be a fabulous dad, that was part of what I loved about him, always, love about him the most, still. I could see him holding my babies, not just making them.

Never part of the dynamic for Matt and me, never. Yet he, I have no doubt, would make a wonderful father to someone else's child. His wife's, perhaps. This I also know, even though the part of him that belongs to me, fits into me is not the man who will be a father.

But it does not surprise me that they are still childless.

—It's a hard thing when you understand what someone is, perfectly.

I deliver the kids to school safely, drop Annie at my mom's for the morning, run back home and pretend to be a housewife for two hours – laundry, fucking laundry, who finds joy and fulfilment in pairing socks? – then meet my dad for our sacrosanct father–daughter lunch. First Thursday of every month when we're in the same city, third Thursday of the month too, when we can fit it in – our ritual since I was . . . twelve? Thirteen? It was at one of these lunches that I officially lost what little religion I had been brought up in. Confessed to my first kiss (but not my first fuck, although I did think of telling him . . . but that would have been too much, even for my dad). Told Dad I had to leave John, but couldn't figure out how to do it. Laughed to him about – well, all of them. Scott. Raj. Pretentious Jason and overly ambitious Aldrin. That weird guy from Ghana who really wanted me to pierce my tongue and clit. Tried to explain to him why I was going to marry Alex.

Never told him a word about Matt.

We face each other across a wobbling round table in the basement of The Unicorn. Dad's staring at a steak sandwich. I'm poking at an awful Caesar salad.

'What the fuck was I thinking?' I say. 'Fish and chips. Fish and chips. The only thing we ever order here.'

'Sometimes change is good,' my father says. I give him a suspicious look.

'But not when it comes to pub food,' I retort. 'You know what? I'm not eating this. I'm going to order fish and chips. You?'

He cuts into the steak.

'Not so bad,' he says.

My dad. Stellar dad, incredible – and incredibly patient – husband. But will never, ever admit he made any sort of mistake. As he masticates the sandwich, I'm filled with gratitude for his place in my life – for his awesomeness as father. As grandfather. And I wonder if this will be one of our very rare really *honest* conversations – or one of our companionable silent lunches when we just chew and enjoy each other's company without talking – or one of the painful, shallow ones, in which one or the other of us has something profound to share but can't figure out how to breach it, and so we talk at length about nothing.

I wish to share . . . *nothing*. I feel my angst and turmoil and mindfucked state retreating inwards where I can wall them off. And I tell him – that Lacey thinks she and Clint are ring shopping, but I think they're just ring *photographing*. That I can now do four unassisted pull-ups ('but then I want to die.'). That Henry's got a loose tooth. That Alex is in a mad pre-Christmas rush – 'Everyone wants to try to close before Christmas. But it means all these late nights.' And how much I'm dreading the annual law firm Christmas party. 'I swear, they get worse every year.'

Dad laughs and nods and sighs in all the right places. If he can tell that I'm withdrawn and not talking about anything real, he doesn't betray it. And that's why I can always be with him. My mother will also sense it, discern that I am in angst and turmoil. But she will poke, and poke, and poke until I run away screaming. Dad never will. I can stay with him even when I retreat.

Today, I realise I'm not the only one who retreated. He's sitting across from me also full of something he can't share.

I take one of his big, callused hands in mind. Kiss his knuckle.

'What was that for?' he says.

'I love you,' I say. 'Always.'

And I see a glistening in the corner of his left eye. No. No fucking way is my dad about to cry. No.

It's gone.

'I'm going to have to retire next year,' he says instead of crying. I let go of his hands, fold both of mine under my chin.

'No, really? When did you get so old?' I tease.

'Sometime between my third and fourth grandchild,' he teases me back. 'You know how proud I am of you? How much I love you, all of you?'

This, again. So out of character.

'I know,' I say. 'You don't have to tell me.' I close my eyes. Fuck. Fine. I'll do it.

'Everything OK?' I ask. 'At home? With you and Mom?'

I have had the nerve to ask this question . . . oh, three times in my life. Once when I was sixteen, and realised, after coming home from summer camp, that my parents hadn't spoken to each other at all in the four days I had been back. Once when I was nine months pregnant with Cassandra and hyper-sensitive, and suddenly noticed, acutely, painfully, with a tinge of horror, that even when they were allegedly joyously anticipating the arrival of their first grandchild, my parents weren't so much speaking to each other as shouting at each other. Or rather my mother was shouting. My father . . . hiding. And once, five years ago, when my dad started smoking again and my mother put herself on a ridiculously restrictive diet . . .

The answer, always: 'Well, you know how it is, Jane. She's not the easiest woman in the world to live with. She goes through her episodes. But I love her. And always will.'

No answer at all. And yet answer enough that I am always afraid to ask.

Dad is looking at his hands, his terrible steak sandwich. I wait for 'You know how it is'. Instead:

'I'm sorry.'

'What?'

'I'm sorry,' he repeats quietly. 'I know . . . I saw you. Noticing. Reacting. On Monday.'

I nod. My belly clenches.

'It won't happen again,' he says. 'If I can help it.'

And again. No answer at all. And yet answer enough that I wish I hadn't asked.

We finish lunch in silence. He holds me a little longer and tighter than usual when I kiss him goodbye.

My phone buzzes as I get in the car. Text from Mom. 'How was your lunch with Dad?' 'Great,' I lie and type. And lean against the driver's-seat headrest, my eyes closed. I need to go pick up my kids. Make supper. No text from Alex alerting me to clients sabotaging the evening tonight. No emails from my clients upsetting my schedule. No message from Matt.

And that's good.

I need . . . equilibrium. I need . . . I need to spend a night enveloped in the cocoon of my family, my husband, my children, my real life. I need to anchor. I need . . .

. . . I need to not wish that there was a message. I need to get a fucking brain.

I've been here before. And I've stopped it. And I will stop it again. I have so much to lose. Everything. A family with four children. What does he have? Joy. I pause. I have always been unfair to Joy. Superior, mildly contemptuous – either for her blindness and oblivion or her willingness to endure a series of betrayals so she could wear the crown of Matt's girlfriend, then Matt's wife. Jesus. Is that what he thinks about Alex? Superior, mildly contemptuous? Dismissive?

I don't want to think about any of this. Any of it. Ever.

I push the thoughts away. Hard.

Alex and I are fucking awesome parents. I chant this to myself silently as I make dinner. As we don't yell at the children, much, while they show off for Daddy at the dinner table. As he cajoles the boys into clearing the table and loading the dishwasher. As he reads *Captain Underpants* to the boys. As he says, 'I've missed too many bedtimes in the last little while' to me while I mop up the flood that is our bathroom after four children bathe in it. I read *Winnie the Pooh* to Annie. Cassandra, too grown up at this moment for my comfort, is curled up in her bed reading *Anne of Green Gables* to herself.

We are fucking awesome parents. No longer chanting.

Knowing. Believing. I slip into bed, not tranquil, no, definitely not tranquil, but . . . certain of this, at least. We are really great parents, Alex and I. And the children are all asleep, and he is going to come into the bedroom, and I will . . .

'Jane?' He pokes his head into the bedroom. 'Boys are asleep. I'm going to pop down into the office for a bit before bed. Review the latest drafts of the documents so I've got a head start for tomorrow.'

'Of course,' I say.

And he's barely gone when I pull out the laptop. And check Facebook.

Busy day?
—No.
—I've been . . . avoiding being available.
Ah. And why?
—Because. I am struggling, finally, suddenly, with reconciling this, what you do to me, with my real life. And my real obligations. Which I want and need to preserve. Do you understand? A husband. Four children. A really fucking great life.
Yes. I understand.
Jane.
Do you remember – the last time we saw each other. It was the only time you were ever in my condo in Montreal. On the balcony. Everyone else was in the kitchen.
—I remember. The last time.
I had you alone for only a few moments. I looked at your legs and asked if you were wearing stockings.
—You put your hands under my skirt.
You gave me the most withering, pitying look. Pulled away. Do you remember what you said?
—'Get your fucking hands off me.'
Yes.

—I was pregnant with Cassandra.

I figured it out – a few months later. At the time, it was such a slap – your first real rejection of me. You would not look at me the rest of the night. And I never wanted you more. Of course. Perversely. I wanted you then. I wanted you always. I want you always. But I always want you . . . tied to someone else.

—Ah.

I believe this is what you want as well. It used to be. Is it still?

—I am struggling. See, I remember that moment, so very well. I remember how you looked at me. I remember how I felt with your hands on me. And I remember . . . I remember realising that if I was going to do this properly – if I was going to be Alex's wife, and the mother of his children – I had to stay the fuck away from you.

—And this bothers me, this: you and Joy, you still have no children?

No. We've been trying to conceive, half-heartedly, the last year or so.

—Half-heartedly?

Utilitarian, reproductive sex is boring. You know I'd think that. But, Jane, and this is what you are asking: I am not looking for an out of my marriage. I am not looking to destroy yours. I am looking to fuck you senseless when I come. Use you. And leave.

Is that blunt and honest enough for you, my forever lover?

—Tell me you're not having a mid-life crisis, are not frustrated with your marriage, aren't . . . oh, fuck, I don't even know what. What do I want you to tell me? *This: this is about us. Always. An opportunity. A gift. A chance to come together again.*

And you want it as much as I do.

—You are always corrupting me.

We were always corrupting each other. I think, deep down, you're more a harlot than even I.

—Bastard.

At least, that's my fantasy.

—I want to run. That's what I do with you, what I've always done with you. Enjoy a little, suffer a little, then leave. That's my MO.

Yes. The running. Your MO, as you put it. Well. Have you enjoyed enough? Tell me to fuck off and go away. Maybe I will.

—Maybe?

No. Probably not. You've admitted already it's too late for you to start playing coy.

—I am promised to you.

I don't chase. It's undignified. You are promised to me.

—And if it's everything we've been imagining, we will repeat it in another 10 years.

With great pleasure.

Now quickly.

Tell me what you'll be doing in eight days, my lover.

—I will be your fuckslave.

Again.

—I will be your fuckslave . . .

—my lover

Your master

—Presumptuous.

You will be on your fucking knees before me, my whore. Say it.

—Yes.

Good.

8. Xo

—8. Xx

I'm so fucked.

Day 5 – One night

Four days ago, I was sane.

Today I am mad. This is how my day starts. Wanton as soon as I am awake, wanting, aching. No longer pretending. I turn on my laptop and email and Facebook only for one thing. Work? What work? Calgary is asleep, but Montréal is stirring. And, oh, my lover. Yes. There he is. And here we go. The countdown. And fuck. A client pings me on Google chat at the same time. Lovely.

7
—7
Instantly hard
—Fire in my belly
Get my email?
—checking
—fuck
This was me. This morning, thinking of you.
—oh yes
— . . .
—I am distracted
—I have a client on Google chat right now
I like the thought of you being innocent and
professional on one side lusting on the other
More corruption of you.
—by you

And me alone.
Confess your actions last night.
—I rehearsed what it would be like.
—Walking into the lobby
—Barely able to stand on my fuck-me heels
—Standing in the entry, looking for you
—Play by play
—Oh, lover, 7 days
I would let you stand there a good while. To enjoy the sight of you prepared for me. Let others enjoy it too.
—As soon as I walk in, they're all looking at me. They know what I'm there for. I exude it.
Your long legs on show, cock-sucking lipstick and fuck-me heels leave no doubt.
—Are you requesting cock-sucking lipstick?
Demanding.
—demanding, of course
Lots of eye makeup. All the better when it runs, teary eyed.
Purposeful. Professional.
Ready to use.
—Tell me that all day, no matter what you do, part of your mind will be tormented by pictures of me.
No small part.
Pictures of you, at my feet. In debasement.
—Jesus, Matt.
I'm putting you to work as we speak. My hands on my cock, my mind turning them into your mouth, your pussy.
—There will be nothing left of you in 7 days.
Soon I'll abstain. Right now my morning cock needs seeing to.
And that's your fucking job. Do it.
With one hand you're stroking me, innocently typing with the other.

—yes

—writing to a client

—very professional, formal

—he doesn't know I'm naked, at your knees

Occasionally you lean over to spit on my cock to keep it slick. Professionally. Almost disdainfully.

—I'm distracted, multitasking you know

My multitasking slave

It's easier to type when I bend you over the desk to fuck you. Now you can use both hands. Get more work done.

—efficient

—you got impatient

—Wait, I really need to go through this with my client . . .

Fucking hot

I tell you to read aloud what you're typing

So I can hear your voice quaver

Interspersed with grunts and moans

—I read to the rhythm of your cock's movement

I tell you to type 'I am Matt's fuckslave' just to see it on screen.

The words hang there. Tantalising.

—We both stare.

—I start to delete.

—(I just really typed and deleted that in my Google chat. Fuck. What's wrong with me? Flirting with danger.)

How did that feel?

—I almost came.

Do it again. All caps.

And cum.

—wait . . .

—typing

—. . .

—cumming . . .

Good
—now you
Mmmmmmmm
Done
—I cum on command for you
As do I apparently
—There is power in submission . . .
Shot up to my neck
—I get up on my tippy-toes, lick it off
You are thorough. Diligent.
Dedicated.
—(how can I come this much in 24-48 hours and still be unsated?)
(Lucky me. Hopefully this mystery will never be solved.)
—We should go do stuff. Get dressed. Work.
—It's like the languor of leaving a well-used bed . . .
Languor.
Your mind turns me on so.
—the idea of your tongue on my nipples makes my toes curl
And yes. Work. Clothes. Reality. Nipple.
—7 days.
Seven. But you're mine. Already.
—utterly
Always.
In all ways.
Have a good day.
—It has a lot to live up to.
I have every faith. Xx
—xo

I breathe. Shower. Dress. Race down the stairs after Alex, his phone in my hands, catch him at the door, 'You left this in the bathroom again, love!' Marshal kids out of bed. Breakfast. Clothes. School run for all four today, because it's a preschool morning for the squirt. Everyday, ordinary things. Real life. At which I'm looking through a distorted lens, a curtain. Seven days. Seven days.

The phone buzzes and I swear my clit screams. My mouth parched. I stare, unseeing. Then crash, so disappointed. Nicola. Texting. Me? I raise my eyebrows, surprised, because Nicola does not really like me, never has. We're 'friends of friends', frequently in the same physical space together, but hardly soulmates. Her text says it all: 'Jane? Are you there? No one else is around. I. Am. Going. Mad. Need to talk to someone!'

My disappointment, my wetness anger me. And so I dial her number as an act of atonement.

And she spews. So much unhappiness and so much anger there. And it's just; I cannot deny her this anger, her right to be angry. The rat-fuck bastard is acting like, well, a rat-fuck bastard. Refusing to take the co-parenting-after-separation seminar. Refusing to negotiate an interim financial agreement. Refusing, I realise suddenly, to accept that he is in the middle of a divorce.

'He still hopes this is a separation,' I say, but Nicola doesn't hear me, she finishes the sentence differently:

'. . . not to take the responsibility for anything!' she cries. And she shouts and screams, and then, abruptly, switches gears and starts talking about the skank. Because none of this would have happened if it weren't for her. If she hadn't approached him, if she hadn't chased him. If she had acted the way a woman should – if she had respected *Nicola*, another woman, *a wife*, the *rights* of a wife . . .

I hold the phone away from my ear, but I still hear. And every few seconds make a sympathetic noise. A perverse part of me imagines she is Joy. A masochistic, martyred facet of my psyche casts her as Alex, saying all of this in his head – because he is a man, and he is Alex, and he would never bare his soul like this, no more would I. In both scenarios, the calumnies are cast at me, not at Matt. Of course, at me.

Just as Nicola, angry, angry though she is at the cheating rat-fuck bastard, is angrier still at the intern-skank, and sees her as the catalyst. He was weak and unable to say no, *she* was the instigator, the catalyst. If she hadn't seduced, invited, aggressed . . .

Jezebel.

How very Christian of Nicola, I think, and then, I think this: flip it. So. For me – am I weak and unable to say no? If Matt hadn't come – if he hadn't seduced, invited, aggressed . . . would I have sought him out? Or another?

It is a very, very interesting question. So interesting, I hold the phone away from my ear and sit on the floor to ponder the answer.

What is happening here? Is it me? Him? Us?

I wanted you then. I wanted you always. I want you always. But I always want you . . . tied to someone else.
—Ah.
I believe this is what you want as well. It used to be. Is it still?

I rejected Matt, consciously, effectively, once. But fully. With Cassandra in my belly. My commitment and love for Alex and the family we were starting were the most important, the only things in my universe. And what followed? Ten years. Almost eleven. Five pregnancies. One near-death experience, four babies. Swollen belly, milk gushing from breasts. Extreme joy. Exhaustion. Love. Motherhood. Monogamy. Monogamy without much struggle, without much reflection, because there wasn't much room for anything else. And yes, happiness, fulfilment. Other lovers, other desires? I barely had time and desire for Alex. It was all . . . babies. Toddlers. Obligations. Never enough sleep.

Nicola's two kids are Cassandra and Henry's age, I think, maybe older. Is she at this place? I suddenly wonder. Coming

69

out of the cloud cast by reproduction . . . no, wait. It is her husband who strayed. I am mixing stories and metaphors.

I am looking for justification.

I am looking for an argument that ends like this: I deserve this night.

Fuck it. One night. Eleven years of pregnancy, and babies, and breastfeeding and faithfulness and monogamous sex and no real transgression or temptation, eleven years of duty. Fuck it. One night. I deserve this one night.

I'm going to do it. And I'm not going to feel an iota of guilt about it.

Done.

Shut the fuck up, brain.

'And is that too much to ask, Jane?' Nicola's voice echoes in my ear.

'No,' I say firmly. 'It's not too much to ask.'

'Thank you,' she says. 'Thank you. I know this – I just needed to hear someone else say it.'

'It's not too much to ask,' I repeat. And then I add, 'You'll get through it.'

'Of course I will,' Nicola says. 'I will. Because I am awesome. And not an immoral, cheating skank.'

She hangs off. I touch my forehead against the cold tile floor.

Fuck it. One night. I get one night. And I get flooded with relief. The dilemma, the angst, the search for the guilt, disappears, recedes. One night. The climax. In, what, eight days? Seven days. And one night. And then, it's over, and real life takes over again.

One night.

It's my mantra for the rest of the day. I field one more telephone call from Nicola, and listen to her patiently, guilt-free, without feeling the need to atone, judge or rush, as she repeats everything she said in the earlier conversation. I make all the right responses, all the right noises. One night.

I get one night.

I pick up Annie from preschool. I take her out for lunch, and then to the library for story time. We read books. Mem Fox. Robert Munsch. Mo Willems. She laughs so hard at Elephant and Piggie that she wets herself. While I'm changing her in the bathroom, she hiccups, hiccups and throws up lunch – sushi – all over herself. Me.

One night.

I get one night.

'Why does the car smell like vomit?' Henry asks, wrinkling his nose, as the kids load into the car. Annie bursts into tears.

'Annie's sick,' I say. 'Hush.'

'Disgusting!' Eddie says. 'And she smells like pee, too!' Annie cries louder.

'You smell too, Mom,' says Henry.

I sigh.

'Sorry, Mom, but vomit does smell really, really bad,' Cassandra offers. Annie's now wailing at the top her lungs. I rest my forehead against the steering wheel.

'If you're really lucky, Annie will cry so hard she'll puke again,' I mumble through gritted teeth.

Eleven years of pregnancy, and babies, and breastfeeding and faithfulness and monogamous sex and no real transgression or temptation, eleven years of diapers, vomit, snot, sleepless nights, given to all of them freely, unresentfully, fully.

One night.

At home, I clean Annie up and proactively put her on the couch with a puke bucket beside her. Send the boys to Lacey's to play with Clayton. Ask Cassandra – nose in book already – to keep an eye on Annie while I clean myself up. Then go to check how badly the car stinks. Disgusting. Ugh. So tired. But. Kind of at peace. Unconflicted. Not happy, exactly, but . . . OK. Thoroughly OK, and no longer covered in vomit.

The phone rings and I look at it, and it's Nicola again, and I have done my duty by her today, and will not go through a third conversation with her. I let her go to voice mail. But the phone tingles while I am still holding it in my hand, and my clit tingles too, and it's Facebook, and it's Matt. My lips start to part in a smile, and I prepare to be caressed by a lover.

But then, the world ends, immediately:

Heart-breaking/soul-saving news. My Calgary trip is off. Fucking lawyers. Fucking clients. We're pulling all the work – fuck, fuck, fuck.
I am truly sorry. And fucking pissed.
The adjective of the day is: livid.

I don't write back. What is there to say? The world has ended. Everything is over. He's not coming.

I am safe. I cannot transgress.

I can't breathe.

Day 6 – Obsession

I can't breathe. Or sleep. At 5.30 in the morning I give up. Get up. Go downstairs to pretend to work. And I write . . .

—Oh lover I miss you already, and four days ago I
didn't even know there was anything to miss

And I go offline, and turn off the phone, because I don't want to suffer.

I channel the insomnia into a mad explosion of work, then surprise Alex with pancakes for breakfast.

'Is it wrong if I like the effects of your insomnia?' he asks.

'No.' I shake my head. 'Enjoy without guilt.'

Ha.

I try to get in touch with the guilt within me, but there is only heat and desire. And regret. Such woeful regret when I let myself feel it, I again lose my breath. I do not need to be any more in touch with those.

Because it's Saturday and they can sleep in, the kids are of course up early. I feed them pancakes when they come down, then wrestle the younger two into snowsuits and chase everyone outside. The snow is fresh and clean. We make snow angels. Try to make snowballs. Run.

I run, throw. Breathe. Try not to think.

Alex is pulling out of the driveway as we come back. He stops, gets out. Kisses all around. 'I hate working on Saturdays,' he murmurs into my ear. 'You know that, right?' I shrug. Brush my lips against his neck.

'Every December,' I whisper. He helps me load the kids into the van, then gets back into the hatchback. Drives away.

I rest my head against the frame of the van. Cold. So cold.

'Mom?' Cassandra, ten years old and so tall and allowed to ride in the front seat when the roads are good, leans over. 'You getting in?'

'Yes. Let's roll.'

We get to my parents' house with enough time for Mom and me to share a coffee before I take off for the gym. There are cardboard boxes everywhere. 'We're going to decorate all-out today, sweeties – we're in the second week of December already, really, and I'm so behind!' she tells the kids. And suddenly, I realise, yes, she is behind, my Christmas-crazy mother who starts the process of Christmastifying her house on November 1, and is 'finished' by December 1. The tree is up – but it's undecorated. The Christmas village: still in boxes. Cassandra and Henry start taking things out.

'Wait for Gran!' my mom trills.

'Is something wrong?' I ask. Look at the clock. Got to be in the car in two minutes. Gulp the coffee.

'Why would anything be wrong?' my mother says in an unnaturally pitched voice. Fuck. Something's wrong. I look at the clock again. She catches my eyes straying.

'Go,' she says. 'We are going to have a great time decorating the *entire* house. Don't hurry back.'

Fine.

I make it to the gym without rear-ending or side-swiping anyone again, a miracle. Nicola's not there, and I think I might be relieved she's not. Or I might just be horny. Jesus-fucking-Christ. I'm absolutely soaking. What the fuck is wrong with me?

I mop. Change. Ponder having a shower before the session . . . walk out. The gym looks fuzzy.

'Jane!' Jesse's voice. My head snaps. 'You looked like you couldn't find me,' he says. 'So. Any requests for today?'

He seems very, very far away. 'Yes,' I say finally. 'Make me lift heavy shit and not think. Exhaust me.'

'I can do that,' he laughs. I hope he's as dense as I think he is. Sweet and dumb, right? He cannot pick up on the unleashed storm that is me right now.

'Jane!'

'What?'

'Stop now. Rest.'

'OK. What next?'

'On the bench.'

'What?' I fucking jump up two feet.

'On the bench,' he says. 'Chest flies. You hate chest flies. And I'll give you a heavier weight than normal to boot. You asked to be exhausted, remember?'

I sit at the edge of the bench and watch while he goes to get the weights. 'Hey, Jesse,' I say. 'How long have you known me now? More than a year, right?'

'Almost two, actually,' he says.

'Right,' I say. 'So – well, you don't really know me very well, because it's always just here, and we have limited conversation. Lift this. Rest. Et cetera. But – well, tell me this. Give me some adjectives that describe me.'

'What?' Jesse looks uncomfortable, and for a brief moment I wonder if perhaps he does not know what an adjective is.

I am unfair. Because he's so pretty.

'Well—' He crouches down beside me. 'Lie down so I can give you the weights.' I lie down. On the bench. Fucking hell. 'You're very . . . disciplined. Committed. Dedicated.' He places the weights in my hands.

'Jeezus fucking Christ, how heavy are these?' I yowl. Heave the weights upwards.

'You're a really, really good mother,' Jesse continues. 'The left arm is going too deep – pull it up sooner. The way you talk about your kids – it always makes me smile. Inspires me, really. Well – and it's part of that dedicated thing. How many clients do I have who, at any excuse, don't come? Too busy, too sick. No babysitter. When your babysitter falls through, you come with the kids. And they're great kids. And you're so patient with them.'

'Fucking hell, Jesse, I am going to die here.'

'Although you do swear too much. One more – you've got it.'

'Ugh.'

He takes the weights from me and I curl into the fetal position on the bench.

'You swear too much,' he repeats.

'Not an adjective,' I mutter.

'Was I only supposed to use adjectives? Well – yeah. Disciplined. Dedicated. Patient. Outspoken . . . but kind of reserved at the same time, which is an interesting combination. And . . .' I stop listening. Other adjectives are going through my head.

Hard.

'. . . one of the strongest women I know, actually, physically and mentally,' Jesse says. And flashes me a lovely smile. I have no idea what he just said. My thoughts are in a hotel room in which I would have been a week from now – and in which I will now no longer be. And . . . feeling no relief. Just regret. Such overpowering, crippling regret. And lust and desire and . . . Oh, fuck. If I were ruler supreme of the universe, I would be in that hotel room right now.

'Jane?' Jesse asks. 'Are you going to get off that bench?'

Eventually.

Fuck. One night. I wanted that one night. So very, very badly.

I finish the workout. Drive back to my parents' house.

My mom can't wait to get us out of the house, which happens sometimes, so I gather up the kids – Eddie doesn't want to leave, of course – and drive straight home. The kids want to chill, so I let them find books, movies and computers. Throw in laundry. Ponder supper. Avoid work and the computer for a while. Scrub the bathroom. Promise to read books in a few minutes.

Check Facebook.

5.30 in the morning? Could you not sleep, my lover? In the span of six days, I've become one of those people who check their Facebook mobile every 11 seconds. Obsessed.
Today's obsession, made worse by the fact that I won't get to feel it: the sensation of your hair between my gripping fingers.
Freshly shorn to serve me better. I'm developing a preparation fetish.

Instantly wet. Or, rather, wetter.

I am losing my mind.

Why is he writing me? Tormenting me? It doesn't matter. None of it matters. He's not coming.

Read books to kids. Do stuff. Then it's time for Cassandra and Henry's piano lessons. I think, as I do every Saturday – what was I thinking? Piano lessons on Saturday? Why? But it's the last one before Christmas break. Fine. Distraction. Good to have things to do, places to go. I won't write back.

Load kids into car. Think about leaving the phone behind. Except that would be irresponsible. Winter. Icy roads. I could have an accident. I need the phone with me. Right.

'Jane!' Lacey dances out of her front door and around her Mini. Clayton is with her, smiling shyly at Cassandra. 'Jane, look!' and she thrusts a hand, huge flickering diamond on her finger, into my face.

Oh, my fucking God. A diamond. A ring. He did it. *She* did it.

'Oh, Lacey!' I hug her.

'It's not exactly me, is it?' Lacey says, extending her hand in front of her and looking at the ring and finger critically. 'A little too . . . white.' She laughs. 'But Clint insisted this was the one.'

'It's stunning,' I say. 'And the date?'

'The day I nail that man down to a date,' Lacey says. 'How many years did it take me to get him to propose? And how many months to get the engagement ring?' She's not frustrated or bitter. She's, if anything, ecstatic.

But that's Lacey. Perfection. Happiness. No matter what.

And to her, in some way, Clint must be perfection too. I can see it, sometimes, physically anyway. He is built like a linebacker or a hockey enforcer. He fills doorways. Casts a large shadow. 'I'm big, and so I need big men,' Lacey likes to say. 'You know, I don't want to think they're gonna break when I wrap my legs around them.' The visual of Lacey with her legs wrapped around Clint, and him carrying her up the stairs to her bedroom, makes me smile; the one time I heard Lacey say this right in front of Clint, it made him hard. Instantly.

He moves like an athlete, dresses like a businessman. And, for whatever reason, is a retail store manager, of a Target-like big box store. And seems perfectly content with his lot in life. The work doesn't go home with him, except in the form of an employee-discounted wardrobe. Lacey says that the guest bedroom in his two-bedroom condo is essentially a walk-in closet. 'With beds for the boys in the middle.'

'The boys' are Lacey and Clint's son Clayton, just a few months younger than my Cassandra, and Clint and Sofia's five-year-old son Marcello. When Lacey's happy with Clint, she calls Sofia 'the other wife'. When she's despairing of him, she calls her 'that woman'. Clint has both boys every weekend,

Friday night to Sunday evening, and the occasional weeknight as needed by the moms. He's the most conscientious, involved part-time dad I know.

He's also a star employee. His store has the lowest staff turnover in the chain, and consistently the highest sales, despite its less than stellar location in northeast Calgary. The low staff turnover is a no-brainer: all the adolescent girls, single moms and part-timer retired grandmothers stay to dream of being seduced by him; all the pubescent boys and plotting men stay to reap the benefits of working with so many horny females.

I don't know that any of this is true. But that's what Lacey says and it seems plausible.

'Of course, he doesn't sleep with any of the employees,' Lacey tells me. With what I think is touching faith and innocence, given what she knows about and has gone through with Clint. Until she adds, 'He just sleeps with the customers.'

Well. Yes.

That's how Lacey and Clint met, at his store. Lacey was there with a girlfriend, sorting through dresses on the clearance rack, she says. 'And then this incredible hottie, in the sexiest three-piece suit I've ever seen – and I'm allergic to suits, honey, never liked them before, not a bit – this hottie strolls by and looks at the dress I'm holding and says, "That would look absolutely wonderful on you." And I press it against me, and I say, "Not too skimpy?" And he says, "No such thing as too skimpy for you."'

The girlfriend considerately melts into the background. Jealous? Or resigned? Lacey doesn't recall; the girlfriend disappears from her story the moment Clint enters. Lacey takes her haul, including the too skimpy dress, to the changing room. With the promise to show it to Clint. He suggests she use the wheelchair-accessible family changing room that's just beside his office. He sees her in the dress. They disappear into the office.

Nine months later, Clayton is born.

'You always get what you want,' I tell her, the ring still in my face. Lacey smiles.

'Eventually,' she agrees. 'I am a long-term player.'

'Eventually.' I smile. 'But that's all that matters, right? Endgame.'

'Everything OK with you?' she says. She looks at me carefully. 'You're losing weight,' she pronounces. 'But not in that "I work out with a hot trainer to melt the baby fat" way. In a sickly, peakish, "not eating enough" way.'

She stares at me some more. Disconcerts me.

'Um, no, I don't think so,' I protest. 'Probably just tired today. And not at my best.'

I drive away a little faster than necessary.

I will not cyberfuck on a Saturday afternoon during my kids' piano lessons. Even though there will be nothing else to do in the waiting room but fiddle with my phone . . .

Fuck.

I have no self-control or will. Annie sucks on markers and colours, and Eddie fiddles with his Gameboy.

I take out the phone.

—Sleep was elusive.
what have you done today
—suffered
I am in withdrawal.
I tortured myself by rereading our missives.
—The extent of my desire for you is obscene.
I like that word
—Madness
I'm on a conference call. Because of the Friday disaster.
Fuck. Can't even concentrate on what I'm saying.
—I'm writing to you from my kids' piano lesson . . . so fucking wrong
—I was with my trainer this morning. When he told me to lie down on the bench . . .

80

I wonder if he could sense your heightened state.
—I don't know. I don't think so. Possibly he just
thought I was insane. I was not myself.
No. You were mine. Are mine.
Fuck. You bring out my dominant side to a nearly
frightening degree.
—frightening
—appropriate word for this
my anger hasn't abated. I thought it would by now.
—the build-up . . .
—so hard to let go
Especially when I don't want to.
—I'm glad
—that you don't want to.
I need to see you. Send me a photo.
Now.
—Now?
Of your face, Jane. Do it. Fucking now.
—sent
god you look good
—thank you
that mouth
will you keep your glasses on?
—do you want me to?
yes
brainy sexy hot
this isn't helping my anger
—they might be hard to clean if you cover them with cum
—I guess that didn't help either
I don't care
—Tell me about your anger.
It's a hot heavy feeling.
in my stomach. in my cock.
I want to fuck you so angrily
need to use you to release.

81

—I want you to use me
—I feel the bruises on my wrists from where you gripped me too hard
the marks on your thighs where I fucked you so hard
I can't take this. I have to have you
send me more of you
—I can't
—there are . . . considerable logistical difficulties in the taking and the sending
—did I mention I was in the kids' piano class?
Later then.
Fucking reality calls me as well: another emergency meeting.
now go cum for me
—At my kids' piano lessons?
Wherever the fuck you are. Now.
—Fuck you. Go to your meeting.
I'm going. Take more photos of you. I want to suffer more. And I want you to suffer with me. xx
—xo

Fuck. Mad. Mad. Clearly losing my mind. At home, I find myself moving from task to task without focus or concentration. Marie texts me. Still no word from Zoltan. What should she say? She's texted him again. Should she text him to say it's over? And more . . . I don't respond. What can I say? Truly, I give not a fuck. Tepid little *faux* affair. Not real. Not real. She calls – I don't pick up. I am a bad friend. I don't care. The text from Alex telling me he's going out for drinks with the deal team and won't be home until late barely registers.

I suffer.

Sleepwalk.

I hear Alex come in late, as I'm reading Annie to sleep. Hear him moving around in the kitchen. Heating up food. Dishes clinking in the sink. Then his head pokes into the girls' bedroom. He gives Cassandra – quietly reading a book – a kiss. Another one for Annie. A third for me.

By the time Annie's asleep, so is Alex. And I, shaking, shaken, sit in bed beside him and do yet another unforgivable thing. One night. It would have been just one night. One night, and over. And now what?

I get up. Lock myself in the bathroom with the phone. And take photos.

Send.

It's very, very late in Montréal. But he's waiting.

Holy fucking hot.
The open mouth. Yes.
—the things I do for you
—slut
The things you'll do for me. Slut.
—promises
Looking at you again. (Carefully)
Hold your fuck-me heels up to the camera.
—oh god done
And so well done
I WILL have those on your feet, pointed at the ceiling.
—My stomach is in knots
—I feel sick with desire for you
Did you like showing yourself to me?
—no
Good.
—this is so fucking sick
Yet we can't stop.
Addicted.
—I don't think that's the right word even
—compulsion
The dark cousin of obsession.
Those heels are fucking hot. To be blunt.
—yes

—I get wet putting them on
put them on
—on
how do you feel
—slick
obedient
—angry
good
—resentful
even better
—Jeezus
I want you to get fucked in those heels tonight.
—do you?
—what am I thinking while I'm getting fucked?
—in those heels, by someone else
Me. Watching you perform for me.
Making you work.
My shameless whore.
—Scripting me, directing me?
Letting you know when you can cum.
—stopping me when I really want to
'Wait for it.'
—oh fuck
you can't cum but he keeps pounding you
'Fuck her harder.'
'Harder.'
I stand up and take my cock out inches away from your face.
—out of reach
just barely
—I make that sound
I know which one.
'Cum on her ass. Now.'
I shoot my cum onto your glasses.
You are covered at both ends.

'Now you can cum.'
—can I use your limp cock?
No. I want to see you cum by submission alone.
your face glazed and eyes wild
—without a touch
—just from the scene, on your command
Now.
—now
you are so beautifully, submissively obedient
—fucking hell
—this is unreal
I hope you just came.
—without a touch
—I am soaking through my leggings
good
—I can't wait another 10 years to see you
you won't have to
Now go. Fuck him. In your glasses and in the heels.
Now.
—Jesus.
Fucking now. Orders. And tell me about it in the
morning.

I take my leggings and panties off in the bathroom and put
the fuck-me heels back on. And walk, very slowly, into the
bedroom.

Mad.

Interlude: She only belongs to those who take

She doesn't quite know what to say or how to say it. The day is unfolding and the thoughts and feelings of the night and morning escaping.

There was this: a cock in her mouth, ramming against her throat, interfering with her breathing, thrusting so hard she did not suck or lick, she just struggled to breathe.

There was this: a rapacious appetite, bite marks on his thighs, her face worshipping at his groin, her eyes closed, her thoughts in a dozen places at once, but always coming back to the moment, the smell of sex, the sound of self-control breaking.

And there was this: 'Fuck me hard, harder – I want to feel like you will break my pelvis,' and the sound and sensation of bone against bone and pleasure and pain commingled.

And there was release, toe-curling, soul-freeing release. Finally. She had cum for you so many times in the past six days. But she had not released like this, not in all that time. Always something holding her back, just enough so that, at the end of it, she remained unsated.

And when she fell asleep, you came to her, and you demanded. Everything. And she didn't even try to fight you any more, broken and hungry and knowing that this was fulfilment for her. Not having to ask. Not having to explain. Coach. Just to be taken. As you wanted to take her.

She woke up . . . happy is not the right word. Happiness is no longer possible: happy is what she had before she had this. But: almost relaxed. Almost sated. Able to contemplate the day ahead without a fire consuming her from within. For a while.

At the back of her mind, letting this thought simmer:

A few weeks ago, she spent a weekend alone in Vancouver. On one of those nights, she had dinner and too much wine with a man she knew wanted very badly to sleep with her – and she went to her bed virtuous and alone, and not at all tempted. On another night, she spent the evening and much of the night, including four hours alone with him in her hotel room, with a man she very much wanted to sleep with. There was no transgression, no hint of one, even though she knew exactly what she had to do to get him to cross the line: she knew what he was waiting for, and what he needed to see or hear from her to escalate things.

She does not like to ask. Or encourage.

She belongs only to those who will take.

What would you do if you had her alone for four hours in a hotel room?

She dreams of that every night.

Day 7 – I hate you

Thank you for the story. It was . . . entrancing. I could feel it all.
—You're welcome.
Now finish what you started.
—What?
I wake up to that in my inbox. Now I'm hard. Finish me. My fuckslave.
—Fuck. I'm not the only one going mad here, am I?
No. Both fucking insane. What will you wear today?
—What do you want me to?
I want you to dress like my whore. Slutty enough to make you blush and feel slightly shameful. Knowing I'm watching. Skirt a little too short. Breasts on display. No panties.
I sit across the room and watch you. I make your face burn with shame just by staring into you.
My slut, my slave. Mine.
—Yours.
—Utterly.
Now tell me what you're going to wear. And it'd better be something that makes every man who sees you want to fuck you.
—A dress. At first glance, demure, even conservative. But when I stand in profile, you notice it hugs every curve.

—And you notice it's cut so that you can't help but stare at my breasts.

—And when I sit down, the slit on its side and its shape means it runs much too high up my thighs.

Love the stealthy slut approach.

—And you know there's nothing more under the dress.

Yes. I enjoy watching my fuckslave toy with men.

Fills me with pride.

Check your email. Sent you another reaction shot.

—Jesus. Looking at this in my kitchen is so wrong.

So fucking wrong.

Wear stockings under your stealth slut dress. My cock demands it. I don't care if you have to drive somewhere today and buy some. They are an essential part of your uniform. Wear them very high on your thighs.

—Yes.

Yes, what?

—I will?

Yes, master.

—Role-player.

Your fucking owner, whore. Stockings. I want pictures. They will make me want to cum on your thigh. Tall, lace-up-at-back ones, do you remember? You wore them for me once before . . .

—I remember.

Get those for me when I come.

—You're not coming.

I will fucking come. Get the stockings. I will lace them up for you. Then I will send you down to the hotel bar. Make you wait for me. All eyes lusting at my whore.

—I'm in hell.

Good.

Your shameful submission is the most erotic thing I've ever imagined.

89

—10 years ago, 20 years ago, you couldn't do this to me, not this
—not like this
—not to this extent
I know
Now tell me what you are
While I cum.
—your fuckslave
More. Word-fuck me to the finish.
—I am your fuckslave
—I live for your pleasure
—Use me
—Harder
—Rougher
—I need this to be barely consensual
—I am in your room, and suddenly coy, demure, backing away
—Be rough
—Mark me and make me scream
—and cum for me
Holy ffffuck
Tremors
Aftershocks
Legs still shaking
—the fuckslave feels powerful
you made me gush
all over my chest
—Sated?
For the moment
—well
And now reality kicks in and I realise I'm an hour late for brunch with the in-laws.
—Life beckons.
It does indeed.
—Goodbye my lover.

—You will be fucking with my mind all day.
Stay warm, my lover. Thank you for this morning's service.
xo
—xx

I'm shaking when I log off, shaking and wet, and so sick with desire my stomach is in knots and my eyes are burning. I hear Alex moving upstairs and I listen . . . but he does not come down. Bathroom door creaks. Silence. Silence. And then, finally, the shower. And I move. Upstairs. Bathroom door. Lean against it. Listen for the kids – sleeping. And I slip into the bathroom, into the shower. My hands on his chest. 'Good morning.' 'Oh, love, yes.' 'Fucking insatiable, are you possessed?' 'Maybe. Yes. Don't you like it?' 'God. Harder. Yes. Like this . . .'

The water runs cold before we're done, and Annie's pounding on the bathroom door – 'Are you there, Mommy?' – finally brings our session to an end.

'Thank you.' He nuzzles my neck. I knock his phone off the sink counter as I reach for the door. Pick it up, put it back on the counter.

'You've got to be more careful with your toy, love,' I say, for the possibly hundredth time since Eddie put Alex's Blackberry in the toilet four years ago.

He flushes. Reaches for it and makes a motion as if to put it in his pocket. He's naked bar the towel wrapped around his waist. I laugh.

Let Annie in.

'Where were you?' she demands, latching onto my leg. 'Why are you here? What are you doing?'

'Waiting for you,' I tell her. 'What else? Everyone else up?'

They are. Watching TV. Eating cereal. I mother. Make bacon and eggs. Brush hair. Throw in laundry, unload the dishwasher. Remind Alex we're having dinner with his mother. Ignore a text from my mother ('How are you guys today?'). Ignore a text from Nicola ('Guess what the rat-fuck bastard did now?????'). Look at the text from Marie and raise my eyebrows.

- Guess who's got a new boy toy?

I feel . . . generous. And playful.

—Nicola?
- LOL. You don't get boy toys when you're enveloped in bitterness and hate.
- Goddess energy. That's what attracts boy toys.

The people who say texting does not communicate emotion, nuance – they don't text enough. I can feel Marie's smile. I can almost smell her pheromones.

—Over Zoltan, are you?
- Who? The dickless dickweed with the tiny withered penis that he never even got to use on me?

Guess she's over him.

- So over. What are you doing? Can we grab a coffee so we can talk?
—Sledding at Confed Park? In 45?
- Perfect. I'll bring the mochas. You get the Timbits for the kids.

I leave Alex lounging on the couch, texting on his phone and watching Netflix. 'We'll be back in two, three hours, and we can leave for Okotoks right away,' I call as I shepherd the kids into snowsuits and out the door. 'Love you.' 'Love you too,' he calls to my back.

The mocha's still so hot it burns my lips; Marie-in-the-flesh is beaming even more powerfully than her texts did. 'Is Alex working today again?' she asks, by way of making small talk and showing me she has self-restraint and cares about *me,* that she does not just want to jump into talking about *it.*

'No, decompressing,' I say. 'JP?'

She shrugs. Then smiles.

'Working, or, you know, claiming he's working,' she says. I nod, throw a glance at the sledders. Cassandra is dragging Annie up the hill. Henry and Eddie are fighting over who gets the 'good' sled. Marie's kids are watching to see how it all shakes out. I turn my attention back to Marie, who's rolling her eyes. Every few months, this is Marie's dominant mood: suggesting, never overtly, but pointedly, that perhaps JP is fucking around. With the implication that she's free to do what she wants to do. Because he already is.

'Their profession is so convenient, isn't it,' she says now. 'Late nights. Client meetings. Emergencies. Deadlines. Weekends at the office.'

I used to think, when I was first getting to know her, that she was trying to bait me. Get me to defend Alex – or, worse, get me to worry about Alex. About the late nights. Last-minute emergencies. All that. The intimacies with the office wives; the fuck-buddy exchanges among the associates. Now I know it was always about her. And JP.

And her desire for the boy toy on the side.

She's just about bursting; her self-restraint used up. She is ready to talk about him . . . in one – two – and . . . now.

'So,' she says. 'There I am. On fucking Facebook again, because this is how I'm dealing with not texting or retexting or checking to see if the dickweed texted me – by trolling on Facebook and commenting on people's stupid status updates and watching fucking cat videos, when – guess who pings me?'

Marie and I are late-life friends. We have no school or university friends in common. Nor any work colleagues. The question is, I suspect, rhetorical.

'Who?'

'Guess.'

Or not.

'Someone I know?' I ask. She nods. Her mouth curls into a smile. A smirk.

'Oh, yes,' she says.

It's a small pool.

'Someone at the law firm?' I ask. Which would be as stupid a thing as possible, on his part and hers, but these things are rarely rational. As I know.

She laughs.

'You'll never guess,' she says.

'Fuck. Fucking tell me,' I say. 'Who?'

'Paul,' she says. And, as I don't react, she repeats, 'Paul!'

'Paul?' I ask. And as I'm about to ask, 'Who is Paul?' I am reminded that Paul is the name of Nicola's cheating rat-fuck bastard husband. 'Paul?' I repeat. 'That Paul? I mean . . . Nicola's Paul?'

Marie bites her lips and grins and laughs.

'That Paul,' she says. 'Isn't that insane?'

Insane. Yes. Paul. Dorky Paul, who fifteen years ago managed to convince Nicola to fuck him, marry him and have his children. And six months ago, started a torrid affair with his 25-year-old intern. And now is making Marie laugh and grin and – Oh, my fucking God, she is giggling and blushing – like a Japanese schoolgirl.

I don't understand women. I don't understand people.

'Paul?' I repeat.

She starts to tell me, to explain, and as she talks and I process, I start to understand, a little. It's not really about Paul, so much – is it ever about the actual man for her? – as it is about Marie. Vulnerable, angry, smarting from rejection – or perceived rejection. Frustrated, restless. Getting a ping from the ex-husband of a woman she's probably as tired of hearing complain about her divorce – no matter how justified her complaints might be, my superego inserts sternly – as I am. Maybe, the ping comes just a little bit after JP's acted like a real ass – taunted her, hurt her. He does that. And so, there she is. Hurt, rejected, angry. Vulnerable. And – ping. 'Hey, Marie, I know you have to be on Nicola's side here more than mine, and I understand that, but just wanted to reach out. Miss my old friends.' Oh, yes. I can see it. And a conversation ensues. This that and the other. Life. Children, complications. Marriage is hard. Monogamy's a struggle. And how are things with the skank?

'You didn't call her a skank, did you?' I ask.

'No, of course not.' Marie's appalled. 'Her name's Deirdre. Isn't that a pretty name?' She looks at me sideways, slyly, and her eyes challenge me to remind her that, when Nicola first told us the story, and the skank's name, Marie's contribution to the conversation consisted of 'Christ, what a name. Did her parents want her to grow up to be a whore?'

I let it go. Let her continue.

'And things are not so good with Deirdre. Of course. Because, well, she wasn't looking for a . . . permanency, you know.'

I know. Deirdre, the ambitious intern, was looking for a fuck, and possibly a short cut to workplace advancement, although, as this is the second decade of the twenty-first century, we pretend women don't do, or need to do, such things any more. But there it is. She did not want a husband. Stepchildren. Or even a permanent boyfriend in his forties.

Marie takes me through the saga quickly. 'So this started when?' I ask. She shrugs. 'Oh, it's been going on for ever,' she says. 'Well . . . three days?' In texting terms, for ever. Children, marriage, complications, monogamy. 'He says the more he processes all this, the more certain he is that he's definitely polyamorous,' she says. 'Deirdre is.' Oh, fuck. Here we go again. Marie was mildly insufferable when she was introduced to, and enamoured with, the concept of polyamory. And I was thrilled when she finally laid it to rest, deciding that 'the French had it right after all.' Don't want to go through this with her again.

'It was just such a treat to talk about all this with someone,' she says. 'With someone who's had the same struggles, you know? *Really* talk.'

And she talks about the talks. And I wonder if Paul really is this articulate when he texts – it's possible, I suppose, although my experiences of him in person are of a cripplingly awkward, inarticulate introvert – or if I'm just hearing Marie's filter, Marie's interpretation.

But filtered or real, she feels – heard. Understood. Valued. Attractive. Desired. Attracted?

They're not sexting or cyberfucking. 'Yet.' But. The conversations are getting more intimate. More intense. More frequent.

'There's probably a message waiting for me on my phone right now,' she says, slyly. She's so happy. Fey.

She terrifies me. With her . . . emotionality, vulnerability. Stupidity.

I don't dare make analogies, comparisons. Judgements.

I listen.

My reward is an embrace after the sleds and kids, wet, exhausted and whining, are packed back into the vans.

'Oh, Jane,' she says. 'I don't know what I would do without you. It's so good to know you have someone who will always listen.'

Now I'm hard. Finish me. My fuckslave.
—Fuck. I'm not the only one going mad here, am I?
No. Both fucking insane.

I can't judge, criticise. But holy fuck. Marie. What are you thinking?

I say nothing, of course. I hug her back.

And I hope Nicola neither texts nor calls me today.

All the kids need a change of clothes when we get home, and Alex is impatient and nagging. I throw snow suits, mitts and hats into the dryer, scramble for new shoes for everyone . . . then race upstairs. And dress for Sunday dinner with my mother-in-law. Like Matt's slut. In a tight, short dress. Stockings.

No panties.

Your shameful submission is the most erotic thing I've ever imagined.
—Fuck you. I can't believe I'm doing this.

'You look so pretty, Mom,' Cassandra says as I put on my coat.

'Out, out the door!' Alex says. And doesn't notice what I'm wearing at all. Well. That's probably just as well.

I am dutiful wife, mother, daughter-in-law for the rest of the night. I am. My thoughts stray, every once in a while, but, physically, I am there, I am present. As I always will be. And I think of Marie's current insanity, and mine . . . mine does not seem so mad by comparison. Or so futile. Or so . . . unjustifiable. Marie will, perhaps, in the end fuck Paul. (Why? How? Yuck.) But . . . Matt isn't coming. There is no event. I rejected him before, I got over him before. And I will again. All I am doing now, all I have now is thought crime. Fantasy. Albeit with a partner. And I know, from years of monogamous exertion and years of intermittent thought crime, that this – that thought crime – burns out. Always. Think of fucking someone long enough, dream of it often enough, let it play in your head like a tape enough times as you bring yourself to orgasm – or have your partner of many, many years do so – and you habituate it. The newness, the strangeness, the allure disappear. And reality returns, and satisfies again, sufficiently. For a while. Everything burns out.

This too will burn out.

It must.

Hopefully before I completely lose my mind.

When we get back home and I put the kids to bed – and Alex disappears into the office for his Sunday-evening 'catch up' – I decide to lose it, just a little, one more time. Still dressed in my stealth slut dress, stockings. Log on. Green light, he's there.

—Lover.

Lover. Whore. Have you cum for me today?

—Oh yes.

Tell me.

—When you and I finished this morning, I took Alex to the shower . . . down on my knees, his cock in my mouth, my eyes closed, thinking of you

—pushed him down to my pussy, begged him to lick me

—then me on all fours, the shower water running cold, his cock behind me—I demanded he pull on my hair

—collapsed bottom of tub water so cold unable to move thinking of you looking at me

Demanding bitch

So incredibly sexy

I want to watch you

And I want to see your outfit. All of it

—not easy to do

Anything worth doing rarely is

—demanding

Extremely

—disintegrating

Do as you're told.

—I will comply . . . eventually. Maybe.

Answer properly.

—Make me.

You need a good cock slap across your cheek

—Which cheek?

Your ass. Then your face if you're still stubborn.

—This will burn out, right?

—If we do this enough, binge like this, it will abate?

Let's find out.

Now do as you're fucking told.

—. . .

—I hate you

I see that.

So gorgeous.

—I hate that when you type 'do as you're fucking told'
I almost come.

*And I love that you almost cum. We are the perfect
counterparts.*

*My favourite is the last one. Your garters. Of course I
want more.*

Insatiable

—greedy

A glutton.

Devouring you endlessly.

—I'm on my bed, wantonly spreading my legs for you

—Seriously questioning my sanity

Panties?

—none

All day?

—yes

—for you

Dedicated.

I am lucky to own you.

—You are.

—Jeezus

Also questioning my sanity.

And I want to see your pussy.

—It's good to want things

I won't order you.

—thank you
Don't want to overwork you.
—Pacing can be good.
I'm going to go cum on your gartered thigh now.
Now that you can show me more of.
I am devouring your angry photos, again.
Why is forcing you so fucking hot?
—Because you're twisted.
Perhaps because it exposes the real you. Or my fantasy
real you, if that makes any sense.
—Nothing makes sense. But you? Is this the real you,
or a role you're playing with me?
I wish I knew. My god, what if it is.

I hear footsteps. The bathroom door.

—I have to go now
Show me your cunt, Jane
—Jeezus
—I can't, not now
—I have to go
You have the night.
Go. I release you
—Bastard. Cum on my thighs before you fall asleep. I'm
gone. xx
xo

Alex pokes his head into the bedroom.
   'Waiting for me?' he asks. 'After this morning? Not sated?'
   I smile at him and pull my dress up to my waist.

Day 8 – Too far

Alex sleeps like the dead. I don't. Give up, get up. Do paperwork. Send an SOS into the ether, too early for even Montréal to answer:

—Awake. Aching.

When he answers, a few hours later, Alex is already up, moving around, getting ready for the day. Coming in and out of my line of sight. I don't care. I engage.

Tell me you haven't been awake since 3 a.m.
—4 a.m. Midnight. All night. Restless.
—I did manage to work. Made up for the negligence of yesterday.
Any other accomplishments?
—No.
A shame
—I don't think I can do that, not even for you.
—It's not just logistics, although that makes a convenient excuse.
Is it a step too far?
—maybe
—but
—when I see you
—maybe you can do that

Among much else.
Did you put your arousal to good use this morning?
—aroused wrong word
—restless
—mad
—shaking
—and you?
Frustrated
Thwarted
Full of rage and cum.
Feel like a danger to the public.
—yes
Keyed up
Volatile
—volatile
—and vulnerable (me)
Service me.
—What do you want?
Too much.
—yes
—I relate
—(shaking)
Tell me all the things I can do to you when I have you in front of me.
—Jeezus.
—I will kneel at your feet, my face resting against your thighs.
—Your cock against my forehead.
—Your hands in my hair.
—You will keep me there, every once in a while taking one hand from my hair to my mouth.
—You won't let me touch you, or myself.
—We will just be.
—You want to see how hard you can get just standing there, with me at your feet.

In your place. A tableau of submission.
—still so still
Your warm breathing against my balls.
—your hair tickling me
—I let out a very quiet, very weak moan
—you love it
Stick your tongue out. Slowly.
I feel it on my balls. Reaching behind them. So wrong.
So debasing. Not even using you to suck my cock.
—Alex is in the kitchen. I have to go . . .
Tell me who you are
—Your fuckslave
My whore
—utterly
—oh fuck
—on my knees
—I can smell you
Your hungry tongue swirling on my balls. Heating them
up. I smother your face.
—I don't think you'll be able to be stoic and torment
me much longer.
—I rub my face against you.
Go offer to suck his cock.

What the fuck? I stare at the words at the screen. Jesus. Matt. Alex's lips brush my temple. 'Have a good day, love.' He goes down the stairs.

—He's gone. Do you want me to follow him, or service
you?
Follow him. I will cum to the thought of you being
loaned out.
—Jesus. What's wrong with you?
Everything. Admit you love it. And hate it in equal
measure. Now go do what you're told.

103

And – insanity. I run after Alex. Catch him at the front door. Wrap my arms around him, and then slither down to his groin.

'Jesus, Jane, what are you doing?' Unzip his pants. Cock in my mouth. Take it voraciously, aggressively. His hands in my hair, his orgasm almost soundless, almost immediate.

'Jesus, Jane,' he says again, pulling me up. Kisses my lips gently. 'Oh, Jesus. I have to go . . .'

'I know. Have a good day,' I say. Shut the door behind him. Lean my head against it, and then bang it. In-fucking-sane. What have I just done?

My laptop, on the kitchen table, open. I run up the stairs. He's waiting. I type.

—done

—oh fuck

—I have dribbles of his cum in the corners of my mouth

—and he might think I'm possessed

—which may be an accurate description of the situation

So erotic possessing you.

—Did you cum?

Indeed.

Picturing how you would offer. Coyly or bluntly. I chose blunt. Without much enthusiasm. Obedient.

—I was pretty enthusiastic. You were standing just below the landing, in the shadows, watching.

Enthusiastic obedience. A professional. Also fucking hot.

—The line between reality and fantasy is becoming dangerously blurred.

—Have a good real life day my lover.

And you as well (her master says, scrambling into his clothes, late again).

—xo

xx

I've lost my mind. Completely.

I need to end this, now.

I've never wanted anything more desperately in my life.

I feel undone. Lost.

Mine.

I pull myself together sufficiently to get the kids fed, dressed, out of the house. Deliver them to school – all four, it's Annie's preschool morning again. Brave mall crowds to do the final bit of Christmas shopping: promise myself there will be no more shopping. And, in a moment of weakness and self-immolation, agree to visit with my mom after I pick up Annie at noon.

I've spent most of my sentient life fluctuating between feeling mildly irritated with my mother and irrationally angry. Today, I am angry *and* irritated – angry about how she treats my dad, irritated that she managed to manipulate me into coming over this afternoon. Angrier at myself, because I suspect a sick part of me doesn't want to be here just because it wants to be available to *him*, and what the fuck is wrong with me?

The house smells like decadence and Christmas. My mother's baked a mountain of cookies and, as always, starts stuffing Annie's mouth with them as soon as we come through the door. She fuels my anger and irritation just by being and I feel my face go tight, tight. I sit down. Stare at my coffee cup. Try to control myself. I know my anger is unreasonable. I know I am always unfair to my mother. And not just because she tells me so, constantly. She's right. I love her, of course I love her. But I am Daddy's girl, always was. And in our family of three, my father and I were always the Allies. The co-conspirators. The evaders. The hiders. The ones who watched each other's back – who tag-teamed, who strategised – and, she was always, always alone.

I realise, perhaps for the first time ever, that this must have really sucked for her. Fuelled *her* anger and frustration?

I look at her now, moving here and there in the kitchen, a whirlwind of nervous energy and activity. Never still. Talking to Annie, talking to me. Talking *at* the appliances. How old is she now? I think 63; she retired three years ago now. Went uber-domestic. Cookies, pies, home-made jams and pickles.

I wonder if it's harder on my dad – if *she's* harder on him – now that she is at home so much more. That she has more time to be frustrated by him. And fewer outlets. And less stimulation.

Suddenly, madly, I wonder if my mother has ever had an affair. She has always had men around her – she was a beautiful woman. Still is, I suppose, and I try to look at her not as a daughter would but as a man would. Yes, still beautiful. Charming when she turns it on.

Does she still turn it on, ever, for my dad?

I don't want to be thinking this.

She's been talking, telling me something, and as I look up at her, she knows, as she always does, that I wasn't listening.

'Oh, Jane,' she sighs. Disappointed. Then looks at me. Carefully. And again. Frowns. 'Oh, sweetie. Are you OK?' Lacey's a little bit psychic. My mother isn't. But she's my mother. She always senses the disquiet and restlessness in me, and because I never share it with her, she always makes the same, the only, the worst assumption. And, there she goes, she makes it now. 'Is everything OK with you and Alex? Are you fighting? You know, there are rough patches in any marriage . . .'

Fuck. I interrupt her immediately; marital advice from this woman I will not take. Ever.

'We're fine,' I say, shortly. 'We're always fine.' I pause. I could ask here: I could say, 'And you and Dad?'

But I don't want to hear it; I don't want to hear either her justification of what I saw here on Monday or her denial of it – or her normalisation. 'All couples fight,' she would tell me. She really likes to say that one; she's stopped yelling at my dad sometimes to say that to me. With a smile. 'Those

106

who fight, love, you know' is another favourite. And then there's this one, 'Where there's passion, there's friction.'

And there she goes. She runs through all three. And more. And she talks still. About how every marriage, no matter how long and how – she says *haaa-pp-eee* – no matter how *happy* has rough patches. And you ride them out, with lots and lots of communication and, well, sometimes you can't, well, it looks like you can't but even that's a rough patch, love will see it through . . .

'Alex and I are just fine,' I repeat, talking over her voice.

Are we?

If we are, how does what I'm doing with Matt fit into 'We're fine'?

And is my mother telling me all this because she can read some of what's happening in me?

Thinking hurts. I push everything away. Drink coffee. Eat cookies. Leave the house unsettled. No longer angry. But confused. Yes, perhaps, confused.

And reluctant to go home, to be alone.

From the car, as we're both waiting to pick up the kids in front of the school, I text Marie. 'River Park? I don't want to go home.' 'Super. See you there in 15.' God. I love her. Always there for me, always. Even if she's texting me in between sexting with Paul.

She's sexting – or at least texting – Paul *while* talking with me, and for that I love her a little less. But. She's distracting me from my own madness, and I am grateful.

'You know what I really like about Paul?' she says, putting the phone away. 'With Zoltan, I was always worried that he thought I was a skanky slut cheating whore. You know? Because he was single and unattached, and . . . well, he didn't have *my* complications. He didn't have as much on the line as I did.'

The kids are chucking rocks into the water, trying to break up the ice floes on the river. The ice rumbles, but not enough:

it's quiet in the park. I think we're sitting too close to the kids to have this conversation. I start walking, and Marie follows.

'I feel less vulnerable, less at risk with him,' Marie says. She sits on a rock. 'He's done it already, you know? Crossed the line. Had to deal with the consequences.' She gives me a piercing look. 'The guilt, frankly, is not nearly as bad as I thought it would be.' She pauses. 'Do you think I should feel more guilty, Jane?'

'For what?' I'm startled. Genuinely so. Because I'm a selfish, self-centred bitch and even though I've heard her words, I have no idea what Marie has been talking about.

'For . . .' Marie pauses. 'Everything. For not loving JP enough to just be satisfied. For not being honest with myself and him enough to talk about this. For not having the guts to actually have a real conversation with him about . . .' She stops.

'Jane? Are you listening to me?'

Go offer to suck his cock.
Follow him. I will cum to the thought of you being
loaned out.
—Jesus. What's wrong with you?
Everything. Admit you love it.

'Jane!'

'I'm sorry.' I focus on her. Listen. And then start to fade out again as she runs the tape she's been playing to me for years.

It goes like this. Marie has intermittently wanted out of her marriage almost the entire time I've known her. It's a sentiment that it's been hard not to unilaterally applaud. Paul's a dork and a cheating rat-fuck bastard, but JP is a jerk, wanker and asshole. He berates and criticises Marie for everything – the state of the house, the sameness of the meals, the behaviour of the children, the imperfectly scrubbed bottoms of his

108

precious copper pots – and thinks it's OK, because once a month or so he comes home with flowers. Invariably ends his pissy texts to her with 'I love you'. Pinches her ass when other people are looking, to show them, and her, how much he loves her.

I dislike him quite intensely.

'Jeezus, if you ever talked to me like JP talks to Marie, I think I'd have you shot,' I told Alex after our first – and only – dinner party at their house. 'On second thought – I'd kill you with my bare hands.'

Alex didn't say anything. Then, 'We never have to do this again, right?'

'What?'

'Have a fucking couples' date with JP and Marie,' Alex says. 'Yes, that was hell. I know she's your friend. Courting him, however, is in no way necessary to my career. We may work together, we do not have to socialise together. Never again?'

'Never.'

JP's at least a decade older than Alex, Marie and I. Not that that's a reason or excuse or explanation for anything. Lacey and Clint are a good fifteen years, more, older than us, and they're not lame or intolerable. Clint's a slut, but not a jerk or wanker.

So. When Marie rants and raves about how being married to JP sucks – how she wishes she had the courage to leave, how she feels trapped, undervalued, frustrated and so on – I nod. And make sympathising noises. Do everything short of telling her to just shut the fuck up, pack a suitcase and go.

Because when you yourself are a mother of four children and buy into the benefits of the intact nuclear family – at least on some level – that's crossing the line.

I think.

Maybe JP would be better as a part-time dad who had to compete for his children's love and affection.

I'm not sure that Marie would be happier as a single mom. Nicola sure as fuck isn't. But maybe Marie would be. I don't know.

In the meantime, she dreams of torrid affairs, and is sent back to the misery of her marriage by the flaccidity of the real thing.

How fooling around with Nicola's cheating soon-to-be-ex-husband fits into this matrix is a bit harder to decipher. But none of Marie's flirtations and excursions of the heart and loins have ever made much sense to me. The first one – the first one she told me about, at least, but as she tells me everything, I assume it was indeed the first one – happened when her youngest was two. It was a 'one-night stand', she said, her one night out away from the family while she was visiting her parents in Toronto. A 'hook-up' with an old boyfriend that 'went too far'. 'Horrid, shameful, will never do it again,' she said, weeping. She made herself miserable over it for months and months – accepting every unacceptable thing from JP as her 'just deserts', because she was a bad, unfaithful, undeserving wife.

It was some six months afterwards that I found out the 'one-night stand' consisted of a couple of kisses in a pub parking lot.

I have never been able to ascertain if they were really stellar kisses – and so their memory was so erotic that it trebled her guilt and angst – or such terribly tepid kisses, so disappointing, that she couldn't believe she'd 'risked' her marriage over them.

Six months later, she was intensely texting with another old boyfriend, meeting this one for an occasional coffee. The interaction consisted almost completely of her complaining to him about her husband – and him complaining to her about his wife. She thought it was leading to a torrid affair – possibly divorce and remarriage for them both. It ended with him starting up a real affair somewhere else. And, indeed, leaving his marriage. But not for Marie.

Then came . . . I don't remember. Another one and another one, all variations of Zoltan. Hot. Intense. Petering out, leading to nothing. Too often on the men's initiative, with the lover, or rather would-be lover, ending it – or just withdrawing. And Marie, heartbroken, devastated. Until the next time.

Always next time. Always willing, anxious to take the risk again.

Sometimes, I think I get it. Sometimes, I think it always ends like this because this is what she courts. She seeks out men who will ultimately reject her – or whom she effectively rejects with her need, her emotional volatility and her vulnerability, because she does not truly want to cross that line. Because she does not know what she wants: to leave JP or to stay. To work through this, or to have things explode.

I do know this: I don't think she wants a secret, discreet affair that unfolds quietly, parallel to, in the shadow of her marriage.

I don't even think she wants fireworks, passion, the type of madness Matt ignites in me – if it stays contained, separate from the main plot line of her life.

I think she wants a train-wreck. A crisis, a climax. A tremendous, crashing, emphatic end to her marriage, one so messy and crazy that it will be circumstances dictating the outcome. Not Marie. Not Marie making the decision to walk – or the decision to stay. But JP casting her out, walking out because of what she's done.

Leaving her 'no choice'.

But – as she pushes towards this train-wreck, she intermittently pulls back. Changes her mind. Decides JP, the marriage, the intact family is what she wants.

At least until the next temptation . . .

'What do you want?' I ask her, abruptly. She looks at me, confused. 'What do you want?' I ask again. 'From this?' I point to her phone, in her hand again, exchanging another text with her new would-be lover.

'To fuck,' she says bluntly. 'I want to fuck someone other than my husband. I think monogamy and marriage suck. They're boring. I. Want. To. Fuck. Someone. Other. Than. My. Husband. There. Clear enough for you, Jane?'

And she storms off. Angry.

I watch her go, and I ache for her.

And, suddenly, I ache for me.

The scene from this morning plays out before my eyes.

Go offer to suck his cock
Follow him. I will cum to the thought of you being
loaned out.

Fantasy and reality blurring. Thought crime involving Alex – my life, my husband, my love, my trust. Too much. I am so not in control and so not clear – can't talk about lines crossed or lines uncrossed. I see no lines. I see nothing. I only feel; if I were a man, the Greek chorus of Nicola's supporters, Colleen and all of them would say I am thinking with my cock. So. I am thinking with my clit, with my pussy. Fuck. If that. Thinking?

I need to stop.

Now.

I look at the children at the river's edge. Marie's further up the bank between the trees. My Cassandra, so tall – two more years, maybe three, and she will be as tall as I am. Henry, a photocopy of Alex. Eddie, who has my dad's smile. And Annie, my last, most unexpected gift, my embodiment of perfection. And I remember when, and how, and why, I said, 'No' before.

He remembers it too. He told me.

Do you remember – the last time we saw each other.
—I remember. The last time.
I had you alone for only a few moments.
—You put your hands under my skirt.

*You gave me the most withering, pitying look. Pulled
away. Do you remember what you said?
—'Get your fucking hands off me.'*

Cassandra in my belly. Motherhood before me. No room in
that life for my forever lover, for the moral ambiguity that
excited and drew us towards each other no matter who else
we were coupled with.

*I wanted you then. I wanted you always. I want you
always. But I always want you . . . tied to someone else.*

Oh, fuck.

Is there room in my life for him now? No. Not if he blurs
into my reality like this, assaults me, overwhelms, threatens
my sense of reality and self. No. He can't be here. We can't
do this.

*I am not looking for an out of my marriage. I am not
looking to destroy yours. I am looking to fuck you
senseless when I come. Use you. And leave.*

But he's not coming.

And this mindfuck? It's worse, more intense, more damaging
than one night in a hotel room.

I can't do this.

I've stopped before. Walked away.

I will do so now.

The thought and that purpose stay with me through the
rest of the afternoon. Marie, angry and sullen, barely talks to
me, but I don't notice. I think only about what I have to do.
We separate in silence. I drive home, focused. I find Matt
online as soon as I come home. I need to do this now, before
I talk myself out of it. Now.

I grit my teeth. 'Get your fucking hands off me.' The new

variant. Softer and gentler, perhaps. I feel my resolve waver
– fuck, I want him. I want this.

I will stop it.

Now.

—Are you there?

In work hell. Fucking reality.

—What happened?

Consequence of my mind not focused on task at hand.
Nothing to show for days' worth of 'thinking'. Fuck.

—I won't be long. Listen. This morning . . .

Too much?

—Too much. And you, in trouble at work. I think . . .
too intense. I do not want to damage your life in a real
life consequence kind of way.

Nor do I with you. Perhaps this morning was a little too
close to the flame.

—Not just this morning. All of it. This is . . .
unsustainable. No longer a 12-day countdown to a
one-night thing. Something different, and harder.

You want to stop?

—Want? No. But we have to. To preserve . . . sanity.
Reality.

Fuck.

—You know I'm right.

I wait. A minute passes. Two. Five. Seven. What do I want
him to say?

Yes.

A wise choice. We are heading for disaster. It has never
been quite like this, has it? Fuck. Will you miss me?

—Stupidly and utterly.

I will picture you constantly. A 24-hour performance.

—Jeezus.

114

—Stop.

Stopped.

—Goodbye, Matt. Oh, fuck. I'm gone.

Jane. Lover. Always mine. Go. xx

I log off. It's done. It's over.

I walk away from the computer, tears in my eyes. They don't go away, keep coming back. 'Fucking hormones,' I tell Alex, as I cry into the dishwasher. Make it, somehow, to bedtime. After.

In bed, I press my face against the pillow. Cheeks wet still, again. Why, when I've done the right thing, do I feel so fucking bad?

Day 9 – Jonesing

I wake up jonesing.

At 4.30 a.m.

I stare at the clock and calculate. Three hours until I can count on the kids to wake up and give me something to do. Six and a half hours until I get to the gym. Twelve hours until . . . oh, fuck. How can this be so hard?

I feel fourteen. Broken. Stupid. Mindless. Lusting for the unavailable, uninterested boy, counting the hours until I might hear from a crush . . . Except it's worse, because back then, I was much better at self-deception. I lack that tool right now; I know exactly what I'm jonesing for and why.

And I know where it is, how to reach for it.

But I won't.

And I hate it.

And it makes me horny.

I look at Alex. Sleeping beside me, stretched out, chest moving up and down. How long has it been since I've woken him up in the middle of the night to fuck?

I move the covers off him. Undo the drawstring on his pyjamas. Nuzzle my face against his groin, his soft cock. Enjoy his smell. It's always been one of the things about him that's turned me on the most, always, always, his smell. I like it when he doesn't shower right away after a workout. When he comes back home from a bike ride or a run, moist.

Smell's one of my triggers with Matt too.

116

—I still remember the way you smell. It's all around me.

And vice versa.

The sweet scent of you
you are delicious

I lick my husband's cock slowly and gently. It responds immediately, of course, it always does. I take the tip of the head
into my mouth. Alex moves, groans. Deeper.

'What?' he stirs. 'Oh, Jane. What are you doing?'

'I can't . . .' I say, his cock still in my mouth, '. . . sleep.'

'Oh, God,' Alex says. 'Thank God for insomnia. Don't
stop . . .'

I don't.

But when he moves to go down on me, I push him away.

'Just for you,' I whisper. 'I'm going to get up and work.
Finish up what I planned to procrastinate on until this evening.
I've got that thing at Nicola's tonight.'

'OK,' he says. Falls back asleep.

I go to my computer; bite my lips, don't check Facebook.
Don't look at my phone.

'Porridge?' Henry pokes at his bowl. 'Why did you make us
porridge? Can't I have Gorilla Munch?'

'It's not porridge, it's a blueberry French toast-muffin medley.
I was inspired and it's delicious. Eat it.'

'You aren't eating yours,' Cassandra points out. 'Mmm.
Actually, it is delicious.'

'There, see? How often do I make you guys a hot breakfast?
Eat. Enjoy.'

'I like cereal,' Henry says plaintively. But he takes a bite.

The children are very uncooperative, wanting nothing from
me. I hyper-focus on the coming session with Jesse. I'll ask
him for . . . chin-ups. All the crap I hate.

117

I will not lie down on the workout bench to do chest presses. Or anything.

Kids to school. Annie to my mom's. Gym.

I'm not sure how I make it to the gym without crashing into someone or driving off the road. Fucking hell. Triggers everywhere. Everything making me think . . . or not think. I stumble into the gym unseeing. Spend too much time in the changing room staring at myself in the mirror. Who is this crazy woman?

I put on my ugly, baggy sweat pants, and an even uglier, scraggly T-shirt. One of Alex's old T-shirts. Nice. I look at myself in the mirror, this time to see . . . What? Righteousness, virtue? Moral satisfaction? Discipline?

I see a gaunt face, shadows under the eyes, pain, misery.

I see a mouth getting ready to engulf a cock.

I'm so fucking fucked.

I body-slam into Jesse as I walk out of the change room, blind. He catches me before I fall, and I stare at him, stunned. Barely there.

'Jane, you OK?'

No, not really.

'I'm fine – just disoriented.' I look at Jesse. His forehead's furrowed; he looks very concerned. So sweet. Which means I must look like shit. Of course. I shake my head vigorously. Resist the urge to slap my cheeks.

'Make me work,' I say. 'Awful, horrible things. Stop me from thinking.'

'I can do that,' Jesse says. Gives me a careful, measured look. 'Let's start with push-ups. Go.'

I drop down to the floor.

And realise that I pay a large, muscular man a substantial amount of money every week to make me go down on my knees and do things I don't really want to do.

I do not relish this insight.

He takes me at my word, and chooses one god-awful, exhausting exercise after another. When I'm hanging from the bar doing leg-ups – perfect, I hate these as much as I hate push-ups – I almost stop thinking about Matt. These are hard. They hurt. One. Two. Three.

'I've thought of a few more adjectives,' Jesse says abruptly.
'What?'

'A few more adjectives,' he repeats. 'To describe you. You put me on the spot the other day. I'm not . . . I don't have stuff like that ready to go.'

Five. Six. He's a sweetheart. I wish I could remember what the fuck I asked him the other day. All I remember is jumping when he told me to lie down on the workout bench.

'Intelligent,' he says. 'Articulate.' He delivers that one carefully. And then – 'Intimidating, that's a very good one for you.'

'Ugh,' I grunt, pulling my legs up. Inhale. Exhale. 'Intimidating? Even here, to you? Ugh. Or just sort of generally?'

'You kind of ooze . . . confidence and . . . the other word I had, self-possessed. And confident. Some people might call it arrogant, but it's not, it's just – you're . . .' He pauses. Awkward. 'You're you.'

Sweet, dumb, deluded, imperceptive Jesse.

'Ugh.' I hang from the bar. 'I'm me. At this precise moment, Jesse, it's not such a great thing to be.'

'Well, I like you,' he says. Simply. And turns bright red.

Ah, 26-year-old boys. Sweet. And so imperceptive.

But I'm mildly cheered up. If Jesse doesn't see it, then perhaps I will manage to get through the rest of the day – the rest of the week – the rest of my life – without the entire world pegging me for a jonesing whore.

Maybe.

Alex makes it home with three minutes to spare for the kid hand-off. 'Have fun,' he says. Pecks me on the cheek. 'Be good.'

'Of course.' I blow kisses all around. He's taking the kids out for burgers, then for an evening swim. I'm getting together with friends for the express purpose of getting Nicola drunk.

The original goal was to get her drunk and laid, but that proved a little more complicated to arrange. Next time.

And I realise that, as I'm getting chauffeured there and back, I can get myself gloriously and blissfully drunk as well. And perhaps sleep.

Time passes faster when you sleep.

Ping. My phone. Text from Marie.

- There in 10.
—Ready.

'Jane? What the hell are you doing?'

I turn my head in surprise. Marie and I are standing in the middle of Nicola's neighbourhood market, fulfilling our promise to arrive laden with food.

'What?'

'You were supposed to get food while I did the liquor-store run!' Marie wails.

'I did!' I protest. My cart is full. I point. 'Black Forest cake, napoleons, this awesome cheesecake thing, those delicious German apple pastries – I forget what they're called, but look at them. Fucking luscious. And I got two kinds of ice-cream – caramel toffee and chocolate cherry. To die for.'

'That's all dessert!'

'Well, of course,' I say. 'We're going to eat dessert and drink wine. If Alex ever leaves me for one of his articling students, this is what you show up on my doorstep with. And wine. You got wine, right? Not de-alcoholised beer?'

'I got some de-alcoholised beer,' Marie says. 'And wine. But, fuck, Jane, people will want to eat something other than cake.'

'Fine,' I say. I toss a hunk of Brie into the cart. Then a pre-made chickpea salad. 'There. Get a baguette if you want to.'

I check on Marie's alcohol purchases before we pull away from the vicinity of the liquor store; they're adequate.

'Are you OK?' she asks.

'I'm fine,' I lie.

'It's just, you know, the desserts,' she says. 'Did you and Alex have a fight? No, of course not. Omigod, are you pregnant *again*?'

'Jeezus fucking Christ, no,' I say. Momentarily horrified. My hand on my belly, my mind rolling through the past week-plus of marathon fucking with Alex – suddenly and blissfully thankful for the vasectomy that he ran to get pretty much as soon as we found out I was pregnant with Annie, because clearly the one he had after Eddie did not take.

'I comfort drink, I don't comfort eat,' I snap. 'This is for Nicola.'

'Ah, Nicola,' Marie says. 'Poor bitch.'

Alex is right, I decide. I do not really like women. My affection for Marie and my mild lust for Lacey are anomalies; the uncomfortable relationship I have with Nicola is more the norm. Even Marie, for whom my affection and attachment are deep and genuine, wears me down with her . . . femaleness. And looking at her, in this moment, I accept that I find most women too needy and too clingy – even when they haven't just been dumped by a rat-fuck bastard of a cheating husband – too demanding in all the wrong ways.

I hear Matt laughing in the back of my head and want to slap him.

I am not judging Marie for sexting with Nicola's ex-husband.

I'm just annoyed by her.

She picks it up.

She stays in the car when she pulls up in front of Nicola's house after I get out. She passes me the bags and packages from the back seat. Does not open her door.

'What's going on?' I ask.

'I'm not going,' she says.

'What?'

'I'm not going,' she repeats. 'I just can't be there – with all those women, being all sanctimonious about marriage and fidelity and crapping on Paul and calling the girlfriend names all in the name of female solidarity and delivering pap about how, sure, monogamy is hard but what does a responsible adult do? He sucks it up and does the right thing, he keeps his fucking pants zipped up . . . I just can't do it.'

I get that.

It would be awkward enough for Marie to sit there surrounded by the Greek chorus of sanctimonious faithful and/ or betrayed wives if she was just sexting a stranger. But she's on-course to fuck Nicola's ex-husband.

'I don't know how you can do it,' Marie says, looking at me sideways. I shy away. I've told her nothing. But she knows me. Can she see this in me? What I've done, what I've stopped, what I'm regretting so intensely right now it's making me physically ill? 'How you can sit there and listen to them – and then not judge *me*?' But of course. It is, always, about *her*.

'I have been planning to down two bottles of wine for the last . . . thirty hours,' I tell her. 'I'll cope. And you I love. No matter whether you keep your pants zipped up or not. Anyway, aren't those leggings?'

'Goof,' she laughs. 'I'm going to go to Chapters and read and blog,' she adds. And I know she's lying, she's going to pathologically check her messages, and sext. 'I'll come pick you up. Midnight?'

'Don't be silly. Someone else will give me a ride, or I'll cab it. Go.' She blows me a kiss. Screeches out of the driveway.

Everyone else is already there. My dessert-heavy food delivery is lauded – 'Why waste calories on broccoli?' Nicola quips to show us how together and happy and determined to party she is. And the wine flows, and the conversation.

Not all of it is about the rat-fuck-ass-wipe-bastard *aka* Marie's new lover, who is currently 'forgetting' to invoice on a regular basis and thus contributing zero dollars a month to the upkeep of his two kids and soon-to-be-ex-wife. We also talk about our children and their accomplishments, foibles,

122

struggles. Fitness. The heartbreaking federal by-election. But the phone with pictures of the girlfriend (unflattering in her nakedness, and badly made-up to boot, Colleen pronounces) is passed around.

Again, I decline the opportunity to look.

'She's not that attractive,' someone says. Sincerely, or to please Nicola?

'No,' Nicola agrees. 'Does that make it better or worse? I don't know. Would it be better to be left for someone clearly . . . hotter?'

It's a good question. Would it?

She's younger. Twenty-five. Openly polyamorous. Aggressively sexual. In both Nicola and Paul's versions of the story, she goes after him. And I believe that – there is no conception of Paul that I have in which he is capable of chasing and seducing a woman.

I wonder if Nicola went after him, fifteen years ago. And if so – why? What did she see in him then? Can she still see it now? Or is she too angry, too betrayed, too broken?

The women do the Oprah thing and support Nicola fully and unconditionally in whatever she says, vents and feels. The resulting conversation is confusing – a surreal combination of ripping the rat-fuck bastard to shreds (I'm starting to forget his real name again – Paul, right? Paul, before he was the rat-fuck bastard, he was Paul, and to Marie he is Paul still – or rather again) and a celebration of the innate and total fabulousness and awesomeness that is Nicola. No one attempts to explain how someone as fabulous and awesome as Nicola is – 'And you are, you are so awesome!' Colleen intones, the high priestess of this mass – ended up with the rat-fuck bastard in the first place. And no one considers that in underscoring the rat-fuck bastard's lack of judgement, lack of general attractiveness and overall past and present ick-factor, we're effectively questioning Nicola's judgement and attractiveness.

After all, she chose the rat-fuck bastard in the first place.

And Marie's choosing him now. What the fuck?

I drink.

And I drink some more.

Life is insane.

I remember a hundred disparate moments. And then, just one. Who was my boyfriend then? It was long before Alex, I don't remember. It doesn't matter. Matt was already with Joy. Or maybe still with Lizette. No, Joy. Maybe even engaged to Joy already? Whatever. Always coupled to someone else, each of us.

In this memory, we are all out, a dozen of us, maybe more – but neither of our official significant others is there. That happens often. Odd, that. Do they know, and do they give us space? Is the universe indulging us? Are we just ridiculously lucky? Or just opportunistic? Irrelevant.

We are . . . clubbing. Drinking. Is it St Paddy's? Oktoberfest? Some excuse to play to excess.

A bar. I am sitting in Matt's lap, his hands under my skirt, when someone puts the box on the table. Pops it open. Four little squares on a tissue.

'Perfect acid,' he mouths. 'But only four. Who's riding?'

We are, really, a comparatively clean crowd, even at our wildest. Pot at parties is pretty much the extent of it, and not that often either. There are exceptions – wild-eyed Jason who is never fully there, poor Justin, who is always either hungover or waiting to be hungover. But most of us toke up a bit here and there, and drink ourselves into oblivion only occasionally.

I've never dropped acid before.

Matt takes a hand out from under my skirt – the other slides deeper into me – reaches for the box, takes two of the squares.

'How do you do this?' he asks. His first time too. The hand that's inside me doesn't miss a beat. An explanation. Matt puts a square on my tongue, another on his. 'Let's fly, lover,' he says.

The rest go to . . . the guy who brought them. Who was it? I don't remember. Who gets the fourth one? Matt's

124

roommate at the time. Who was it? I cannot remember. So self-absorbed. Still Tim, or another? They follow Matt and me out of the bar as we leave. 'How do we know it's working?' I ask. Matt shrugs. 'Doesn't matter.'

As I look at the memory, it occurs to me, suddenly, that the friends we left behind . . . what do they think? They all must have known, because we were never discreet. What did they think?

I didn't care then. I won't care now.

We all four of us go to Matt and Tim's apartment. Looking at walls and paintings and posters. Flipping through books. Drifting here and there. TV on for a while. Music.

Matt and I end up on the roof, with a blanket.

No clothes.

He caresses one nipple for hours, hours, hours. Then pushes me down to his cock. 'No mouth,' he whispers, 'just your face.' And then his hands on me, inside me. Stretching me. 'Does it hurt?' 'Yes.' 'Mmmmm.'

Enter Tim. With a carton of ice-cream – I remember, Heavenly Hash. He sees – what? Matt's erect cock. Me splayed. And he reaches for me, I remember seeing the arc of his hand, moving so, so very slowly, and Matt saying lazily, 'I'm not sharing today.' And pulling the blanket partially over me . . . but leaving my breasts exposed. And then . . .

'You can feed her ice-cream,' he says, 'while I finger her cunt.'

Jesus Christ.

'Jane?' That's Nicola. I look at her, glassy-eyed. 'Want to tell us what's eating you?'

'Not even a little bit,' I say. 'This is your day. But give me more wine.'

After the cab drops me off at home, I take a few moments to sit on the cold tile floor of our entryway before crawling up the stairs on all fours. I do not wake Alex up.

Fortunately, I also don't vomit.

Neither do I sleep.

Day 10 – Thrice Broken Home

Wednesday, December 12

In the morning I hold on to my coffee as if it were a lifeline, and appreciate Alex not saying anything about how awful I look.

But when he asks if he should drive the kids to school, I almost bite his head off.

'I'm fine,' I say. 'I didn't have that much to drink. I just didn't sleep.'

'Again,' he says. 'How many nights has it been, Jane? Maybe you're getting sick.'

But he's too busy and rushed to press me, and he leaves. And I'm grateful.

I run the kids to school. And – errands? Fuck it. I go home. Crawl back into bed.

Don't sleep.

Drink more coffee.

Finally, pull out my laptop. Turn on all the usual things. Stare at the screen resentfully. Don't want to work.

Ping.

I jump.

Marie.

- Jane? I promise I will never ask you to do anything like this again, but I really need this.

It's good to be wanted. Needed. Fucked. Jesus. My head pounds.

—Shoot.

- But tell me if I'm crossing the line. Or shock you.

—I'm completely unshockable. What's up?

- OK. He wants me to describe my boobs. I don't know how to do it.

—You've been sexting for years, and now this comes up for the first time? I mean, it's pretty simple in terms of what he wants: he wants to hear they're hot.

- But are they hot? I mean, I know how to describe my other sweet spot and what it likes in lush detail. But my boobs? Saggy, flabby, like deflated balloons, but hot in a push-up bra or when held up together. I suck at this! Help me describe my hot sexy titties. I'm just self-conscious, because he's such a good writer. Such a good writer, Jane. I read him, and I drip.

This, I think, is clearly the result of JP's boob obsession. And his not-so-subtle messaging that Marie's post-baby breasts are not good enough. Wanker.

—Jesus, you do suck at this.

—Hot sexy titties is a good start. Do it like this:

—soft

—just a little more than a handful

—hiding behind black lace

—Then, describe your lingerie – not what you're wearing, but your dreamiest, hottest fantasy lingerie

—Then: nipples so erect at the thought of your tongue

—got it?

- You're a little evil

—I'm a thwarted *Penthouse Letters* writer.

- Will you edit a draft if I send it to you?

—Yes.

- I love you. OK, give me a few minutes . . .

I wonder if this falls in the category of things all friends do for each other? Or have Marie and I stepped into some kind of cyber-sin vortex where only bizarre, bizarre things happen? I check work email; find a polite way to tell a client that poor planning on his part does not constitute an emergency on my part, today is bad, but I can turn things around tomorrow, will that work? Suddenly, I realise I haven't eaten. Make myself an egg, stare at it in disgust. Do a half-ass job cleaning the kitchen. Don't think about the fact that, although Facebook is open, I will not hear a ping from Matt.

Ping.

It's Marie again.

I did not jump, and my clit did not tingle.

- OK I promise to never make you edit or read my smut again, promise, promise. OK, how about this: more than a mouthful, less than a handful. Squished against your face. Hard nipples poking you. Wanting for you to do that sucking and licking like you describe. I love to have my boobs sucked and licked, mmmmm. I want to add something about they're soft enough to squeeze ever so tightly around your cock, do you think that's OK? Or should I just say, technically speaking 36C, and leave it at that?

God, she really does need help. All right. This I can do:

—Do it like this, in little bits, and if you can, wait for his response between each one. Ready?
—Salacious
[then wait for a response – which will be mmmmm or tell me more or . . . salacious? or I like . . .]
—more than a mouthful, a perfect handful
[his response – wait for it!]
—black lace hiding erect nipples

—tempting and tantalising

[his response – maybe he asks you to be more explicit, or will say something like, tantalise me]

—Pressed up close against your face softly brushing up against your lips.

—Crush them . . .

—What do you want? *They* are waiting to feel your tongue, your hands.

—Or . . . perhaps they want to wrap their succulent softness ever so tightly around your cock . . .

—But keep it short, baby. Short prolongs the back-and-forth.

- He doesn't do short. He goes on and on. For paragraphs!

—But you don't have to. Short. Salacious. Keep him wanting more.

—Oh, and Marie? Always leave before he does.

- Jesus, Jane. You know what? I'm really, really glad I never dated you in high school.

—You're welcome.

This is funny.

—Shut up.

Is this how you played me, Jane?

—It wasn't a game, you and I.

No. Is that why you ran?

—Yes. Now get the fuck out of my head!

After I get the kids back from school and Annie back from my mom's, and as I wait for Alex to come home, I need to start discharging my dutiful daughter-in-law obligations. Lucky me, I have three sets of in-laws. Well, two sets and a single. All courtesy of Alex's serial monogamist father, who bequeathed to my children three sort-of-grandmothers on the paternal side.

There's Alex's *'real'* mom, whom the serial monogamist left when Alex and his sister were seven and four. She lives in Okotoks, a small town that abuts Calgary – a suburb in denial, really – works as a part-time librarian, saves for retirement and is, 30-some years later, still recovering from her marriage to the bastard. Or so I think, given that this incredibly good-looking and intelligent woman hasn't gone on a date in all the years I've known her.

We're going to a movie and dinner with her tonight. Except for the being in a restaurant with a four-year-old part (the elder three are fine), I'm almost looking forward to this duty. Alex's mother is fine. She adores me, her grandchildren. She doesn't know I've been cyber-cheating on her son.

Fuck. But I'm not any more.

I just want to.

The children call her Nana. Alex's father's second wife they just call Jeanette, as he does. We will be visiting her *en route* to the suburb – er, small town. When I met Alex, Jeanette was his stepmother. No children of her own. Super-focused on being a great stepmom to Alex and his sister. Failing – in Alex's eyes at least – thoroughly. Alex resented her so extremely, we debated for weeks whether she would get to come to our wedding. He refused to let me send her birthday cards, until Cassandra was born. The biggest fight of our marriage, to date, came when he found out I sent Jeanette and his dad a happy anniversary card . . .

Jeanette – to Alex's father 'Jeanie-girl', gag – currently lives with a man she wants the kids to call Uncle Christian. I call him Jeanette's friend. Alex pretends he doesn't exist. There was an Uncle Brian until a few months ago, and an Uncle Greg three or four years earlier.

We visit her once a month or so. Well, maybe more like once every six to eight weeks. Most of the time, I do this on a weekday, with the kids. Occasionally, on a Saturday, with Alex. Each time, Alex threatens to stay in the car. Each time, I say nothing. This woman was married to his father when our first two children were born. She's never missed a birthday or Christmas card for any of them. I let him work through all of this on his own; he usually follows me in. Twice he's stayed in the car. On those occasions, I tell Jeanette a client called and Alex is taking the call in the car.

Clients. The perfect excuse for everything.

When I get angry about it, I tell Alex he doesn't get to deprive her of grandkids just because his father is an ass, and he can suck it up and suffer through coffee and cake with her eight times a year.

He grimaces, and occasionally concedes that now she is no longer married to his father, he likes her much better.

But before I discharge my duty to Jeanette, I have to discharge the one to Alex's father. I grab the laptop – do not check Facebook – and turn on Skype.

I used to do this on Saturdays too, but I got tired of watching Alex disappear into the basement as soon as he heard his father's voice.

Life's a bitch. The birth of our first child turned into an olive branch between Alex, his father and Jeanette. Jeanette acted as if her whole life's purpose was this: to be the grandmother of Alex's child. And when someone loves your child that much, it's darn hard to hate them. She made up for the pronounced lack of enthusiasm exhibited by Alex's father, who felt 54 was 'too young' to be a grandfather. Still, his first-born and only son had procreated, and at a respectable age. There was a degree of paternalistic pride involved, and even more after Henry was born. It helped that baby Cassandra looked ridiculously like a new-born Alex, and Henry was his total photocopy. An unprecedented amount of family engagement followed. Jeanette insisted we have a 'family' dinner at least once a month. She sent us home with so many leftovers, I hardly ever had to cook. 'You take care of that baby, that's the important thing,' she'd coo if I protested. 'You fatten her up for the next time Grandma sees her, her little precious.

Here, give Grandpa a kiss before you go, sweetheart. There he is, waiting for a kiss from his precious little munchkin.'

Alex would smile. How could he not? And he didn't mind coming back the next month.

But then Jeanette was replaced by Claire, and Alex stopped talking to his father altogether. We found out about Claire at the now regular family dinner at which we planned to announce that we were expecting our third child. Typically, Jeanette was the one burdened with the task of explaining why Grandpa wasn't there. And wouldn't be there again. Ever. Nor, ever again, with her.

It kind of sucked ass all around.

But.

'Grandpa's on!' I call, and three of the kids run to crowd around the screen. Except for Henry, who hides under the table.

The conversation, held once a month or so ever since my father-in-law moved to Vancouver Island with the third wife, always follows the same script. 'Grandpa' and Claire appear on the screen, side by side. They look and smile. The kids say, 'Hi, Grandpa! Hi, Grandma Claire!' 'Just Claire,' Grandpa corrects them mechanically. Claire smiles a stiff and pained smile. I never correct the kids when they call her Grandma Claire, even though she hates it – and Alex hates it.

I like that it makes her angry.

Claire is maybe . . . five years older than me? 'Grandma Claire' indeed. Childless. Very blonde and always perfectly made-up. Nice tits, not affected by pregnancy and breast-feeding, always on partial display. I try not to call her Barbie.

'What have you guys been up to?' Grandpa asks.

'Not much.' 'Stuff.' 'We went swimming.' 'Daddy got us a new video game.' 'We've read Harry Potter.'

'Things are well here,' Grandpa says. 'The weather's a bit more damp than we like, but it's a small price to pay for getting away from the snow.'

Six fucking years of this. I am an absolute paragon of a

daughter-in-law. Does he know this? Does he know that the only reason he gets this conversation with his grandchildren – his *only* grandchildren – is because I facilitate it? That if it were up to Alex, he'd never hear from them, ever?

Maybe. Maybe not. He probably doesn't care. Selfish bastard.

'Why do you keep on doing it, then?' Alex asked me one time when I bitched about the shallowness of the interaction.

'Because,' I said through gritted teeth, 'I will not be the one who ruins our children's relationship with their paternal grandfather.'

'You're just going to let him do it himself as they get older and more discerning?' Alex asked.

'Yes.'

The conversation grinds to its usual painful close, and the kids scatter. I lean in to say goodbye and disconnect. Grandpa's already leaving. It's a duty for him too, and he's done it, and he's gone.

'Jane.' Claire's pretty face fills up the screen. Her hair is smoother and blonder than ever, her makeup immaculate.

'Claire,' I say. She hates me. She never talks to me.

'I've been reading your blog,' she says.

Oh, fucking hell. Did I write something about fucking in-laws on there recently? I probably didn't. I limit my blog to innocuous, funny 'kids do the darnedest things' stories, with only the occasional, and generally non-relationship-ending, excursion to the soapbox.

'I was reading the post where you compared your pregnancies,' she says.

I wait.

'Do you know which I mean?' she says.

I shake my head.

'You said . . .' She pauses. 'You said your first was a walk in the park, and you could have run a marathon the day before labour. The second was tougher. And the fourth almost killed you.'

133

'The third almost killed me,' I correct. 'The fourth was a vasectomy gone wrong.' And the universe's greatest gift to me. 'It really, really almost killed me.' And for a moment, I close my eyes, because I'm thinking about the pregnancy I didn't write about, the one between the first and the second – the real second pregnancy – and what it did to me. To us. I feel tears under my eyes. Blink them away.

Open my eyes, look at Claire. She's staring at me. Face pinched.

'You said . . .' She pauses. 'You said you think of yourself as a poster child of why women should have babies in their twenties instead of their thirties, never mind forties.'

Did I? Sure. Sounds like something I might have said. God knows among the things that make me incredibly happy right now is that, when I turn 40, there will be no diapers or tantruming toddlers in my life. Breeding early for the win!

I wait for Claire to get to her point.

'I'm forty-three,' she says.

And here it is.

'Do you think . . . do you think it's too late?'

Why the fuck is she asking me?

Her 64-year-old husband shuffles across the screen in the background. She leans in closer to the computer.

'There are plenty of women my age having babies,' she says. Her voice vibrates with urgency.

Fuck.

This is a clear violation of the third-wife/I'm-not-really-your-daughter-in-law relationship.

Fuck, fuck, fuck.

She's staring at me, waiting for me to stay something.

Fuck.

'There are,' I agree.

'You know some too, right?' she says. Urgently. Again.

'Of course,' I say. What does she want to hear? I shake my head. The universe has apparently decreed that this is how I atone for wanting to be Matt's whore. By counselling my father-in-law's third wife about late child-bearing.

Fine. I'll play.

I tell Claire about sexy Lacey, who had her first baby 'by accident' at 16, one planned child in her early thirties during what she calls her 'exploratory marriage' and then another accidental conception at 42. I tell her about Hetta, my lesbian friend who took her first male lover at 43 for the express purpose of getting a child, and got one. I tell her about Jocelyn, who ended up with triplets courtesy of fertility treatments at 40 . . . and then conceived naturally and accidentally at 46.

But I am not telling her what she wants to hear. I can see that from the tightness around her eyes and mouth.

And suddenly . . . I know what she wants to hear. Oh, fuck. Oh, fuck. Why from me?

'When I first met you, I was sure I didn't want – I didn't want to be, you know, like you,' she says suddenly, bluntly, rudely.

'A breeder?' I say, matching her bluntness. This is no surprise, of course. Claire's contempt for my leaking breasts, round belly/sagging belly/round belly, baby-puke-splattered shirts and abandonment of purses for diaper bags filled with Fisher Price toys, bags of snacks and sippy cups instead of lipstick and makeup cases, was thinly veiled at best.

But while Annie did just puke on me five days ago, these days such incidents are rare, anomalous. My babies are growing up, my belly's flat. And while I'll never have porn-star boobs again, they no longer leak. I feel a flash of triumph and superiority over Barbie. No sippy cups or diapers in my purse any more. And I have babies and she don't, nah-nah-nah-nah. Then try to shake the feeling away. Unfair. Unreasonable. But. There it is.

'Yes,' Claire looks away from the screen. Turns back to it. 'Is it too late for me?'

I know what she wants to hear.

I do.

Tell her.

'You know it's not too late for you,' I say. 'But. It's too late for him.' My eyes go left. To her 64-year-old husband, shuffling about in the background.

Claire's cheeks flush. I look at her face, and then I look down to the laptop keyboard. And I type.

—It's too late for him.
He's still virile. Fertile, she types back.
—You know that's not what I mean.
—He's 64. When your baby is born – 65. Turning 70 the year your child goes to kindergarten. Eighty-fucking-three when he graduates high school.
—It takes more than virility to be a father.

I stop typing. Look at Claire. She's looking down at the screen. She looks at me. I type again.

—It's not too late for you.

'Well, thanks, Jane, goodbye,' Claire says in a high-pitched, odd voice. Her face disappears.

'Fuck,' I say.

A pair of small arms wraps around my neck. Cassandra rests her chin on my shoulder.

'What did you do, Mom?'

I just told your grandfather's 'my biological clock is ticking' third wife to leave him.

'Nothing,' I say.

But I forget that my ten-year-old is observant. And a quick reader.

'Oh, Mom,' she says. 'Are you going to tell Dad?'

'No,' I say. 'No.'

'He'd understand,' she says.

'I don't think he would.'

'He'd forgive you,' she says.

I have a moment of dissonance. Are we talking about the same thing here?

'I'm pretty sure he wouldn't.'

'He hates her,' Cassandra says. 'He can't stand Claire.'

True.

But.

Nobody wants to be the product of a thrice-broken home.

Are you thinking of me, my fuckslave?

—Constantly.

Good.

—I hope this is half as hard for you as it is for me.

Harder.

—Pretending to talk with you in my head is not helping.

No. Fuck your husband. Take your mind off me.

—And who are you fucking? Your supermodel wife? The waitress who served you lunch and noticed you smiling at her? A stripper in a back alley off St Catherine's?

Does it matter?

—No. All that matters is that it's not me.

Once we come back from dinner with Nana and the kids, tired but happy, go to bed, and Alex puts away his phone, I take the advice of the demon in my head. It's a brief and business-like encounter that brings me no relief. As Alex collapses into my arms post-orgasm, I'm briefly tempted to whisper in his ear, 'I think I just sanctioned the break-up of your father's third marriage. Sorry, babe.' Instead, I roll away from him. Fall into a restless sleep in which past and present, reality and fantasy, desire and hate get so thoroughly mixed up I wake up crying.

Day 11 – Unconditional

Today, I choose not to be miserable. Today, I will be part of nobody's drama, not even my own. Today, I will fucking rock.

I turn off my cellphone and do not turn on my laptop, and I use the landline to call Lacey.

'I'm pulling the kids out of school and going to the mountains,' I tell her. 'Want to come?'

Her laughter envelops me like a lover's embrace; it is exactly what I need; it is joy.

'I've got Marcello too – no kindergarten today and Sofia couldn't take the day off,' she says. 'Will we all fit in your van?'

'The beast seats eight,' I tell her. 'Thirty minutes?'

'Thirty minutes,' she agrees. 'But, Jane, honey? Just so we're clear – you're not going to make me hike through snow or anything like that?'

'Well . . .'

'I don't hike,' Lacey says emphatically. 'I will sit in the car and drink cocoa and wait for you if you absolutely must hike, but just so you know, there is no scenario today in which I am hiking. I'm putting on five-inch heels just to make sure.'

And I laugh.

On the way to the mountains, Lacey talks wedding. She shows me the ring at least a dozen times, from different angles. She thrusts the phone, with pictures of cakes and dresses, in front of my face as I drive – always at the most curve-filled moments.

I softly swear, as a red velvet wedding gown – 'White is so cliché, especially if the bride's maid of honour is going to be her thirty-something daughter!' Lacey says – is thrust before my eyes just as I have to navigate a 90-degree turn.

'Oh, Jane, am I driving you crazy?' Lacey asks. 'I'm so sorry. But you know, I'm so, so, so very excited.'

'I know,' I say. 'I begrudge you not. Really.'

'But you don't understand,' Lacey says. I half-turn to check on the children. Marcello and Annie have both dozed off. Each of the older boys is glued to a gaming device; Cassandra has earphones on and is listening to an audiobook.

'No,' I agree. 'Don't misunderstand me – I understand, or I think I understand, why you and Clint are together. I don't question that. At all.'

'You don't understand why I want to get married,' she says. 'Why I care.'

I nod. That, I do not understand at all. After so many years of making it work – somehow – without the bonds of matrimony . . . why now? What for? Why bother?

'I'm not sure I understand either,' Lacey says. 'Maybe I just want the party, the dress, the ring. The cake! I like cake.' And she laughs.

'Maybe,' she adds, more serious, 'I'm afraid of growing old. Alone.'

'But he will never leave you,' I say. 'Since he's met you – he has always come back.'

'Maybe I want something to ensure that,' she says. 'Something that I have, some connection between him and me, that no one else has.'

'The wedding band,' I say.

'The wedding band,' she echoes. 'Geez, Jane, you've made me all glum. We need tunes. And look, some cute ski-bum hitchhikers, let's pick them up.'

'We have six kids in the back seats,' I remind her. But I slow down, so she can ogle.

'Danish,' she pronounces. 'Definitely Danish.'

'Delicious,' I murmur. And Lacey laughs.

She waits in the car with coffee while I run the kids through a mild hike. And marches in her stiletto heels – 'You didn't think I was kidding, honey, did you? Five inches!' – down the main strip of the Banff townsite like she owns it. The tourists turn their heads. Japanese and Korean cameras snap. Ski bums from around the world get hard-ons, and their girlfriends feel immediately inadequate. I walk in her wake, enjoying the ambience.

'Look at all those boys giving you the eye,' she whispers in my ear, her lips brushing my hair, as we pass a group of wind-burned snowboarders.

'Me?' I laugh. 'Lacey, no one sees any other woman when she walks beside you.' But as I turn back, I'm willing to admit a couple of them might have noticed Lacey's handmaiden, even though she's wearing snow pants and a puffy jacket.

Pheromones.

They can smell you a mile away.

—Fuck off, lover. Get the fuck out of my head.

It was your idea, lover. You were always the one into arbitrary rules. Limits. Boundaries. Running away. Me, I just needed the safe word.

—Fuck the fuck off. You will not ruin my life.

My favourite part about road trips is, always, the drive back. The children are exhausted: when they were littler, they would all fall asleep, and I would enjoy an hour, sometimes two, of complete silence. Bliss. They're older now, so awake. But still exhausted. And quiet. And lazily poking at their games and iPods.

'Now tell me,' Lacey commands as we pull out of the townsite and onto the highway. 'What do you need?'

I turn my head sideways and look at her, my beautiful

140

neighbour, personification of love, lust and lack of judgement, and tears leak out of my eyes.

'Perhaps unconditional acceptance,' I say. Stupid.

Lacey's beautiful eyes blink.

'I was asking, pastry or apple,' she says. 'But unconditional acceptance, that I can give you too.' She leans over and pecks me, very gently, on the cheek. 'Talk?'

I shake my head.

'Oh, honey,' Lacey sighs. 'Do you know what your challenge in this lifetime is?'

'Just one?' I quip.

'Just one,' she says. 'Pardon me for going all pop psychology queen on you, but you have severe intimacy issues.'

I laugh.

'You do,' she insists. 'You're lucky you moved in next door to me, and I'll sit in anybody's lap. Otherwise . . . well, tell me, Jane. Who lives in the house on the other side of you?'

'Um . . .' I search my head. Fuck. People. Surely I've seen them. Blue car. 'Unfair,' I counter. 'They're never out of their house. Ever. On the other side of you, I know the Chius . . .'

'You know the Chius because I know the Chius and you've met them at my parties,' Lacey counters. 'The point is. The people on the other side of you? The Joneses, actually – how hilarious is that, they're actually called the Joneses? Anyway – they're in and out of their house as often as you are. You never look at them, smile at them. And you would have never made an overture to me. Except that I'm obnoxious and I sat in your lap.'

'Untrue,' I say. I noticed Lacey the moment she stepped – sauntered – out of her car. And into my driveway. And, figuratively, I suppose, sat in my lap. Fuck.

'So the question is, my dear friend and neighbour,' Lacey says, half-pouting, half-laughing, all-Lacey, 'what are you afraid of?'

I let her question hang in the air for a long, long while.

141

'It's not that I'm afraid,' I say finally. 'It's just that I think I'm a little frightening.'

'We all are,' says Lacey. She pecks me again. 'Unconditional acceptance, honey. Here. I give it to you. Now, stop being moody and let's put on some tunes. Oh. And start eating again. You're looking gaunt.'

I love her.

So very very much.

I let tears drop on to my cheeks and lap all the way home and she doesn't say anything. But after we unload the kinder, she pulls me close to her and holds me. And I rest my head on her shoulder, just long enough to feel a moment of relief.

'Thank you.'

'Unconditional,' she says. Smiles. Then laughs out loud as Clayton wallops her with a snowball.

The day is almost over, I realise, as I follow the kids into the house, where they've shed snowsuits and mittens all over the entryway. I holler at them to come back and gather them up. Check to see that the slow cooker slop is ready. Text Alex: home for dinner? Text back: three minutes away. Holler, 'Chilli ready in five!' to the kids.

Look at the phone hatefully, resentfully.

Check Facebook.

Fuck reason. Come back to me. Now.

The feeling of delight and desire that shoots through me stuns me. I am . . . transfixed.

Oh, my fucking God. Yes.

Alex at the front door. I log out. Feed the troops. Eat. Or try to, anyway. Make myself chew, swallow.

Swallow.

Fuck reason. Come back to me. Now.

Oh, yes. Now. But. Reality is. And there is kitchen clean-up, and book reading and bedtime. And finally, the kids in bed, the littles asleep, the older two reading to themselves . . .

'Do you want to watch a movie with me tonight, Jane?' Alex asks, stretching out on the couch, and reaching a long hand for me.

'No, baby, so exhausted – I won't make it through,' I say. 'I'm just going to read for a bit, and then go to sleep early.'

'OK, love,' he says and clicks the remote. I kiss his cheek. And disappear into our bedroom with the phone.

Come back to me. Now.

And I write . . .

—Here.

He's waiting.

Tell me you suffered.
—oh god
Tell me.
—I was going through the days in 15 minute increments. Working so hard not to think of you, you were all I could think about.
And now?
—Want you. No terms.
—Tell me you were tormented. Just a little.
Fuck I was tormented. Am tormented.
And frustrated.
Thwarted.
Denied.
I looked at your 'I hate you' email, the pictures, a dozen times. Sometimes just the subject line was enough to stir.

—I got drunk, for the first time in months if not years, just to sleep.

—And it was what? Not even three days. Jeezus fucking christ.

I like the thought of influencing you, tormenting you by my absence.

Crossing distance, and years.

—When I closed my eyes, I'd hear you whisper, 'Now do what you're fucking told, and I'd . . .

You'd what?

—I'd buckle.

Good.

Now tell me what you are. What you still are.

—I'm your fuckslave.

—With apparently no fucking will or self-control where you are concerned.

—and fucking pissed about it

—And what are you?

Your master

With a hard cock

—Check your email.

Stroking my cock as you type. Fuck. Is that you, right now?

—yes

Such a bold whore. I approve.

A tempting target.

—Are you aiming already?

I think you may need it on your face. It's been days since you've submitted.

—Too many.

—Will you let me lick you first

(Not alone)

Has he fucked you while I couldn't?

—(safe?)

(Barely. Don't care.)

Answer me.
—I don't know. I don't remember. Does it matter? All I wanted was you – longing, for the wrong thing.
So wrong.
I like how you sent me your photo, unbidden.
Eager.
—Broken.
—Do you remember . . .
—We were in your apartment one day, God, 15 years ago, maybe more.
—On your bed.
—And you asked me what it was I wanted. And I said . . . I can't remember the exact words, but it was something about how you had to figure it out, that you had to make me – I did not want to have to tell.
—I remember, I said, 'You have to find the key.' And you got angry. 'What key? Tell me.' But, of course, I wouldn't. I couldn't.
—Fuck.
—I think you've found it.
I know that I have.
Maybe I've been searching for the key this whole time.
—It disturbs me.
—(that you've found it)
—And it both pleases and disturbs me that you've been searching.
Why are you disturbed?
Do I frighten you now?
—Yes.
—And excite me beyond the realm of what I thought possible.
—Which is also frightening.
This is the real me.
I know that now.
As natural as breathing.

This is what you feel. The reality of me.
—Tell me what you want.
Wanting you. To get on your knees.
—for you
For me alone.
Unless I lend you out.
—You make me ache.
—You always watch.
Always.
Ensure you're being obedient and thorough.
Knowing it would reflect on your owner.
—I hate being owned.
—And it makes me so hot to read you say that.
—Jeezus Christ, Matt, what have you done to me?
Broken you.
Fixed you.

I don't hear the stairs creak; I don't hear anything until the bedroom door opens. Alex.

—I have to go. xx
I understand.
I'm loaning you out to him. Fuck him to please me. xx

When Alex sits on the bed, I slide up behind him and wrap my arms and legs around him, my tongue licking around his ear, down his neck, my hands fumbling at his cock immediately.

'Jesus,' he moans. 'What's up with you?'

'I think today,' I whisper between nips at his neck, 'you need to get the fucking of your life.'

'Yes, please,' he groans. Turns to face me. And later, much later, as he rolls off me: 'Oh, my fucking God. If this is peri-menopause, I hope it lasts for ever.'

I fall away from Alex exhausted, sated and revelling in the thought that however mindfucked I was, *he* couldn't make it through three days without me either. The bliss this thought induces in me makes me sick. I feel hate and contempt swell up inside me, for myself. For him. For us.

And then the bliss returns. And, exhausted, I sleep. Don't dream.

Day 12 – Depraved

I've got Facebook open on the laptop as I'm wrestling kids into clothes and tidying up the kitchen. Purely to be available. I'm not even pretending it's for anything else. I don't care about Marie's moral dilemmas, Nicola's angst, Lacey's wedding plans – she's posted a dozen photos of potential dresses and wedding cakes. Someone's kid lost a tooth? Whoop-de-fucking-do.

I'm waiting for this:

Get over here.

How does he know that this is exactly what I wanted to hear, right now? That I don't want a 'how was your night?' or even that increasingly powerful 'Tell me' that turns my knees to jelly? Today, in this moment, this is what I want. And so I respond, immediately:

—Here.

And then, because I am mad, totally mad, but also in synch, and I know what he wants right now as he knows what I want right now, I give him the word I know he craves.

—Here. My master.

And it's exactly what he wants right now too, and I lose my mind. And fuck, so does he.

on your fucking knees
—down
Turn away from me. On all fours. Now put your face to the floor.
—oh my fucking god
Keep that ass up.
—weight on elbows
Relax your pussy. Let it open for your master.
—yes
Keep your fucking face DOWN.
—I'm sorry
Now beg to be used.
And start every sentence to me with 'Your whore says.'
—Your whore says, please fuck me, my master. Please.
I lean over and spit on your pussy to make you wetter.
—Jesus.
First I want to hear you cum.
I slide two fingers inside you
—oh, jeezus, I raise my ass higher, to take them deeper
and immediately start working your g-spot.
—(Moaning)
Finger fucking the front wall of your pussy . . .
harder than you ever knew you could take it.
—tears in my eyes, my forehead aching from the pressure of the floor
My hand slick with your pussy juice.
Look how quickly you're going to cum for me. What a well-trained little whore.
—so quickly
—but you know I cum on command for you
—shall I?

Cum for me, my little slut.
—My upper body slumps more, my ass pulses upward, and I explode in shudders. My knees splay, I collapse.
Utterly used.
—But I still want you, so badly.
—Do you want me to say it again?
Yes.
—Your whore begs, please fuck me, my master.
—Use me. Utterly.
One hand holds my upper body up while the other grips your hair and forces your face into the floor while I use your pussy.
—oh god, I push back against you, because I want to feel you ripping me apart
The side of your face pressing down. You are helpless. Shameless.
Take my fucking cock, slut.
—yes
—all that matters is that you want to use me
Tell me what you are. Out loud with every stroke.
—I . . .
—am . . .
—your . . .
—fuck . . .
—(I gasp a deeper breath)
—slave . . .
—I . . .
—am . . .
—your . . .
—whore . . .
Take off your panties.
Right now.
—In life?
Yes.

I'm lifting up my skirt and sliding my hand into my panties as Alex walks into the kitchen. My hand drops. The laptop lid slams down.

So. This is what I am now? This is what I do?

Fuck. Insane. Right. This is why I wanted to stop this.

I lean against the stove, my knees shaking. My wetness soaking through my panties.

'Why's the laptop on the stove?' Alex asks, conversationally.

'Facebooking with Marie,' I say. Voice hoarse. Jesus-fucking-Christ.

'Any pancakes left?' he asks. I shake my head. Close my eyes for a millisecond, find myself.

'You're late today,' I say. Conversationally. Surely, conversationally.

'Another late night tonight, I think, so I thought the client owed me a sleep-in,' he answers. Pours coffee. 'Do you want me to run the kids to school?'

'No!' It comes out too loud. But, Jesus. I don't want to be alone. I can't be alone. In the house. No. Not right now. Not after that.

'No,' I say again. 'Annie's got a library field trip and story time and I'm volunteering. I need to be there anyway. But thank you.'

'I just feel I haven't been, you know, there for you guys very much,' Alex says. 'Not pulling my weight. Not . . . present.'

I turn around to fully face him. And kiss him.

'It's like this every December,' I say. 'Fucking clients. Fucking year-end. Not your fault.'

Marie texts me as I'm unloading the kids in front of the school. I watch Annie take off on her own, not waiting for Cassandra. Feel one of those stupid pangs – in September, I had to walk into the preschool room with her every single morning. Now she doesn't even wait for her sister.

I check the phone as it buzzes again.

The old message:

- Jane! Help!

And 45 seconds later:

- I know you're there! I'm three cars behind you. I see you! Talk to me!
—Do you want to come out and talk to me?
- No. I can't. I'm texting with Paul.
—Jeezus. Then why are you texting with me?
- He's being really hot. So hot, Jane. He says, hold on, I'm going to copy this . . .
—Stop. Don't tell me. I can't hear this. What do you want from me?
- You're so much better at this than I am. He wrote, oh, so fucking hot, Jane, 'I want to inflame your desire, I want you writhing in your car, sopping wet, waiting for only me.' What do I write back?
—'I want to suck your cock now.' Fuck, Marie. I don't have the time for this right now.
- You're just sitting in your car! Jane, please! You know I suck at this . . .
—Fine. 'Oh, lover, as I read your texts, rivulets of my pussy juices stream down the insides of my thighs. Tell me more.' And then just 'Yes' and 'Mmm' as he word-fucks you. You can do that, right?
- Geez, who peed in your cornflakes today, Jane? Anyway, thanks!

I pull out and around and as I drive past her car, I see her head bent over her telephone.

Judge her. I dare you.
—Shut up. Go away.

She's alone in her car. Where were you this morning?
On all fours, ass raised in the air for me on your kitchen
floor.
—Fuck off!
Depraved.

There are probably pills I can take for this.

There are rivulets of something or other streaming down
my thighs. And my cheeks. My face is as wet, as flushed, as
my pussy.

I'm still shaking and . . . fuck, wet, dripping, when I get to
the gym after dropping off the kids. But sufficiently calmed
that I'm also angry, appalled . . . but oh, still so fucking
aroused. Jesus. Peri-menopause? Or simply not being 'finished'
– the result of being interrupted, of not coming when he . . .
The changing room is empty and as I slip off my jeans, I slip
my hand into my panties, and . . .

'Jane!'

What the fuck now? I grab my sweats with both hands and
whirl around to face Nicola.

'Are you just working out, or do you have a session with
Jesse?' she asks.

'I'm too lazy and undisciplined to ever work out on my
own,' I say.

'Oh,' she says. 'So, you're with Jesse.'

I nod.

'Oh,' she repeats.

My mood switches, immediately, from maddened lust to
just mad. I fucking hate women. She wants to say something.
She wants to ask me something. Why won't she? As she opens
her mouth again, I think that if she says, 'Oh,' for the third
time, I will whack her with my water bottle.

'I was wondering,' she says instead, 'I was wondering,' she
says again, 'I was wondering,' she says a third time, and I grit
my teeth, 'would you mind sharing him?'

What?

My eyebrows rise up and I stare at her. She flushes.

'Would you mind sharing him?' she asks. 'It's cheaper – you know, it's cheaper if there are two, and . . .' She stops. Humiliated, and, as I feel my rage receding in the face of her vulnerability, I see her reaching for her own rage, her rage against Paul, which she will use to ward off her humiliation. Her humiliation at going from being, if not quite one of the one per cent, then from a spot of such ridiculous financial privilege that economising on a gym membership or a session with a personal trainer was about as much in the cards as needing to rely on the 10-per-cent-off days at Safeway to manage the grocery budget, to where she is now. Wrangling over child-support cheques, kiting the credit cards, maxing the line of credit, while her ex fucks his intern.

And sexts Marie. Although that, Nicola doesn't know yet.

I see her rage building and – I need to stop it. Now. I cannot bear to hear it explode. I cannot endure another crucifixion of Paul – another vilification of the skank.

But I will not share Jesse.

I reach for my purse. My wallet. Pull out a handful of twenties, don't count them.

'Here,' I thrust them at Nicola. 'It's my "Have a Happy Divorce" present to you. I think that's good for three, maybe four sessions with Jesse. Book in after me.'

And I slide into my workout clothes and run the fuck out of the locker room as fast as I can.

It's not until I'm flat on my back on the gym floor and Jesse's counting me through jack-knives that I realise that my attempt to reconcile my selfishness with the desire to do Nicola a good turn just added to her humiliation.

I am that dense, that obtuse.

And I feel a flash of guilt.

'Hey, Nic!' Jesse nods in her direction as she walks past us, and then starts stretching nearby.

Too close, frankly, for my comfort. Is she mocking me or offering me a chance for atonement?

I glance at her and receive a look of such rage and venom that I close my eyes. Recoil back.

Fuck her. I don't want to share. And neither does she. Else she'd have let her husband fuck the skank, at least for a little while.

She'd probably have drawn the line, though, at him doing Marie . . .

'Jane?' Jesse pops into my line of sight. 'Focus. Your form's terrible today.'

'Sorry.' But I struggle to find focus for the rest of the session. I am ashamed . . . ashamed that I hurt Nicola. Shamed by my still throbbing arousal. Ashamed of what else? This spike of selfishness? My possessiveness over Jesse?

Sweat pouring off me, I push self-knowledge away. Stretch in the gym until I see Nicola leave the changing room. Then shower, change and race like a madwoman to meet up with Annie's preschool class for their Nutcracker drama story time at a local library.

Survive a telephone conversation with my mother. About what? Not a clue. Blood is pounding in my ears. I am . . . how did Jesse put it? Unfocused.

Or, more accurately, focused on the wrong things.

Kid pick-up. Balmy winter day – 'Can we stay and play at the playground, please, Mom, please?' 'Why not?' and I sit on the bench and watch them. Marie's beside me. Texting, not talking. Every once in a while, giggling. 'Don't worry, Jane, I don't need you to script for me any more, I'm getting the hang of playing the way he likes,' she whispers. I shudder. Not sure why. Just – unsettled.

Finally, everyone back in the car. Still shaken. Unsettled. Selfish. Oh, my fucking God, so fucking selfish. Getting harder to push that self-knowledge away. But unwilling to surrender to it. Fighting.

I like that.

—I think you are driving me mad.

Just a little. Do you want me to stop?

Self-knowledge. And so, in my head:

—Not yet.

Chinese food pick-up, because I know I am incapable of boiling, cooking, chopping. And finally home. I pull into our driveway just as Clint is pulling out of Lacey's. And my phone rings in my hand before the key's out of my lock.

'Sure,' I tell Lacey. 'Come on over. I'm slopping Chinese on the table.'

'I'll bring popcorn,' she says. 'And wine.'

And five minutes later, she and Clayton are at our table, bowls full of noodles and rice and black bean ribs and ginger-fried chicken, and the boys are shouting and showing off and Cassandra looks exasperated and Annie overstimulated, and I feel the throbbing in my head recede, to be replaced by the quotidian throbbing that's the result of too much child noise – so instead of making the kids help clean up after the meal, I boot them to the living room with the bowl of popcorn. 'Will you make hot chocolate?' Henry begs, and I say something non-committal, which he interprets as a yes. And they're gone.

Lacey pours us more wine. I start putting the leftovers away.

'Do that later,' Lacey says. It's a command, really. She means, 'Sit down, and listen.' And I do. Bracing myself for another wedding story – pictures of cakes, rings, gowns, perhaps venues.

Instead:

'Sofia's pregnant,' she says.

The wave of *déjà vu* that hits me is so strong I close my eyes. We're here, in my kitchen – what, a bit more than four years ago. I'm very pregnant with Annie. Utterly exhausted by Henry and Eddie. Ravaged with guilt at neglecting Cassandra.

I'm sitting and drinking tea and watching Lacey clean my kitchen – after feeding me the supper she brought over for me. And all the while talking. About Clayton's new teacher. The day's wacky clients at the spa she runs. The municipal election. Her fantasy of a Christmas in Hawaii. And then, in the middle of it all, inflection barely changed:

'Sofia's pregnant.'

She's known for a few days now, she tells me. She's still processing – although that's not the word she uses. 'Still dealing,' she says, that's what it is. 'Still dealing.' 'I knew, of course, that they've stayed in touch, got together every once in a while,' she says. 'I'm not the jealous type at all, you know,' she says. And she says – how surprised she is by her feelings. Her anger. Her surge of possessiveness. 'I want to believe that if you really love someone, you set them free,' she says, and the statement, on the surface so banal – so worthy of a fridge magnet or a Facebook meme, although this first 'Sofia's pregnant moment' comes before we're all living on Facebook – seems profound on her lips. 'I want to be the person who can do that. Who can accept him completely, as he is. But this is harder than I thought.'

She says . . . she thinks it would be easier for her to accept a confession of sexual or emotional infidelity. 'I'm not naive, Jane, I remember very well that he was still officially with Sofia when he and I met,' she says, 'and I know the type of man he is, and how much he likes women and sex and . . .' She pauses, trails off and then repeats, 'I'm not naive.' But it would be easier, so much easier, she says, to accept a confession of infidelity not accompanied by the *fact* of a child.

The *fact* of a child. The expression, despite its pathos, makes me smile.

Clint's child . . .

'That's so much more real,' she says. 'I can't dismiss it as just a fuck.'

'The fruit of a fuck,' I say.

'Multiple fucks,' she says. Sighs. 'A relationship. Like ours.'

I remember – I ask her, what did Sofia do? When she found out about Clayton?

I don't remember what Lacey said then. But clearly Sofia eventually forgave.

My kitchen. Now. Four, five years after the first 'Sofia's pregnant' revelation. Are we going to have the same conversation?

No.

This time, it's at least a little different.

'I told him he had to leave,' Lacey says. 'That I needed time to think. That I couldn't believe – right now – right now. After he asked me to marry him, finally. As we're planning a wedding. After he's given me the ring. That I couldn't believe I had to deal with this shit again. Dealing with the reality of Marcello is quite enough, thank you.'

The first time I've heard Lacey swear. The closest to bitterness I've ever heard her come. And it's not her, and she retreats from it. Immediately.

'I love him very very much,' she says, and I know at this moment, she is talking about Marcello. 'And I love that Clayton has a brother. And I even – you know, I even really like Sofia.'

Of course.

'But I'm not sure I can go through all this again. And perhaps again,' Lacey says. 'How many children am I going to have to accept? Am I in a – what-do-you-call it, polygynous relationship? Am I going to be one of two wives? For ever?'

She doesn't expect any answers. I pour her more wine. Finish cleaning up after supper as she talks, vents. Doesn't cry. And then:

'And the strangest thing,' she says, 'I haven't told you the strangest thing. The other thing.'

I wait.

'She's not even sure it's his,' Lacey says. 'Because, of course, she's got a boyfriend.'

Of course.

'The "real" boyfriend, that's what Clint said. The real boyfriend. What's Clint?' Lacey asks.

'The lover,' I say.

'The lover?' Lacey echoes. 'The baby-daddy. Well. So – she doesn't even know if it's his. But she wanted to tell him – and have him tell me right away – because of the wedding,' Lacey says.

Of course.

I hear tears in her voice. And I'm grateful that she does not want answers or commentary.

Because what the fuck does one say to that?

Finally, she's talked out, spent. 'I need to go, be alone,' she says. 'Have a bath.' I offer to keep Clayton until bedtime. 'No, I need him with me,' she says. And I understand. She calls for him, and all the kids clamour in. Shouting. She shepherds Clayton down onto the landing, to the door. Turns to me.

'When's Alex coming home?' she asks. I peek at my phone. Yes, a text.

'Late,' I say. 'Late. The usual December rush.'

'Oh, honey,' Lacey says as if I'm the one who needs to be pitied, and hugs me. I let her hold me. Feel the throbbing in my temples return.

Lock the door behind her as she leaves.

Force myself to focus on real life. Everything that needs to be done gets done. Bath. Bedtime. Books. Long shower. And in bed.

Text Alex:

—Good night, baby. I love you. Chinese leftovers in fridge.

Turn off the phone. Turn off the light. Close my eyes.

Open them. Grab my laptop.

159

—What are you doing here?

Can't sleep. Wanted to relive this morning. Are you all right, lover?

Safe?

—Safe, yes. All right, not so much.

Shaken?

—Yes. So much.

Tell me you dripped with lust for me all day. Used, but unfulfilled.

—God. Yes.

My shameless slut.

—Yours.

—Fuck, so yours.

Who'll do anything for me.

Won't she.

—She wants to say, 'Within reason.' Or 'I'll do anything you ask me to so long as it's something I want to do.'

Tell the fucking truth.

—Anything.

—Always.

All caps. Shout it.

—ANYTHING

—ALWAYS

—Terrifying and still unwelcome though that admission is.

I value it all the more for the resistance.

Whore. Tell me this is your true self.

—This is my true self. But I think it only exists in relation to you.

Say that again.

—All of it?

The important part.

—Your whore says, this is my true self. And it exists only in relation to you.

Your master is proud to own your true self.

To own you truly.

160

—Role-player.
Deny it. Can you?
—. . .
—In this moment, you more than own me. You create
me.
I like that. I am your will.
—You are. Too much.

I stare at the screen. Aching. Longing. And then, this thought,
again. Terrifying. Because – reality. His cock, in the past, has
filled me. So totally, so powerfully – I thought. His hands have
caressed, played – savaged – every part of me. There is no
part of my body that hasn't felt him, experienced him, taken
him, been pleasured by him – suffered to please him. In reality,
in the past. But fuck. This thing, this thing that's happening
now – these words on a screen, these sensations in my mind
– they eclipse our past reality.

Completely.

And our physical reality of the past . . . it was not meek.
It was always . . . powerful.

But this. This is so much more.

And so, when he finally comes – and he will come. Or I
will go. And it will be real again after – what, more than ten
years? Almost eleven.

And it will be terrible.

Because how can it ever match this?

And this thought: maybe we both like it better this way.
Just in my head, in his head. An all-encompassing mindfuck
. . . without the physical limits of reality. Crow's feet and grey
stubble. Loose breasts. Aching hips. Middle-aged bellies and
imperfections and the unpredictability of going off-script and
all those rubs of gritty reality.

And then what? I shudder.

And then, this thought: perhaps, if it's terrible . . . if it's
not this intense . . . if it's less encompassing, if it's messier,

161

duller – that will not be a bad thing. Because . . . unsustainable. Insane.

I want to tell him this. I want him to think about this too. To suffer and worry.

I type:

—Do you know . . .
Yes?
—. . . there's a part of me that simultaneously worries and hopes that when we meet 'live', it won't be this intense.

His response, immediate:

Listen, whore. When I see you, I'm going to fuck your mouth deep and hard, hands sunk in your hair. Force-fucking you until your eyes water.
Time enough just to catch your breath and a cock slap in the face before your throat goes back to work.

I read and I teeter, immediately, on the verge of orgasm. Depraved. But I'm looking, longing for . . . what? Reassurance? Something more.

—And it will be better than this? even more intense than this word-fuck?
Word-fuck falls short. That's what we used to do, when we were too young to know any better.
Mindfuck comes close.

And he starts to read my mind:

Seeing yourself, your hidden self, now your exposed self, so depraved. So used.
So eager to serve me.

Shocking yourself with your eagerness, your desire to submit to me. Your affinity for your true self.
—And you. Do I release your true self?
You know you do. This side of me, it comes out the most for you. It always did. Before I knew what it was.
—And when I am on my knees before you, in reality and not just in this mindfuck, and you shove your cock in my mouth . . . will your true self shock you? More than it shocks you now?
I'm counting on it. Now go. Sleep. Recover. So you are rested and ready when I have need of you tomorrow.
xx
—xo

I log off . . . almost sated. Almost calm. And, for the second night in a row, sleep like the dead. Not happy, but . . . fuck. Pleased.

Depraved.

Day 13 – Obligations

I wake up, rested and restless, relieved and randy; the relief and reassurance of yesterday night still present, but receding. I hear Alex in the shower – and no one else yet awake – and I reach immediately for my phone. The morning is almost over in Montréal, and maybe there is a message for me already. Maybe. And then I let myself self-deceive and wonder if Marie's up, and if she's messaged me about something, and maybe I should ask her what she's going to wear to the party tonight, or maybe she will ask me what I'm going to wear . . . Will I dress for Matt? And if I do, if I let him dress me for tonight, whom will I shock and whom will I titillate? – and I let delicious and decadent and illicit feelings swirl in me. And then I see the date.

Oh, yes. Oh, no.

It would have been tonight. Relief gone. Replaced by instant lust.

This is the day Matt would have been here – spent the previous day servicing clients – and the night at . . . where would he have stayed? The Sheraton? Le Germain? The Palliser? Wherever. Irrelevant. The Ramada Inn, for all it matters.

Fucking me.

I hear the water in the shower stop, as I type, without thinking, just carried away by . . . nostalgia, memory for what wasn't? desire? regret?

—It would have been today.

164

I push the phone away as Alex comes into the room.

'You're up ridiculously early for a Saturday,' I murmur.

'Couldn't sleep,' he says. 'Although it was a ridiculously late Friday night. Jesus. But everything's on track.' He sits beside me, towel wrapped around his waist, droplets of water on his shoulders, in his hair.

'Dreading the party?' he asks, suddenly.

'No.' I shake my head. Try not to wish for him to go away. He sits beside me, rests his head on my shoulder.

'It won't be so bad,' he says. 'The food's always good.'

I want him to leave so I can see if Matt's messaged me back. Fuck. Real life first, amoral whore.

I wrap my arms around him. Smell him. Seek tranquillity.

Check my phone as soon as he goes downstairs to make coffee.

Nothing.

An hour later, two hours later – nothing.

It shouldn't matter. It's Saturday – a day on which it makes sense that it's harder to connect. Weekend. Constant presence of husbands, wives. But . . . I want him. Every morning, I touch him . . . How many days has this been going on? Thirteen. This is day thirteen, unlucky thirteen. But this would have been *the* day after, or the day of – we never settled details. And it matters. Oh, God, it matters. I can't believe how much it matters. I want him. Right now. Today. So badly. The day unfolds, the children wake up, are fed, amused – we take them swimming. A full day. A day in which I should not be aware of the heaviness or the silence of my fucking phone, but I am.

The message is waiting for me when we leave the swimming pool. Yes, I check it right in the change room, still dripping.

My time is not my own at the moment.

I am stupid.

Unthinking, unreasonable. It's a Saturday, a family Saturday – a Saturday I'm spending with my own family, my beloved family, my children who mean more to me than anything, anything else. Do I have time for a session of cyberfucking? No. No, I don't. In seven minutes, I will be in a car with my husband and my four children. What the fuck is wrong with me? Why does this message – a carefully worded 'I am not alone and I cannot talk' (cannot fuck) message – feel like a slap in the face, a dismissal? Suddenly, I am again a thirteen-year-old girl rejected by her first crush, standing in the dark, alone, at a junior-high-school dance, and I want to weep.

I am in-fucking-sane.

My time is not my own at the moment.

Neither is mine. Suck it up, princess. What did you think? Did you think that he'd spend the whole of today fantasising about what would have been? Well, yes. Yes, I did. Because when I woke up this morning, when I realised what today was – that was my plan. Oh, fuck. Insane. Shake it off. Real life. Real life matters and real life comes first. Do you know what this message means, you stupid skank? It means his wife needs him. It means . . . utilitarian, reproductive sex. It means a twelve-hour wait in the ER because one of them, or a friend, or a parent, is sick. It means there's a work emergency. A cat needs to be taken to the vet's. Oh, fuck, it means grocery shopping. And putting up shelves and cleaning the garage and trimming the Christmas tree. It means – real fucking life always trumps, and always will trump, this. Whatever this is. And that's the way it's supposed to be. This. Is. What. You. Want. Real life first. Some kind of limit on the obsession and compulsion.

Fuck, fuck, fuck.

All I want is him between my thighs. Or at least in my head.

I turn off my phone. I don't give a fuck if Marie tries to reach me. If my mom feels a desperate need to text me with

166

questions about what she should cook for the kids when she has them for their mega-sleepover on Monday. Alex is next to me, and I will not spend the day waiting to hear from Matt.

I. Will. Not.

As the kids, hungry and exhausted, fight in the two back rows of the minivan while we drive to pick up Alex's mother who's babysitting them while we go to the Christmas party at Alex's firm, I remember precisely why I've always run from Matt, always played with him only when coupled with another – and frequently, fucked someone else when I just wanted him. And this is it. I hate feeling like this. And no one else ever made me feel like this. This broken, this obsessed, this irrational.

This owned.

—That's what I do with you, what I've always done with you. Enjoy a little, suffer a little, then leave. That's my MO. *Yes. The running. Your MO, as you put it. Well. Have you enjoyed enough?*

I don't know. Have I? But maybe I've suffered enough. Maybe I do need to stop this. There is no way this scenario can end well for me, is there? Best case: we cyberfuck a few more weeks. He comes to town. We fuck for real. I withdraw, shaken, bruised. Sated. Or not. Worst case: I'm reckless and stupid and Alex finds out and I hurt him so terribly, terribly he never forgives me. Everything in between: nothing but variations of Jane getting kicked in the teeth. Matt withdrawing, realising he can't maintain his reality with me in it. Joy finding out, freaking out – being hurt, leaving. The two of us finding each other oppressive, unbearable. So many ways for this to end, all of them bad.

Fucking moron. Run. Leave. Stop this.

I don't want to.

'Jane?' Alex asks. 'Why are you moaning?'

'I think I'm going to throw up,' I say. And when he pulls over, I stumble out of the car and retch into the ditch.

I feel much better. Not well. But better. Self-awareness sucks and suffering sucks. But there are worse things.

I don't turn on the phone when we get home. And although I think only of Matt when I dress, I leave it all behind – including the phone – when we leave the house.

Mostly.

Alex's law firm throws the worst Christmas parties. Apparently, there's an actual fun Christmas party for the lawyers and staff – spouses *not* invited – earlier, in November. The lawyers-and-significant-others Christmas party is god-awful. The men all wear the same suit. The women all wear too much perfume and jewellery. Everyone drinks a little too much – and yet not enough. The conversation is a combination of insincere compliments and irrelevant anecdotes.

I keep on reading that law schools are graduating more than 50 per cent female students these days, and waiting for this statistic to make an appearance at Alex's workplace. But no. Not yet. The 'baby' lawyers – the students and associates – are, indeed, half and half, and perhaps even more so. But go up the food chain five, six years, and most of the little girls disappear. By partner level, it's predominantly male – and the *powerful* partner level (Alex isn't quite there yet) is all male. The support staff, by contrast, is almost all female. A made-to-order recipe for a dysfunctional workplace.

Apparently it's somewhat different in the *Toronto* office – what isn't? – but in Calgary, it's boys, boys, boys. Which means that the really awful thing about this Christmas party is that it's not lawyers and spouses, it's really partners and *wives,* associates and wives, a smattering of associates and husbands.

Alex suggests I hate his law firm's parties because I hate lawyers. It's not true. I hate the wives.

When Alex was still a snot-nosed associate, and I was at the first of our many, many god-awful law firm social gatherings, one of his senior partners told me that in his experience there were two kinds of 'legal wives'. There were the helpmeets who were effectively their husbands' (husbands', not spouses' – why bother hiding the gender-twisted reality in non-sexist language?) practice managers. They were the true networkers and business development specialists, he said. They ensured the couple's role in the community. They threw the parties, attended the luncheons, made connections with the charities, the boards, created the opportunities for their husbands to meet the *right* people.

'And then there were the wives who chose to lead their own lives.' He sighed. Looked at me suspiciously.

Then: 'Those marriages hardly ever last,' he said sadly.

I accidentally-on-purpose spilled my red wine on his Armani suit.

He was, as it turned out, wrong. As I watched Alex's colleagues' marriages fall apart over the – God, how many god-awful Christmas parties has it been? Twelve? Oh, my fucking God, *twelve,* almost twelve, when did that happen? – over the last twelve years, it was clear that the helpmeets got divorced at just the same rate as the wives who 'chose to lead their own lives'. The partner pontificating on the legal wives to me – he dumped his *second* helpmeet three or four years ago. His third wife, however, is also a helpmeet.

Some women, apparently, are undeterred by the experience and evidence of Bluebeard's earlier wives.

I am not a helpmeet. I am also not, in their eyes at least, one of the 'wives who lead their own lives'. Most of them are also lawyers, or other professionals with six-days-a-week, twelve-hours-a-day type jobs. To them, I'm a boring housewife – my freelance job incomprehensible, irrelevant, unimportant. To the helpmeets, I'm lazy and incompetent. As a result, every year, at each Christmas party and every other painfully boring law firm event, I am shunned equally by both sets of wives.

Woe is I. Not. It's all right. I shun them right back. Although I'd enjoy my half of the shunning more if they tried courting me. Instead, Marie and I usually retreat to some semi-private corner and talk about everything *but* the practice of law, the latest United Way fundraising campaign and the terrible service at the Tribune. Gag. And when we're not pregnant and nursing, get stinking drunk.

We met at one of these awful Christmas parties, Marie and I. Alex and I had been married . . . months, barely. He had just switched firms. Was already thinking it was the biggest mistake of his life. But there he was, in a suit that cost as much as our monthly mortgage payment. And there I was, in a dress off the clearance rack at Winners.

I had just been introduced to, judged and found wanting by some senior firm wives. Then spilled wine on a grey-haired, dandruff-shedding partner who pinched my ass (not to be confused with the pontificating partner who would go on to marry and divorce three, maybe four 'helpmeets': I would spill wine on him at another gathering). Then endured a series of god-awful 'The reality of the Calgary market' conversations with Alex's less intelligent contemporaries, who understood neither simple math nor complex economics, but read all the financial papers. And, as I refilled my wine glass one too many times, got hit by one of those 'What the fuck have I done with my life? Am I going to have to socialise with all these awful, awful people until the day I die? Is this my social circle? These – these are Alex's and my "people"?' feelings, the intensity of which made me reel.

Wine glass in hand, I almost ran to the oasis offered by a cluster of potted plants in the corner of the room.

Where I slammed my head into the wall. Once. Twice.

'Girlfriend.' A slightly slurred voice spoke in my ear. 'Stop that. And drink some more wine.'

And there was Marie. Sitting against the wall, her black, sequined – clearly very expensive; I was starting to realise that any item of the partners' wives' clothing was worth exponentially more than my entire wardrobe – dress crumpled, a bottle of red wine in her hand.

She leaned forward, shaking the bottle in my direction. I took it from her, took a swig.

'Jane,' I said.

'Marie,' she said. 'Are you hiding because Bob pinched your ass?'

'No. Well, he did. But mostly I'm hiding because the wives hate me. Or I hate the wives. I haven't decided yet,' I said. Slid down the wall and sat down beside her. 'You?'

'They hate me, because I'm the new trophy wife,' Marie said. 'Apparently, they get over it come the next divorce – they direct all the venom to the new one, and I join them, and that's how I break into the group. That's what JP says. There.' She pointed through the foliage. 'My not-so-trophy husband.'

'Oh,' I said.

'You're a first wife?' she asked.

'And last,' I said. Marie laughed. 'Cute,' she said. Handed me the bottle again. I drank.

And that was how I made the first, only, female friend of my adult life.

We spent the rest of the night behind the potted plants – I went out to snatch another bottle of wine from the bar later; she teetered out to grab a third at the night's end. I'm not sure if JP noticed where his 'helpmeet' was or wasn't; if Alex did, he made no mention of it. He seemed to have a good night.

'Do you know which one's his fuck buddy?' Marie asked me, as I pointed out Alex to her in a group of junior associates, drinking, laughing and looking a wee bit awkward together. I raised my eyebrows. Marie was working hard to shock me all night.

'I don't know that he has one,' I said.

'Yet,' she said provocatively.

'Perhaps,' I shrugged. I looked at the circle of lawyers, the women among them, carefully. 'None of them really seems like his type.' I paused. 'Or mine. Except maybe that one – the long-haired one in the mini?'

'Your twin,' Marie offered, not rising to my subtle bait. 'That's Susan. She's sleeping with the head of the department. She doesn't do associates.' She paused. Decided to bat at the bait. 'And I don't think she does girls.' Provocative again.

I shrugged. Took another swig of wine.

I didn't see Marie again until the next year's Christmas party – JP and Alex were in different practice groups and different demographic groups – by which time we were both sporting pregnant bellies. Despite our perfect sobriety, we had a great night again, feeling superior over the non-reproducing females and sexier than the post-reproductive ones. And we saw each other again. And again.

We amused each other. Understood each other – well, I understood her, and she *thought* she understood me, which was foundation enough for a friendship until we got attached to each other. And then, we were friends simply because we were friends.

There are worse bases for relationships.

Marie's how I endure each god-awful Christmas party, because my relationship with the wives has not improved as I've become a more seasoned one: I'm eternally out of sync, my life choices and life phases incompatible. My ability to pretend to be interested in their dull lives negligible.

I instinctively flock to her. Look for her. Because although Alex and I enter together, as do all the not-currently-divorcing couples, we split up almost immediately. He is claimed by the handful of colleagues he actually enjoys spending time with socially, then pulled into huddles by others who have a pressing matter to discuss with him, then into a group of juniors who see him as powerful enough to curry favour with . . . yet young enough to be approachable. I engage in active avoidance of the helpmeet wives, who are busy exchanging horror-nanny/best new diet/ 'meditation is making such a huge difference in my life' stories. When they approach me, I try to be kind to the new wives, but, because I'm me, I probably come across as patronising and insufferable. The handful of husbands is even more lost and awkward, and too much work, so I studiously avoid all of them.

I realise, suddenly, that Lacey is right. Not only do I have severe intimacy issues, I might very possibly outright hate people. Fuck.

I fend off the mildly inappropriate advances of one or two of Alex's already inebriated colleagues; suffer through an awkward conversation with a new snot-nosed associate who hasn't yet learned I'm not a helpmeet or an intangible asset to the firm. None of the older ass-pinching partners ever attempts to approach me any more; if I haven't actively ruined their suits with red wine, they've seen me do it to others.

Through it all, I search for Marie.

I see her.

She's standing just off to the left of the cold buffet table. Concentrating. But, of course, not on the table. On her phone.

Fucking hell, the girl is texting. I feel the absence of my own phone suddenly. And I'm furiously glad I don't have it, because I would check it. I would check it, and once again I would read

My time is not my own at the moment

and this thing passing for a moment of equilibrium and peace would pass. But just the thought makes me feel stupidly, bitterly disappointed. And, again I know this stupid, bitter disappointment should be a warning bell to me: a sign that I'm doing something . . . well, stupid. Today, in this moment, if not exactly for the first time, but certainly most clearly, most acutely, I know, I *know*, that I'm doing something that will not end well for me, however it plays out. I should be acting like an intelligent, thinking woman instead of a wanton slut who, a week ago, was planning to spend *tonight* being fucked every which way in a hotel room by a man not her husband. Oh, my fucking God.

I need to get a drink.

'Jane?'

Standing in front of me is . . . Shelley? Susan? One of the associates from Alex's department. We've met. At these parties. At the handful of 'team' dinners. I think she's possibly even been at my house. I think she dropped off Alex's dry cleaning. Possibly an actual client file. But no, I think it was shirts . . .

I can't remember her fucking name at all. I smile. And it probably looks like a snarl.

'How are you?' she says. Beams. Why the fuck is she talking to me?

'Fine,' I say. 'You?'

'Fine,' she beams. 'Merry Christmas.' And she starts to reach for me to embrace and kiss me and I duck away.

'Merry Christmas,' I say. Desperately look over her shoulder for Alex. Spousal SOS. Today is not a good day for me to make nice with your little work helpmeet, be she your office wife or wannabe fuck buddy. Where are you?

'The kids must be really excited for Christmas,' she says.

I nod.

'They're such cute kids,' she says. 'I love seeing their photos all over Alex's office.'

I smile. But I know it's a grimace.

'Are you guys planning to go away over the holidays?' she asks.

I shake my head.

Oh, my God.

I am a rude fucking bitch. I am 'one of the wives', putting a little newbie in her place.

Except, of course, she's not a new wife. She's a lawyer. Which makes her . . . well, Alex's office wife. Or one of. Or aspiring to be. Fuck. Still. Polite. Be polite, bitch. Game face on.

'And what are your plans?' I finally manage to say. She beams again and explodes into a recitation of all the files she's working on with Alex, and how busy they are trying to wrap this or that up before Christmas, and how she hasn't made any plans because she wants to be available to him *completely* in case things go over . . .

I finally spot Alex and try to catch his eye, except it's unnecessary, because he is looking across the room – at Shelley-Susan – at Shelley-Susan talking to me – and he looks horrified. Not in a 'Poor Jane must be suffering' kind of way, but in a 'What is that slut doing talking to my wife?' kind of way.

If this was a movie, this would be the moment for a montage: clips of Alex fiddling with his phone, 'Hello's' that sound odd, 'I have to work late tonight' messages, and enlightenment flooding the poor deceived wife.

Except it's not a movie, it's my life, and this is Alex. Still. I try to look at Shelley-Susan in a different way.

'Is it Shelley?' I ask. 'Or Susan?'

She flushes.

'Melanie, actually,' she says.

'I'm sorry,' I say. 'I'm terrible with names.' And this time I make the conscious choice to be a bitch and cruel. 'The last one was Susan, I think. So your plans for Christmas, then, are lots of late nights at the office with the father of my four children?'

Melanie-Shelley-Susan's cheeks turn almost the same colour as her lipstick.

I feel my lips starting to curl into a smile. I'm about to start laughing hysterically.

Alex appears at my elbow. Inserts himself into the space between me and Melanie-Susan.

'Are you having a good time, love?' he says, wrapping an arm around me, and kissing my temple. Then my mouth. Well. This is also interesting. But then, this is, perhaps, the father of my four children reminding his office wife of her rightful place.

'I wasn't,' I say. 'But then Susan – I'm sorry, Melanie found me. And the night got better.'

Melanie is on the verge of tears, and I'm suddenly on the verge of feeling embarrassed and ashamed. Alex gives her a look – angry? worried? – and I see him wondering if he should ask what we were talking about, and I see him decide he doesn't want to know, and I see him have no fucking clue what to do next.

I decide to be a helpmeet, for 90 seconds at least.

'Will you two excuse me? I need to catch Marie before she disappears,' I say. I slip out of the arm Alex still has around my waist. Face him and rest both hands on his lapels. Ponder giving him a 'He's mine!' kiss on the lips, but instead, just touch my head to his chest. Loving. A hint of submissive. Then I look up and smile at him, not submissive at all, triumphant, really, and the hysterical laugh rises from my belly to my throat, and I let it escape, just a little, as I slant my eyes at Susan. Melanie.

'Good luck,' I say to her. And I know it's the cruellest thing I could have said. And I'm mildly ashamed. But mostly glad.

Marie's still texting when I reach her. Her eyes mildly glazed, her lips open.

I know my arrival will not be welcome.

And it's not.

'Jane,' she says, barely raising her eyes from the phone. 'Oh, Jane.' She reads, and grins like an idiot, and looks at me. 'Oh, Jane. I'm so happy.'

This is one of those points where a friend either hugs or offers unconditional joy and support – or, if she is made of strict moral fibre, counsels the other to not be a fucking idiot. I do none of those things. 'Wine,' I say. 'I need wine.'

Marie's still fiddling with the phone as we fill up. Glancing at it.

'I think he's gone away,' she whispers. 'I hate when he does that – he just leaves. Doesn't tell me he's going.' I nod. 'But, oh, Jane, when he's on – it's so good. So *fucking* good.'

I try to be self-aware enough to accept that the reason I want to smack Marie upside the head at this moment is because

—It would have been tonight
My time is not my own at the moment

I am a self-involved, morally bankrupt whore and a hypocrite.
I drink.

'And it's all thanks to you,' Marie gushes. 'Ever since you
helped me draft those texts? That's exactly what he likes.
Loves. Oh, Jane.' Glances at the phone. Which is silent.

I drink again.

Shudder. Am I like this? Jonesing for a message from a
phantom, not even a *real* lover? This – I let the word come,
and I embrace it – pathetic?

Self-awareness truly sucks.

Alex appears behind me. Hands around my waist. 'Home?'
he whispers in my ear. 'God, please,' I say back, tone unmod-
ulated. 'Unless we're leaving because you think I've had too
much to drink, in which case, you know, I feel I ought to offer
a token protest,' I add as we navigate the room. 'God, no,'
he says. Looks at me. 'Did you have too much to drink?' I do
a brief mental inventory.

'No,' I decide. 'But I think I was about to start tossing it
back with a little too much abandon.'

'You never really enjoy these,' he says after a pause. 'I do
appreciate . . . I really do appreciate you coming. Always. To
all of them.'

'Of course,' I say, surprised. 'How could I not?'

He says nothing until we're at the car. He opens the passenger
door for me. As I slide into the car, my frustration with Marie
ebbs. I experience a brief but poignant pang of regret at what I
might have been doing tonight. And another, shallower one at
the day's radio silence – and full admission to self that what I
would have really liked to be doing today – tonight – was role-
playing and word-fucking with Matt about what tonight would
have been like in life. I would have really, really liked that.
Perhaps as much as, perhaps more, than I wanted the real thing.

But. Real life. And, truly, how many opportunities for *that* type of encounter did today offer me? The five minutes in the morning that I was awake before Alex came out of the shower? The five minutes he was downstairs making coffee? The fifteen minutes he was in the shower before the party? In the car or swimming-pool changing room with all of my children? Fuck, fuck, get a grip! If we had connected earlier in the day, would I have been doing what Marie was doing during the party? Would I?

I like to think I wouldn't.

But I suspect I'm lying.

And I knew what I was capable of, which was why I left the phone at home.

That's something. Isn't it?

There is a lesson there for me. I'm sure of it. I try to follow it . . . I can't find it yet.

'You're very quiet,' Alex says suddenly. I look at him. Shrug.

'Tired,' I say.

'What did . . . what did you and Melanie talk about?' he asks after another long pause.

And I laugh.

'She asked me if our kids were excited over Christmas, and if I had any plans for going away,' I say. 'And then she said her plans for Christmas involved being available to you at all times.'

The car jerks sideways.

'Jesus!' Alex slams on the breaks.

'I'm paraphrasing,' I say. 'In the perverse state of mind I was in, it sounded like she was feeling me out for permission to have an affair with you.'

'Jesus,' Alex says again. 'Jane. You didn't think . . . You don't think . . .'

'My beloved husband,' I say. 'Any woman who thinks she has to ask my permission to go after you – I am so not worried about that. It was . . . amusing.' I pause. 'I am sorry – if it

178

ever arises – I was harsh. To her. She did not deserve . . . I was cruel, on purpose, and I'm sorry.'

He says nothing, until we pull into our garage. And then, as he gets out of the car, he gives me a lingering look.

'You're sorry you were harsh to a woman you thought I might be having an affair with?' he asks.

'No!' We don't seem to hear each other. 'No. I'm sorry I was harsh to a young, insecure woman who was . . . just trying. It wasn't necessary.'

We stare at each other across the car. Then enter the dark house in silence.

The children are asleep, and so is Alex's mother. We briefly debate whether he should wake her up and drive her home now, or let her sleep. Decide to let her sleep. He disappears into the bathroom. I find my phone. Plug it in to charge it.

And, automatically, click it on. And as I do, it buzzes.

Apologies for the radio silence
Today has not been a good day. For so many reasons.
Real life stress and woe. Not very conducive.

There are a lot of things I want to say. My head whirls—the look in Alex's eyes when he sees me talking with Melanie, Marie texting at the bar, her angst over being left hanging, the storm inside me, what I regret, what I want, what I don't want. And what I want is at times clear and at times fuzzy, but suddenly, and very clearly, I know exactly what I don't want. And so, I type:

—Real life first. Always. And, Matt – do not think of me as an obligation, OK? Ever.
Never. That is a promise.
You are a gift.
—Yours. Good night, my lover. xx
Good night. xo

Day 14 – Do *what you're told*

Sunday, December 16

I wake up . . . content. Mildly irritated at my husband. Physically exhausted and just slightly hungover. Sufficiently morally ambivalent that I make pancakes for everyone, my mother-in-law included, instead of checking email or Facebook. It is Sunday, after all.

Alex, Cassandra and Annie all leave to take Alex's mother home. The boys run over to Lacey's to play with Clayton.

I caress the keys.

Good morning.
—Good morning. I'm alone.
Mmmm. Delicious surprise.
—Are you alone?
No.
Beside me in bed. Awake. Lazy Sunday. We just fucked.
—Jesus, Matt, what the fuck is wrong with you?
I want you servicing me. In plain view.
—Tell me. Does she know what you are?
A sense.
—(What do you want?)
Perhaps she does.
—Alex knew what I was.
Gagging on my cock as she watches . . .
—But I think he may have forgotten.
What were you?

—Morally fuzzy, unpredictable.
—Lacking too many of the normal inhibitions.
I think you've reminded him lately.
—Yes
—I blame you
—and your cock
—Just the memories, re-imaginings of it
—You are a dangerous man
I am.
Tell me your most vivid memory of my cock.
—Memory?
—I think . . .
—the first time I put my lips on it
—I don't remember where. I think there was a party.
Lots of people. You pulled me into your bedroom. Or *a*
bedroom.
—I remember how scared I was.
Scared?
—Scared. I was 18.
I must have always been a bit scary.
—The effect you had on me always shook me profoundly.
—And see, I always knew exactly what you were
—and what you could do to me
—So: my lips on your cock. You hard instantly. Drops of
precum there, as if they were there always
—Its curve
—It shocks me how vividly I remember that curve
What am I?
—You? Ruled by your cock and desire
—Completely amoral when it comes to sex
—Fucking promiscuous, mildly sociopathic
—And capable of controlling me too completely
—So.
Check your email.
Taken just now.

181

—and such a head
Worship it
—I'm nuzzled against it.
—Tracing the veins and ridges with my finger, my tongue
Have to run to reality now, sadly. She is getting up.
And I must do the same.
Get up. Do life. With a hard cock.
—Enjoy. The discomfort.
I'm trying. Failing.
xo
—xx

And. My email pings. Panic. New numbers, new arguments. Can I do a quick read, shoot it back in 30 minutes? Of course. Why not? It's a Sunday in December, Christmas countdown, what else would I be doing today? Do these people never take any days off? The house is empty, my lover is taking his hard cock elsewhere, what the fuck is wrong with me?

Work. Read. Think. And settle. A little bit, anyway. Reality is. Reality anchors. Numbers are predictable, decipherable, reassuring.

Time passes.

Ping.

Becalmed?

I was. The selfish bastard. Anger rises in me in overwhelming waves. At myself. At my immense stupidity. At keeping Facebook open while I worked. At the rising heat in my belly and groin. Such desire. Oh, fuck. My fingers touch the keyboard. Angry. Compelled.

—I was. Until now.
Good. I feel like I'm walking around with a loaded pistol.
—Fire.

*Earlier, it was a ridiculous risk. I admit it. Questioning
my own grip on sanity a little.*
—It will burn out.
—It has to.
are you dressed
—No. Still in nightgown.
Report.
—Black. Cotton. Really not uber-sexy.
Short?
—Yes.
Accessible?
—Yes.
Enough.
I want you out in public today, dressed like a slut.
—Feeding your jealously?
Yes. Stoking the furnace.
*While at the same time reminding yourself of your
subservience.*
*You will flaunt yourself at other men. They will look at
you. Desire you. And you and I will both know you are
only mine.*
And then, when you come home: you will tell me.
—I hate you.
Tell me.
—Two words.
—Buckling knees.
—Hate and love commingled.
how exposed
—I really hate you
Hard. Tell me why.
—Because
—two words
—and a fire in my belly
powerless
—angry

183

Ping. What the fuck? Oh, Jeezus. Nicola. Why is she messaging me? Fucking hell.

- Guess what the rat-fuck bastard did this time?
—What?

I skim over the words. The gist: frozen bank accounts. Swollen line of credit. Missed credit-card payments. Inaccurate – and this seems to be what angers her the most – portrayal of the divorce on his match.com page. ('He's on match.com? What happened to the skank?' I type, while I think, 'What is he doing with Marie?' 'Oh, they're still together. I think he's just covering his bases.') Finally, I do read this:

- One day, months from now, I will ask you why I didn't
kick him out years ago
—Because you're freakin' awesome. And you try to
make things work. And because you're a good mom.
- Thank you. I needed to hear that.
—I need to go.

I need to go because I'm cyberfucking my lover in the other window. What would you say if I said that to you, Nicola? In-fucking-sane. And a hypocrite.

And I'm back with him. Inside the madness. And my bliss.

Who are you angry at? At yourself, or me, or equally?
—me, you
—mostly me
let me shoulder the blame
you are powerless before me
and I am taking advantage
—Arrogant.
very
I know how to work you

and I know you want to be worked.
I should be easier on you.
—will you be
—or is it too much of a power trip still
of course I enjoy it
but I don't wish to burn you out. Or cause harm.
I am demanding. But not cruel.
—I am hating you a little less
—except that makes me want you more
—so really, I can't win
then get on your knees
—fuck
—and?
Grab your wrists behind your back.
Open your mouth and stick out your tongue.
Invite me – beg me – to fuck your throat.
I'll allow a pillow under your knees . . .
. . . but only because I want to fuck your face for a
long time and don't want any complaints.
—oh my fucking god
—fuck my throat
—please . . .
Take my fucking cock.
pulling your hair, up and down, jerking myself off with
your throat
—dear god
—gagging
—tears in my eyes
good. make you slippery, sloppy. wet everywhere.
humiliated
fucked
—used
—hungry
Mine.
—yours

Still angry?
— . . .
I hope so
my unwilling fuckslave
—too weak to describe what i feel
—I lay my head on your thighs
No rest for you.
I put you right back to work.
Allowing a breath every . . . once in a while . . .
—Your definition of not wanting to cause me harm or
burn me out is . . . interesting.
—it's harder to balance now – I ask to use my hands
Are you outside right now, exposing your too short
skirt? Are you stroking the cock of some stranger on
the street because I told you to? That would be
burning you out.
You are getting off easy. And getting off.
Call me and cum for me.
514-978-5679.
—Seriously?
—Now?
I am always serious with you.

I stare at the screen. At the keyboard. Minutes pass.

Do what you're fucking told.

The doorbell rings. I slam the computer lid down. Alex back?
The boys back? No. Fucking neighbourhood carollers.

I'm inexcusably rude.

I slowly go into the basement with the laptop and the phone.
I don't know why.

I think I want to hide.

The basement is full of Alex's workout equipment. I go to
my pretty 26-year-old boy toy; Alex, usually alone, sometimes

186

with his buddies, sweats in the basement. Jesse comes by every once in a while to give them technique tune-ups.

I suppose it could be worse. I could be doing this from one of the kids' bedrooms.

I'm not going to call.

Fuck.

Of course I will.

Dial.

'You kept me waiting.'

'I didn't think I'd call.'

'I knew you would. You always do what you're told. Don't you?'

I disassociate from myself – or connect with myself – or lose myself. I don't know what the fuck I do. I do what I'm told. And there, in my basement, on Alex's workout bench, I come – repeatedly – as I have never come before.

And I'm the fucking O-queen. It's not a struggle to satisfy me, really.

Jeezus.

Whore. Shameless. Slut. Fuckslave. You come when I tell you to.

All the words I've read, in my ear. In his voice.

Jesus-fucking-Christ.

If I believed in God, I am going to hell.

Thank God I'm an atheist.

What is happening to me?

I'm flying. I'm coming so hard, I feel liquid pouring down my leggings past my knees.

The call waiting cuts in. Beep beep beep beep.

I keep on coming. I drop the phone. Shake, shake, shake. Scramble to find it.

I think I might say . . . 'I have to go now.'

Or maybe just 'Oh, my fucking God.'

And he says, 'Now say thank you.'

I say it. My throat constricts.

'You can go now.'

I drop the phone. Hang up.

The single most erotic, most intense experience of my life.
I am clearly so fucked.

The phone rings.

And I stare at it as if it's a venomous snake or a cobra for
such a long time – surely he's not calling me back? No, he
can't be.

It's my mother.

I don't really like to talk to my mother on the telephone at
the best of times. I love her, God knows I love her, but she gives
awful phone. She sighs and insinuates and leaves things hanging
. . . and gets huffy and hangs up. This is not the best of times.

I don't pick up.

The phone goes to voicemail . . . and then rings again. And
again.

Fuck. She does this sometimes.

'Hello?'

'Jane? It's Mom.' Well, duh. There is insufficient blood flow
to my head, I decide. I lie down on the workout bench, telephone in hand.

Well. That didn't help.

'Are you there, Jane?'

'Yes, Mom. Um . . . now is really not the best time. I've . . .'
Well, I definitely can't tell her what I've just done. But it doesn't
matter. She does not want to listen to me.

'Of course it's not the best time. It's the worst time. But I
need to talk to you now, before you and Alex bring the kids
over tomorrow.'

Tomorrow? Right. Tomorrow, on a Monday, the kids have
planned a sleepover with Gran and Gramps. I don't remember,
I can't remember why on a Monday. There's a reason. A cogent
one. Something to do with my dad's work, Alex's schedule,

and my mother's whims. And because the kids are out of the house, Alex and I are planning to play. Go out for dinner. 'Date night.' Right. Date night. With Alex. My husband. Father of my children. On whose workout bench I just came like a shameless whore for . . . Stop.

My mother is talking.

'. . . and so that's it, we've decided it's the best thing to do,' she says.

I clearly missed something important.

'You did?' I say. My voice reverberates in my ears.

'Oh, honey.' My mother's voice goes all soft and gushy. 'Don't be angry. You know this isn't about you. This is between your dad and me. And it really is the best thing.'

What the fuck?

'Mom? What are you talking about?'

'Our separation,' she says. 'Well, divorce, really. We're calling it a separation, but I need to be frank with you, honey, there is no plan to reconcile, reconnect. It's been forty-three years, mostly wonderful years, and we've raised just the most wonderful daughter and gotten the most terrific grandchildren out of it, but life goes on and . . .'

She's talking in clichés and circles, which is what she does when she is emotionally overwrought.

'You're getting divorced?' I say. 'You and Dad, you're getting divorced?'

'Don't tell the children just yet – Dad's still living in the house, he'll be there tomorrow,' she says. 'He's going to start looking for a new place this week. I'm going to stay in the house. We decided we need to keep the house, for the grand-children, you know. Because of the treehouse and the . . .'

'You. Are. Getting. Divorced?' I repeat.

And then I hang up the telephone.

As it starts to ring a few seconds later, I hang it up again. Then race up the stairs and unplug all the instruments in the house.

I'm standing in the middle of the living room, wild-eyed, when the doors creak and Alex and Cassandra come up the stairs.

'Everything cool, Mom?' Cassandra asks.

'Jesus, Jane, what happened?' Alex asks. And then, 'Annie's asleep in the car. Should I bring her in?'

'I'll tell you later,' I say. 'I'm OK. But I'm just going to go lie down for a few minutes. I'm dizzy. Give me ten minutes, OK? And then get me if you need me.'

'What should I do with Annie?' Alex asks.

'Bring her up to her bed,' I say. 'Or my bed. I don't care. Look. I need to lie down. Now.'

I stagger up the stairs to the bedroom. Bed. Blanket.

I wonder if the universe is trying to deliver some big moral to me here.

If so, I don't hear it.

Do as you're fucking told.

'He's going to start looking for a new place this week.'

What's just happened?

What am I?

Day 15 – Spent

I am the product of a broken home.

I repeat the sentence to myself in my head a few times as I stir my coffee. I'm not sure if it hasn't fully sunk in, or if I'm just so totally, completely fucked up here that I can't appreciate the enormity of what has just happened. My parents will be celebrating their 43rd anniversary – the next one would have been forty-fucking-three – in some . . . courtroom? arbitrator's chambers? I guess probably just a lawyer's office . . . unhitching their union. Split asunder for evermore.

I indulge myself with one of my favourite images of my parents – one I drew on and talked about on *my* wedding day. I had gotten some lame-ass award, and there was a banquet and a dinner, and they were there of course – and I was there chiefly for them, because while I thought it was a lame-ass award, it was their daughter's lame-ass award, and so of course the greatest, most important thing ever to them. They arrived dressed to the nines. Holding hands. When was this? Pre-wedding, so eleven, twelve years ago. Exuding happiness.

One of my colleagues pulled me aside to whisper, 'Your parents are so cute! I keep on expecting them to sneak off into some corner or another for a quickie!'

Not precisely the sort of thing you want to hear about your parents – and not precisely how I described the event when I eulogised it at my wedding – but the sort of thing that makes you think their relationship is, you know, made of stern stuff.

Has a – what are people always talking about? A *foundation*. A solid foundation.

Even if lately they do nothing but snipe and poke at each other.

I managed to tell Alex when I crawled out of bed yesterday. We sat on the workbench – the one I sat on when Matt . . . I let that thought come to me briefly, don't run from it – and I told him, and he hugged me, and said all the right things.

As well as 'They've been so beastly to each other lately, it's frankly a relief.'

Which didn't sound like the right thing, exactly. But it was true.

We agreed to respect their decision not to tell the kids just yet. And I had a cover if I needed one for any emotional distress stemming from my phone-fucking earlier in the afternoon.

I needed one.

Do as you're fucking told.

I am the product of a broken home.

I check work email quickly before the kids wake up. Stare at the fucking Facebook *F*. To check or not to check.

I don't want to.

I'm . . . spent. From the intensity of the phone encounter or from news of the divorce? I don't know. It doesn't matter.

I piddle around with email and Twitter, get cereal for this kid, clean up the spilled milk of this kid, tell the video-game addict to eat breakfast between rounds, shower, defrost meat, disappear into the home office to make a few work phone calls to follow up on yesterday's emergency.

And I don't jump when the phone rings. It's not equilibrium, exactly, it's just – whatever. Trust. I'm in the middle of the biggest mindfuck of my life, but I trust the mindfucker.

The thought is so shocking to me that I say nothing into the receiver when I pick up the phone.

'Hello? Jane? Jane, are you there? Where the hell were you this morning?'

Marie. On the *landline*. To me.

This is a little bit weird.

We may be closer to 40 than 30, but we are fully the Facebook and texting generation. Plus, we're mothers of multiple children. The little buggers never let us talk on the telephone. Why the fuck is Marie calling me? On my *landline*?

'You weren't on Facebook this morning! Or answering texts! I even called your cell!'

Ah, yes. I wasn't.

'What's wrong?' I ask. Marie. My friend. I love her. Support her. Must be there for her, instead of wallowing in my own insanity.

It's chaotic, because she whispers – the kids must be in the background, perhaps JP also, but surely she wouldn't call me in a panic with JP in the house? Still, I get the gist. Which is: she emailed her new would-be lover some skanky naked photos of herself.

'And it's been twelve hours, and I know he isn't always online, and has a life, but it's been twelve hours, I need an acknowledgement! Did he see them and hate them? Did he . . .'

I am about to become an affair counsellor to a fellow cyber-adulteress.

Surreal.

'Babe,' I say. 'Twelve hours. Do nothing.'

How do I feel when I don't hear from Matt for twelve hours?

Besides the point.

It's been more than twelve hours since yesterday's encounter actually. And I'm fine. Well, not fine, exactly, but . . .

'Do not ask, do not nag. He'll get them. He'll react. Eventually.'

'What if he doesn't like them? What if he thinks I have

old-people boobs? I'm almost forty. I've breastfed two children. I've . . .'

This is the point at which my natural inclination is to tell her that these are all things she should have agonised over *before* she took and emailed the stupid pictures.

But I love Marie.

'You're hot and you have great boobs,' I say, which is true. I've breastfed four children to her two, and my boobs are hot. Well, in the right bra, and at the right angle. In the right dim light. 'Just stay offline. Don't write anything. Don't chase. It's undignified.' I think I'm quoting Matt. Lovely. 'And not sexy.'

'It's really hard,' Marie says after a pause. 'I want to talk to him.'

'Don't fucking chase,' I chastise her. And then listen to her say that maybe he likes that, maybe he wants to be chased? Suppose that's his turn-on? And what if . . .

'Look, you'll do what you want, of course,' I say. 'But . . . if you're not sure – if it's just a case of wanting to get it out of you – just text me with what you want to tell him. Or better yet, just write yourself a note. You know? The diary solution.'

Why am I telling her this? Because she's terrifying me with her need and her vulnerability. Because I want to give her armour.

'That's brilliant,' Marie says. 'OK, I'll write it down, and then I'll have said it, but not sent it. That's brilliant. Jane? Do you do that?'

No. But I was once a very, very exposed and vulnerable teenager.

And now I kind of think I'm a hard-ass.

Do as you're fucking told.
—Shut up.
This is amusing. Again, I ask, is this how you're playing me?

194

—Fuck off. Get out of my head.

I like the idea of you attempting to strategise.

—Oh, my fucking God, stop talking inside my head now!

'Jane? You OK?' Marie's voice comes from far away.

'Yes, yes. Kids, you know. I've got to go. Stay offline. Do stuff. Wait for him. This is not the recipe for true love, this is how you play a player. OK?'

'OK. Thank you.'

'Anytime.'

I drop the kids off at school and ignore my mom's texts inviting me over for lunch or coffee or just a 'chat'. I don't want to deal with the whispering and 'secret' confidences I know my mother will inflict on me, while repeating that she wants to keep things 'normal' for the grandchildren. Not yet. To the gym – today's lifeline. Nicola's finishing her session as I walk through the door, hair plastered with sweat to her forehead, face contorted in agony.

She grunts in my direction, and I run to the change room to effect my switch as quickly as possible so I'm out of there before she comes in so we don't need to talk about the rat-fuck bastard. And so I don't have to see how angry she still is from our last encounter.

Foiled.

'Hey.'

'Hey. Good workout? You look good. You've lost weight.' Life is turning me into a liar.

'From stress,' Nicola sighs. Then looks at me sideways. 'Are you getting tired of my whining and bitching?'

There are times when friends tell friends the truth. And there are times when friends lie.

'You are entitled to whine and bitch as much as you like,' I say. Nicola sighs. I don't think she believes me. I'm right.

'You're a terrible liar,' she says.

'You are entitled to whine and bitch as much as you like about the rat-fuck bastard,' I repeat. 'And yes, the people around you might get tired of it, and wish that you'd get over it. You know what? Who gives a fuck what they think? This is about you. You can be as self-centred and self-indulgent here as you like. Fuck us and our desire for you to move on because your unhappiness inconveniences us.'

'I don't just whinge,' Nicola says. 'I've – I've totally taken control of finances. I'm not sitting around destitute while he tries to be a deadbeat dad. I'm pulling in income however I can. I'm economising.' She leans over and whispers, 'But Jesse's too sweet to economise on. I'm not ready to give that up yet.'

'Sweet,' I agree. 'Speaking of Jesse, I've got to go. Be you. Be awesome. And all that.'

'I love you, Jane!' Nicola calls to my back.

She doesn't really. She doesn't even like me. It's one of those obnoxious things people say. For the record, I do not love Nicola. At all.

But I do love Marie.

And Lacey. And her earlobes.

But I digress.

Jesse.

'Abs, arms or legs today?' he asks. 'We did full body last time, so take your pick.'

'Abs,' I say promptly. Abs are easy. For abs, I get to lie on my back most of the time. It's relaxing, almost.

I like you on your back.
—I know.
Although I like you on your knees better.
—I know that too. Are you always going to be here now?
Maybe.

196

I start crunching. And then planking. And then obliques. And side planks. And . . .

'You look different,' Jesse offers suddenly.

'What?' I've got one hand in the air, one on the ground and my legs contorted all around me. 'Crooked?'

'No, I mean – you look more in your skin,' he says. 'You know. More yourself.'

I stare at him. Really? Today you notice I'm more in my skin? Today? The day after I phone-fuck my 'the more wrong it is the hotter it is' mindfucker of a cyberlover and find out my parents are splitting up? Today I look more in my skin?

'I didn't like to say anything,' Jesse says, 'because I know how private you like to be.'

Thank you. I think.

'But you've seemed quite unsettled the last couple of weeks or so,' Jesse continues.

Well, that he got right.

'But today – you seem more relaxed, more yourself than for a long time,' he says. 'Know what? We should stretch. I've been dying to stretch you for at least ten days, but you kept asking for hard work-outs. One more set of abs, and we'll stretch.'

Awesome.

I melt into the floor as we stretch and I realise I am indeed, for the first time in days and days and days, totally physically relaxed.

I guess the phone-sex orgasms did achieve something.

I really hope it wasn't news of my parents' divorce.

It had to be the phone-fucking.

Which is probably not the moral the universe meant for me to get from the experience.

But I don't care.

Six hours later, I'm at my parents' house. 'Is it going to be weird, like last time?' Cassandra asks. 'Gran kept on hugging us and telling us how much loved us.' 'Constantly,' her brother echoes. 'And she does,' I say. OK. First encounter with divorcing parents. And go.

My mom is fluttering around the kitchen, as always a bundle of nervous energy. 'I am so lucky to have my grandchildren with me, all my grandchildren!' she trills. 'I am simply the luckiest grandmother in the world!' My dad sits at the kitchen table, head bent over a bottle of beer. I kiss the top of his head. Rub his shoulder. 'You know I know, right?' I whisper. He nods. He looks at me, and the sadness and . . . guilt? Jesus, the guilt in his eyes pierces me. Oh, Daddy.

For a brief moment, I'm eight.

Will I get out of there without a heart-to-heart with him? I must.

My mother pulls me away. 'I bought the children's Christmas presents today,' she whispers. 'I can't wait to tell you what. Can I tell you? Can I show you?' She drags me into the den. I look at the stack of Apple boxes.

'Oh, my fucking God, you bought each of them an iPad.'

'Don't swear, Jane, it's not ladylike.'

Neither is getting fucked in the ass on a workout bench.
—Maybe now is not a good time for this.
Of course not. That's why I'm here. It reminds you I own you.

'Did you buy me an iPad?'

'You always resent it and complain when I buy you expensive Christmas presents,' my mother says defensively. 'You can use one of the children's if you really want.'

'Would you have bought me an iPad if you had divorced before I had children?' I ask, which is stupid, because there were no iPads before I had children. Still. I'm starting to feel a little annoyed with my mother.

'Jane, you have every right to be angry and disappointed, but there is no call to be rude,' my mother pronounces and huffs out of the room. I stick my tongue out at her back.

No manners. Product of a broken home.

At dinner, Alex asks if I want to talk about the divorce. 'No,' I say. 'No,' I repeat. 'Anything but. Do you think Lacey and Clint will actually marry?' 'No,' he says with a laugh. 'Not if Clint plays things the way he's been playing them. Why do you ask?' 'I'd like Lacey to be happy,' I say. 'Lacey's always happy,' Alex says. 'As I'm happy – right now – to be here with you. Without four additional sets of ears. So I can tell you how adorable you look. Without a child making grossed-out puking noises in the background.'

I smile at him.

I love him.

I do not look adorable and I do not want to look adorable.

I want to be told I look hot and fuckable. And I want to be told that he will not leave me after 43 years of marriage, no matter what.

But.

I kiss the knuckles of his hand. And we have a lovely romantic dinner.

And a night without needing to do bedtime for four children. Alex draws me to him and kisses me, gently but thoroughly, as soon as we walk through the front door. 'I am thrilled to have you all to myself for the entire night,' he whispers as he kisses my neck and my earlobes. Pulls my breasts out of my dress, my bra.

I wonder if he'll take me on the workout bench.

He leads me upstairs. Undresses me. Kisses and caresses me. I relax against him, into his curves and angles. I kiss all my favourite spots, and his favourite spots. Nip playfully every once in a while.

'You're not as voracious as you were last week,' he whispers into my ear. 'I'm glad.'

'Why? Was I scary?'

'I was a little scared I would not be able to keep up,' he says between ear nibbles. 'Excuse me.' He kisses his way down my torso to my belly and my pussy.

Matt's pussy. Christ. Where did that thought come from?

Me. Naturally.

He licks me to a languorous orgasm. I slide down his body to reciprocate.

Now, this is what I like.
—Are you watching?
Always. Put your hands on his balls. Just use your mouth on his shaft.
—Like this?
Yes. Take him deeper.

'Oh, Jesus, Jane, oh, Jane, oh, Jane, oh, Jane!'

And swallow it all.
—I don't want to.
Do what you're fucking told.

Day 16 – Perfect Trust

I missed you yesterday.
—I was . . . spent.
And today?
—Strangely calm.
I'm glad.
—How are you this morning?
Lazy, lusty.
Wish I could stay abed, being served.
I was made for Roman times, I think.
—Yes
—Question
Please
—the effect of the cataclysmic telephone call, in retrospect
A bit of quiet after the earthquake, I must admit.
I think I may have shocked even myself.
And, while I checked in to see if you were trying to reach me – I did not reach out for you either.
—yes
—But now? What?
Pleased. Released.
Still stoked on your spontaneous servitude.
—You are very fond of that word.
—but yes

—I think I'm almost at peace here, for the first time since the beginning
—languid, relaxed
I am glad to hear that, truly.
I do care about your happiness, most evidence to the contrary.
—I know
—Likewise
—I hope you know that one of the things all this shows is that I clearly deposit perfect trust in you.
I know and I'm honoured.
Reality intervenes now, sadly. Wife. Work. Stay warm, forever lover. xo
—Be safe. xx

Alex races down the stairs as I log off – 'Fuck, fuck, my eight a.m., why didn't you wake me up, Jane?' I pour coffee into a travel mug for him and press it into his hand on his second pass through the kitchen. And he's gone. My mom texts to let me know she's *en route* with the kids to the school, and will drop Annie off afterwards. I realise I need to have something to do – out of the house – as soon as she arrives, so that I don't have to endure a talk. I can't do a talk. Not yet. I want my peace, my calm, my 'equilibrium' to last for at least a full day.

I invite myself over to Marie's house, and, when my mother arrives, report my plans to her casually as I transfer Annie from car seat to car seat.

'Thank you.' I peck my mother on the cheek. And know I'm a bad daughter. Know that she wants to talk. Explain. Maybe cry, because crying always makes her feel better. And I . . . I refuse to be there for her.

Annie nods off in the car. I drive through a Starbucks, grab two mochas for Marie and me, and a steamed milk and bear claw for Annie. Go back and get two more bear claws.

'Are you trying to get me fat?' Marie demands as I hand over the loot. Bites into her pastry immediately. 'Oh, God, heaven. Thank you. How did you know?'

'Lacey told me,' I joke. Then I notice her eyes are red. Fuck.

'What's up?' I ask. She shakes her hand, her fingers. Bits of pastry go flying everywhere.

'You asked to come over,' she chokes out. 'What's up with you?'

A tear trickles down her cheek.

Fuck, fuck, fuck.

We're stretched out on her $8,000 designer couch. She's cradling her phone in her hand, but she's focused on me. Annie's in my lap.

'Do you want to watch a movie?' I ask her. She nods sleepily. Marie turns on Nickelodeon. We take our coffees and pastries into the kitchen.

'I always talk,' Marie says. Another tear. 'It's always about me. Tell me. Anything. Something.'

Another tear comes. And another.

So I talk. Awkwardly, unemotionally. Badly. About the phone call from my mom. The 'let's pretend nothing's happening yet, not until after Christmas' strategy they want to employ with the grandkids. My reluctance to talk to her, to hear more.

Marie hugs me and lets the waterworks loose – for me, for whatever is eating her. It doesn't matter. It makes me realise I haven't cried about it. Should I? Do I want to?

I really, really don't even want to think about it.

'How do you feel?' Marie asks, wiping her eyes. And looking earnestly into mine.

'I don't know,' I say. 'Mostly . . . angry, I think. Angry. At my mom.'

'She's the one who left?' Marie asks.

'Of course,' I say. Then frown. It wasn't said. But, of course, in my mother's story, it wouldn't be. It wouldn't be said, or even implied. But. Of course. She is the instigator. Always. She is the one who threatened it, every five to seven years. The last time . . . five or seven years ago, on the clock, her exact quote to me was, 'Everyone's entitled to a little bit of happiness in her life!' And my response, I remember, which made her cry, 'So your life to date has been a vale of bitterness and tears? Thanks, Mom. Makes me feel awesome.'

I'm a terrible, terrible daughter.

Fuck.

I am incredibly angry at her.

I take a long, long gulp of my coffee.

And look up to see Marie weeping, weeping.

And that is not for me, none of it.

'Tell me,' I say.

'I'm so stupid!' she says. 'So fucking fucking stupid! Stupid!'

Eyes red, tears pouring, nose running, she starts to talk. Then stops. Then grabs the phone and scrolls through her messages. Then throws it, angrily, across the room. And looks at me. Devastated.

For this, I need no intuition.

'It's over with Paul,' I say. State, don't ask.

'The rat-fuck bastard dumped me,' she says. 'Dumped. Me! Via text! Without ever meeting! He – that cheating rat-fuck dickless bastard had the nerve – the, the . . . effrontery! – to dump! Me! Me!'

'Marie,' I say. Plead. 'You know he's not worth a single tear . . .'

But she doesn't hear me.

'Do you know why he left? Do you want to know why he left – me? Oh, fine, I know it's stupid to say he left me – we weren't even together. Whatever. Why he won't pursue anything with me, any more? Do you want to know why?'

Honestly – no. Not a little bit. I think my life would be complete, and certainly more tranquil, if I had never known that Marie was sexting with Paul. And finding out how the affair – would-be-affair? That's too strong a word, even fling

204

seems too strong a word – how their *thing* ends . . . no. I don't need to know. I don't want to know.

Words on a phone screen: she is crying over words on a phone screen.

Are you dissing the power of words on a screen, my whore?
—Fuck off.
I'm just amused.
—We're different.
Of course we are.

I don't want to know.

But of course I will learn.

'He said he could not continue to do this until I told JP what I was doing,' she said. 'He said he wanted everything to be, and I quote, "open and above board". He said that his biggest mistake – what wrecked his relationship with Nicola – was not talking to her about Deirdre before. Not explaining. Not asking. He said . . .'

Here it comes.

'He said true polyamory has to be all about honesty and openness and communication,' Marie continues. She's calming down a little. 'He said he's been where I am, and struggled with the desire, and that he chose to act on his desire before communicating with his partner, and that was wrong. He said . . .'

I remember talking about polyamory – not with Alex, never with Alex – with Matt. 'Hypocritical fuckers,' he said. 'I bet they still all fuck around. Illicit fruit and all that.'

'What are you and I then?' I asked. We were talking, as always, in bed. When was this? Post-Joy. Pre-Alex. Post-coital, exhausted.

'We are lovers,' he said. 'Exhibitionist, anxious children come up with rules and primary and secondary relationships and vetoes. We – you and I – take lovers. Are lovers.'

205

Paul, if I understand the saga correctly, had never even thought or heard of polyamory until Deirdre explained it to him. As the reason why he shouldn't leave his wife for her – because he could have it all. Because she didn't want to be his *only*. Or even his 'primary'.

Paul is now a born-again polyamorist. Perhaps that's inaccurate. But an evangelical polyamorist, anyway. An apostle. And as is the case with all new converts, insanely dogmatic.

'He said . . .' Marie says, 'he said, he had the fucking nerve to say, Jane, that he wouldn't "help" – help! – me cheat on my husband! That I owed my husband . . . oh, fuck, what did he say? Truth. Truth! And that I had to have . . . oh, such fine words: clarity. Self-knowledge. Blah, blah, blah. And JP and I had to have trust. Perfect trust! What the fuck is perfect trust, Jane? What is that? I sure as hell don't know.'

And she's calm no more, weeping again.

I know exactly what perfect trust is. Exactly.

But how can I tell her?

Well. I can tell her this.

'I think perfect trust is when . . .' I pause. This is harder to put into words than I thought. What is it? 'It's when you accept everything about the other. All the dark and scary and the . . . the wrong. You don't think about it much, you just . . . I don't know, you just have it. It's being able to expose yourself to a person so completely, you might still burn with shame and embarrassment as you reveal, but never worry about . . . rejection. Hurt. Because he accepts you, unconditionally. All of you. And you never doubt . . . you don't doubt. You just . . . have trust.'

And Marie cries. And cries. And then stops.

'Do you and Alex have perfect trust?' she asks.

'No,' I tell her.

And she looks at me for a long, long time.

She doesn't have to tell me she and JP don't have it either. I leave her unsettled, but caffeinated and supported in her opinion that polyamorists – especially newly made poly-amorists – are self-righteous hypocrites. And that Paul would probably be terrible in bed. Short, balding, pudgy – really. What was she thinking? 'What was I thinking, Jane?' she asks. 'Well – it's because he was so articulate. Such beautiful texts . . .' But she seems to be calmer. For now.

We don't talk about her and JP at all, and that's a relief.

Annie and I do a grocery run on the way to picking up the rest of the kids from school. They're all irritated and exhausted, snappy and fighting – even Cassandra. 'We didn't sleep much last night,' she explains, but I know. Sleepovers at the grand-parents always have that price. As soon as we get home, I turn on Netflix. *The Princess Bride*. Make dinner. Let everyone eat on the couch, and collapse on it beside them. They smear spaghetti sauce on their clothes and the cushions. I use my skirt to wipe off the bigger spots. Classy.

I push Marie and Paul – and my parents – out of my head. I search for my mood of this morning. What was I? Relaxed. Happy. Not thinking. Languid.

'Death can't stop true love. It can only delay it for a while,' Wesley tells Buttercup on the screen.

'Are you and Daddy true love?' Annie asks me.

'Something very like it,' I say. Close my eyes. Still not thinking.

And I'm not thinking when I reach for the laptop.

and now
tell me.
—hungry
—but still, at peace
—is that possible?
It is. And perhaps ideal.
We were . . . unsustainable.
—Indeed
—We still are.

Are we?

The image of you curled up on that bench is forever burned in my mind.

—I am smiling at the memory, warm feeling inside

has your nipple recovered

—mostly

—But right after, I was a little traumatised.

Tell me how you felt.

—Right after?

yes

—utterly owned

—self-less

—and completely questioning my sanity

—(and yours)

what frightened you the most

—that I did what you told me to

—against all reason, discretion and judgement

—that my want and desire were so . . . intense . . .

—there was no room in me to even consider 'No'

Everything?

—I don't understand.

You did everything I told you?

—yes

It was sometimes hard to hear. I'm pleased you were so thorough.

—It was hard to hold the phone

—and talk

—and do

Do what?

I like to see you type it all.

—you want me to type it out

of course

—I'm a little worried that may damage the sense of peace I had achieved this morning

—do you wish to be unsustainable again

of course
but I am rarely wise with you
Still. I do want you at peace.
—hungry
Ask me to release you. Or start typing.
—you told me to rub my clit
—to put my fingers in my pussy
—deeper
—to work it harder
—you told me to put my fingers in my mouth
and you obeyed
—everything
—it didn't occur to me not to
—it was . . .
—so intensely, overwhelmingly erotic
—. . .
—and stupid
—dangerous
compulsive
and meant to be
we are a matched set

Are we? I wonder if he's right. We always fitted. We always gravitated to one another. But we've always been . . . well. Dangerous, I suppose. And I've known it, always. I remember . . .

—I want to tell you something
—from 20 years ago
please
—When I was with John—and after the first time you and I came together . . . and pretty much every time after that, with John, with the others. Even with Alex
. . .
Tell me

209

—that was my MO: be restrained, be in check, be
faithful . . . get increasingly restless . . . increasingly
edgy . . . and then do something incredibly risky
—and then, I would be OK for a while, be able to keep
everything reined in
—be a 'good' girlfriend
*And did it keep things hot at home for you while you
were being good?*
For a while anyway?
—yes
—that was part of the . . . deal with the devil?
Usually always with me?
—arrogant
I did say usually
—often
—always my first choice
—except when you were busy seducing someone else
we and our moral compasses
Did John know? I always thought he did.
—some of it
—he knew about some of you
—it was a turn on: that you wanted me
—it made me more desirable to him, because you
desired me
I totally understand.
I have a raging slutwife fetish.
Sadly, only fantasy
(skewed, I know)
—I loved hearing your voice
and I yours
your sounds when you came . . .
exquisite
—perhaps the thing that affected me the most
—was the contrast between your voice and what it said
—your voice has always been a caress to me

—so sexy, so soft
but this time?
—it was a whip
—with the promise of a caress
—same pitch, same cadence
—as before
controlled
—yes
controlling
—getting off on the control
—I had never heard that in your voice before
—Was your wife still in the house?
Oh, yes.
—. . . appalled you took such a risk
as am I, slightly
—yet – it also excites
I am glad
—did you cum?
I could not
just walked around after with a ridiculous hard-on
—it was just for me then
—thank you
For you
Finally, the instructed thank you
—I said thank you on the phone before I hung up
—. . . gasped it, anyway
I did not hear you
thought you were being shamed into silence . . . or
rebellious
—that came after, the shame
—. . . and then, the release
—But lover. Now – will you be satisfied with taking
fewer risks for a while now?
What do you mean?
—Promise me this: real life first, all around

211

—no doing things that put your marriage at the kind of
risk you engaged in yesterday
because I don't think I can be counted on at all to pull
in the reins, to say no
agreed. and well said.
—good
—thank you
—I would be devastated if the end result here was a
major real life fuck up for either of us
as would I
*perhaps this remote control aspect, that I am away, that
I could not come, is a gift in disguise*
—a gift?
keep us half sane
and real lives safe
—perhaps
—at other times a torment
exquisite torture
—but
—that is what keeps life interesting
Yes.
Savour your release, lover.
I don't want you burned out
on edge all the time
—no
—it was not . . . sustainable
No. We never are. Still. Perfect trust.
—Yes.
Good.
now go enjoy your calm
—thank you
—you too, my lover
I will
—I am so very very glad

—this is happening
as am I
—xx
xo

And perhaps for the first time in . . . two weeks, more, I really am glad.

Which might be proof I'm completely and totally insane.

Alex comes home, exhausted, when I'm reading the kids to sleep. I hear him in the kitchen, the bathroom, the bedroom. He's asleep by the time I come to bed. I don't wake him up. I sleep. So extremely well.

Day 17 – Interview for an affair

I oversleep, and wake up to seven texts from Marie. 'I'm better.' 'Fuck, I'm not. I miss him!' 'Jane, tell me not to be a moron and not text the fucker!' 'No, I'm fine. I'm good. Dickweed.' 'Is it me? Maybe it's me. Maybe this isn't about openness and polyamorous communication crap, but he just didn't want me!' 'Oh, fuck, Jane, what's wrong with me?' and, finally, 'Are you going to that stilts thing?'

Oh, crap. Stilts. I jump out of bed and find all four kids asleep. Late, late, late! I spare a moment for half cursing and half blessing private-school enrichment programmes and their assumption that mothers have no calling in life other than chauffeuring their children around. Race, race, race: clothes, cereal. Brush teeth. Into the car.

'This sucks,' from Henry, my sleepiest head.

'Stilts! Stilts!' from Annie.

I check email as they're bundling into coats. Ah, crap. A pile of analyses I ought to complete this week so they don't ruin Christmas. Actually, never mind. Not crap. Purpose. Focus. I will not think about my parents. About Marie's love affairs. About Nicola's divorce.

And not too much about Matt. Must work. Can't cyberfuck. Purpose.

As I drop the kids off, I start to worry about Annie. A four-year-old on stilts? What the hell are the organisers thinking? OK, so Annie will be there with three older siblings.

Still. I should stay, just in case things go sideways.

Except Annie, the independent fourth child, does not want me to stay.

'Mom!' Cassandra rolls her eyes. 'I'll text you if we need you to come back. OK? Go.'

I go.

I don't want to leave, because if I stay I have focus, purpose: taking care of Annie.

OK. She'll be fine. I'll be fine. I've got my laptop and a stack of reports to review. I find a café. Coffee, I need coffee, no time for coffee before I left the house, caffeinate me now, please. I do not ask for their Wi-Fi password, so that I'll truly work, and I breathe in the beautiful smell of the coffee and take my first sip, so good, so hot, so bitter, almost erotic, when . . .

'Jane! As I live and breathe, Jane!'

Jesus-fucking-Christ, who talks like that?

I am uncaffeinated, and in no mood for . . . this.

'How long has it been?'

I raise my head angrily, resentfully.

'My goodness, you look fantastic! I mean, for a mother of four children, I never would have guessed!'

Oh, fuck. I can't remember her name. But I remember I can't stand her. And I remember precisely why.

Unfortunately, she clearly doesn't remember I can't stand her and thinks this is a fabulous reunion. She plops down in the spare chair at my table – there are three empty tables around us – and puts her bag on the table beside my laptop. Tells me she's drinking soy-milk-no-sugar-green-tea-lattes now, and I hate her even more, even before she takes her iced pumpkin scone out of its paper bag. 'Oh, there's my drink!' she trills and lifts herself out of the chair and runs in tiny unbecoming steps to the counter. Do all women trill now? Is this a new thing? She's wearing purple yoga pants that would probably look OK if they weren't two sizes too small.

I don't spit on her scone, and am pleased with herself.

She returns. Cindy? Sherry? Susan?

'So how have you been?' she asks in a voice I bet she describes as cosy. I tap my laptop and the stack of papers.

'Busy,' I say. 'I'm actually working right now.'

'Well, aren't I lucky to catch you at a coffee break,' she trills. I try not to think how much I hate trilling. Fail. 'So how are you? I'm so, so great. Johnnie's started grade one this year, you know, and oh, my goodness, how wonderful it is to have entire days to myself . . .'

'No, I'm working *right* now,' I say. 'Like here. Right now. On these reports.'

'Really?' she says. 'Gosh. You were always so clever. Well, it's good to keep those professional skills up, isn't it. You just never know. Look at that poor Nicola. Would you ever have thought?'

Jesus-fucking-Christ, make this woman shut the fuck up before I throw my scalding coffee into her face.

'And the worst thing is, the girlfriend? Paul's girlfriend? Well. This is what she does, Jane. She breaks up marriages. She goes after married men. She's one of these possessed Jezebel-type women. Do you remember when we had that terrible scandal at our church two years ago? When our pastor had an affair? Well. It was with her.'

Oh, my God, she's still talking. And inexplicably, I am listening.

'And she just went after him. She did. Not caring he was a Man of God. Married, with children, with responsibilities. She just went after him. A Jezebel, Jane, that's what she is. And when he confessed all to the congregation, it just completely ripped us apart. He had been such a leader, such a force in the congregation . . . and she destroyed it all.'

'She did, did she?' I say. 'And what did he do?'

'Well, at least he confessed,' she says. 'At least he had the moral strength to confess, Jane, if not to resist.'

'Really?' I say. And then, maliciously, I add, 'Don't you think it all would have been better if he hadn't confessed?'

'What?' she stops talking. Stares at me. 'What do you mean, he shouldn't have confessed?'

'Well, just as with Nicola's husband,' I say. 'He didn't really want to leave Nicola. He didn't want to break up his marriage.' He just wanted to fuck a slightly younger, blonder woman. For a while. I should say that. I bet she would leave if I did. But she'll probably leave if I say this too . . . and so I say it: 'It wasn't the affair that broke them up, it was the confession.'

'What are you saying?' she says. Because she's stupid, and doesn't understand me.

'I think if Nicola's rat-fuck bastard of a husband was a little more careful and little less-immediately guilt-ridden – or less inclined to swallow his girlfriend's polyamorous philosophies – he could have maintained his marriage and enjoyed his affair, for a while, until it burned out,' I say. Do I believe what I'm saying? I'm not sure. But I'm enjoying, oh, yes, I'm enjoying the reaction. 'I think your pastor, if he hadn't had his urge to confess, would have maintained his marriage and his job and the adoration of his congregation. And the affair, for a while. That's what I think.'

'Jane! That's lying!'

Well, duh.

I violate rule number one, which is: never argue with people dumber than you. Because I want to annoy her.

'Say you had an affair,' I say.

'But I wouldn't!' she hollers.

'Indulge me. Say you did. Say – with him.' I toss my eyes and head towards a nice-looking, 40-something silver fox who's ordering coffee at the bar at the moment. I look at him for a few seconds. Tall, broad-shouldered, flat belly. Yes, definitely good-looking. A touch of Alex in the eyes and posture, actually. I smile in his direction. He raises his eyebrows.

'Say – you're at one of your church retreats or workshops

217

or something. *Sans* husband. And you and he hit it off, and maybe have a few glasses of wine. And end up in bed . . .'

'People at our church retreats do not drink wine! Or have affairs!' she says, getting up ungracefully. Yes! She's leaving.

'Your pastor did,' I say, not yell, but I'm not quiet either, to her retreating back.

I feel mildly petty. Mildly ashamed of being petty. Mostly pleased with the effect. I turn back to the laptop.

'Excuse me.' It's the silver fox from the bar. 'May I join you?'

There are three – no, four – empty tables around me.

I study him carefully. Yes, definitely a touch of Alex in the eyes and posture. When Alex's hair goes greyish-white, this is what he will look like. I like that. I smile back.

'Please.' I gesture towards the chair.

'I realise I'm interrupting,' he says. 'And I don't mean to be rude. But I did overhear some of your conversation with your friend.'

'Not exactly my friend,' I say. 'And I suppose I was not particularly discreet.'

'Well,' he says. 'I am a great believer in . . . seizing opportunities the universe presents.'

Are you now? I'm becoming a great believer that the universe is an evil fuck that hates me. But to each their own.

'So,' he says, and smiles. 'My name's Craig.'

'Craig.' I smile back. What the fuck am I doing? Ah. This. 'I am immensely flattered. And I am enjoying having you sit at my table, for a while. But I am not currently shopping for an affair.'

He looks crestfallen. And ashamed. And he's regretting his impulse – I can almost see the thought bubble over his head, remonstrating with himself for being stupid, for taking the risk.

I've used up my cruelty for the day. So . . .

'But if I ever start shopping, I'll definitely call you in for an interview,' I say. And smile. Almost like I mean it.

'Thank you.' He smiles back. 'Flattered.'

'Don't be.' I open up my laptop again, look down. I feel him get up. Take a step away. Then come back.

'Jane?' he says. 'I heard your . . . um . . . that woman call you Jane,' he explains. I nod. 'Look, I've got fifteen minutes before I have to go pick up my daughter. And – I get that you're not shopping for an affair. I'm not trying to pick you up.' He lies, but whatever. 'But if I don't find out what your interview consists of, I will go to my grave an unfulfilled man.' He flashes me another smile. He has a nice smile. 'Fifteen minutes. And then I leave, no other commitments or . . . innuendo or anything.'

OK. Work is boring. My mind unfocused. I'll play.

'Well, won't you sit back down then,' I say. 'The interview. Ready?'

He nods.

'Married?'

'Yes.'

'Kids?'

'Two. Boy, seventeen, and girl, fourteen. Boy's a ski jumper. Girl's a black belt in karate.'

'Happily married?'

He pauses, thinks.

'Comfortably married.'

'Discreet?'

'So very.'

'What does your wife do when she finds out about the affair?'

'She's not going to find out.'

'Where do we go on our first date?'

'The private room at Teatro's. *After* the theatre crowd leaves.'

'I cancel because one of my kids has the flu. What do you say?'

'Do you have Children's Tylenol? Or can I drop some off anonymously in your mailbox on the way home?'

'It's your birthday. What do you want from me?'

'An unsigned, handwritten card sent to my office. I'll know it's from you.'

'I have the motherfucker of all days. I text you saying, "Cheer me up." What do you do?'

'I courier you flowers. Anonymously, of course.'

'You have me alone in a hotel room for four hours. What's the first thing you do?'

'Draw you a bath. Chill champagne.'

He really does have a nice smile. He thinks he's nailed it. Poor man. I give him a kind look. Glance over at his watch.

'I think you've got to run now.'

He looks down at his wrist.

'I do. Lovely to meet you, Jane.' He takes half a step back, then comes back. 'Look,' he says. He pulls out a clip, and then a business card. 'This is me. All my contact info. This—' he pencils in another number '— is my confidential cell. If you ever . . . you know, if the situation changes. Call me. Any time.'

'Thank you, Craig.' I take the business card. Glance at the name, the email, the numbers. Put it down on the table beside my coffee cup.

'*Really* lovely to meet you, Jane,' he says. Wants to linger. I put my fingers on the laptop keys, thrust my eyes at the screen. Start to type.

The door jingles as he leaves.

And my phone buzzes.

'You were right, Mom. She's done.'

'On my way.'

I pop the laptop and the reports into my bag. Get up. Become aware of a handful of eyes on me. I look at the two flushed 50-something women in the far corner, the horrified teenage girls right behind me, and the construction worker whose eyes hit the floor as soon as mine rise. I pick up the business card between two fingers, look at it again, then flick it back onto the table.

'Not my type,' I say in the direction of the two flushed women. 'But, you know, he's shopping.' I walk out with a bit of a swagger.

It's nice to be wanted. But she only belongs to those who take. Not those who have to ask.

I get through the rest of the day with perfectly manageable angst.

I like that story very much.
—I thought you would.
He's going to think of you for days. Weeks. Waiting for the phone to ring.
Tormented by my fuckslave.
—Yours.
I want you to call him.
—Fuck. Matt. I threw away the card.
You used to be able to remember a number, any number, after seeing it once. You remember his. I'm sure.
—Stop it.
I like the idea of loaning you out. It's making me hard. So hard.
—Fucking stop it.
Where are you?
—In my living room. But alone.
—You?
Getting into the bath. Nude.
Are you ready to work?
—Yes. But don't make me . . .
I want you to serve.
—tell me
Watch you calmly as you dress for me
You work fast. Efficient. Professional.
From many nights of servicing me.
No conversation.

221

Unless I disagree with a choice you've made.
—no
—that distracts
—where do I keep my eyes
—as I change
On the floor
No, not those boots. The taller ones.
—all right
I don't care how long it takes you to buckle them.
—I feel sly today.
—I put the boots on before anything else.
—I sit at such an angle, you have a full view of my
pussy
—as I buckle
—slowly.
You prop one foot high on a chair to reach the lowest
buckles.
Displaying your pussy to me brazenly.
My shameless fuckslave.
—I steal a look to see if you're watching, how you're
watching.
Look at my cock, if you're going to look up at all.
—I do.
—And then I look away.
You can see it was growing beneath my clothes.
I sip my wine. And watch.
—I turn my back to you
—Leg on chair arch in spine
Your strength has always stirred me.
The way you can take a hard fuck.
You were made to be pounded.
—I'm not very subtle, I'm arranging myself so that my
ass presents at its best.
—I take another peek over my shoulder, to see if
you've had to unzip your pants yet.

You please me with your animal signalling
—are you hard yet, my lover, I want to say
—but of course I don't
Then you hear my belt buckle.
The sound makes you shiver.
—(reading this makes me shiver)
—I'm still just wearing the boots
The soft snap of my button
—I grab the corset quickly
Yes.
I want you bound.
—Just the plain black corset, not too many clasps, I
took too long with the boots and you will not have
patience for too many clasps
the stiff one that stops below your tits
—yes
A whore's corset
—a fucktoy's
Oh yes. My fucktoy's. Of no use save for fucking.
Now get your collar on.
—Fuck. Matt, no. We don't do that.
You do what I fucking tell you to do. Put it on.
—I don't want to.
At that moment you dare to look me in the eye.
Almost defiant.
'Do what you're fucking told.'
My voice is hard.
My cock is harder.
You move. 'Good.'
—Something like a necklace. An almost pretty choker
No. The PVC.
Tonight you're working hard.
You hesitate again.
—it's really hard for me – I don't like that
You never did, until after. My belt, Tim's tie? Do you

*remember when I took Tim's tie off his neck as I was
pushing you into my bedroom?*

—Jesus. Yes.

*And still you hesitate. I've had enough. Faster than you
can imagine I stand up and stride up to you.*

—I don't like props. The boots are . . . sexy. I love that
they excite you. Like my fuck-me heels. They excite me
too.

—The collar . . . I fucking hate it.

*'This is the last time I'm going to show you how this
works.'*

I snap it into place around your throat. Yank.

—tight

—I whimper

it's smooth and cool

—I swallow

—try to make myself relax

Give in

Give yourself over to me

surrender

I tilt your chin to me

What are you?

Tell me.

—can I look at you?

—your fuckslave

Look at me when you say that.

—I look.

Again.

—I am your fuckslave

—nothing more

*I don't even let you finish your last word before I fill
your mouth with cock.*

No waiting to ease you in.

—I don't mind

Right to the hilt.

You can take it.

—I've been waiting to get your cock in my mouth since I arrived.

—It had been too long.

—I gag a little from the force of the entry . . .

You've been trained so well

—but I know what you like

Gagging enough to make you shudder. Almost like an orgasm.

But much experience has taught us both where the line is.

I push you to the line. And then . . . over it.

—what happens?

You gag. You shudder. Spit pours down my shaft and warms my balls and your exposed tits.

—(so wet)

The wet sloppy sounds of you getting face-fucked reverberate

—(and a little mortified)

Tell me why.

—(my hands on my breasts, my nipples so hard)

Mortified how badly you want this humiliation?

—(I am still taken aback by the effect of this on me)

—I want to be at your feet, your cock in my mouth

You belong there.

—my breathing ragged, working on your cock, getting more aroused with every stroke

When I'm weary of using your very skilled mouth I pull out with a wet sloppy sound, slapping your lips with my cock.

'Get up.'

—I'm up

I grab the metal ring at the front of your collar and march you to the hotel room window

'Stand there.'

—Oh, Jeezus, no, you know I don't like this. What the fuck is with you today?

Do what you're fucking told.

—I stand

Legs wide

—eyes shut

'Open your fucking eyes.'

'Tits out. Proud.'

—I open my eyes, but my head stays bent

Arms outstretched, pressed against the cool glass floor to ceiling window

I reach for the curtain chain.

'Eyes front, whore.'

—Please, no

Still you disobey

—I'm trying, it's so hard . . .

With one hand I pull the curtains open, with the other I yank your head back, forcing you to show your true self to the world.

What do you see out there? I demand as I work your swollen wet clit with one hand, the other still gripping your hair.

Tell me.

—(oh my fucking god)

Fucking tell me fuckslave

The shame and the orgasm rock through you, wave after wave that has yet to crest

What do you see in the reflection of the window?

The dark night outside turns the window into a mirror. Reflecting you back on yourself.

Look at yourself.

Slut boots.

Whore corset.

Collar.

And so wet.

And a man's hand working your wet pussy.
—'I see . . . a whore.'
For all to see.
Pedestrians two floors below have yet to look up.
Yet.
Cars. So many passing cars.
—you're still stroking me, and holding my hair, and I'm
not sure which I'm enjoying more
What can any of these good people do with my whore,
right now?
—The shame's an acceptable price to pay.
—'They can look. See.'
'Know you for what you are from a mile away.'
But you know that's not the answer I'm looking for.
'What can any of these people do with my whore, right
now? Tell me.'
—'Anything you wish.'
Yess . . . You shake almost violently now.
—yes
—I can barely stand
—Even with my hands at the window
The window bows in and out with the pressure of your
hands,
and your impending explosion.
'Look at yourself.'
—My forehead and breasts pressed against it, it's so
cold
—I raise my head
Rubbing harder
—oh
—pulling hair harder
'LOOK AT YOUR FUCKING SELF.'
—tears in my eyes
Then you see it.
A car.

Slowing down.
Stops.
—Oh Jesus Christ.
—'My lover, please, that's enough.'
Traffic backed up behind him.
Horns.
—'I don't want them to see.'
—'Please.'
Tension rising.
Give him a good show. RIGHT FUCKING NOW.
—Oh god.
YANK on your hair one last time to put you in your place.
—I lift my head, spread my palms and legs.
—Thrust my breasts forward.
—but close my eyes, think maybe you can't see
Shameless fucking slut.
OPEN your eyes and watch them.
—I swallow
Show them what beautiful eyes my slave has
—Open my eyes, thin slits, tears in corners
—so fucking hard for me
Now the horns have fallen silent.
Everyone waits for my slave.
—I am not an exhibitionist, not to this extent, at all
—I do this all for you
I don't care.
Do what you're fucking told.
—I do it.
—For you.
—Teeth clenched.
—Shaking.
—so humiliated
Do it now. For real.

—I take a deep breath. Eyes open wide. I look at that first car.
Better.
Headlights burning into your body.
—You can tell I'm almost done
—almost spent
—too much
I reach forward with my fingers inside your pussy to work your swollen g-spot
You are ready to burst
All I have to do . . .
—I will explode the second you touch me
. . . is slam your spot then pull my fingers out to let you gush
—I cum and cum, and I cry as I cum, from the relief, both physical and mental
All over the hotel room carpet
—I forget I am still on display
—(I am about not to be alone)
—(front door creaking, footsteps)
You forget everything
—I just cum
Remember this.
Now go swallow some cum.
—I will.
Good girl.
—Oh my fucking god.
—(thank you)
—(he's here. I'm gone.) xo
Thank you. You are such a perfect fucktoy.
I am so pleased you are mine.
Still. You have your orders. xx

Alex leans into me, lips brushing my forehead. 'Exhausted,' he says. 'But absolutely done for the day. Are you coming to bed?' I nod. I want to say, I need a moment. Or, in a few minutes.

But I don't trust my voice. I take his hand in mine instead, press my forehead against it.

'In a minute,' I finally say. 'Just need to wrap things up.'

'Don't work too hard,' he throws over his shoulder as he walks up the stairs. 'One workaholic per family is more than enough.'

I sit, very still, eyes closed. Waves of the mindfuck still rocking through me.

Finally, I go upstairs. I have . . . orders.

Interlude: Practice

She gets offline with you, sick with desire, and goes to the bedroom. He you allow her to fuck is asleep.

She stretches out beside him, and contours her body around his. He's sleeping on his back. She puts a hand on his hip. Leaves it there a while. Moves it lower, rests it against his cock. Then, a few minutes later, slides it into his pyjama bottoms. Rests it very gently on the top of the head. A little stroke with her thumb. Then stillness.

She waits. She knows that's enough, that he will stir. And he does, and moves his hands onto her, and starts to caress her. That's when she slides down under the covers. His hands follow her. Take off those bottoms. They're barely off when she takes his cock in her mouth.

She practises.

She thrusts out her tongue. She takes it deep. She works through the gagging.

She has always loved the size and shape of his cock; it fits her so well. She remembers yours. And she thinks it will be harder to take, like this.

She takes him deeper.

She is very methodical. You would approve. Although she is not following instructions precisely, because he is too languid, too prone. He is satisfied to have her do most of the work. For now.

She is silent. And he is about to cum, and now he pulls her head off his cock and comes awake in an instant, flipping her onto her back. And he enters her quickly, and she comes the moment he penetrates her.

She's surprised.

He does not last very long inside her, because she did her work very well. He collapses on top of her, and breathes into her neck, her ear.

She closes her eyes. And thinks of you.

Day 18 – I take good care of my possessions

Thursday, December 20

I wake up dreading lunch.

My Thursday lunches with my dad are sacrosanct, the third of the month perhaps not as important as the first – but we planned this one back in November. And for me not to go, even after their Sunday bombshell – *especially* after their Sunday bombshell – would be the equivalent of telling him I don't love him any more. And I settle within myself, as I feed and dress the kids and get them ready for their last day of school before the Christmas break, that I do love him. Of course. There is a storm of anger, resentment, confusion, disappointment and a dozen other feelings I dislike raging within me. But. He's my dad. Love him. Not his fault my mother's snapped, gone crazy. I will endure the lunch.

Alex, wisely perhaps, says nothing meaningful to me all morning, but keeps on pressing his lips against my forehead, my neck. We stand in the kitchen, pressed against each other, very, very still for so long, the boys start making puking noises.

'I love you,' he says as he heads out the door. I blow him a kiss.

I decide not to cry.

It won't be so bad. My dad and I, we know how to talk about nothing. We have years of practice.

But yes. It is harder this time. As he sits there – we're back to fish and chips this time – I can tell he really wants to tell me something. He is full of story. Full of explanation. He is just waiting for the sign.

Well, fuck him and his needs. I won't let him.

I know the story.

He's told it to me on several occasions over the years. The first time, when I moved in with John; the second time, when I broke up with John. The third time, when he was worried I might move in with Aldrin. The fourth time, when I told him Alex and I were engaged. The fifth time, some time after Eddie was born but before Annie, when I asked him, after a particularly awful family dinner, 'Is it always like this now?'

'I made a decision when I got married,' starts the story. 'That I was going to have peace in my family. No matter what.'

That's what happens, I guess, when you grow up in a household where the parents stay together and fight together. Incessantly.

And that, in my father's story, is his family. I can't check it against truth, because I never knew my grandparents. Reading between the lines of my father's story, they drove each other to an early grave a couple of years before I reached sentience.

The story's a little different each time, but I've learned this much from it: that my grandmother was a bitter, angry nag. That my grandfather was a philandering (maybe), argumentative jerk. That arguments over everything – including the default temperature setting on the water heater and the best time to re-wallpaper the living room – are all that my father's memories of his parents consist of. That, and yelling at the kids.

'Things were going to be different in my family,' goes the story. 'I was going to have peace. Whatever the price.'

So. My father's never yelled at me. Or disciplined me, much. He's never raised his voice at my mother, or disagreed with her in a substantial way over anything. He's nodded. Caressed. Agreed. Apologised. Compromised. Surrendered.

In the process: infuriated my mother. By his passivity, his apparent indecision, softness. Refusal to engage. Total withdrawal from conflict.

234

I inherited his ability to refuse to engage, through either genetics or modelling and self-defence, because my mother, denied a sparring partner in her spouse, tried to make one out of me.

I always thought I understood my father.

And I understood, if did not always support, his story.

Peace at any price.

And I can't imagine his heartbreak at this moment. That it wasn't enough – that, after 43 years, what he gets out of peace at any price is the end of his marriage.

I've seen my mother teeter on the brink of leaving him every few years, ever since I entered my teens. It must have happened before, too, in those first fifteen years of their marriage when I was too young to really notice the friction. It must have always been there . . . And I've thought of it as the irony of their marriage: that she, the volatile, explosive, demanding, difficult-to-live-with one, that *she* was the one who at times couldn't deal with living with the accommodating, easygoing, 'whatever you want, my love' partner.

And none of it was enough.

I so don't want to hear the story again. I don't want to hear him try to explain that he tried everything and it wasn't enough and it wasn't his fault. I don't need to be any angrier at my mother.

'Jane . . .' my father starts. I raise my hands.

'No,' I say. 'Not now. Let's eat. And . . . I love you. I don't understand. Fine. I don't. But I don't want to . . .' I pause. But I don't have to say any more. He, unlike my mother, understands my refusal to engage.

I wonder, suddenly, if Alex does. Or does it infuriate him, as it does her, but he doesn't throw it back in my face? Does he suffer in silence?

I stab at a French fry viciously and I wonder if my father married his mother –and I sometimes think he did. And if he married his mother . . . what did I do? The thought is profoundly icky and disturbing. I shut it down immediately.

'Dessert,' I say. 'Today, we definitely need dessert. What's the least gross thing on the menu?'

Because she knows I'm meeting Dad, my mother insists I come by and see her in the afternoon, before he gets back from work. I accommodate. I don't want to. But I accommodate. And, as I wait outside the kids' school to pick them up *en route* to Gran's, I seethe. I'm trying to settle within myself that I love my mother, and that I will love her even though, after 43 years of marriage, she has chosen to be an extra-selfish bitch and ruin my dad's life and . . .

Ping.

Oh, lover. How did you know I need you?

Fuck. Not him.

Marie.

The only person I know who can weep via a text. And there she is, weeping into my phone.

Over Paul. The end of the thing, whatever it was – ten days of texting?

I want to write, 'Get over it, for fuck's sake. It wasn't even real.'

Except, of course, I know those jonesing for what is not real still wake up jonesing just for a message, a ping.

I want to write, 'This much pain over Paul? Paul? Really? You've seen him – *Paul*, right? You remember Paul? You remember the things we said about Paul when that marriage first imploded? Things like, "Can ya believe he found *another* woman willing to fuck him?"'

I want to write, 'Shut up shut up shut up.'

Instead I type, 'I love you.'

And she weeps back at me, more, a mixture of gratitude and such intense, mad pain – and selfishness – that I'm not sure what appals me more, her naked emotions or that she is throwing them at me. And I feel the resentment building in me again, resenting that she is doing this to me today, today,

236

when I've just had to endure *not* talking with my dad, and I will next have to endure *not* talking with my mom, about their stupid, stupid divorce, and . . .

Then I realise that, of course, she knows nothing.

Well. She knows what's happened. But, of course, thinks I'm just fine. Because, as she herself accused me in the past, I tell nothing. I do not throw my emotions in her face.

Would it help?

Architect of my own suffering. Whatever. I let the anger roll and boil inside me, my anger at my mother and my anger at Marie intertwining. For good measure, a shot of anger at Matt for . . . I don't know what. For everything. For the first message, for the phone call, for the sudden shot of longing that joins the anger in my belly. For the wetness between my legs, the ecstasy, the complication.

Fucking selfish bastard.

And what am I?

I have my game face on by the time the kids come to the car. 'Where's Annie?' I ask. A jolt of panic. She should be holding Cassandra's hand.

'Gran came and got her at noon,' Cassandra says. 'She said there was no point in her staying in aftercare for the afternoon when she had Grandma at home.'

Another shot of anger. And checked in with me about this? Of course not. Fucking selfish bitch.

By the time we get to my parents' house, I'm vibrating with anger. I endure my mother's embrace, but barely. The table's stacked with baking.

'Annie and I have been so busy this afternoon,' my mother trills. Annie's covered with flour and icing sugar. The kids descend on the table. 'Wash your hands!' their grandma instructs.

I continue to vibrate.

I can't look at her.

'Did you have a nice lunch with your dad?' she asks.

'What?' I say. 'No. No, I didn't.'

And then . . . I lose it. 'What the fuck is wrong with you?' My voice is low, but the kids are there, right there, and I don't talk like this – to my mother – in front of them. Or ever, frankly. 'How the hell was it supposed to be a nice lunch?'

'Oh, Jane,' my mother says, and moves towards me, arms outstretched. I back away.

'Don't,' I say.

'Oh, Jane,' she says. She picks up a coffee cup, and walks past me into the living room, a wall and assorted furniture separating us from the kids. Sits down on the couch. Waits for me to follow. 'Jane, I'm so, so sorry.'

'Sorry?' I shake my head. 'Sorry? You're sorry? Tell me. Tell me this. How could you do this? For forty-three years – more – he's put up with all your crap. All your crazy. All your—' I look around the house, her house, filled with her stuff and her personality and her preferences, her stuff, her wallpaper, her art, her furniture, her *everything,* in which *he* happened to live, giving way to her in everything, everything '— all your . . . everything. He put up with *everything.* And after forty-three years, you fucking end it?'

The cup my mother is holding drops to the floor. Shatters. Tiny pieces, shards everywhere.

'I didn't leave him,' she says. And her voice is cold, and terrible, and my belly contracts. 'I am not the one. He's the one . . . he's the one . . .'

I stare at her in shock.

And shame.

'Of course, he didn't tell you,' she says, and there is such venom and anger in her voice that it makes my own insignificant. 'Of course not. You two just . . . didn't talk. Didn't talk. As always.'

She turns around, and walks out of the living room. Past the kitchen. I hear her footsteps on the stairs. I wonder how a daughter apologises for all the things I've just said.

I clean up the shards of the coffee cup. Pour two new cups. Follow her upstairs.

She's sitting not in the master bedroom but in my old bedroom, on the edge of the sofa bed. She raises her eyes as I come in.

'He sleeps here now,' she says. 'He's been sleeping here for months.'

'Oh, Mom.'

I sit beside her. Hand her the coffee cup. Put an awkward arm around her.

'Why didn't you tell me? Before? When this all started?'

And she looks at me, her eyes so sad, so sad I'm startled, and she says . . .

'I've never been able to tell you anything, Jane. What could I say? And it wouldn't matter. It wouldn't matter. You've always, always taken his side.'

And I say nothing. Keep my arm stiffly around her shoulders. Drink the coffee. Listen to my mother cry.

—I'm having the worst day ever, lover. I need you.

When I tell Alex, he raises his left eyebrow – which I'm starting to find a rather annoying habit, and I try to make myself remember how I once thought it endearing.

'And you're shocked?' he says.

'Yes!' I say. 'Aren't you?'

'No,' Alex says. Shrugs. Looks away from me. 'I always thought that if anyone ever left that freak show of a marriage, it would be your father.'

'Freak show of a marriage?' I repeat. Terse.

'Sweetheart.' Alex touches my shoulder, draws me into an embrace. 'You've called it worse yourself. They were together for forty-three years. When was the last time they were really happy together?'

Images run through my mind: my parents' smiling faces, on

239

my graduations, at our wedding, bending over our kids, family photographs, couple photographs from trips and cruises, always beaming. Alex seems to read my mind.

'They take a great picture together,' he says.

I want to hurt him.

'What they had was better than your father's three wives,' I say. Viciously.

He doesn't flinch.

'I suppose,' he says. 'Or perhaps not.' He lets go of me, sits down in the kitchen chair. 'I have no answers for you, Jane. I'm sorry.' He looks at me, and gives me the little-boy smile that made me fall in love with him. 'It sucks when your parents split up. Apparently no matter what age you are.'

'Mom!' Cassandra runs in. 'Henry and Eddie are fighting over the computer, and I'm so tired of being the policewoman!'

'Coming,' I say. Start walking.

'Jane?' Alex calls after me. I half-turn. 'I love you. For ever. I promise.'

'I know,' I answer.

But I have no 'I love you's left in me today.

The day mercifully ends. Bedtime goes on for ever – the kids feed off my angst and anger. Alex takes over. 'Go,' he says, removing the book I'm reading to Annie from my hand. I accept. But, instead of going to bed, I take my laptop. And disappear into the basement. Curl up on the workout bench. Think about how late it is in Montréal.

But he is mine as I am his. And he is there.

I'm sorry I missed you earlier, my lover. And now?
—I am so spent I want to curl into a ball and weep.
Tell me.
—It's all unsexy awful reality and I'm so fucking exhausted.
Tell me.

—That's not what we do.
You do what I tell you. So now, tell me – what's wrong?

Well, let's see . . . where do I begin? Where do I end? What does it matter? I don't want to talk about my father with my lover.

—I don't even know where to start, my lover.
Would it make you feel better to serve?
—. . .
—No. I am . . . exhausted. Spent. There is nothing of me left for you today. I am so sorry.
Don't be. Are you alone?
—Yes.
Then I will pleasure you. No demands.
—You will?
Yes. I like to take good care of my possessions. And I do genuinely care about your happiness.
—I know.
—(starting to feel a little better already)
(Good)
Now . . . do you remember the first time I licked your beautiful pussy?
—My blunt lover. Oh, yes. The lawn? Oh, yes.
Good. We're walking on that street. Not by design. It's not then, it's now – I'm in town for some client thing, and you meet me, of course. We're walking to the hotel, slowly, because you're dressed more or less like the Eurotrash girl you were back then and you're wearing my favourite fuck-me heels.
—Walking very slowly indeed.
I recognise the street first. 'I think that might be the lawn,' I say. You blush. After . . . what? 20 years? The memory's still enough to make you blush.
—That excites you.

I got excited – and hard – the moment I recognised the street. Can you guess what I do next?

—No. Yes. I don't know. Tell me.

I've had my arm around your waist – caressing your hip, your ass, your thighs as we walked – and I tighten it, and walk you to that lawn.

—Oh, God.

I push you down – not too hard. But emphatically. Sit down beside you.

—Is it cold?

It doesn't matter. You're already hot. As am I. The first time, do you remember, we kissed for a while before I dove between your legs.

—Jeezus Christ, yes, I remember.

I don't kiss you. I position you against me, and I slide my hands under your skirt. I shove the skirt up to your waist – and I'm very pleased you followed instructions, and there is a garter belt there, no panties. Very convenient for me.

—I obey.

You do.

And I reward.

I caress you much more gently than you're used to these days, drawing the tips of my fingers over your lips, your clit, the softest parts of you.

—I like it. I lean into you more.

I shift you, so I can use both my hands. A little less gently now. One hand's fingers sliding into you. The other focused on your clit.

Jesus, you're engorged.

—It doesn't take much when I'm with you.

That pleases me. Always.

Are you self-conscious, worried about all the windows?

—Yes. No. I am when I think about them. I'm not when you stroke me just the right way.

242

Good. They're all around us. Some lit. Some dark. Curtains up. Curtains drawn. Do you remember what that guy shouted?

—'Get a room!'

'Get a fucking room,' I think. Well. We have a room to go to. But this is much more exciting. My little slut-whore's enjoying herself immensely, I can tell by how wet she is, how engorged.

—Am I moaning?

Are you ever. But nothing compared to the animal sounds you will be making shortly. I take off my coat – did I mention I take good care of my possessions? – and I put it down on the lawn, and push you onto it.

—And you?

I go down between your thighs. Licking. Biting. Tongue thrusting. It's been a long time since I've done this – these days, I prefer to watch you while you play with yourself. Or to fuck you so hard you scream. But, mmmmm, this is nice. You're delicious. The smell of you is intoxicating.

Are you relaxed?

—So relaxed.

Good. I'm going to make you cum now.

—On the lawn.

On the lawn. And now, in real life. Put your hand on your clit. Now.

—Jeezus.

Stop typing. I don't want you to type. Read.

Left hand on your clit.

Right hand on your tits.

Gather them up. That's what you're doing on that lawn – playing with your tits, exposed, in full view of anyone who might look out their window.

Your left hand – that's my mouth. I'm leaving your clit now to thrust my tongue inside you.

243

Put your fingers into you.
Deeper. Deeper. Harder, my fuckslave.
I do not treat you as a breakable toy even when I
pleasure you – you know what you're supposed to do.
Yank on your nipples so hard you want to scream. And
again. I want you to make yourself cum just by the
pressure on your tits, can you do that for me? Just a
little longer . . . just a little harder . . . just a small
release, and now, I want both hands on your pussy. In
your pussy. Rub and thrust. That's my tongue, and my
hands, and you're dripping, dripping drowning me.
Cum. Now.
If you've cum, you can type.
—Oh, my fucking God.
Now say thank you.
—Thank you.
Properly. I've indulged you. You know what I want.
—Your whore says thank you. Lover. Master.
Good. Now go.
—Do you want me to serve you now?
No. Do not diminish my gift by seeking reciprocity.
—Dripping. For you.
Go fuck your husband. That's an order.
—Thank you. xx
xo

Alex is in the bedroom, with the lights off. I slide in beside him. On top of him. Wet. 'Jesus, Jane, I'm not sure I've recovered from yesterday,' he whispers into my ear. But he's whispering as he slides into me. And we don't fuck: we slowly, lazily make love, just rocking back and forth. It's easy, it's every day, ordinary. I feel comfort. I fall asleep in his arms, his softening cock still inside me.

I don't think. I don't dream.

Day 19 – Generous

Alex brings me coffee to bed. And my laptop. And my phone.

'I think you need to text Marie,' he says. He looks gorgeous in his suit. I smile at him. Languid. Happy. I look at the screen. There are 24 messages.

'Jesus Christ,' I say. 'They can't possibly all be from her.' He kisses my cheek. Lingers. I look up at him.

'What are your plans for the day?' he asks.

'Texting Marie,' I say as I read through her messages. 'Jesus. Well, not all, but twenty of them are hers.'

'Seriously?' he asks.

'Ah,' I say. Distracted. Reading the seventh reiteration of

- Am I insane? What's wrong with me? And where the fuck are you when I need you?

'Ah . . . last Friday before Christmas . . . anything that doesn't involve going to a store. I suppose I ought to be baking. And wrapping presents and shit like that.'

'Will you see your dad?' he asks. I flinch away.

'No,' I say. 'Oh, fuck. He called you.'

Alex looks away.

'I won't,' I say.

'He loves you,' Alex says. Still not looking at me. Then he glances at my telephone screen.

245

- I think I am going totally and completely crazy.

'What's wrong with her?' he asks.

'I really hope it's not peri-menopause, because if it is, you won't be able to handle it when it hits me,' I tell him. Read the next one, which is more of the same. And the next one. Sigh. 'New plan: I will invite Marie and her kids over to bake with me. She loves baking about as much as I do. We will be miserable yet dutiful together.'

'Good friend.' He nuzzles my neck. 'Good mother. Good wife. Good wife who deserves a husband who puts some thought into her Christmas present instead of running out for something on December twenty-fourth . . . which you know I might be doing . . .'

'Oh, fuck, you mean I need to get you a Christmas present too?' I say. He starts to reach for a pillow to swat me with, remembers the coffee in my hand. Kisses me instead.

I put the coffee down on my nightstand. Kiss him back. Then text Marie and tell her to come over and bake cookies with me.

- Where the hell have you been?
—Sleeping, psycho-bitch. We'll talk when you get here. Don't be insane. Come on over. Today, we bake.
- Do you have white flour and sugar? Because those spelt cookies you made us make last year were disgusting.
—Fuck you. Bring supplies if you don't like what I bake with. But yes, I do have real sugar and flour.
- Food colouring?
—No.
- I'm bringing food colouring.
—Fine. I'll send Henry and Eddie home with you.

Alex. Still reading over my shoulder. He chortles. Gets up and moves to the door, turns around in the doorway and looks at me.

'Jane?' he says. I raise my eyes from the screen. 'He loves you.'

I know. But sometimes that doesn't make things OK.

Even before she arrives, I know I will have to tell Marie something. More than I have, more than I want to, because she's feeling betrayed and disappointed by my silence, over-exposed and too vulnerable because of all that she has shared. So, after the kids get their fill of breaking eggs and spooning and cutting cookies, and we kick them out into the snow while we bake – 'They need to bake and cool off before you decorate them, go, run, run!' 'Do I have to go too, Mom?' 'Yes, Cassandra, get outside for at least fifteen minutes, please? Watch Annie!' 'It sucks to be the oldest sometimes!' 'I know, babe, but you'll get to drive before any of them' – we sit down at the table with coffee, and I tell her. About my parents, about my anger, confusion, my anger at my mom, and finding out it was my dad who left, and how suddenly that's so much worse . . . I don't tell her everything, of course. I can't. But what I tell her, it's enough.

'Jesus,' she says. 'Oh, Jane. You must think I'm such a stupid, selfish bitch.'

And she bursts into tears.

And I hug her and let her cry. And accept that her suffering is real and painful to her. I don't have to understand it. Or even condone it.

'Ask me something,' Marie says suddenly.

'What?'

'Ask me,' she says. 'Ask me what I want. Ask me what I'm looking for. Ask me why I'm crying over that stupid fuck!'

'What do you want?' I ask.

And I can tell she has been rehearsing the answer. Because it comes quickly, immediately and harshly.

'I want someone to want to fuck me,' she says. 'To want me so badly, he doesn't care. That I'm married. Unavailable. Fucked up and confused. To want me so badly, he doesn't care about the consequences. He doesn't want me to be – honest.

247

And clear about what I want. And – have perfect communication and rules and everything all worked out and all that shit. He doesn't give a fuck. He just wants me. Now. In his bed. Against the restaurant dumpster. Wherever. That's what I want.'

She gets up. Looks at me. Glares.

'Judge me,' she demands.

I shrug.

'I won't,' I say.

And then . . . I realise. I can do something about this. Something wrong. Possibly horribly wrong. But. What the fuck. It's Christmas. A surreal Christmas, and an outright sucky one for a lot of people. The Christmas my father left my mother. The Christmas Paul left Nicola, got left – or at least got *demoted* – by his skank and kinda left – but not really – Marie. The Christmas Alex's little associate is going to spend lusting, and maybe more, after my husband. The Christmas I've spent all of December cyber-cheating on Alex. Fuck. What a Christmas.

It might as well be the Christmas Marie finally has a real affair.

'Give me your phone,' I say.

I left the card on the coffee-shop table. But Matt's right. I have a tremendous memory for numbers. And I looked at that personal cell number twice. Each time long enough to remember it.

'Why?' Marie asks.

'Just give me your phone,' I say. I wipe my hands on my pants. Take it from her. Punch in the number. Pause to think. And then type:

—Hi there, Craig. This is Jane, from the coffee shop. Remember me?

I ponder pressing *send* at this point. But I need to set the parameters from the beginning. So I continue.

248

—I'm texting you on my friend Marie's phone. I'd like to introduce the two of you.

Send.

'What are you doing?' Marie demands. She wrenches the phone from my hand. 'Jesus-fucking-Christ, Jane, what are you doing?'

'I'm setting you up,' I say.

'Oh-my-fucking-God,' Marie says. 'You are handing off a lover to me. I don't fucking believe this. Self-restrained, perfect ice-queen-princess Jane has a fucking lover whom she is handing off to me! How pathetic do you think I am?'

'No!' I protest. The phone buzzes, and I grab it back from her. 'I promise you, first, that this man is hot, and second, that he has never ever been anywhere near my –' I pause '– icky girl parts,' I finish. And we both howl. 'One day, I'll tell you how I met him. But it's really not important.'

- Jane. How nice to hear from you. And how odd.

'What are you going to say?' Marie asks. I shrug. Start typing.

—Not so odd. Pretend we're in the coffee shop. Talking. And she walks in. She's a good friend of mine. Very hot. And, shall we say, interested? She joins us at the table. I introduce you. That's all. The medium's electronic, the introduction's a real life thing.

'You're insane,' Marie says. The phone buzzes as we read.

- I'm intrigued.

'And you?' I look at Marie. 'Do I continue?' She bites her lips. Looks at the phone, at me. Nods.

—So is she. I'm about to hand her the phone – excuse myself to go to the powder room or something. Think of this as my Christmas present to you both.

I pause. I kind of want to type, 'And if you hurt her, I'll eviscerate you.' But that might spoil the mood. Instead:

—Be good. Have fun. Jane out.

And I hand Marie the phone.

'What the hell do I do now?' she yelps.

'I think he'll take the lead,' I tell her. And the phone buzzes.

- Hello, Marie. This is Craig. I'm a little weirded out, but more intrigued. You?

'I have to go . . . to the bathroom,' I tell Marie. She doesn't hear me. She's looking at the screen, smiling.

When I come back, her head's bent over the phone, and she's texting. I take the cookies out of the oven. Pop in the next batch.

Supervise the decoration of several batches with all six kids while Marie texts. Glows.

'You're insane,' she whispers in my ear as she hugs me when they're leaving.

'Probably,' I agree. I want to say . . . don't take it too seriously. Or . . . don't blame me when it all goes wrong. But fuck. Whatever. 'Enjoy. For at least a little bit.'

'Oh, I will,' she says. 'I will.'

Lacey sends Clayton over in the afternoon so she can wrap presents, and then reciprocates by taking my entire brood. And I, alone in the house, a pile of unwrapped presents hidden in the laundry room in the basement, a phone tingling with texts messages from my dad, I close my eyes. And choose to be, for the moment, perfectly selfish.

I sit at the laptop.

—I have a story for you.

End-of-the-day of the last workday before Christmas in Montréal. Probably no longer in the office.

Tell me.

I smile. And I tell him.

My generous whore. I approve.
—I'm glad.
Although I would have preferred ordering you to fuck him. Unwilling, reluctant. Doing it only to please me.
—You're sick.
You love it.
Are you alone?
—Surprisingly, yes.
Ready to work?
—Yes.
Because you were so generous, I got you a present too.
—Have you?
She's right over there. Pretty, isn't she? Turn around and eat her pussy.
I want to watch your head bobbing up and down while I fuck you.
—I reach for her slowly, one hand and my tongue exploring her pussy.
I want to see your hand working her pussy as you lap at her clit.
—It's so sensitive, she squeals already.

Tell her what you are. Your voice muffled by a mouthful of pussy.

— 'I'm Matt's fuckslave.'

—I turn my head to see your reaction.

I slap your ass for that.

Keep your eyes on your work, whore.

—It's yours to do with as you will.

I know.

—I pull her lower down so I don't need to support myself with my hands.

—I want to use both hands and my mouth.

Your skills and enthusiasm impress me.

—I have missed having a girl in my face.

—they taste good

—their reactions so much more . . . graded than those of men

Her juices are flowing fast now.

—Her clit between my finger and thumb, my tongue licking around her, darting inside.

It excites you, your pussy is pounding.

'Want to hear her cum?' I ask the other.

—I don't like you talking to her.

Between moans she manages to say . . . 'Yes, sir.' So polite.

—and then?

—what do you say to me?

I slap your ass. Still not fucking you.

—My pussy throbbing and pounding from desire for you.

'Show her how you can cum on command like a well-trained whore.'

NOW.

And don't stop working her pussy.

—I engulf her lips and clit in my mouth.

—I raise my ass and arch my back.

SLAP your ass again. Hard.
—All I need to do to cum is think how much I want
you.
—how much I want you to use me
Do as you're fucking told.
—how I'll do anything you tell me to
Yes. You will.
Prove it.
—and I cum in a streaking, shivering, shaking explosion
—pussy juice spraying
—knees buckling
My juicy whore.
Shameless.
Irreplaceable.
—I drop my head to the floor, my forehead almost hits
it, I collapse so thoroughly.
Valuable.
—yours
*'Stand over her. Straddle her. Your turn to make
yourself cum.'*
She does as she's told.
—Will you fuck me as she stands over me?
To you: 'Tell her to cum on your face.'
—I slowly roll over onto my back
— 'Cum on my face.'
—Does she squat down, or stay standing?
—I want her standing. What do you want?
*Standing. The sight of her legs towering over you make
you feel so dominated.*
—I look up at her pussy
Then your pussy is filled with my cock.
—Spread my legs for you
—Oh
—Finally
Cum on her pretty face.

—I am so hungry for you.

—She does not come as readily on command as I do.

'You should feel her pussy, it's so fucking wet.'

I make her face away from me. I reach over and slap her ass HARD

She cries out.

—I raise my hips a little off the floor, I want to wrap my legs around you and bring you down on me.

—But I worry you won't let me.

Lie there and take it.

—I spread my legs again.

—I put my hands over my face.

'Take your fucking hands away from your face. Finger her g-spot to make her spray all over you.'

—She's too high up

—I have to sit up

You may sit up. Hungry for her gushing.

Shameless

—I slide my finger inside her.

—Readjust my pelvis to ensure you are still able to fuck me.

Fuck her. Hard.

—I'm out of practice so it takes me a while to find just the right spot.

—Another finger. Three.

Her moans tell you the place.

—I have her

—I look at you

Eyes full of mindfucked lust

You are so fucking mine.

—Thoroughly.

Keep looking at me, whore.

—I come from the eye contact

Good.

—a small, delicious shudder

—my fingers still in her pussy
Keep your eyes locked on mine
yes
She starts to clench
Shudder
—She spasms around my fingers.
'Make her cum on your face,' I say, calmly.
—I pull out my fingers and pull her pussy closer to my face.
—Three rough strokes with my tongue on her clit and she cums
—streams
Such a skilled slut.
She screams.
Splashing you.
—Are we done with her now?
—Or will you make me watch while you fuck her?
She's only there to make you angry.
You serve her too. And now you've been gushed.
—Then make her caress you while you fuck me so hard I cry.
—I don't tell you any of this, but you know
—The question is
—will you choose to please me
—or torment me
—or both
Torment.
'Get dressed and sit on that chair,' I tell her
She watches as I pull you to your knees.
Shove your face into my balls to lick them, clean them.
—Your cock, so wet, so hard, slides out of me.
Your face wet and musky from her juice.
—I belong between your legs, I know this.
Yes. You do.
—But that she is watching, it burns me

—humiliates me
—as you intended
You're going to stay there. Humiliated.
—I cannot hide my hunger
Until I'm ready to add my cum to hers.
—My desire . . .
Fuck. Call my phone. Now.

I stare at the screen for a minute. Again? Now?

Do as you're fucking told.

I run down the stairs. Where the fuck did I put it? Kitchen. Stove? I turn it on as I run up the stairs, start dialling the number before I'm back in the bedroom with laptop and phone. And I come, again, intensely, the second I hear his voice. I don't remember what he asks of me, what he tells me. I whisper things, and cum on his command, again. And again. His voice throaty, urgent, mad. I remember this: thrusting my hand, my fingers, into my throat, so he can hear me gag. And that's when I hear him cum. Where? In his office? At home in his bathroom? Jeezus.

'Oh, fuck,' he says when he's come. 'Oh, fuck, my whore. Thank you.' Clicks off.

Cum-smeared fingers shaking, I turn off the telephone. Stare at the ceiling. Oh, fuck. Oh, fuck.

My laptop. He's typing.

Are you all right, lover?
—Shaking.
Intense. Unplanned. And I was just planning to share a reality update with you today.
—What's up?
Holidays, at cottage with the in-laws, from tomorrow on. Through Christmas, maybe until New Year's. No

Internet, unreliable phone service. And limited privacy.
—Radio silence, then?
Probably. I don't know. But likely. Did not want to leave you worried. Neglected.
—You are kind to your whore.
Always.
—I will miss you.
Just a blink compared to past absences.
—Yes. But. You are a potent addiction.
As are you.
—Well. Anticipation and delay have many advantages.
Plenty of time to anticipate
—I shall call it a fast. It will make me feel virtuous.
I like the idea of a virtuous whore.
All the better to corrupt.
—Valmont. *Dangerous Liaisons.*
Always did love that film
—For all the wrong reasons.
Story of my life.

I feel calmer. Grounded? No, not grounded. Relieved, released. I will miss him, yes. But. It will be easier to get through Christmas if I'm not cyberfucking Matt. It will also be easier to hate my father. I let the thought sit there. Face it head-on. Wow.

It's still there.

I hear the door. Children.

—I have about ninety seconds before I am claimed by reality.
—But. Reality, she is a cruel mistress.
In reality, I am a cruel master. And this was a most . . . climactic goodbye. Was it not?
—Oh yes. But now go. Pack. Fly.
Enjoy your downtime, my lover. My whore.

257

—You too. Anticipation. Restraint. Virtue. And all that.
Indeed. Dream of me.
xx
—xx

I wrap a few presents. Make supper. Ignore three calls and five texts from my dad. More from my mom.

I smile when Marie, several hours later, texts me, 'I love you!'

But I cry into Alex's shoulder without explanation before supper. He thinks it's because of my dad. And it might be.

I am not already missing Matt. I. Am. Not.

Day 20 – Rage

'Oh, fucking hell.'

I'm on my knees in front of the washing machine, discovering that Alex has 'helped' me with the laundry. He put my frilly, slutty and lacy things in the dryer (goddammit) and tossed in the load of clothes I had waiting in the queue . . . and added his workout clothes to it. I take out the mass of intertwined lingerie, wires poking, laces entangled, and bang my head against the dryer.

I resist the urge to yell, 'Fucking hell, what have you done!' I love him. He let me sleep in, he kissed the tears off my cheeks, he didn't ask questions, he said no wrong things. He let me hate and miss and suffer without intruding and I love him.

I transfer the wet laundry into the dryer, pulling out those of my things that need to be line-dried. I settle my first flash of anger, and remind myself, as always, how disgustingly lucky I am that these are the big rubs in my marriage. JP fakes oral, wants his wife to get a boob job and puts her down every chance he gets. Matt spends his last morning before his Christmas family vacation cyberfucking me. Fuck. Don't go there. My father . . . don't go there either. Alex. Alex's big transgression? Doing the laundry wrong. In the grand scheme of things – nothing.

I. Love. Him.

I'll complain to him, of course. I'll say, 'Beloved, you just ruined $1200 of my lingerie.' And he will make Bambi eyes

259

at me and say, 'I was just trying to help!' or 'You have $1200 of lingerie?' And then he'll pout, and not do any laundry at all for the next six months.

I'll do it like this: 'Thanks for tossing in the laundry, babe. Next time, though, remember my lingerie never goes in the dryer. That wrecks it. And next time you want to wash your workout gear, just toss it in ahead of my stuff, OK? I don't like to mix the loads.'

And he'll pout and get defensive and not do any laundry at all for the next six months.

I grab the bag of ruined frilly, slutty and lacy things and slowly walk up the stairs.

First-world whine. Not a big deal. Blah-blah-blah.

'Jane!' Alex is yelling. 'Jaaaaaane! Where are you?' Fucking hell. In the basement! Doing laundry! Crying over my ruined bras! Reminding myself how much I love you!

Ground yourself, woman. Now.

'I'm here.' I finish climbing the stairs. 'What's wrong?'

Because Alex doesn't normally yell.

Oh, fuck.

He's standing in front of my laptop, pointing at it.

I experience another moment of acute anger at the evil bitch of a universe, chastise myself for my immense stupidity at leaving – what? Facebook? My email? Oh-my-fucking-God, it was Photo Booth, he saw the photos – before I notice that he's pointing at the Skype screen.

I go limp with relief.

Absolutely limp. But my armpits and palms are moist.

'It popped up,' he says. 'I was just walking by, it popped up. I wasn't messing around on your laptop.'

He sounds a little defensive, and rightly so, because it always bugs me when he touches my laptop – and not just since I have crime to hide.

'You don't need to apologise,' I say. Then look at the laundry. 'Babe, you put my lingerie . . .'

'Fuck your lingerie!' Alex snaps. 'Jane – read this. Just read this.'

I come closer. Lean in.

'Dear Alex, and Jane.' I take note of the comma. Classy.

'Your father asked me to tell you this, as he does not "know how" to do it himself. We have split up. I am moving out. My new contact information is claire2012@gmail.com . . . Jane, please email with your personal email and cell number, I do not have that in my contacts. Thank you, Claire.'

'Oh, beloved,' I say. I drop the laundry bag. Wrap my arms around him. 'Oh, Alex, I'm so sorry.'

And thank you, Claire, for not including a 'Jane will understand' or 'Thank you, Jane' in the message.

'Why are you sorry?' Alex accepts the embrace, but stays stiff. 'Are you sorry that my father is a horrible, horrible human being who can't make his third marriage work? Are you sorry that I am half him, and so likely to dump you for a woman Cassandra's age at some point? And then dump her for, I don't know, the fucking school crossing guard's younger sister?'

'I'm sorry you're upset,' I say cautiously. How did he do this for me, when my anger at my dad flared? He did all the right things. How did he know? How come I do not know how to do this for him?

Would it help if I tell him I'm pretty sure it was Claire who did the leaving, not his father?

'I hate him,' he's saying. 'I fucking hate him! You know, I get that he and my mom, I get that they were the worst thing ever. That the best thing for me and Jen was that they got divorced, and we got to spend a good chunk of our childhood away from him, from them together. I get that – they didn't work. I didn't get it then. Well, you know.' I know. God, that I know. 'And Jeanette . . . whatever. I was unfair. Fine. OK. I don't know. I hate him.' He slams my laptop lid down. Hard. 'I fucking hate him.'

I'm still behind him, arms on his chest. What do I do? Am

I supposed to make him talk? I don't really want to; I don't want to scratch at the scabs. And it's not about Claire and his father. Is it? It's about Alex and his father. Just as my refusal to answer the texts from my mom isn't about my mom and my dad, but my mom and me. And the pain and darkness in my belly – not about what my father did to my mom. Or why.

Why is life so fucking complicated?

Cassandra runs down the stairs.

'What happened?' she asks.

'Claire left Grandpa,' I say, and Alex actually hears me, and looks at me, eyes wide. 'Cass, I need you to keep Annie and the others out of the trouble for a bit, OK? Daddy and I have to talk.'

My too-old-for-ten Cassandra nods wisely and runs back upstairs.

'I don't want to talk,' Alex says sullenly. He sits down on the couch.

'I know.' I kneel down beside him. Put my head against his thigh. 'I want you to go downstairs. To the gym. Lift some heavy stuff. I'll spot you.'

'I don't want to,' he says. Still sullen, like a little boy.

'I know,' I say. 'Don't bother changing. Just go.' I get up. Pull him up. Push him towards the stairs, and follow.

I watch him do a few deadlifts. Pull-ups. When he sits down to do bicep curls, I kneel down at his feet again. Loosen the drawstring of his pyjama pants.

'Jesus, Jane,' he says.

'It doesn't solve anything, I know,' I say. 'But, you know. It feels good.'

'God.' The dumbbell clangs to the floor. His hands in my hair. I lick at the head of his cock methodically. Dispassionately.

Professional. Unenthusiastic.
—Shut up and leave. Now. This is not about you.
It's always about me.

262

I'm not full of lust or desire. Or even anger or frustration. I am empty. I am not here. I'm not sure he's there either. My tongue on his cock, my lips around his shaft, my hands on his balls. I count as I engulf him – a seven-slow, three-fast pattern. Just because.

He pulls me up off his cock, a rarity but hardly a surprise, as I'm probably giving him the worst blowjob of his life. His lips on mine. Teeth. Pain. And then he turns me around and bends me over the bench.

I come, instantly, quietly, but he does not know.

He bends his body over mine.

'I'm so angry,' he whispers in my ear.

'I know,' I whisper back. 'It's OK.' I'm not sure what I am giving him permission for. I simply am.

He stays folded over me, very still, for what seems like for ever. And then, awkwardly, inelegantly, without preamble or preparation, thrusts into my ass.

Mindful of the children upstairs, I grind my teeth together and scream only into my throat.

Alex does not like anal sex. How many times over our years together have we done this? Twice? Never for long, never successfully. He is not good at it, he is not skilled and at this moment he is inconsiderate, and I do not enjoy this. At all. My body is tense and I fucking hurt.

But it's not about me right now.

I close my eyes, and I think about what I did on this workout bench a few days earlier, when my parents were still 'happily' married and Alex had no new reason to despise his father. My thoughts race. Searching for distraction, for sensation. Something to hold on to, to focus on.

The memory comes.

My body relaxes.

I remember – the first time Matt did this to me. And how John facilitated it. I still don't know: was he wilfully blind, completely trusting or just . . . complicit? Was I a horrid, cheating skank of a girlfriend, or did he know what I was doing and either chose to ignore it or was turned on by it, the way Matt still gets off on watching his women get fucked by other men?

I was too young and inexperienced to figure it out.

But whatever it was, I took advantage of it. Too often.

This is me, on the telephone. Matt's phone, Matt's arms around my waist, one snaking up, the other down.

'. . . so I thought I'd just crash at Matt's,' I'm saying. It's 2 a.m. and I woke John up. He's groggy. Why wasn't he out with us? I can't remember. He often wasn't. Exams, work, not in the mood. 'Neither Chris nor Patrick can drive. We've all had too much to drink. They're all crashing there too. One of them will drive me home in the morning. Or I'll catch the bus when transit gets going again.'

This is the game I'm playing, and this much I know: John can offer to come pick me up, and if he does, I will go home.

In fact:

'Or do you want to come pick me up?' I ask. 'I'm sorry, I know I already woke you . . .'

'You don't mind staying at Matt's?' he asks. He wants to get back to sleep.

'I've got dibs on the good couch,' I say.

'OK, hun,' he says. I fucking hate it when he calls me hun. 'Thanks for calling. I'll see you in the morning.'

And twenty minutes later Patrick's on the good couch, and Chris is on the floor with pillows, and Tim's in his room with his girlfriend. And I'm naked in Matt's bed.

'I love that you have permission to be here,' he whispers, his tongue in my ear, in my mouth, working its way lower. And he flips me over, quickly, aggressively, and I feel the tip of his cock press against my anus and I jerk away.

'No,' I say, and pull away. The weight of his body drops on me. Pins me.

'I want to,' he says.

'No.'

He rolls off me, flips me back onto my back. And his face disappears between my legs.

Of all my lovers, past and future, no one does this better. I wish I could teach John to do this (later, I will occasionally wish Matt could have given Alex pussy-licking lessons too). And I don't know what it is – the combination of tongue and fingers, lips and knowing just when to nip and when to thrust and when to caress, or perhaps just the incredible level of enthusiasm involved . . . and I stop thinking and I come, and come, and come . . .

I'm still coming when I realise I'm back on my belly, and Matt is smearing pussy juice into my asshole, his fingers probing me.

'Matt,' I say.

'Please me,' he says. Cajoles. His voice is soft, gentle, not insistent. His finger's gentle.

'It will hurt, and I'm scared,' I say. Echoing words I exchanged with John a few months ago. And it was over. The end. And he never asked again.

Matt's other hand caresses my clit, and an orgasm that I thought was finished gently restarts. I moan.

'You know it pleases you to please me,' he whispers.

'It will hurt,' I say.

'Yes,' he says. 'I'll need both hands to start. But then I will put one in your mouth. And you will bite. As hard as you need to. And scream.'

'The guys . . .' I say. I feel the head of his cock pressing against me.

'They all know I'm fucking you in here,' he says. And he's in and I let out a cry and his hand clamps down on my mouth and then slides, sideways into it. I bite down, hard, and he cries out too. And for a moment, we're still and silent.

'Can I move?' he asks. 'Are you ready?'

'No,' I say. 'Scared. It hurts. Tense.'

'Relax, my lover,' he says. And moves once. Shifts his body weight a bit, and repositions his hand in my mouth. 'Bite. Scream. Think —' he thrusts harder and groans '— how much it pleases you to please me.'

'Presump-tuous,' I groan. My teeth graze his hand. I close my eyes. I'm an athlete, I can make my body relax on command. Right?

'Think of John effectively giving me permission to fuck you,' he whispers. '"Sure, you can stay at Matt's after you've been out drinking all night with him and his friends. What could possibly happen?"'

'That's your turn-on,' I whisper.

'And yours,' he retorts. Thrusts. I bite down on his hand, hard, and listen for his cry. It does not come.

'Think of that time I mouth-fucked you in the gondola,' he says. 'Do you remember?'

'Yes.' There are tears in my eyes. He takes his hand away from my mouth. Slides it under my body. Onto my pussy, my clit. Oh, Jesus.

'In such a hurry to get to the hill, he didn't wait for you to get your rentals,' Matt says. 'Stupid bastard. But I did. Do you remember how quickly I shut that door so no one else would get in?'

'Yes.'

'And how quickly my snow pants were unzipped?'

'Oh, God.'

'Do you remember what I said?'

'No.'

'Liar. What did I say?'

'Oh, God. "Please me."'

'Mmmmm. Yes. And you did. Oh, you did.'

He's thrusting in and out of me now, rhythmically. Hard. There's still pain. Some pain. But the hand on my clit doesn't stop moving so there is pleasure too.

'Better?' he asks.

'Yes,' I whisper.

'Do you like it?' he asks.

'No.'

'Tell me what you like,' he says.

'No.'

'Tell me,' he says. The strokes, and the force of his hand below, increase.

'No. Fuck off.' I grit my teeth, close my eyes. Do not think of the gondola. The roof. His bed. This moment. His cock. My weakness.

'Tell me how much you like pleasing me.' Insistent.

'I hate you.'

'Oh, fuck, yes.' And that's how he comes. And I come, my lips bleeding.

A few minutes later, he slides out of me, rolls me onto my side and eats me out for fucking hours. We sleep for a bit. Fuck again in the morning. I don't get back home until late afternoon. I can barely sit down for the next two days.

'Jane?' Alex's face is pressed against my back. 'I'm so sorry, my love. I'm so sorry. Are you all right?'

'I'm fine,' I say. 'Are you still angry?'

'So fucking very,' he says. Sweat or tears on my back. 'Jane?'

'Yes?'

'I am not and never will be my father.'

'I know. Beloved, I know.'

We stay in the basement, draped over the workout equipment for another hour, until Cassandra knocks on the door and asks, plaintively, how much longer she needs to take care of the 'children'.

'Coming,' I say, getting up.

'By the way, Daddy,' she says. 'Your phone was in the bathroom again, by the sink. You have new messages.' She hands him the phone as I walk out. Retrieve the bag of ruined lingerie from the living room, take it to the bedroom to see what I can salvage.

'Jane.' Alex is standing in the doorway.

'Yes?' I look up.

'I was just reading news stuff and email,' he says. I turn more fully, stare at him, uncomprehending. 'In the bathroom. On the phone. Just reading.'

I stare at him a little longer. Still confused.

'OK,' I say. 'Why are you telling me?'

He stares at me. 'Because,' he says. 'You know.'

I don't. And then, suddenly, I do.

Fucking men.

'Alex,' I say. 'I would never check the messages on your phone. Or have suspicious thoughts about what you were doing in the bathroom.'

'Sometimes I wish you would,' Alex says. Oddly, wistfully. He sits beside me on the bed. I rest my head on his shoulder.

'Do you want me to pretend to be a jealous wife?' I ask.

'I don't have to pretend to be a jealous husband,' he says.

His words hang between us, suddenly heavy and ominous. I take my head off his shoulder. Get up. Mildly angry.

'That,' I say, 'is really not my problem.'

And I leave. Not seething. But not happy.

It's a miserable, miserable day, made more miserable by our – at first painfully silent – car ride to Okotoks to see Alex's mom, because he decides he needs to tell her, right now, today, in person. I don't argue. Of course. While we're in the car, there are six telephone calls – no voicemails – from my dad, three texts from my mom ('Are you OK?' 'I'm worried about you!!' 'Remember, Jane, I love you very much xoxo') and another handful of texts from Marie. Excited. Erotic. Borderline obscene. I can tell at a glance. I look at them, but don't really read.

'Who the fuck is texting you?' Alex snaps as my phone buzzes yet again. I'm driving. 'Again?'

'My father, my mother, Marie,' I snap back. 'Take your fucking pick.' We glare at each other. My phone's between us, on the front seat. I grope for it blindly. Don't hand it to him: chuck it. Now, seething. 'Check. Read. Go nuts.'

I keep my eyes on the road. But in the periphery of my vision, I see him, phone in hand, not looking at the screen.

'I'm just going to turn it off, OK?' he says finally. 'I'm sorry, Jane. I'm . . . I'm not myself.'

'I know,' I say. 'I'm sorry too. Hard day.'

Telling Alex's mother that her ex-husband left his third wife – not the highlight of the day, perhaps, but certainly not its most difficult task. If anything, she's mildly amused. If that. If I didn't think that she was putting on a game face for Alex's sake, I would think she was uninterested.

Her reaction first confuses her son, then, I think, soothes him. And I am grateful. I hold her tighter and kiss her with more affection than usual when we leave.

On the drive back, Alex puts his hand on my knee. Traces his fingertips up my thigh. Takes my hand off the steering wheel at one point and kisses my fingers. My wrist. I smile at him, half-turned.

'Gross!' Henry shouts from the back seat.

'Shut up!' Cassandra says. 'It's romantic.'

It's not. Not really. But it's ritual and it's comforting. It's a return to us, a reaffirmation of everything we are, of what really matters.

By the time the kids are in bed, I'm drifting back towards peace and comfort. Fuck his dad. My dad. We're fine. We're just fine.

And then, as he slides into bed beside me, he ruins it.

Hands me his phone.

'What?' I ask.

'My phone,' he says. 'I un-passworded it. If I leave it lying around anywhere – you are free to look at it. At anything.'

I refuse to take it.

I do not want this. Not one little bit.

'Alex,' I say. Patiently? Or voice tight? I'm not sure – it echoes, resonates in my ears like it belongs to a stranger. 'You are a lawyer. Clients email and text you confidential information all the time. You don't fucking un-password-protect your phone. Are you insane?'

'No!' he says. He's still holding it out towards me. 'I just want you to know . . . I have nothing to hide.'

'My love,' I say. With tenderness, I hope, and not exasperation. 'Why are you doing this?'

He looks at his feet. For a long time.

'That's what they say you should do,' he says finally. 'To show you have no secrets. Give your spouse access to everything.'

I think of my password-protected laptop. Phone. Facebook and Gmail accounts. My moment of fear when I found him looking at my laptop this morning. My anger in the car earlier. The lack of Internet in the Laurentians, and thus the emptiness of what he might have perceived as my grand gesture of disclosure when I tossed my phone at him.

My complete lack of incentive for reciprocating his self-disclosure.

'Oh, my Alex.' I embrace him. Still don't take the phone. 'Why do you do this to yourself?'

He folds into me. The phone falls from his hand onto the bed.

'I don't want to be my father,' he whispers. I hold him for a long, long time.

'You never will be,' I whisper back. 'And I will never leave you. Or let you leave me. So. Just . . . love me, OK? You don't need to strip naked for me.'

We fall asleep holding each other, the phone tangled somewhere in the bedsheets between us.

Day 21 – Permission

The kids celebrate the Sunday before Christmas by waking up at 6 a.m. and stampeding *en masse* down the stairs.

'Who needs an alarm clock?' Alex groans. Rolls out of bed. 'Staying in bed?' I pull a pillow over my head in response.

When he's gone, I realise I have tears in my eyes. I don't think about why. Reasons enough. Still. I am not pleased with myself.

When I finally get up, I channel disquiet into breakfast. Eggs. Bacon. Pancakes. And waffles. Cassandra walks into the kitchen as I'm throwing dishes onto the table.

'Holy cow!' she exclaims. 'Who's coming over for breakfast?'

'Lacey,' I say promptly. 'Call her, sweetie, or pop over. Ask her and Clayton and whoever's over there to come.'

I need a hit of Lacey. I need to be enveloped in her arms.

'Probably just Lacey and Clayton,' Cassandra says. 'I don't see Clint's car in the driveway.'

No secrets in our neighbourhood.

Seven minutes later, we're all around the table – the boys and Annie making a ruckus, Cassandra staring at Lacey's earrings and dress with admiration and envy, me forcing food down my throat.

'Eat more.' Lacey heaps more eggs onto my plate. And suddenly I notice there is no diamond ring glittering on her finger.

When she leans over to refill my coffee – hostess always,

271

even in my house – I spot it on a thin chain around her neck. She sees me look, and pops it under her top.

'A story for later,' she mouths. And when the kids leave us to watch a movie, I wait for her to tell me.

But first she insists on doing the dishes. And makes me eat more. Makes another pot of coffee.

I wait.

Alex comes back into the kitchen.

'Remember how I said your neglectful husband was going to have to go out on December twenty-fourth to do Christmas shopping?' he says. 'Well, I'm a day ahead of schedule. Can I disappear for a few hours?'

'With or without kids?' I ask.

'God, without,' he says. 'Please.'

I give him permission. He kisses me. Disappears.

Lacey finishes the dishes and, finally, she sits opposite me at the table. Pours out the coffee.

'I can't put it back on just yet,' she says. And the rage that's been flowing through me intermittently finds a new target. I know exactly what he's done, the bastard. Of course. And it doesn't make it any better that I always thought that this is what he would do: that I never believed he would, finally, marry Lacey. That I was always sure that, after letting her plan and indulge, in the end, he would run. And run in what a spectacular way: creating a situation so untenable for Lacey that she would be the one to walk.

There is a part of me that recognises that my anger at him makes no real sense. What does it matter?

But the part of me that loves Lacey – that loves my mother – is so fucking angry.

So angry I miss the story and hear . . .

'. . . so I finally said, well, I won't make you take back the ring, but I'm not wearing it on my finger until I figure out what I want to do,' Lacey says.

'Oh,' I say. What?

272

Lacey shrugs expressively.

'I know,' she says. 'I know you would tell him to go to hell. Heck, you would have told him to go to hell the first time he made a baby with her.'

'The first time,' I echo. A part of me wants to laugh hysterically. 'I forgave him the first baby' Lacey is effectively saying. 'The second one is a little hard to stomach.'

But is that what she's really saying?

No. Because she is Lacey.

'I did break up with him, the first time,' Lacey says. 'Remember? And how long did that last? Three weeks. Twenty days, actually. I can do without him for about twenty days.'

I wonder what Sofia's 'I'm able to do without him' metric for Clint is. And does she think of Lacey as the 'other' girlfriend, the other 'wife', or does she think of herself as the one on the side? According to Lacey, Sofia has always been more off-than-on than Lacey . . . but she's been around for longer. Clint was with her – or at least tumbling back to her intermittently – when he met Lacey.

And made Clayton with her.

A circumstance that Lacey used to explain her ultimate reaction to the *first* 'Hey, baby, Sofia's having my baby but it's you I really, really love' situation.

'First, I was angry, so angry,' Lacey says. 'Of course. So angry. Not even, you know, because she was pregnant. But because he had been telling me for months – for years – that he wasn't with her any more. Well, clearly he had been with her. And probably repeatedly.'

Yes.

'Which,' she says, reading me, 'also would have made me angry. But, you know. I forgive. A lot.'

'But then—' she shrugs, and no one shrugs quite like Lacey '—I thought . . . I believed . . . I know. We are meant to be together. We have been together for lifetimes. Coming together. Fighting. Ultimately working things out.'

I say nothing.

'I know you think it's all crap,' she says mildly, without rancour. 'But. I believe. And. Well. After we were apart – what happens every time we are apart – I realised I want him in my life. No terms.'

'Well, but now you want him in your life on marriage terms,' I say. The diamond ring has popped out from under her collar and glitters. She reaches for it, twirls it.

'So this time,' she says, 'this time, I knew he was with her sometimes. And with others. Because, you know. That's him. And I have not . . . I have had my fun too, you know.'

I didn't, actually. But I am not surprised.

'But another baby's a little hard to absorb.' She puts into words what I've been thinking. 'Especially while we're planning a wedding.'

I nod. This I do understand. And I also understand this:

'It probably happened *because* you're planning a wedding,' I say.

And Lacey tilts her head.

'What?' she says. She gives my throwaway sentence much too much consideration. 'Say it again,' she demands.

'It probably happened because you're planning a wedding,' I repeat.

'Oh-my-God,' she says. 'Oh-my-God. You are so right. Oh-my-God.' She gets up in a gorgeous, fluid motion. 'Can I leave Clayton here for a while? I've got to go.'

Yes, she does. This I understand too. And she will do this: call Clint. Text Clint. Fuck Clint. Forgive Clint.

If he's still game – marry Clint.

I watch through the window as she crosses my lawn and driveway to get to her front door, and I see her take the ring off her neck and slip it back on to her finger.

Oh, Lacey.

I text Alex the shorthand of what just happened. He texts me back.

- Only Lacey. BTW, are your ears pierced?

—Yes. But I hate earrings. How can you not know that?

The phone vibrates in my hand as I read. It's my father calling. And I am not talking to him. Possibly never ever talking to him again.

Lacey, I know, would forgive him. Perhaps not be angry in the first place. But I am not Lacey.

I would like to be like Lacey, a little bit.

Fuck.

I check the voicemail: six of them, maybe more, from my father.

All variants on the same theme. He's sorry. Can we talk?

I don't want to. I so don't want to. But.

I type, 'I'm home alone with the kids. Come over.'

And there he is, 45 minutes later. Covered by my children, who adore their Gramps beyond all reason. As they hug him, kiss him and wrestle him, he throws me a 'See? I am a really good grandfather. See?' look.

Fuck him.

I leave the living room and go to the kitchen. Start making another pot of coffee.

'Jane.'

He's standing three feet behind me. I feel his presence.

'My sweetheart,' he says.

I don't turn around.

'Jane, I'm so sorry.'

'What for?' I ask. The coffee grinder whirrs. My voice sounds funny. I am not crying.

'What for?' I repeat. Half-turn my face. He looks at me, then backs away to the kitchen table. Sits down.

'For . . . everything,' he says. 'For leaving. For not telling you earlier. I told myself you knew – that your mother had told you. And you . . . I was so happy.' He stops. He doesn't know how to articulate it, but I'm his daughter and I know exactly what he is thinking in this moment: I loved him. I accepted him. I was angry and shaken, but I loved him. I forgave him – or it looked like I forgave him. And it was so easy, so convenient to think that I knew everything and still accepted him unconditionally.

Unconditional acceptance. Big deal.

I leave him sitting at the table looking at my back until the kettle comes to a boil. I pour the water into the cafetière. Then stand there the four long minutes needed for it to be drinkable. Pour coffee into two mugs. Add cream and sugar to his.

Carry them to the table.

Set them down carefully.

Sit down.

Am I going to ask him why?

Yes.

'What happened?' I ask. I'm looking into my coffee mug, not at him. 'What happened to "I was going to have peace in my family at any price?"'

And I know the answer before he speaks it. Because, after all, I've been there, with them. I've seen it.

'There has not been peace in the family for a very, very long time,' he says. 'You know this, Jane. You have asked me . . .' His voice trails off.

I should accept this. Stop here. Hug him. Love him. Let him be my dad. Unconditional acceptance. I can give this to Marie. To Lacey and Clint. Even, sort of, sometimes, to Nicola in her anger and Paul in his stupidity.

I need to give this to my father.

But. Not quite yet.

'Why now?' I ask. 'Why . . . after forty-three years? Just before Christmas? Why now?'

And when he tells me, haltingly, slowly, badly – I get up and walk out of the kitchen. Into the living room. Slide between the children on the couch – 'What are you guys watching now?' '*Elf*, again!' – pull them around me and close my eyes.

276

'Jane . . .' He stands in the doorway.

'You have to leave now,' I say.

'Jane, my sweetheart,' he pleads.

'Leave my house,' I say. 'Now.'

The kids start to turn their heads away from the movie; I see Cassandra's brow furrow.

'Dad,' I say. 'You know what I need right now. Please go.'

And he's gone.

I should call Alex. Text Marie.

I sit on the couch surrounded by my children and struggle to understand my father as Will Ferrell's overgrown *faux*-elf character tries to make his father love him.

I should definitely not call my mother.

So I text her.

—He told me.

The phone rings two minutes later, and it's her, and I realise I asked for this. Perhaps I even want it. So I answer it, and, cradling it between my ear and neck, retreat back into the kitchen. Two mugs of untouched coffee still on the table.

'Jane, my love,' my mother says. And she – the wife being left, the one who is suffering, becomes the comforter, automatically, because she is the mother, my mother. She says – what does she say? That she will be fine. That he loves me and the kids, so much. And – and here I laugh, I actually laugh – that 'men do these things.'

'Are you angry?' I ask her.

'So fucking angry,' she says. It's the first time I've heard my mother swear. 'So fucking angry, Jane. But I will be fine. And you will forgive him.'

'Will you?' I ask her.

'Probably not,' she says. And I laugh, hysterically.

I spend the rest of the afternoon practising how I'm going to tell the story to Alex. I might say this: 'Hey, guess what?

Not only did my father leave my mother after forty-three years of marriage, he left her for someone else. Just like your jackass of a father. Do you still like him?'

Or I might say this: 'But wait, it gets better. He wasn't actually having an affair, oh, no, not my Puritan, perfect, honest, upright father. No, that would be . . . ungentlemanlike. Uncouth. He's met someone he *likes*. Someone he would like to *get to know better*. Someone he'd like to ask out for a coffee, dinner. But he can't because he's fucking married to my mother so he had to leave her! He left my mother so he could ask someone else out for a fucking coffee!'

Or this: 'My father left his marriage of forty-three years so he wouldn't feel guilty about maybe-sort-of flirting with a sixty-year-old widow.'

Or, perhaps, this: 'My father has totally lost his mind.'

Or . . .

I wonder if Alex will defend him. He loves my dad, always has. What will he say? Will he say, 'Surely, Jane, you can understand how your father couldn't live a lie?' He will say, 'Forty-three years is a long time, Jane.'

If he says, 'Surely, Jane, after forty-three years, he deserves a chance at a little bit of happiness in his retirement years,' I will scream.

If he says, 'But he had to be honest, Jane. Can't you understand that?' I will leave.

As I pound chicken breasts with a metal meat mallet into barely edible mush, I try to articulate to myself why I'm so angry.

I was angry when I thought my mother left. Because 43 years is a long, long time and walking out on that . . . fuck. Why? Why would you do that?

I was angry when I learned he left. Because 43 years is a long, long time, and he put up with everything in those 43 years. Everything.

I am infuriated right now, because he left not because he

278

was done – his cup of patience runneth over – not even because he found something else . . . but because he wanted to be *free* to pursue the opportunity to find something else. He left 43 years for . . . what?

A 'maybe' coffee date.

Not a mad, passionate love affair. Not something better than my mother. Just . . . potential. A maybe.

A fucking maybe. An opportunity.

I hope the little widow – I picture her as five foot zero, with a white beehive hairdo – turns him down flat.

Or strings him along for a couple of months, and then breaks his heart.

I hope he dies alone, miserable, celibate and full of regret.

I hope he goes crawling back to my mother . . . and that she kicks him in the teeth.

So angry.

So so angry.

The anger stays with me the rest of the day as I move through all the quotidian tasks, cleaning the kitchen, feeding the children, listening to Alex's account of the insanity that was the mall on the Sunday before Christmas.

The children ask to stay up all night, and I have no energy to fight them. And what does it matter, it's Sunday, it's almost Christmas. La-di-dah. Bath, tooth-brushing and into their rooms, with books and gaming devices. The boys ask to borrow my laptop so they can watch *Elf* again in bed. I give it to them. Annie crawls into bed between them. Cassandra goes to her own bed with *Anne of the Island*.

'Do you want to watch a movie as well?' Alex asks. 'Come. On the couch. With me.'

I don't. I so don't.

But I go.

He tries to make a choice that pleases me. *Love Actually*. 'It's got Colin Firth and Alan Rickman in it,' he says. 'You'll love it.'

I hate it.

'Alex?' As Emma Thompson's character throws a fit over the Alan Rickman character's lame attempt at an affair, I hit the pause button on the remote. 'Alex? I need you to promise me something.'

'Anything. The moon,' he mutters, and reaches over and strokes my arm, then my breast, gently. 'So long as it doesn't involve me ever having to go to a mall in December again.'

'Promise me that no matter what happens, our children have one set of parents. For ever,' I say.

'I promised you that on our wedding day, remember?' he says. Calm. Eyes on the screen, not on me. 'The big discussion about how I wanted to leave out "till death do us part", and you insisted that if you were going to marry me, it was for ever and ever, and not until I decided – or you decided – you wanted something else? Remember? To you I pledge my troth and all that?'

'I remember.' I smile at the memory. Saying 'to you I pledge my troth' was funny and we both laughed as we said it. So did our friends. I have a sudden, too sharp, image of Matt's face. Laughing. I remember when he pledged eternal faithfulness to Joy, I had to look down at my shoes. And bite my lips. 'What I mean, though – that you promise me we stay married no matter what. No matter what I do, what you do – this marriage, this family is for ever.'

'What are you talking about, Jane?' He's looking at me now. Not happy. There's a crease in his forehead.

'Stupid shit,' I say. Tears circle in my eyes. 'Do you want me to stop?'

He looks at me. He wants me to stop. I close my eyes. And my mouth.

'No,' he says, suddenly. 'Talk to me, Jane. Tell me.'

Those two words, in his mouth, in his voice. I shudder. But I talk.

I tell him why my father left my mother.

I tell him why Nicola left Paul – or Paul Nicola, depending

280

on how you assign blame, interpret motivation. How that marriage ended.

I tell him how I think Marie and JP's marriage might end. Because she's unsure, restless.

I tell him how much Lacey is capable of forgiving.

I go back to talking about my parents. Because that's the one that's really ripping me.

'Forty-three years of ups-and-downs, sure, of building and rebuilding, of life – all of a sudden, over, because my father didn't even think it honourable to think lusty thoughts about some sixty-year-old widow unless he left my mother. Who he hasn't even . . . and may never . . . Where the fuck is the sense in that?' I ask.

'What are you saying?' Alex asks.

'That if he had just . . . got it out of his system, gone on a few dates – seen her wrinkles close up a few times, been on the wrong end of *her* nagging – that maybe my parents wouldn't be doing this. He wouldn't have left. They'd be celebrating their fiftieth a few years from now.'

Alex shakes his head. He doesn't believe me, I can tell. But I want to finish the thought, the argument. 'And Nicola. Look at Nicola and Paul, two people who will now be miserable and fighting for the rest of their lives over assets and parenting plans and who gets which holidays and all that shit. And why? Because she couldn't ride it out. He didn't even want to leave, right? He just wanted to . . .'

'Well, then he shouldn't have fucked the intern,' Alex says reasonably. 'Sometimes, things are just that black and white, Jane. This thing is.'

'It's not,' I argue. 'Because people want things – get restless – frustrated – bored – whatever. Those are all normal emotions. And monogamy's hard. And sometimes boring. And often frustrating. And – throwing away fifteen years, forty years, whatever, because of . . . well. I won't do it. And you don't get to either.'

'Jane? I'm no expert on family law, but I think you've just sanctioned any future affairs I may have,' Alex says. 'But, love . . . I said nothing to even suggest I sanction any affair you might have. Do you understand?'

Oh, Alex. Yes. I understand. The curse of my fucking life, that I understand completely and so self-deception is denied me.

I laugh.

He sidles closer, kisses me on the forehead. 'But, Jane . . . all those marriages? They were all fucked up. Nicola and Paul were a disaster. You know that. JP's a jackass. Your parents – your parents have been fighting for years. Decades. And Clint and Lacey – Jesus-fucking-Christ. Who wants that? And us – Jane, we're great together. We're nothing like any of them.'

I shrug. Nod.

'I know,' I say. 'But. You know. I still want you to promise me.'

He says nothing.

I unpause the movie.

Emma Thompson continues to freak out at Alan Rickman. And he takes it.

Finally:

'Jane?' I turn my head. Meet his eyes. 'I want you. For ever.'

I smile. I kiss him on his still creased forehead.

'I love you, father-of-my-children and husband-till-death-do-us-part,' I say.

We watch the rest of the movie in silence.

When we go upstairs, the kids are all asleep, even Cassandra, her book on the bed. We turn out the lights. Go to bed.

Still silent. It takes Alex a long time to get to sleep. And I lie beside him. Frustrated, angry, aching, wanting to wail on my dad, my mom. Everyone.

And wanting to fuck Matt.

And not wanting or caring for permission to do so.

Day 22 – Striptease

The children sleep in, and so do we, which means we're in a mad rush to get out to Okotoks for Christmas Eve brunch with Alex's mom. Alex's sister lives in Texas, and they 'share' their mother for Christmas: one year in Calgary, one year in Houston. This year, it's Houston. But we always get together on Christmas Eve, even on Calgary years. My mother won't let go of Christmas Day at her house, ever. On Houston years, after brunch, we drive Nana into town, to the airport.

Alex is driving like a maniac.

'Baby, we're never going to get there if we're dead,' I choke out at one point as he charges across three lanes of traffic on Deerfoot.

'I know,' he says. 'It's just – you know.'

I know. He doesn't want to be late. Saturday's game face notwithstanding, he thinks it might be a tough Christmas for her. He's a good son. Father. Husband.

His phone rings. And then rings again. And again.

'Jesus,' he says. Digs it out of his pocket.

'No fucking way,' I say. Take it out of his hand, as it rings again. 'You are not talking on Deerfoot. Not in this mood.'

I click it open.

'Oh, Alex, thank God I got you,' comes the voice, and I know it's Susan-Shelley-Melanie. 'I just got the papers back from . . .'

'It's Jane, Alex's wife, here, Susan,' I say. 'He can't talk right

283

now. Driving. Is it appropriate for me to take a message, or is it confidential and do you want to text him or leave a voicemail so he can get back to you in about thirty minutes?'

I don't look at Alex's face but I see his knuckles tighten a little on the steering wheel.

There is no sound on the other end.

'Susan? Or was it Shelley?' I ask. I fucking know it's Melanie. 'Are you there? Is this a real emergency that justifies interrupting his Christmas Eve with his family, or can it wait until, you know, Boxing Day?'

Her voice, when it finally comes, is frosty, stiff.

'It may be Christmas Eve, but New York is still working,' she says. 'I'm still working. As his senior associate on a critical file, it's my . . . my . . . responsibility to keep Alex in the loop on all the . . .'

'Fine,' I say. I'm not sure why I'm smiling. I guess I'm small and petty; I goaded her and I'm enjoying the reaction. 'It's a real emergency. He will call you back as soon as he stops driving. Have a Merry Christmas. Susan.'

I turn off the phone. Alex changes lanes for no reason at all.

'Her name's Melanie,' he says finally.

'I know,' I say. Think for a minute. 'That was my impersonation of a somewhat possessive, bitchy wife. Ticked off to be called by her husband's newest –' I pause, because I'm about to say fuck buddy, and I have four children in the back seat '– office wife on Christmas Eve.'

'I rather liked it,' he says. Reaches for my hand.

I wonder how he would have reacted if I had said fuck buddy.

I read the texts from Marie while the kids start building their Christmas Lego from Nana, and can't decide whether to be pleased or appalled. The thing – affair – sexting – with Craig is going . . . well. He's attentive. Sensual. Romantic. Oh, wait.

284

More than sexting – he's a quick mover, and I think I approve. They're meeting for coffee. Oh, fuck, already met for coffee: 'JP's taking the kids Christmas shopping for me, and I'm meeting him for coffee. OMG, skank, skank,' gloats an early text.

And later: 'FAN-TAS-TIC. I will tell you about it tonight.'

Tonight?

And I remember that, weeks ago, we had both agreed to do a Mom's Night In type of thing on Christmas Eve at Nicola's house. Her kids would be with Paul. She was planning to be hysterical and suicidal. Colleen promised we would all be loving and supportive.

I text Marie, 'You're planning to go?'

Marie: 'Sure. I think it's OK, now that I'm not, you know, doing anything with Paul.'

Sure.

And she adds: 'Carpool? In your wheels? I want to drink.'

Fuck. I so don't want to go.

'Fuck,' I say out loud, and Alex and his mother both fall silent – they're talking, not about Alex's father and Claire, of course not, they're talking about books, movies and global weather trends – and look at me. 'I'm sorry,' I apologise. 'But fuck. Sorry,' I apologise again. 'Baby –' I turn to Alex '– Marie's reminded me. I had promised to go to this Mom's Night In party at Nicola's. On Christmas Eve. Why did I do that?'

'Because you're a good friend,' Alex says. Leaves his mother's side. Comes and sits on the arm of the chair I'm in. Pulls me close to him. 'You told me when you planned it, I remember. First Christmas Eve without her kids. Super-stressed. It's a good idea, Jane. Go.'

I tilt my head to look at him.

'Go,' he says. 'You've been pretty much single-parenting all this month. How many nights, days away from the kids have you had? Go. We've had our big Christmas Eve celebration this morning. It's fine. We'll do movie night – that's all we'd do if you stayed home, right? Or maybe I'll let them play

Minecraft all night. Do all the things Mom doesn't let them do.' He grins. 'Go.'

'I don't want to,' I say. But I mean it a little less. Press my face against his belly. Smell him. Love him.

Alex's mother smiles at us. Then gets up and disappears into the kitchen.

'Go,' Alex says again. 'And come back . . .' He pauses. Holds me a little tighter. 'Come back lusty,' he whispers. 'They'll all be asleep. I'll be waiting.'

I press against him harder. Fuck. I love him. I love him so very, very much.

I also love Marie, I remind myself sternly as I pick her up, and see, from the way she opens the car door, that she has things to tell me, and wants to burden me with them all before we get to Nicola's.

I love her.

I will listen.

'Tell me,' I say as soon as she closes the car door.

'Alex OK with you skipping out on Christmas Eve?' she says instead. I nod. 'JP's a bit grumpy,' she says. 'I shouldn't have done the coffee *and* the evening out. He doesn't usually take the kids for this long.'

'It's past eight – aren't they effectively in pyjamas, and probably watching TV?' I ask. 'Not exactly a hardship.'

'Yes, well, you know,' Marie says. I know. It's JP and he's a jerk. I brace myself for a recital of his shortcomings as a father, and wonder if Marie will once again tell me that he managed to go through two babies without changing a single diaper, *ever*. Instead: 'He gets a little jealous of me. You know. Possessive.'

This is new.

'Does he?' I say. Marie nods.

'Sometimes, he can be very intuitive,' she says. And while I keep my eyes on the road, I feel my eyebrows retreat into my hairline. She's used a lot of words to describe JP to me over the years. Intuitive? Never.

'I think he can pick up on this thing,' she continues. And now I turn my head and look at her.

She's glowing.

Total post-coital, had-the-fucking-of-my-life glow.

This thought jumps into my head: the look on the face of every girl who's ever walked out of Matt's bedroom – or hand-in-hand with him from a public washroom in a bar.

I quash it.

Look at Marie again.

'The coffee went well?' I ask.

She colours. Smiles. Keeps on smiling.

'So well,' she whispers. 'Oh, so well, Jane. He was . . . he was *amazing*.'

Her lips part, her tongue curls and I flinch. Brace myself for details I don't want to hear.

'He brought me *flowers*,' she says. 'Flowers! And when I said, 'Oh, I can't take these home,' he said I didn't have to – he just wanted to give them to me. For me to enjoy *getting* them.'

Turned on, fuckslave? Shall I bring you flowers?
—No. I don't want flowers.
What do you want? Tell me.
—No.
Tell me. I'm just in your head right now, and no one is listening.
—Your cock in my mouth. Your hands on my shoulders, slamming me against a wall.
Yesss . . .

'Jane? Are you listening?'

I pull my attention back to the moment, to Marie. 'Yes,' I say. 'I'm listening. Did you like that?'

But of course she did. She liked everything. He played her – perfectly, beautifully. Caressed her ego. Said all the right things. Put himself on the line: suggested the time and place for their next meeting. 'Lunch at Charcut,' Marie says. 'You know?' I know. And before she says it, I know what's coming. 'And do you know why Charcut? He said it's because Hotel Le Germain is right on top.'

I should be glad that she's pleased. But suddenly I'm terrified, and appalled at what I've done. And she seems to me so fragile and so vulnerable. And he . . . fuck. He's going to give her everything she wants – everything she thinks she wants – and he's still going to hurt her. Because, well, she's Marie.

'He said, "Just so we have the option,"' she's telling me. '"When the chemistry's there, there's no point in waiting, wooing," he said. "One has to seize opportunity. More, one has to create it," he said.'

I've never seen anyone swoon before, but this is what it must look like. Marie, as she sits in the passenger seat beside me, is swooning.

I push back my fear and terror and try to be happy for her.

'And will you?' I ask. 'Seize the opportunity? Create it?'

Marie looks at me. Glowing. Pre-coital glow, I guess.

'Yes,' she says.

She's still glowing when we arrive at Nicola's.

I still feel bad about how I acted towards Nicola on the day I wouldn't share Jesse, and our hellos are awkward. I expect things to get even more awkward after she opens my Christmas present, which is a gift certificate for twenty private sessions with any trainer at the gym. But Nicola is, again, grimly determined to be happy. She hugs me as if we are bosom friends from a nineteenth-century novel, and kisses my cheeks when she opens the card.

'Oh, Jane,' she says. 'And I just got everyone bath salts.'

'Life is cyclical,' I say, stupidly, but she nods as if I had said something very profound. And then, another hug.

'Thank you so very, very much,' she whispers. 'I'm just so much happier when I see him.' She holds me a little too long, and I want to extricate myself. 'And not just because he's so gorgeous and delicious,' she adds.

I pull away abruptly.

'Exercise helps,' I say, wilfully blind. And navigate my way to the snack table.

We let Colleen bring the food today, and it was a mistake. There's steamed broccoli and kale chips and sprouted-almond hummus.

'I thought we'd eat clean because of the gorge-fest tomorrow,' she says, slightly defensive when she sees me eyeing the table. 'Life's all about balance, isn't it?'

'Is it?' I say. I expect it is possible to eat and enjoy kale chips. But as part of a 'this is my first Christmas alone and my first Christmas Eve without the kids' kinda night for Nicola . . . I would have brought cake. Ice-cream. Chocolate. Nicola comes to the table. 'Mmmm, delicious,' she says, spearing a broccoli. Colleen looks at me in triumph.

There is only one bottle of wine too, mine, but fortunately Marie brought the ingredients for Caesars. And while Colleen abstains on principle, and I limit myself as the designated driver, Nicola and Marie are soon fully lubricated. Sign: Nicola starts whispering to me how hot Jesse's ass is. I shudder.

'Jane! You are such a prude,' she says to me, thrilled with her audacity. And . . . what? For the first time, maybe, since this thing with Paul has come down, aware of her . . . availability? Freedom? She was so caught off-guard by the affair and the resulting 'I want an open marriage!' conversation that this may be the first time she is going there.

Interesting.

Probably, I think, good for her.

But the truly prudish Colleen – four years post-divorce and not just still single, but still so scarred she refuses to even think or talk about pursuing either a relationship or a lover – does not like this. She does not want to talk about Jesse's ass – 'And all the rest of him – and I do mean *all*,' Nicola's saying. She wants to talk about the rat-fuck bastard, Nicola's, and so by extension hers, and pain and suffering. And she'll succeed, because this aspect of Nicola is new and just emerging, and most of her is used to railing and complaining.

And soon, too soon, we are back on well-trod ground.

Tossing back another Caesar, and now teary-eyed from it, Nicola's recounting the beginning of the betrayal. Colleen is filling the role of Greek chorus adequately by herself. Marie is mixing more drinks. And thinking what? I turn to look at her as she takes out her phone, reads something, smiles. Our eyes meet. She sticks out her tongue at me and then winks.

I listen to the play-by-play, 'And he did this, and then I said this, and then I found out this, and then . . .'

Then the mandatory 'That is not polyamory!' rant, because Nicola is now an expert.

'What he is,' Colleen interjects, as she always does, 'is a cheater. A cheater who got caught and latched onto an interesting-sounding excuse.'

Marie chokes on her Caesar.

'Rat-fuck bastard,' she says, and for a terrible moment I'm afraid she's going to burst out laughing. Instead, she takes a bite of a celery stalk. Carefully does not meet my eyes.

How do you feel when you are with these women, lover?
—Mildly morally ambiguous.
Mildly? I'd prefer you to feel an utter slut. Ashamed. Degraded. Pussy throbbing with lust for me while they . . .
—A little bit of that.
Good.
—Pervert.
Two of a kind.

290

This habit of talking with him in my head is not healthy and I should really control it. I focus back on the conversation. Nicola is now verging on weepy. Well done, Colleen.

'And you know, I think I could have forgiven infidelity, I really could have,' Nicola is saying.

'Of course you could have.' Colleen has her arms around her. 'It's the lying . . .'

'Yes!' Nicola shouts. 'It's the lying – lying . . . and then lying about the lying . . . and then by the time he told me the truth, I had no trust that it was the truth . . . and it really wasn't . . .'

'It's not about the affair as much as it is about the lying,' Colleen pronounces, as if she is delivering the Sermon from the Mount. Marie, phone in one hand, drink in the other, flushes, and as Colleen opens her mouth – it looks grotesque, her tongue thrusting out as if she is about to lisp an 's' – I interrupt her.

'Bull-fucking-shit,' I call. 'Bull-fucking-shit,' I repeat. 'Of course it's about the affair. It's not about the lying. If it was about the lying, then you would have said, "Baby, fuck whoever you want, just be honest with me about it in the future." Maybe not embraced polyamory or whatever it is he thinks he's doing, but . . . Anyway. It's not about the lying. It's clearly about the fucking.'

My perfectly sober and rational self remembers that only a few days ago I drove a woman away by telling her, 'It wasn't the affair that broke them up, it was the confession,' and is amused by this self's outburst. But I'm not contradicting myself. If it really was about the lying, then once the lying was confessed, disclosed, the fucking would be forgiven. But how often does that happen?

Nicola and Colleen stare at me. First shocked. Then angry. Colleen sends me a dirty look that says I have violated the code of the sisterhood of outraged, righteous and wronged wives *and* their supportive friends. It's an evocative look: she manages to imply that it's just a matter of time before I'm where she and Nicola are right now, and *then* I'll be sorry.

The conversation I had yesterday with Alex flashes through my brain and I wonder if it's worth repeating. But no. Why bother. This is not what they want to hear.

I should stop talking now.

Marie, phone now out of sight, gives me a look too. Ambiguous. She does not want to commit herself to my side. No, not at all. Does it matter to her if it's about the affair or if it's about the lying? Perhaps it does.

'He lied because he thought you couldn't handle the truth,' I say. 'And he was right. Wasn't he? What did you do when you found out? You freaked and railed and felt betrayed and wronged – and you ran.'

'He was a cheating, lying rat-fuck bastard!' Colleen shouts.

I really need to stop talking. Just one more thing:

'And a bad liar,' I say.

Marie thrusts a drink into my hand. 'Shut up,' she hisses.

'So you would rather – if Alex was cheating, you'd rather he was just really good at lying about it?' Colleen demands. 'You'd rather just not know?'

'If his priority was staying with me – keeping the marriage intact?' I ask. 'Yes. I don't need to know. I don't want him to tell me.'

My choice of tense surprises me, and I remember the call from Melanie. If she is more than an office wife, do I care?

Yes. I care. But there is a world of difference between caring and . . .

Colleen is red with anger, and she's calling me a liar again. Nicola's just silent, eyes glassy, staring at us.

'I'm not saying I wouldn't care,' I say. 'Fuck, of course I'd care. And I'd suspect, probably. Worry a little bit, yes. But – see, if his priority was us, if we were the most important thing, and if his goal was preserving us . . . Fuck. No, I wouldn't want him to tell me. I wouldn't want him to engage in an emotional striptease to either ease his conscience or burden mine.

'If I couldn't handle it – if I couldn't take knowing it all . . . I'd rather not know,' I repeat.

And Nicola bursts into tears, horrible, horrible tears.

'I'm not saying Paul isn't a rat-fuck bastard,' I say. Lamely. 'It's just . . .'

'You're worse than the polyamorist skank,' Nicola sobs out. 'What's wrong with you, Jane?'

Ever so much.

I shut up. Watch Colleen comfort Nicola, Marie mix another drink.

What's wrong with you, Jane?
—You.
No. I'm just your trigger.
—Fuck.
We will.

We will.

Interlude – I'll let you play with her

She came home late, with just enough wine in her to make her lusty.

The house was quiet when she came home, and he who you let her fuck was drifting off to sleep. She untied her skirt and straddled him. 'Do you want me?' she whispered. 'Or do I need to fuck myself with the vibrator beside you while you sleep?'

He wanted her. If not before, then immediately. He pulled her down closer to him, and slid his hands to her pussy, caressing her clit and lips and kissing her face and neck and breasts for a long while before sliding into her. He is always a gentle, considerate lover. And she was wet and ready, but gentle and considerate was not what she wanted.

'Fuck my ass,' she whispered in his ear. He increased speed, his hands suddenly on hers, pressing them hard into the bed. She stared him right in the eyes. 'I want you to fuck my ass again,' she said.

She does not talk to him like that in bed, ever, you know.

Without a word, he pulled out and slid a finger into her asshole. The other hand fumbled inside the bedside table drawer for lubricant. She pulled her knees up to her chest to tilt her hips forward. And he thrust in, not so gently, and she cried out in shock. He thrust in and out slowly, one hand holding her hip, the other working her clit, sliding inside her pussy. She closed her eyes and relaxed. And she thought of why she asked him for this, and she thought of you bending her over the dryer in a laundry room while a party raged upstairs, and she thought of herself on her knees before you – in so many different places. And suddenly, your cock was in her mouth, and it was as real as the cock in her ass. And desire built and built and built until the sensation of his cock in her ass was all pleasure, and she felt ready to cum and she opened her eyes and looked at him and said, voice hoarse, 'Cum now. Fast, hard. Now. Now.' And he said, 'Christ,' and came in her ass, on her command, immediately.

As did she.

When he pulled out, she cried out in pain again, and he wrapped his arms around her, one crushing her breasts, the other caressing her ass cheeks.

'I can't decide if I need to exercise less to have more energy for you, or more, to get stronger,' he whispered.

'Am I too much for you?' she whispered back, drowsy, on the edge of sleep. 'I may need to take a lover.'

'Never,' he said.

'A girl,' she said. 'A girl's OK, isn't it? I'll let you play with her.'

'Never,' he said. 'I love you too much.' And he does. She is his world.

'I love you too,' she said. And she does. She truly does.

But she fell asleep thinking of your cock.

Day 23 – Worst Christmas Ever

The kids are sitting amidst a mountain of shredded wrapping paper and gift bags before I realise we didn't get a single picture of them yet. I make them crowd under the tree.

'Alex, can you snap a pic? Even just on the phone?' I ask.

'It's in the bathroom again, Daddy,' Henry says.

'You're lucky Annie doesn't do with phones and things what Henry and Eddie did when they were her age,' Cassandra says. I laugh. Didn't she just say that to him yesterday, the day before? Or was that me?

'I keep on telling him that too,' I say.

Alex flushes and I look at his flush with interest. 'Peanut gallery,' he says, then lopes up the stairs. I arrange the kids, the presents and the mountain of garbage artistically. The bracelet that's Alex's present to me dangles on my arm. The artsy book that's my present to him is on the floor. I put it up on the couch, sit beside it. Watch him take a picture of our ridiculously gorgeous children.

He sits beside me when he's done, engulfs me in his arms. Kisses my neck. 'We've done good, hey,' he says, looking at them too. 'Mmmm.' I kiss him back. Peace and contentment shoot through me, suddenly and thoroughly, and I close my eyes.

'Mom!' Cassandra says. 'We have to go to Lacey's! It's after eleven!'

Lacey's Christmas morning brunch is a neighbourhood

tradition, and for Cassandra perhaps as important a part of Christmas morning as the present rip-a-thon.

'Go.' I wave at them. The kids run over to Lacey's still in their pyjamas, the boys clutching their Lego sets, Cassandra carting her 'new favourite book'. Annie demands a piggyback from Alex. 'I just need to run to the bathroom, sweetums,' he says, and, phone in hand, disappears up the stairs. Annie covers me with sloppy kisses. 'I love Christmas,' she says. I hold her tight. I still love Christmas too. Christmas morning. The brunch with friends.

The Christmas dinner with my divorcing parents may be a bit of a strain. But no. It'll be fine. They'll both put on game faces for the kids.

Alex pounds down the stairs. 'Come on, my munchkin.' He scoops up Annie. The phone's still in his hand; I watch him glance at it, at me, slip it in his pocket. Scowl, then peck me on the cheek. 'Let's go party.'

The associate, I suspect, has sent him a 'Merry Christmas' text, and he's not sure if it's appropriate for him to respond to it. My beloved.

At Lacey's, the table's covered with mimosas, chocolate-covered strawberries and mountains of pastry. A fruit plate worthy of a Roman banquet. To show how casual all this is supposed to be, Lacey's still in her pyjamas – full makeup, of course – with the loveliest lace kimono on top.

I kiss her.

She melts into my arms, her breath warm on my neck. She whispers, 'Merry Christmas! Oh, Jane, I'm so happy!'

Clint is sitting at the table. In a three-piece suit, and the most gorgeous tie I've ever seen on a man. He gets up and solemnly shakes hands with me, without looking at my face or boobs. Gives Alex a brief shot of eye contact. 'Merry Christmas.'

I sit, strategically, close to the chocolate-covered strawberries and far away from the tray of mimosas, and chill as neighbours

I don't much care about come and go. 'Merry Christmas.' 'What a gorgeous day!' 'Like a postcard out there!' 'Was Santa good to you?' Alex sits beside me. Disappears. Comes back.

'The kids OK?' I ask.

'What? Oh, yeah, fine, the boys are all building their Lego in Clayton's room.' He sits down beside me. Takes my hand in his and caresses it. Twirls my wedding ring around my finger.

I decide he texted her, and now feels guilty about it. Oh, my Alex.

I keep my shawl of contentment wrapped around me.

And realise – of course not. He didn't. And feels guilty about *that*.

—Never think of me as an obligation, OK? Ever.

Lacey crouches down beside us. She's full of wedding plans. I focus on her happiness. On Alex fiddling with the ring on my finger. Lacey whips out her phone to show me pictures of cakes.

I'm holding her phone when mine buzzes. 'Jeezus, sorry,' I apologise to Lacey, Alex. She waves it away. 'Someone sending you Christmas love,' she says. 'It's all good.' I pull it out to turn it off. The message is from Marie. 'Are you there?' So much for Christmas love. I sigh. Mild exasperation. The next text comes as I'm preparing to put the phone, text unanswered, into my pocket. 'I didn't get a Merry Christmas text! Is it over? I think it's over!' Jeezus fucking Christ. Is she insane? Or twelve? I type, 'No. Merry Christmas. xoxo.'

The phone disappears into my purse. I try not to roll my eyes. Instead, I look at the phone in Alex's pocket, and at his fidgeting hand.

I could say, 'Baby, just text her, I don't fucking care.'

But. He would care. That I don't care.

And perhaps I care.

I'm glad, I am actually really, really glad that I do not have the option or opportunity to text Matt. I am grateful, truly, for the radio silence and lack of Internet in the cottage in the Laurentians.

I make myself listen to Lacey, but my mind keeps wandering off. To Marie. And her intermittent wish that JP would have an affair so that she would feel justified in having one. But would she really be pleased if she noticed he was texting with his girl-on-the-side on Christmas Day? Or longing to hear from his mistress while he sat next to his wife? I turn to look at Alex and try to catch myself in self-awareness. What do I feel? What do I want? What do I want to know? What do I wish he were doing?

'Why are you staring at me like that?' Alex asks. I shake my head.

'Just thinking,' I say. 'Drifting. Actually . . . Baby?' I lean towards him. 'Can I see your phone a sec?'

He hesitates, perhaps a second, no more. Hands it to me. Password protection is back on. I raise my eyes to his.

'Seven-three-six-four,' he says. I type it in.

And there it is.

From 10.35 a.m., when we were all around the Christmas tree together.

- Merry Christmas, Alex. I hope you have a wonderful day, and a very, very Happy New Year. Except, of course, I'm sure I'll see you before that. Clients. I will let you know if anything else urgent happens today. Anyway. Merry Christmas.

Oh, the poor girl.

And. No text back from Alex. He meets my eyes. Shrugs. I start to type.

'Jesus, Jane, what the hell are you doing?' He starts to reach for me. Stops. I turn the phone so he can see the screen.

'I haven't pressed send yet,' I say. Show him the screen. We read:

- Happy Saturnalia. Do not check email or voicemail today. Enjoy your day OFF. That's an order.

'You don't end messages to her with x's or o's, do you?' I ask.

'Jesus, of course not,' he says. 'She's a colleague.' He watches me press *send*. 'So,' he says after a pause. 'Yesterday – a jealous, possessive wife. Or an impersonation thereof, anyway. And today?'

I shrug. Think.

'A generous, experienced woman, with complete confidence in her long-term play,' I say finally. Alex raises his left eyebrow. Laughs, but not like he means it. Leans in and kisses me, and, taking his phone back from my hand, strides off in the direction of the mimosa tray.

I turn my attention back to Lacey. Her delight in the wedding planning is . . . should be . . . delightful. Her capacity for forgiveness, for love is amazing. Unreal. I force myself to enter into it. And then I raise my eyes to look at Clint. And realise that I still don't believe this wedding will happen. I don't believe he will go through with it. I don't believe he will marry her. When push comes to shove – after ten years, after Clayton, after all she accepted, forgave, waited out, after the first child by the 'old' girlfriend and the current child by the same 'ex-but-clearly-not' girlfriend, after all that – no. It's not going to happen. He's going to break Lacey's heart and utterly, completely disappoint her.

Suddenly, I feel awful.

Nauseated.

I can't stay here.

I can't watch this.

I follow Alex to the mimosas.

'We need to go call the grandparents,' I whisper. And feel him stiffen.

'We're seeing your parents in a few hours, and we saw my mom yesterday,' he says. 'And she's with Jen today.' Jen. Alex's sister. 'She doesn't expect us to call.'

'Jeanette,' I say. 'Your dad.'

He's silent.

Then: 'No.'

'Alex,' I whisper. 'Christmas.'

'No,' he says.

'I'll call them with the kids. You stay here,' I suggest.

'No,' he says. 'My father does not get a Christmas telephone call this year.' His eyes bore into me, challenge me, then drop to the floor. But he has not yielded. I know this.

'OK,' I say. 'OK, that's fine.'

I look back at Lacey. She's sitting in Clint's lap, and he's caressing her thighs. She looks content. He looks . . . hungry.

Fuck.

I don't know.

Maybe it will work. Why not?

I sneak a call to Jeanette later in the day, hiding in the basement with my cellphone, while Alex is getting ready to go to my parents' house for dinner. She's pathetically grateful, and doesn't ask to talk to the kids or Alex; nor does she ask anything about Alex's father. I wonder if she knows? Would he have called her? Would Claire? 'Merry Christmas, Jane,' she says. 'I love you all.' 'I know,' I say. She invites us for brunch, a post-Christmas brunch. Boxing Day? The day after? I demur. We can talk about it later. Hang off.

And read the twelve texts from Marie. For fuck's sake. What is wrong with this woman?

Punch in her number.

'Jane!' she yells. Then drops her voice to a whisper. 'Please tell me I'm completely insane.'

'You're completely insane.'

'Please tell me to get myself the fuck together.'

'Get yourself the fuck together.'

'Please tell me . . . oh, God, I don't know what I want you to tell me. What's wrong with me? What the hell is wrong with me? Why am I so fucking rattled, and needy and unreasonable? Why do I need this much attention and hand-holding and reassurance?'

'Peri-menopause?' I offer unhelpfully.

'Jane!' Marie screeches. 'Whatever. Maybe. Make me stop!'

'Marie. It's fucking Christmas Day. Get a hold of yourself. Be present for your husband and children. And stop acting like a fucking whore,' I say. 'Is that what you need to hear?'

'No,' she says. Weeps. 'I am so unhappy. I can't stop crying.'

'Because you didn't get a "Merry Christmas" text?' I ask.

'No,' she sobs. 'Because . . . What? Yes, honey, I'm coming. I have to go. Merry Christmas, Jane.' She disappears.

I wonder if I am this crazy from the outside looking in.

Maybe.

But I think I hide it better.

My parents, apparently, are capable of hiding nothing. Every fourth word out of my mother's mouth sounds like a swear or snarl directed at my father. My father doesn't look at my mother at all. His teeth are clenched so tightly I wonder how he manages to chew. They hug and kiss all the children, and my mother bursts into tears on my neck as we exchange holiday greetings. Annie bursts into tears at the same time, for reasons not immediately apparent.

The turkey's overdone. The stuffing's burned. The mashed potatoes are cold. So announces my mother as she throws each platter on to the dinner table. Alex flinches visibly. My father opens another bottle of wine. Cassandra's eyes fill with tears.

'So,' I say, with supreme effort. 'We had a great morning. The kids let us sleep in until nine, can you fucking believe that?'

'Jane!' my mother screeches. 'Swearing! In front of the children! At Christmas!'

'Oh, sorry, it seemed to me we were doing Christmas without social niceties this year,' I snap. Then turn horribly red. Apparently I too am capable of hiding nothing, in this context, anyway. 'I'm so sorry. Nine o'clock. What a treat. And then . . .' I list the Santa hoard. Dangle my bracelet. Talk about the spread at Lacey's. Desperately search for something else, anything, to say.

Alex grabs my hand under the table and squeezes it.

My love, my partner.

'Clint told me the most interesting thing,' he says. And shares the world's most boring story about retailing trends in menswear at Christmas. I stare imploringly at my dad. Who nods and laughs. 'I believe that,' he says. 'Why, one time, when I was shopping for . . .'

My mother slams a dish of sweet potatoes – 'not enough cinnamon!' – onto the table.

And all of a sudden a shot of longing so acute reverberates through me, I am sure everyone can feel it. And on its heels comes the equally sudden, and unwelcome, realisation that if I'm feeling this, if I'm feeling this empty, restless, unfulfilled, so filled with longing and desire and anger and angst, then so is Matt, and if Matt is feeling this then he is fucking someone else. Not his wife, because the licit fucking does not alleviate this need. Someone else. Anyone.

Knowing someone perfectly sucks.

That's the way it's always been, the way it will always be. Why I was never his girlfriend; why I am not his wife and can't imagine a scenario in which that role would be bearable. And what I feel is not jealousy or possessiveness but something more encompassing: angst, such angst that it is not *my* body at this moment that is below his. And with that feeling comes . . . shame. Shame at the knowledge of what my desire is, and that this desire has no pride and no self-respect. That it just wants. And as my mother complains about the inadequacy of the cranberry sauce and my father viciously butchers the turkey,

303

I am on Matt's bed. How many years ago? So many. He's already with Joy. I'm nominally still dating Aldrin but already sleeping with Alex. But at that particular moment, with Alex – doing what? interviewing for an articling position, maybe, or studying, or at a conference – and Joy at some yoga or meditation retreat, I am on Matt's bed.

It's one of our intermittent 'rule' periods, during which we – usually me, in a new relationship and determined to be a 'good' girlfriend this time – set up arbitrary boundaries about what it's OK for us to do. So: clothes on. No penetration. My shirt is unbuttoned and my bra loosened, my skirt pushed up around my waist, and my panties pulled down to my knees. His shirt unbuttoned, jeans unzipped. But we're not having sex.

We're word-fucking. Jeezus. Did we always? I guess we did. Our hands caress, a little, but we're word-fucking, the tension and the sex entirely in what we're saying, sometimes ebbing as we take a break from fucking each other with words to talking about . . . Joy's complete aversion to even talking about anal sex. Alex's eagerness – but handful of bad habits – as a lover. Aldrin's unattractive possessiveness. Sometimes rising to a pitch as we take each other through the current ultimate fantasy. I'm a little wet. He's a little hard. We're languid. Lazy.

The phone rings.

He reaches for it around me.

'Hello,' he says. Takes my hand, puts it on his cock. 'Oh, hi, Lee.' Lee's a mutual friend. Perhaps friend is stretching it. One of our social circle. We both know her. I dislike her, but not sufficiently to actively avoid her. We're frequently at the same bars, parties. 'I'm at home, obviously. On my bed. Where are you?' I look up at Matt, eyebrows raised. He leans over and kisses one of my eyes. Then repositions both my hands on his cock. Starts more actively caressing my breast. 'In the bath . . . I like that.' I jerk up and he puts a hand across my mouth. 'What are you doing? Oh, yeah? Are you? And thinking

304

of me . . . well, you know I'm very flattered. Tell me more.'
I raise my hands to his hand and try to wrench it off my
mouth. He tucks the phone between his ear and shoulder and
uses both hands to push my head to his cock.

And I take it. I take him in and out of my mouth, slowly,
as he talks to Lee. 'And then what . . . and now? Are you
going to make yourself cum? Mmmm.' When I stop, his hands
push me back onto his cock. Otherwise, they stroke me – my
pussy, my ass, occasionally my hair.

'That's a girl,' he says. 'Faster and harder, until you cum. I
want to hear you screaming for me.' And I guess she does,
because as I lift my head, he holds the receiver away from his
ear. 'Well, you're welcome, hun,' he says. 'Sweet dreams.'

I move away from his cock to his face as he puts the phone
away. He looks at me, half-smiling, half-defiant. All pleased.
Hard.

I want to ask, have you ever done this to me? Instead, I
say, 'If you ever do this to me, don't ever fucking tell me.' He
sinks his fingers into my hair and pulls me to him. Lips crush
against teeth. And then he's on top of me, and inside me. I
struggle to get out.

'Fuck your rules,' he growls. 'You know we need this.' And
as always when it comes, the sex is so intense, and sating, and
exhausting, and overwhelming, that when it's over, I think I
will never ever need to fuck again.

'So, is Alex the one?' he asks me afterwards. 'Is it true love?'
I lift my head from his chest to look at him. And marvel that
perhaps he knows me as well as I know him, because at the
time I still have the tag 'Aldrin's girlfriend'.

'It might be,' I say. 'It's certainly something. Powerful.'

He looks away from me. 'I'm thinking I will ask Joy to
marry me,' he says. 'When she comes back.'

'You'll make beautiful children,' I tell him.

'We'd make terrible parents,' he says, looking back at me,
and I know he's not talking about Joy and himself.

'Can you make her happy?' I ask.

'Yes. I think so,' he says. I want to ask, will you be happy? but that seems patronising, so I don't. He answers anyway. 'As happy as I can be.' Smiles in a lopsided kind of way. Endearing. Annoying. 'And you?'

'I'll work to make him happy,' I say. 'I worry . . . I worry I won't be able to do it.'

'What?' he asks. 'Monogamy?' I nod.

'I'm pretty sure I won't be able to do it,' he says. 'But I think Joy is willing to . . . not see.'

I believe that.

Is Alex willing not to see? I'm not sure. I am in Matt's bed as Aldrin's girlfriend. Of course, Alex is perfectly willing to fuck Aldrin's girlfriend. His feelings about Matt fucking Alex's girlfriend, Alex's wife . . . I suspect those will be different. They always are.

'I think, if I am with Alex, I will have to do the real thing,' I tell him. He raises his eyebrows. 'If I'm with Alex. I will have to. Be monogamous. Faithful. Truly.' Matt's silent and waiting. Interested. 'Alex . . . took his heart out and gave it to me, to do with as I will. And that's . . . that's amazing. Sexy as hell . . . and scary, and a huge responsibility. If I am with him, if I am really with him, I will have to be faithful. Truly faithful.'

'Can you do that?' Matt asks.

'I will try,' I say. And I mean it. 'Plus, we're going to have babies. Lots and lots of babies. I think that will help.'

Matt laughs. And then, he asks, 'So is this the last time then?' And grins. And slides off his jeans all the way. 'In which case, my twisted lover, get your lips around my cock just one more time. For old times' sake.'

And I do. And he comes. And then we fuck again, more patiently. And while we're fucking, each of us engages in the self-deception that this is indeed the last time. Tomorrow, monogamy begins.

Aching, sated, we hook up with Aldrin and others, including

Lee, to see a movie. Lee keeps on looking at Matt. His eyes slide past her as if she does not exist.

My mother disappears upstairs after dinner and, with a certainty I do not relish, I know she is crying and I know that a dutiful daughter should go upstairs and comfort her. Instead, I get Alex and my dad to clear the table, do the dishes and package up the leftovers, and put Cassandra and Henry in charge of setting the table for dessert.

'We'll do the presents as soon as Gran's ready,' I tell Eddie and Annie about a dozen times. I refill my dad's wine glass half-a-dozen times.

'Are you trying to get me drunk?' he jokes feebly once.

'No, just trying to get your teeth to ungrit,' I retort.

Finally, I go up the stairs.

My mother is sitting in the master bedroom, in the rocking chair she bought when I started having babies, so I would have a quiet and comfortable place to nurse. Her makeup is smeared, her eyes red.

I stand, awkwardly, in the doorway.

'We've cleaned everything, and set up for dessert,' I say.

She nods her head.

'Are the kids anxious to open presents?' she asks.

I nod my head. Then realise her eyes are still fixed on the floor, so she can't see me.

'Yes,' I say.

'Give me two more minutes,' she says.

I should hold her, hug her, comfort her.

'OK,' I say, and walk out of the room. Close the door behind me.

She's downstairs in three minutes, eyes too bright, fresh lipstick on.

'Who's ready for Santa!' she calls out, and the three littles run to the tree. Cassandra follows them at a more restrained pace.

'She got each of them iPads?' Alex whispers to me as the wrapping paper comes off. 'Jesus. What are we going to get?'

'I'm hoping for a *25 Secrets to a Great Marriage* kind of book,' I whisper back. Alex chortles. 'What did we get them?' he asks. 'Don't tell me,' he says. '*Co-grandparenting After Divorce*?' I asked for it, but I give him a dirty look anyway. He takes my hand and kisses it. And looks very serious and interested as my mother opens her completely inoffensive and subtext-free gift of cosmetics, bath salts, candles, and other pretty things and my father a bottle of aged scotch and manly glasses.

Alex and I get a gift certificate for two nights at the Banff Springs Hotel, where we spent our wedding night. 'Free babysitting by Gran included!' my mother trills.

I finally hug and kiss her. Peck my dad on the cheek.

And herd everyone into the car as soon as we finish eating dessert.

'I don't think I've ever been so grateful to get back home,' I whisper to Alex as we get the kids into the house.

'Me too,' he whispers back. 'Worst Christmas ever?'

'Pretty much,' I agree. The kids are exhausted, cranky, reverberating with the vibes. I decree immediate bathtime for all, followed by immediate bedtime. 'But Mom! It's Christmas!' a chorus whines. 'I want to try out the iPad more!' 'Dad said he would load apps for me!' 'Moooom!' 'Possibly a movie in bed on my laptop later,' I half-promise. 'But first bath. Pyjamas. Brush teeth. And go!'

They go up the stairs grumbling. Alex brings the Christmas dinner leftovers and presents in.

My phone rings.

'It's probably your dad!' I call to Alex. Because I don't think his father even has Alex's cell number.

'I don't want to talk to him!' he calls back. I pull the phone out of my jacket pocket. Oh, fuck. It's a 514 area code. Which I've dialled twice. But, of course, recognise. Immediately. Intimately.

Panic.

Why is he calling?

'Jesus. What's wrong?' I don't wait for a hello. My voice is shaking. My legs, rubber.

'I'm sorry.' His voice. Oh, yes. My toes curl. 'Check Facebook. It's, uh, time sensitive.'

And he's gone.

I hear kids fighting and splashing in the bathtub. Alex shuffling in the kitchen. The phone in my hand is hot, burning my hand. I log in to Facebook.

I have a major client fuck-up happening right now. Emergency meetings scheduled for morning of twenty-seventh in Vancouver. I leave Montreal tomorrow morning. Hit Calgary airport at noon. I don't board the Vancouver flight until 6:15.
6 hours. My fuckslave. My lover.
Will you come?

Day 24 – Six Hours

Wednesday, December 26

I have no plan. I'm probably not going to do this. I realise my moral compass is skewed, but leaving my four children in the care of my husband on the day after Christmas while I go fuck my mindfucker of a sick lover in an airport bathroom isn't something I am going to do. I don't really want to leave them with my divorcing and not-speaking-to-each-other parents either. My mother-in-law? Yeah, no.

I'm in bed, eyes closed. Alex, insanely, is up. Which means coffee is ready. Which is good. A phone rings. Not mine. 'Hello?' I hear Alex. And then – 'For fuck's sake,' he says. 'Seriously? Today? . . . No, I understand. I'll be there in forty-five minutes. OK.'

He brings me up coffee with apologies. Fucking clients. He's so sorry.

I shrug it off. 'We had no plans for today. Go.'

'I was going to give you a day off,' he says. 'I thought I'd take the kids to a movie.'

'Clients,' I say. 'Go. I know you have to.' He sits on the side of the bed.

'Is it weird that I sometimes wish you'd resent my work more and complain that I'm not home enough?' he asks.

'Yes,' I say. 'I'm like the fucking dream wife. Go.' He kisses me. Goes.

Well. And definitely not my parents. So I'm not going. The universe has decreed.

310

I grab my telephone. Call Marie.
Then check Facebook.

En route. On time.
—I will be there.

It takes about 40 minutes to drive to the airport, and I unload the kids at Marie's at 11.23.

'Are you sure this is OK?' I say as they disappear yahooing into her basement. 'It's too much. It's for too long.'

'For Christ's sake's, Jane, how many babysitting hours do I owe you?' Marie snaps. 'Go! Meet your deadline, and assuage your guilt by coming back with pizza so I don't have to make supper.'

'I love you,' I tell her. Sincerely. Ponder, again, if I should tell her, as she tells me? This is what women friends do, right? They share these things? She tells me everything. In fact, at this very moment, she is reverberating with need to tell me what she did, what she didn't do and what she is planning to do. With – what's his name. Craig.

But.

There's only so much perfect trust to go around.

Secrets are hot.
—They are. But secrets only stay secrets if you don't tell.
So don't tell. And hurry the fuck up.

And then Marie says . . . 'Why are you wearing snow pants?'

'It's December in Calgary,' I say. 'It's cold.'

By 11.30 I'm back on Deerfoot. In the airport parkade at 11.59.

I'm not really going to do this.

I'm going to pull out and go back and get my kids from Marie's and go home. Right?

I park. Take off my boots. The snow pants.

Take *his* – they've been his since the first time I told him about them – fuck-me heels out of my purse. Smooth out the little black dress. Slide out of the puffy winter coat.

I open the car door.

Fuck, it's cold.

What I'm going to do, I'm going to go meet him at the gate. And what will happen is we will smile and giggle nervously, and things will be awkward and weird. We will have a drink in the lounge. Maybe he'll touch my thighs.

We are not going to go to a hotel room and fuck.

How fucking cliché.

Of course not.

I step out of the car.

I walk through the parkade, across traffic. Into the terminal. Towards the gate. Suddenly, I catch sight of myself out of the corner of my eye in a mirror. I stop, turn and stare. Hi, Jane. This is you at 70, looking at you right now. What does she want to remember from this moment? Does 70-year-old you conquer temptation? Stay faithful? Remember this as the time she almost . . . or regret this as the time she didn't?

I look at my reflection.

She doesn't see me.

She's not thinking.

She wants only one thing.

I close my eyes. Bite my lips.

And I keep on walking towards the gate.

The flight's arrived, the luggage is already on the carousel. There's hardly anyone waiting, hardly anyone there. But passengers are starting to trickle through the door. And soon, Matt will come. And it will be weird and awkward. But OK.

Mindfuck of biblical proportions.

Perfect trust.

I wait.

And then, he's there. I smell him, feel him before I see him. I recognise his walk, his saunter, before I look at this face. Shiver. Shudder.

He heads straight for me. No hesitation.

I feel my lips part into a smile.

And then I bite them, because I think it might be a lascivious smile inappropriate to public places.

And then he's in front of me, one hand around my waist, on my hip, on the hem of my dress, under, the other on my neck, in my hair. His breath on my ear, tongue on earlobe. Lips brush my neck, then mark my skin.

'Let's go,' he growls. 'Hurry. Before I push you down onto your fucking knees in front of all these people.'

Awkward? Weird? Apparently not.

And what happens? A near-run through the terminal. Hotel-room lobby. Door. Room. The door slams. 'Do you remember what you're supposed to say?' 'I hate you. Now fuck me.' 'Oh, yes. Six hours. Jeezus-fucking-Christ, finally.' His hands everywhere, and his lips and tongue. My back against the wall. 'First, release. Because there's no way I'll last six hours otherwise.' 'Yes. Anything.' 'Anything?' 'Anything.' 'Now.' Urgency. Insanity. Screaming. The world totally and completely disappears. Six hours. Madness. Everything happens. *Everything*. 'What are you?' 'Yours.' 'My what?' 'Your whore.' 'Oh, yes . . .' His belt, my hands, his hands in my hair. Pushing me down. I tumble. A noise: something falls. A lamp? 'I don't fucking care.' Something breaks. Pounding on the wall. 'Tell them.' 'Shut the fuck up! We're busy!'

The carpet is rusty, patterned, ugly. It imprints on my knees. Elbows. Hips. Face. 'I ache.' 'Good. But I suppose we should make it to the bed. Can you get up, my slutty lover? Or do I drag you?' 'Fuck. Drag me.' Softness of pillows. Hardness of headboard. 'Hard again. No rest for you.' 'Jeezus.' 'You know what's next. Go to the fucking window. Now.' 'No.' 'He thinks she likes being dragged.' 'Oh-my-fucking-God.' Hands, cock, tongue, pussy, nothing but sensation, lust, desire. Primal fucking. Pleasure and pain commingled.

For hours.

'Lover?'

'What, my bruised fuckslave?'

'Your flight boards in ten minutes.'

'What? Oh, Jesus Christ. Give me my belt. Although I like it there, so very much. Fuck.'

'Pants first?'

'I suppose. Come here. Dress me. But . . . quickly.'

'All right.'

'Will you be all right? Dressing yourself, cleaning up?'

'Yes.'

'Was I too rough?'

'Yes.'

'I think I want you again.'

'I see that. Eight minutes. Belt. Go.'

'Going. Say thank you, fuckslave.'

'Thank you, my lover.'

'Master.'

'Thank you, my lover-master. Now, go.'

Mindfuck of biblical proportions.

Perfect trust.

Oh, my fucking God.

My phone rings when I'm eight minutes away from our house. I toss it into the back seat and Cassandra grabs it. 'Hi, Gran,' she says. 'We're just coming back from our friends' house. Mom's driving . . . uh-huh. Gran's asking if we want to come over for dinner,' Cassandra reports.

'It's seven-thirty, and we just had pizza at Marie's,' I remind her.

'We've just had pizza,' Cassandra tells the phone. Listens. 'Do we want to come over for dessert?'

I want to go home and lie very still in a dark room for a while.

'Ask her if she has dessert or if we need to stop at Sunterra to pick it up,' I say. 'And then call Dad. See if he wants to meet us there, or if we should bring him something home.'

I speak mother-daughter code. Despite the horrific Christmas dinner, despite my behaviour over the past two weeks, I am, deep down, a dutiful daughter. At least sometimes. And Mom clearly does not want to spend an evening alone with Dad . . . and her need is greater than my need to never be in the same house with the two of them again. And . . . also . . . atonement? Maybe. I sigh. Drive to Sunterra.

We arrive with cheesecake, ice-cream and whipped cream. Mom's eyes are heavily made-up. And red. She chatters as she makes tea. I set the table with dessert plates.

'Where's Dad?' I ask.

'They called this morning, said he could have the keys to the apartment early,' Mom says, her back to me. 'So he's gone, he took a suitcase, and he's gone.' Her shoulders hunch and she cries. I stand behind her. Wrap my arms around her. They throb. Rest my head on her shoulder.

'I'm all right, I'm fine,' she says. 'It's just . . . you know. It's basically still Christmas. Forty-three years, almost forty-three years – could he not have stayed another four, five days?'

'Oh, Mom.'

I hold her tighter and she cries. And cries.

Until Henry runs into the kitchen. 'Are we ready to eat? Where's Gramps? Why's Gran crying?'

'She's hurt. But she'll be all right. Just let her cry. Go get the others, everything's on the table,' I say.

Tea and dessert do not make anything better. We wash up. The kids turn on the TV, have a fight over channels. I turn off the TV. 'Give me five minutes, and we're heading home.'

Or are we? Mom suddenly seems very very small, and very alone, in her five-bedroom, four-bathroom house.

Forty-three years. Has she ever been alone in that time? In this house?

I find a *The Grinch Stole Christmas* DVD and put it on for the kids. And I call Alex to tell him the kids and I are staying the night at my mom's.

'Does that mean I don't get my dessert until tomorrow?' he says.

'Being an adult sucks,' I commiserate.

'You OK, Jane?' he asks.

'Not really,' I say. 'Being an adult sucks. But. She's less OK.'

'Do you want me to come get the kids?'

'No. Family sleepover. We'll all bunk down in the living room in sleeping bags, with a fire in the fireplace, and watch Christmas movies half the night.'

'I love you,' he says, and I feel the affection pour into me.

'I love you too,' I say. And I mean it. I always mean it.

I'm barely aware of my body's aches and sensations as I fall asleep. But in my dreams I relive every moment of my six hours with Matt. Over and over and over again.

Day 25 – Evidence

Tell me.
—Aren't you in an emergency client meeting?
Conference call. Boring. Do what you're fucking told.
You know what I want. Tell me.
—Everything?
Everything. I want to see you type it.
—Do I start at the gate?
No. 'I hate you . . .
—'I hate you. Now fuck me.' And oh, God, you grab
my hips and slam me into the door, and hoist my dress
up – I don't know when you undo your belt and
buttons, I don't see it – and you're inside me. One hard
thrust. I scream,
I say . . .
—'I'm going to be selfish first, because there's no
fucking way I'm going to last six hours otherwise.'
*That might have been my favourite part . . . except for
the ones that followed.*
Tell me.
What next.
—You came in minutes. Splattering my thighs. I slid
down against the door to the floor. You left me there,
walked over to the bed. 'Undress for me. You know
how.'
—Are you still there?

317

Yes. Still on call. Still reading. Type.
—I took off my clothes. 'To the chair.' I sat down,
spread my legs. You gave me instructions . . . on what
to do.
—On exactly what to do.

'Jane? Where are you, sweetheart?'
'I'm just on the computer!'
'Oh, Jane.' My mother stands at the door, comes in.

—Oh, fuck. Real life. I have to go.
I understand. But Jane?
—Yes?
That was pretty fucking real.
—Yes.
Till later, my lover. My whore.
—Till later, my sick soulmate. xx
xo

Mom looks OK. Not great, but OK. She's holding two cups
of coffee. 'I thought you'd be ready for another one,' she says.
Sits down beside me on the sofa. Looks at the laptop. 'You
work too much.'

'I only do as much as I am willing to,' I say with a shrug.

'Thank you,' she says after a long pause.

I really don't think 'You're welcome' is the right thing to
say.

'Of course,' I say. Give her a pat on the knee.

'You'll head straight to the gym from here?' she asks. Dad's
gone, but life and our weekly routine go on.

'I'll leave early, and swing by Alex's office on the way, if
that's all right? Deliver him his dessert.'

'You're such a good wife. And mother. And daughter,' says
Mom. And bursts into tears and runs from the room.

I log out of Facebook.

318

Fucking hell.

Good wife. That's me.

I swing by the house quickly to grab my workout clothes and a change of clothes for the kids. Then downtown to Alex's office with cheesecake, whipped cream and a bottle of Lactaid pills.

'God, you are a fucking dream wife,' he tells me. Kisses me. Pulls me into his lap. I flinch. 'Too bad I have a meeting in ten minutes.'

'I need to be at Jesse's in fifteen,' I tell him. Kiss him back, moving very slowly. 'Text me if you'll be late for supper. I'll try to make something sensational to make up for yesterday.'

At the door, I turn around.

'Well, probably not sensational,' I amend. 'But, you know. Hot. And not out of a box.'

I don't like to lie.

Nicola's in the changing room when I get there. She looks god-awful. And she knows it. Our other friends would hug her.

'Do you need to talk?' I offer. I don't want to. God, I don't want to.

'Know what I need, Jane? Do you know what I need right now? I need a man – any man – hell, I'll take a manly woman at this point – to just tell me that I'm attractive and desirable and not gross and yucky and . . .' She takes a breath. 'I'm sorry. I'm just so tired. So tired of looking for solutions and finding the positive and talking to therapists and lawyers and accepting people being kind to me and . . . what do I need?'

'An orgasm?' I ask. This is not a me-and-Nicola kind of conversation. Except for that one time I inappropriately asked her about the rat-fuck bastard's anal sex fetish.

'Yes,' she says. 'Preferably one facilitated by a real live human being. Whatever. Not gonna happen while I'm this psychotic mess. You don't have to tell me – self-pity is not sexy.'

And she storms out, slamming the door.

I follow shortly, and Jesse and I both watch as she exits the gym, head down, arms swinging.

'She wasn't focused at all today,' Jesse sighs. 'I'm not sure I did her any good.'

'Did you grope her ass, by any chance?' I ask. He's shocked. Aghast, actually. I don't care. 'Because really that's the only thing that would have done her some good.'

'Push-ups,' Jesse says, and I know he's saying that just to punish me. Push-ups. Fucking hell. One . . .

'Do you know how hard I work to maintain proper professional conduct and contact with all these women?' Jesse hisses in my ear as I rise. Two . . . 'My entire clientele – I think I do three men. Four. The rest – women. Women in their twenties. Thirties. Forties. Fifties. Oh, and the occasional jailbait fifteen-year-old that her vain, uptight mother thinks needs to lose weight or tone up. I don't know which are worse. The ones in their twenties – or the teenagers – who think any man who looks at them or, God forbid, touches them, even though it's his fucking job, wants to do them. Or the ones in their fifties who just don't care what you think or anyone thinks, they just get off on being touched, they want it to be slightly inappropriate. And I have to not see any of it. Misread all of it. Maintain this . . .'

'Jesse? If I do one more push-up, I'm going to vomit.'

'Rest.'

I stop. Sit and hug my knees to my chest.

'Maintain what?' I ask.

'A professional distance,' he says. 'At all costs. It's all – muscle and bone, and tendons and ligaments. It's all . . . business.'

'Mmmm,' I nod. 'I get that. Is it hard?'

'Not any more, not most of the time,' he says. 'It's part of the job, right?'

320

'So . . . could you consciously, professionally, callously – thinking of it as therapy, as part of the work you do for a client – just, you know, build Nicola up a little sexually?' I ask.

He looks at me as if I am insane.

And I probably am.

'What?' he looks at me again. I'm hot, sweat trickling under my hoodie. I pull it off.

'I just can't imagine how much it sucks for her right now,' I say. 'Well, and you see it, too. But it's just the worst thing. You were talking about the horny twenty-somethings and the menopausal matriarchs. But in the middle are women like me and Nicola. She's a little older than me, and her kids are older, so I bet this is even more pronounced for her – I'm not sure if it's an age thing or a life-stage thing – but, you know, late thirties, early forties, with the strength of motherhood and experience behind them, with the release and freedom that goes from those intensive years of caring for babies behind them, the reclaiming of the body, coming into the height of our power . . . This is when we get our testosterone surge, you know? This is our time to be sex goddesses. Not as bumbling, awkward adolescents, not as anxious twenty-something bar-hoppers – we've done that, we've found ourselves, paired up, then lost ourselves in motherhood, and then found ourselves again . . . And so, for Nicola, at what should be this glorious moment, to get dumped by a rat-fuck bastard . . . a rat-fuck bastard she always assumed *she'd* be the one to walk out on . . .'

Jesse stares.

'Look at her,' I toss my head in the direction of a pretty twenty-something . . . runner, I bet, she has the lean body of a runner. She's not wearing much, and she's lovely. But self-conscious. Exposed, but self-conscious. She keeps on sucking in her non-existent stomach, looking at herself critically in the mirror. 'Do you think she's sexy?' I ask Jesse. It's a rhetorical question, but he bristles.

321

'I've just told you, I practise *not* thinking like that,' he snaps.

'Fine.' I shrug. '*I* think she's lovely. But look at her. She doesn't know the power of her body yet. And I remember being like that – I wish, in retrospect, that I had appreciated and loved and been confident of my young body more. It certainly had some advantages over this one . . . But I think maybe you can't. Maybe you need childbirth. I created life, Jesse, is there anything more powerful than that? And I watched my body grow life, and transform itself so totally. And transform again. And there are the stretch-marks and the loose skin on my belly, and no one will ever say I have porn-star boobs again . . . But my sexual awareness, my sense of self – on every level – what it is now, it is so much more than it used to be. And for Nicola . . .'

I'm not sure what my point is any more. I pause.

'Frog-leg sit-ups,' Jesse says in an odd voice. I lie down. And groan. I've forgotten the tenderness.

'You OK?' he asks.

'Fine,' I mouth. And start curling. Oh, fuck. I think it's the hips. I feel hot hand imprints on them slamming me down into the bed, into the floor. The wall. Or my ass. My back, frankly, doesn't feel so great either. Fucking heels. And . . .

'Side plank,' Jesse says. I arrange my body, paying attention to its tenderness. The wrists, they hurt. The shoulders, ditto. The core's OK. That I owe to Jesse. But I still grimace.

'Rest – and other side,' Jesse says. His eyes are on me still, odd.

I decide to continue the exposition. Talking takes my mind off the pain.

'So there we are, or rather, there Nicola is, a woman hitting this stage of life – blossoming sexually in a way that makes puberty looks like some prairie church choir dress rehearsal. And just as this is happening, your rat-fuck bastard of a husband dumps you – for a pert-boobed intern who doesn't need to dye her hair blonde to hide the grey – but does anyway, to make it, I don't know, *shinier* – with a fetish for anal sex. And he tells you all this. In grotesque, open detail. He tells you how much he wants her, and why – and when you draw the line, when you force him to choose, he chooses this new thing over you. Actually, he doesn't even choose the new thing, does he? Just the potential of the new thing, a taste of the new thing, because in the end the new thing doesn't want to be his thing at all, just one of his things . . .' I trail off. I reach the stage of planking where talking is impossible and grimace more, groan and start to shake.

'How does that make you feel?' I gasp out. And collapse before Jesse says 'Rest.'

Which he doesn't say. He just stands there, staring at me.

I should probably not be explaining Nicola's current sexual needs and frustrations to our mutual trainer. I briefly see their next training session, his hand on her ass, uptight Nic letting out a yelp, and Jesse saying, 'But Jane said you wanted me to!' I realise that yesterday's experience has clearly unhinged me mentally and I need to shut the fuck up. I close my mouth, stand up to stretch . . . and catch sight of myself in the mirror.

My forearms, my upper arms, are covered with bruises, some imprints of fingers, clear hand marks. The marks on my wrists from Matt's leather belt are raw, scabs starting to form. The thin red line around my neck is probably least obvious; I only see it because I know it's there, and the memory of him clipping the PVC-covered metal band around my neck ('It's engraved. What do you think it says, fuckslave?') almost makes me cum on the spot. Other than that line, my neck is fine – just that one brush of the teeth delivered at the airport gate. My shoulders, however, barely covered by the workout tank top, are a mess. His palms, right there, as he pushed me – oh, yes . . . I make a massively conscious effort not to think what my thighs must look like. Or my ass. Fucking hell.

I leap for my hoodie and pull it on. Jesse stands there, staring.

Probably transfixed not by my exposition of a divorcing woman's sexual crisis but by the evidence of Matt. On my arms. Everywhere.

Oh, fucking fucking hell.

'You'd feel like shit,' I supply the answer to my rhetorical question, because really I've gone too far now to stop, and I need to distract him. 'You'd question your self-worth – and certainly your sexual self-worth. And when you were sweating in the gym with your hot twenty-six-year-old trainer, you'd really want him to, accidentally-on-purpose, caress your ass.'

The silence is deafening. And Jesse is redder than he's probably ever been in his life.

I am a moron.

Mentally unhinged.

'I should not have said anything,' I backtrack. 'I'm sorry. I'm off-kilter, and seeing her so down made me more so, and I'm just saying shit better left unspoken.'

'You often do that,' Jesse says after a pause.

I don't argue.

'What next?' I ask. 'Make me lift heavy shit. So I shut the fuck up.'

'Boot-strappers,' he says. 'Take off the hoodie. You'll get too hot.'

'I'll be fine.' I start hopping.

'Take it off,' he says. I ignore him. One. Two. Three . . .

'So,' he says. 'You think of me as your hot twenty-six-year-old trainer?'

I choose not to answer. Eight. Nine. Ten. Eleven.

'The marks on your arms,' Jesse says deliberately. Repaying bluntness with bluntness. 'Are they from Alex?'

I choose not to answer. Which in a way is a way of answering, isn't it?

Fourteen. Fifteen. The burn starts. Sixteen.

'How do your wrists feel?' Jesse's voice is uneven. 'Right now?'

Eighteen. Nineteen. Twenty. I grind my teeth.

'This must really, really hurt.'

I break pace for a moment to look at him.

His sweat pants are loose, but not loose enough.

Apparently he's not gay.

But at this point, I probably can't ever introduce him to Lacey's late-blooming seventeen-year-old daughter when she comes to town to visit her mom.

'Ten more,' he says. Professional. 'Maintain your form.'

When I'm done, curled up in a ball on the floor and hurting everywhere, he sits on the floor very close to me.

'You want me to give your girlfriend an ego boost,' he says. 'By . . . what? Showing her a little extra attention?'

This is my chance to apologise again, to reiterate that what I raised was totally inappropriate, and clearly stemming from the mental disarray caused by my once happily married parents' divorce. Or the fucking I endured last night at my forever lover's hands. Cock. Oh, fuck.

'Yes,' I say instead.

'By . . . what? Doing something like this?'

He puts a hand on my ass. Intuitively, or rather, inevitably, because they are everywhere, over the imprint of Matt's hand. 'Like this?' he asks. And presses.

I fucking yelp.

Leap up.

'No,' I say. 'Not quite like that.' I pause. Take his measure. 'You know what? I was out of line. It was inappropriate. As inappropriate as . . .' I pause. He's flushed. And still hard.

I should stop talking. Now.

'She's hurting,' I say. 'I feel bad.' And then, I add, 'And I feel . . . generous today.'

We lock eyes. Jesse raises his eyebrows. 'You are full of surprises today, Jane.'

I shrug. Turn around and leave.

I might need to find a new personal trainer. A new gym. Fuck.

I want to text Marie, but I'm not quite sure what to say. 'I just asked Jesse to sleep with Nicola. In retrospect a bad idea. Fuck.' Nice opening. 'Also, he's inferred much too much from the state of my arms.' Wait, I definitely can't tell her that. Oh, fuck.

Instead, I text my mom. 'How are you?'

And then my dad. 'How was your first night in the new place?'

And then Alex. 'I love you. But I'm thinking take-out for supper again after all. Sorry.' And then I start to text, 'I might need to find a new personal trainer.' But I delete that one.

And then Nicola. 'You're fabulous. In every way. Go seduce an 18-year-old boy.' It'll probably make her laugh. Or hate me. I just don't know.

And finally, I do text Marie. 'Coffee? Caesars? Come over con kinder in 45?'

My dad texts me back first. 'Want to come see the new place?' That's an easy one. No, not even a little bit. But I'll have to do the dutiful daughter thing shortly. In the interim: 'Not today. Soon.' And, in a sudden return of my anger and resentment, I add, 'You call Mom today?' And that's the end of that conversation.

Marie and I spend the afternoon watching the kids destroy my living room and drinking Caesars. I share nothing. She shares too much. Craig is 'too too everything'. They've set a date for the Charcut-Le Germain meeting, right after Christmas. She's swooning again, and in the middle of her raptures over Craig I decide that her marriage to JP is effectively over. It's just a matter of time. The intensity of her attachments and desire for a string of insipid and generally unappealing would-be lovers exhausts me. And I am unfair. I should understand. I should empathise. And I don't, because . . . I pause and wonder how badly I want to chase self-awareness, but there is no need to chase it, because it just comes. I don't empathise because I am utterly selfish. So wrapped up in what fulfils me and its power that I don't see that Marie's chasing what I have. That perhaps if I didn't have it – if it hadn't come to me as it did – I would be like her. Chasing. And settling for vapid imitations of the real thing.

The real thing. What the fuck is that?

My arms, wrists, back, thighs, pussy, everything hurts.

Each move reminds me. Of the real thing.

I am not jonesing for a Facebook message fix today.

'Jane!' Marie snaps. 'Why do I even bother talking to you?' She drops her face into her hands theatrically.

'Tell me,' I say, mechanically. 'Tell me.'

And she does. Again. Craig. Craig. Craig. She does not remember Paul's slight or Zoltan or what's-his-name who came before. Craig. Craig.

And I wonder if she will meet him at Charcut. And follow him upstairs to a room at Le Germain.

Or if this will be another go-nowhere play.

I wonder if Marie reads too much online porn. Or bad chick lit. I realise I've never asked. I start to open my mouth to ask and realise, yet again, that this is not what she wants or needs to hear. And I clasp her hand, and pat her knee.

'Oh, Marie,' I say. 'I understand.'

Fucking liar – me, not her. But what do I say? Do I say I see her heading for a precipice? That I see the end of all of this being an explosive, ugly termination to a marriage she's been unhappy with for years? That whatever affair she finally manages to execute or confess to JP will be simply an excuse for an exit? That she's doing her best to provide JP, not the gentlest and most understanding of people in the first place, with a wealth of emotional ammunition in what will be a tremendously ugly divorce?

I want to tell her all of this. And more. How vulnerable she is making herself. What she could do instead. All sorts of things.

But who am I to tell her? How can I tell her anything? I cannot.

I cross my arms on my chest. My palms touch, through my sweater, the places where Matt's hands dug into me 24 hours ago.

I think I come at the memory.

I accept that I am a total hypocrite.

I listen.

The kids are asleep when Alex comes home. I'm not, but I lie wrapped in covers in the dark, breathing softly, hoping, for the first time in weeks, that he will be too tired to reach for me. I listen to him undress. Slide into bed. His lips touch my forehead . . . and he rolls away. Sleeps.

I ache. Remember. Dream.

Day 26 – Blame

I wake up before Alex. Shower with the bathroom door locked. Hope I heal fast. Tiptoe downstairs to make coffee. Don't think about how I feel. What I want. Don't think at all.

Coffee. Laptop.

I hesitate for perhaps 30 seconds.

Fuck it.

—Lover.

Good morning.

—How is your crisis?

Abated. I am about to soak in a hotel room jacuzzi.

Bathe with me, my lover. How is your body?

—Remembering you. Acutely.

And when she remembers me, how does she feel?

—she is wet

—and scared

Scared of what

—the things I let you do to me

Willingly

Completely

—and regretful, a little

Thoroughly

Why regretful?

—what would it have been like if you had unlocked me like this 10, 20 (that is terrifying) years ago?

—But

—I don't think I would have been . . . ready.

The timing is perfect

You are ready now

—Yes

Are you ready to serve?

—I may still be exhausted.

I don't fucking care. My morning cock needs taking care of.

—Demanding.

Always. I bought you a present yesterday. I'm thinking of you in it and it's making me hard. As is looking at the pictures I took of your lovely pussy.

—Jeezus. Don't talk about that.

—What is my present?

You'll see. As for the other: a little late for shame and shyness now, don't you think, my fuckslave? Now – to work. I ate at sushi restaurant last night. Supremely tacky. Wooden boats. Actual Japanese servers. Uptight clients in suits.

—Sounds . . . hellish, actually.

It was . . . stimulating. You were there.

—I was?

Yes. They were so fucked up, they needed an analyst of your calibre. So you were there. I barely nodded at you in acknowledgement. Although, of course, I knew you.

—Bastard. But a few minutes later, you texted me.

— 'Go to the bathroom.'

How did you know? But of course. You were there.

—What next?

I met you in the hallway outside the washrooms. As you'd been instructed to wait.

Without a word I grab your neck and drag you into the men's room.

There's a random Asian man washing his hands at the sink.

330

'Get the fuck out.'
He leaves, hands dripping.
—I'm so shaken . . . shaking. I can hardly stand up.
I push the trash can against the door to lock it.
'Get down on your fucking knees.'
I force you to the floor.
—(Are those always going to be the first words you say
to me when you see me, lover?)
(That's a promise.)
—I sink to the floor, the pressure of your hands almost
unnecessary because I'm so undone.
I cannot wait to see you down in your rightful place.
Again.
—Are you wearing a belt?
'Undo my jeans, fuckslave. Fast.'
—I fumble.
Quicker.
—Belt. Button. Zipper.
—And your cock.
Unleashed. SHOVED into your mouth with no preamble.
—you come out hard
—so aroused
Immediately working your mouth hard.
No warm up.
—so hard
—your hands in my hair
No thought for your pleasure.
—no, you are thoroughly focused on your release
Jerking off with your pretty head.
Fucking myself with your face.
'No fucking teeth.'
— 'Sorry,' I mumble, the words an excuse to spit you
out a second, catch a breath.
—My hands, one cupping your balls, the other pressing
against your belly.

331

'There's a good slut.'
Cock slap your face while you pant.
'Back to fucking work.'
—As I take you back in my mouth, an irrelevant part of my mind wonders if my stockings are going to rip to shreds on the floor.
I hope they are. I want my clients to know you're my whore.
The sounds of your wet mouth getting fucked reverberate in the small cramped room.
—Do you worry that the random Asian man will send someone to the bathroom?
No. He was too scared.
He knew not to.
—He was too jealous.
Though he's probably listening outside the door.
—He would have loved to have the nerve to do what you did, to the woman he wants.
—But he never will.
Keep your tongue thrust out.
Yesss. Take my cock deep in your throat.
—I do.
Not that you have much choice.
—I move my hands to your hips, to brace myself, stabilise myself.
You can feel my balls tighten.
—The tip of my tongue touches them when you thrust in.
My cock gets even harder, bigger.
—you're so close to coming
—I am so hungry
—you're using me, but
—I want this, so very, very badly
'I'm cumming down your throat so you'll be presentable.'
Ready fucktoy?

I don't wait for a reply.
Just force your face to the hilt of my cock and pump
cum down your throat
Pump
—I choke
Pump
Nmmmmmmmm
—Swallow
I keep you forced down
—Tears in my eyes from the pressure
Swallow
Don't miss a fucking drop
—Lick
—I curl my tongue around the slit in your relaxing head
I squeeze the last drop from my still hard cock into
your mouth
—I keep my mouth on it
—lick
I grab two paper towels and hand them to you. For
your makeup.
—you've made a mess of my face
'Do up my jeans. Fast.'
'Very good job my little fuckslave.'
—I press my face against your softening cock before I
zip you up.
—Belt.
—Still on my knees.
I push the can out of the way, throw open the door.
The Asian man bolts.
—Jesus
—I spring up
not before he catches a glimpse of you on your knees
—I move, run to the women's washroom.
I walk out. No sense arriving back at the table at the
same time

—I first lock myself in a stall, and sit down, head on my knees.

—Breathe.

—I'm not sure I can make it back to the table.

The taste of cum overwhelming all your senses.

It permeates you. Will everyone know?

I fucking hope they do.

—I'm sure I can't ever look at you again, without a picture of what just happened being writ on my face for everyone to see.

—The smell of you, of me, of sex, is all around me.

When you finally gather your courage and return, I hardly look at you for the entire meal.

You feel so used.

And all feels right in the world.

You discover you are famished.

—Do I?

—I rather thought I'd struggle to swallow anything.

Best meal of recent memory.

—Every bite tastes of your cum.

—. . .

Wow. I liked that.

—I hope you're very, very hard right now my lover.

Deliciously so.

Painfully so.

Now make me cum for real. Type for me . . .

'Jane?' Alex is stumbling down the stairs.

—Real life. xx

'Baby?' I turn to him as I switch screens.

'You left your phone upstairs,' he says. He's holding the phone towards me, sleepy and angry. I feel, for a moment, fear.

He's angry.

But. Not angry enough.

'What?' I reach for it. Force myself to relax.

'She called four fucking times,' he says. 'Four. Fucking. Times. Please tell her what time it is.' He thrusts the phone into my hand. And disappears, back upstairs.

'Marie?' On the other side there is crying and wailing. And the sound of something falling. And finally, Marie's voice.

'Jane, I need to come over. Right now. Right. Now.'

'Of course,' I say. 'I'm here.'

The kids are still in pyjamas when Marie and her two arrive. The boys crowd around the computer. Cassandra retreats to her bedroom with an iPad. Annie refuses to leave my lap. Marie's eyes are red. And, for the first time since I've known her, she's not wearing any makeup. Or, possibly, pants. I look again.

'Are you in your pyjamas?' I ask. Astounded. There are women who leave the house in pyjamas. Marie would never leave the house in . . . yoga pants. Or flats.

'It's over,' she says. 'It's all over.'

I shake Annie off me long enough to fetch and hand Marie a cup of coffee. And wait. It could be all over with – what the fuck's his name? Craig. She could be just talking about Craig.

'Everything is over,' she says. She takes the coffee cup and gives me an ugly, ugly look.

Anger. Fear. Yes. And not residual fear – I am afraid of this. Of her. I take a step back.

'Let's move into the kitchen,' I say, and take the coffee cup away from her. I have a vision of coffee scalding my face and arms. Put it down on the table and pull a chair out for Marie. Sit down. Annie scrambles back into my lap.

She probably shouldn't be here.

'Why don't you go watch a show with Cassie, OK, babe?' I ask. She shakes her head. 'I'm not asking. Marie and Mama need to talk alone. I'll be right back,' I tell Marie, as I piggy-back Annie upstairs.

When I come back, she's gulping coffee. And crying.

Oh, fuck. What has she done?

'I told him everything,' she says, finally. 'Everything.'

Oh, fuck. What *has* she done?

'Everything? Who?' I repeat, I ask. But I know. So much . . . and yet so little. But so much. And of course, Marie made it . . . so much.

'I showed him the texts and the conversations,' she says. 'And the pictures I took and sent. And . . . everything. I told him *everything*.'

I look at her more searchingly now. Carefully. Red eyes. Shaking hands. But what I'm looking for . . . bruises. Because JP . . . and the crying . . .

'And do you know what he did?' she says. Shrill. There is hysteria in her voice. And it rises. 'Do you know what he did?'

No. And I don't want to know. But. I love her.

'Tell me.'

'He said . . . he said . . . he said if that's what it took for me to be happy, then he was OK with it!' she delivers the sentence standing up, then collapses back into her chair.

I don't understand.

'But isn't that . . .'

'He said he was OK with it,' she yells. 'OK with it. With all of it! Any of it! Anything I wanted to do! With anyone! If it made me happy . . .'

'But isn't that . . .'

'How could he fucking do that to me? How could he?'

I don't understand. I don't understand anything. I am clearly an emotional cripple.

'But you said . . .'

'You keep on saying "you said"! Stop that!' she yells. Slams her hands on the table. Gets up and walks in circles around my kitchen.

'And it's all your fault!' she suddenly cries, stopping in front of me.

'How is this my fault?' I want to take a step back, but I stand my ground. And then think . . . OK, maybe it is my fault. I was definitely an enabler. I looked after her kids for her lunches. Her attempted one-night stands. I scripted her fucking sexts. I listened to everything.

I set her up with Craig.

But I never told her to *do* any of it. Least of all to tell all to her husband.

'That's unfair, Marie,' I say.

'I don't care!' she yells. 'I don't care! How could he do that to me? How could you do that to me? Fucking fairy-tale marriage, a husband who adores you . . . and what the fuck do you do? I know you have something happening. I know! I knew before you set me up with your . . . what, what should I call him? One of your cast-offs? And how many have there been, Jane?'

Now, I'm mildly appalled. Frustrated. Oh, my Marie. But what's coming out of her mouth is not about me. It's about her. I'm just a convenient target.

I close my eyes. Forgive her.

She's still yelling.

'You never talk about anything, you never tell me anything, but I'm not fucking stupid, Jane! I see your face when your phone pings. I see you walking around with this smirk on your face like you've just come out of a bedroom and you still feel his hands on your body . . . I see that . . . and I see you . . . I see you . . . and I wanted that . . . I wanted that too. And it was never . . . it was never . . .'

And she sits back down.

'I wanted that,' she says in a hollow voice. 'I thought I wanted that. But it turns out that's not what I want at all. Not at all.'

'Oh, Marie,' I say. And I still don't understand. But I know it's not about me – however Marie's spinning things right now, whatever she's inferred from my behaviour in the last few weeks – her angst, her restlessness, it all pre-dates my mindfuck with Matt. I know this. She doesn't – but it doesn't matter. It's not about me.

It's about her.

So. I ask.

'What do you want?'

She looks at me, with big red-lined eyes, and tears streaking down her face, and suddenly, I get her tragedy. The full depth of her pain, her angst. She doesn't know. She still doesn't know. She still doesn't know if she wants to stay in the marriage. At what price. All she knows is that this permission from JP is *not* at all what she wanted. But she hasn't accepted, she hasn't allowed herself to admit that what she wanted – what she has been courting for years – was an explosion of anger from him at her betrayal. And . . . an end.

'Did you want him to get angry?' I ask. 'Did you want him to . . .'

'I don't know,' she says. And she's spent. And she's going to say it. 'I don't know what I want. I don't know anything.'

And she cries some more.

I make more coffee.

I make nothing better for Marie, of course, but let her cry and rant and tell me it's all my fault another dozen times, and then apologise for it twice, even though she doesn't really mean it. I send her on her way with a Christmas card and a bottle of Jäger. 'Is this good?' she asks, looking at it suspiciously. 'God-awful,' I say.

I make the kids watch *Elf* again. And then *The Santa Clause*. Ponder whether I need to stay on call for Marie today and decide that I do. And so pick up on the first ring when my second mother-in-law calls. And agree to come to brunch the next day. Although I'm with it enough to insert the caveat that Alex may have to work.

'Of course,' Jeanette says. 'Of course. Although if he could make it, I would be so happy to see him.'

'Of course.'

The kids, fortunately, are thrilled. Their dad, I know, will not be. And so I don't tell him when he comes in through the door. Five minutes later, the doorbell rings and Lacey, Clint and Clayton arrive with boxes of Thai food. 'Surprise!' Lacey calls. 'Neighbour potluck!'

'Oh, babe!' I fall into her arms, and, without a thought, kiss her earlobes. Both of them. 'Oh, you have saved me!'

'I am a little bit psychic, as you know,' Lacey says. 'We've also brought wine.'

'Bless you.' I shepherd them upstairs. 'Alex! Clint and Lacey are here with Thai!'

'Great,' he says. Not like he means it. But he hugs the kids and embraces me, and shakes Clint's hand.

'What's eating Alex?' Lacey asks, as she helps me spoon out food onto paper plates.

'I don't know,' I answer. 'We haven't had a chance to talk – he got back from work about five minutes before you rang the doorbell. Some work shit? This is always a weird time of year: some client or other bets everything on closing before New Year's, or even Christmas. The result, stress.'

We both turn our heads to look at Alex. He and Clint are sitting next to each other, wine glasses in hand. Not talking.

'That's why men will always die sooner than women,' says Lacey. 'They stress, but they don't talk. They don't *share*.' I smile at Lacey. Who shares everything. And I think of Marie, who apparently shared too much. My lips go stiff.

'Sharing is overrated,' I say. Alex hears me, looks at me. Forehead creases.

'What's that, Jane?' he asks.

'Sharing, talking, incessantly communicating, telling *everything*,' I say, delivering plates to the table. I pick up my wine and raise it. 'To blessed silence.' Clint, without making eye contact with me, joins me in the toast. Lacey laughs.

'Well, this will be an entertaining dinner party!' She titters. She really titters. For a moment, I love her a little less. 'Blessed silence, ha!'

But Lacey is present, so there is no silence. She makes Alex laugh, and even Clint, after a third glass of wine, starts to offer one-line contributions to the conversation. But mostly it's Lacey, full of stories of Christmases past, tying everything to the Christmas present, the planned wedding, and – because Lacey tells everything, always, and never tries to hide anything – the latest speculations on Sofia's and maybe-Clint's baby.

'So the other guy is really pushing for her to get a prenatal paternity test, did you know there was such a thing?' she says. 'He can't wait for it to come out to know – he needs to know now! Why? If she's willing to wait – and Clint's willing to wait – why can't he?'

Clint flushes an unbecoming red.

Alex shakes his head. What do you say to that?

By the time Clint and Lacey leave, Annie's passed out on the couch, and Henry and Eddie are over-tired and insane. I tell Cassandra how amazingly grateful I am that she can just read herself to sleep, and chase the boys into bed. They're asleep in minutes.

Alex is in bed. Morose again.

'Oh, my baby,' I say, sitting beside him. I'm not sure what to say. So I lift up the covers, and tug at his pyjama bottoms.

'Jane? Fuck. Jane. A blowjob is not the answer to everything,' he says. 'Oh . . . Jesus. Don't stop . . . we can talk about . . . we will talk . . . later.'

I take him into my mouth and throat easily. He doesn't fuck my mouth; I fuck him. There is nothing here of the intensity or anger or whatever it is that manifests in Matt when he drags me into the men's washroom at – but that didn't happen. Reality.

I suck my husband's cock and try not to imagine myself on my knees in a Vancouver sushi restaurant.

Fail.

He comes quickly. But not happily.

He pulls me up and wraps his arms around me. Buries his face in my hair. I stroke his hair and back.

'This is the point at which the wife says, "Tough day, honey?"' he says from inside my neck.

'Ah,' I say. 'Tough day, honey?' I ask.

Silence.

'Not so much for me,' he says finally. 'But . . . ah . . . did you talk with Marie today?'

'More than, she was here most of the morning,' I say. 'Remember? Those four morning telephone calls?'

'So you know?'

'Know what?' I ask. I'm not obtuse. I'm just . . . cautious.

'JP came to see me,' Alex says.

Awkward. The husbands working together. Different departments and all that, but. Not close friends, not colleagues. But. Partners.

'Did he,' I say.

'He told me,' Alex says.

This is going to be a very slow, painful conversation.

'For fuck's sake, Alex,' I snap. 'He told you what? A, I wasn't there. B, I'm not a fucking mind-reader.'

'But you're Marie's best friend, so of course you know!' he snaps back.

'Know what? I know what she told me. I do not know what he told you.' I drop my voice, remembering sleeping children. 'And beloved? We are not going to have a fight over Marie and JP's fucked-up marriage.'

'So you know,' says Alex. 'About the guy . . . and the other guys . . . and the thing . . . and everything.'

Everything? Can anyone know everything? I probably know more than Alex, because I can't see JP, no matter how distraught, telling his partner that he gave his wife permission to fuck around. Or that she showed him the skanky pictures of herself that she sent to her would-be lovers. Or the texts she had been exchanging with them. What would he have told Alex, actually, I wonder?

Perhaps he said, 'Marie wants to have an affair.'

Perhaps he said, as Marie yelled, 'Jane set up Marie with her ex-lover.'

Oh, that would be just perfect. Very JP, in fact. I can see him doing a paternalistic mentor/big-brother shtick. 'I just thought you should know, Alex . . .'

Bastard.

'Some of it,' I say. 'Probably not everything.'

Silence. And then . . .

'JP says it's your fault.'

Fuck. Of course. Thank you, universe.

'Does he now,' I say. 'Funny. Marie said the same thing. About twelve times. I did not appreciate it from her, either.'

'I told him to stop talking and get the fuck out of my office,' Alex says. 'Jane?'

'Yes?'

'Is there anything you want to tell me?'

'No.'

Silence.

'Really and truly?'

'Yes.'

He's silent. My yes is not enough. I search inside myself for more. What does he need?

I speak calmly. Carefully.

'There is nothing I want to tell you. There is nothing I need to tell you. Except that you are my husband, the father of my children, and this is till death do us part.'

'Jane?'

'Yes?'

'Remember what you said, that other night? About . . .

342

monogamy, marriage. Sometimes being hard. Frustrating. Boring. And today, about some things best being left unsaid?'

'Yes?'

'If you had to tell me . . . if you wanted to tell me . . . would I have a lot to forgive?'

There are parts of my body that still feel on fire from the six-hour fuckathon I had two days ago with my forever lover. And I was just imagining his cock in my mouth as I was blowing you.

'No.'

I hear the furnace powering up. The pipes in the bathroom creaking. If I strain my ears, I think I can hear the funny not-quite-snoring snorts coming from the girls' room. That's Annie.

'Till death do us part, no matter what, my love?' he says finally.

'Till death do us part. No matter what,' I echo.

It takes him a long time to fall asleep, and he holds my hand, tightly, through the night.

Day 27 – Endurance

I wake up too early again. And I want to . . . I want to talk to Matt. Not fuck. Talk.

Time zones work in my favour.

—Lover.
Where were we?
—Interrupted. Thwarted by the universe.
Worst universe ever. What happened, my lover?
—Are you superstitious and inclined to believe in signs?
Depends on my moods. I'm superstitious in bursts.
—And right now?
Not so much. What happened? Tell me.

And I tell him. I tell him about Marie, her *faux* affairs, her latest attempt at one and my role in it, her disclosure, her husband's reaction and her own. Her attempt to pull me into it; last night's conversation with Alex. I tell him about my parents. Alex's dad. Jeanette. And, for good measure, about Nicola, the skank and the rat-fuck bastard. The Greek chorus of self-righteous cheater-hating wives. About my stupid conversations about Nicola with Jesse.

Everything. Too much. When I'm done, I stop typing.

And?
—That's it. How can there be more? Well, my next-door-neighbour's fiancé may or may not have impregnated his on-again, off-again other girlfriend while planning their wedding, but that's really the happiest plot line in my life right now.
Other than ours.
—Oh yes?
Lover. One question. Are you feeling guilty? Over us?

And I stop. And think really hard about this, which is hard, because for the last 27 days I have felt much, but have worked hard to think – about us, about guilt, about consequences – as little as possible.

Finally:

—No. If anything, what I feel is guilt over feeling guiltless.
Good.
—Worrisome.
We may be missing those genes.
—Do you? I keep on expecting it to kick in with a vengeance at some point.
But until then?
—Lust.
Good.
—Here we are, discussing messy life and guilt and morals, and I just want you to shut the fuck up and shove your cock in my mouth.
Even better.
We can drown ourselves in each other's lust.
My slut. My shameless whore.
—I blame you.
Choke on me.
DEEPER

345

—Spit dripping out corners of my mouth, barely able to breathe

I want to fuck your face so hard

—I want to be used by you until there is nothing left of me

Frighten you as you're struggling to take me

—no awareness, no self

—I want to feel your power

You're just a mouth

A cunt

Mine.

—I exist, in those moments, only for you, for your pleasure

—for your use

I feed off your submission. Take power from you.

—I lose myself in you

I fucking felt you cum, right now. Did you?

—Yes.

Good.

Unfortunately, reality calls me. Are you better now, my lover?

—Yes, my twisted counterpart. Still worried about our sanity and morality or lack thereof. But better.

My present should arrive today. Dress for me. Send me photos. And think of my cock in your throat when you need a distraction.

xx

—xo

The box from Vancouver arrives while Alex is in the shower. 'Saturday delivery?' I say, to say something. 'Yup,' the courier says eloquently. It's big. I know, without opening it, it will contain boots. Thoroughly inappropriate-to-wear-in-public slut boots. And smile. Put the box, unopened, in my closet. Decide to think of what's inside as a New Year's Eve present for Alex.

When I tell Alex we're having brunch with Jeanette, he looks, for a moment, like *he* wants to shove something down my throat. But then he nods. 'She is a good grandmother,' he says. And looks at me. 'And you,' he says. 'They never tell you. I never tell you. But I know that if it weren't for you, I'd never see them. Any of them. Possibly not even my mom.'

'You'd see your mom,' I say. 'You're not an asshat. We'll be brief, eat and run. We've got to go get your mom from the airport anyway – we can't stay long.'

Neither one of us says it, but we both think it – and we never have to see Claire again. Sometimes, there is a silver lining.

Jeanette is dancing on air, the definition of fey. I attribute it to Alex's presence – and his endurance of her hug. She kisses all the children.

'Where's . . . um . . .' What was his name? '. . . Christian?' I ask when Alex steps out of earshot.

'Oh,' she says. 'He's . . . he's gone.' And pirouettes – I swear, she pirouettes – into the kitchen.

The table is resplendent. So says Cassandra. 'Resplendent,' Annie echoes.

'Wow, Jeanette, you've really gone all-out,' I say. 'This is beautiful.'

'Nice tablecloth,' Alex says. Then adds, 'It looks familiar.'

We sit. And that's when Jeanette drops the bomb.

'I have a surprise for you,' she says. 'Kids? Look who's here!'

And as Alex says, 'If it's "Uncle" Christian, I'm getting the fuck out of here now,' his father walks into the room.

I disassociate, as a defence mechanism. The kids whoop and run to Grandpa – Grandpa live is a treat and much more appealing than Grandpa on the computer screen. They hug him, even Henry. Kiss him. There is cooing, and shouting, and over it all, Jeanette's voice: 'What a Christmas surprise, hey, my darlings? What a Christmas surprise!'

Alex is sitting very, very still. I'm so aware of his stillness, it hurts. His chest isn't even moving. I'm afraid to look at him.

And then, in one smooth motion – he brings out his phone. Types. My phone beeps.

- I'll be in the car.

And he's gone.

The children are still covering Grandpa, and Jeanette is still pirouetting. But she sees her stepson's exit, and I see tears swirl in her eyes and I see her look at her ex-husband. Ex-ex-husband? And then at me.

'I'll be right back,' I say. 'Give us a few minutes.'

'I'm sorry,' she whispers. She steps away from the spectacle of her ex-husband and the kids and right up to me. 'I'm so sorry. We thought . . . and I thought . . .'

'Some things don't really work as surprises,' I say. 'Look – start eating without us, OK? The kids are starving. I'll be right back.'

'Will you bring Alex back?' Jeanette asks. Wistfully.

'I don't know.'

He's sitting in the driver's seat, very erect.

'My love,' I say, as I slide in beside him. 'Oh, my love.'

'Tell me you didn't know,' he says.

'Not a fucking clue,' I say. 'You have to ask?'

'What am I supposed to do?' he says.

'He's your father,' I say. 'I think . . . I think you're supposed to say, "Merry Christmas."'

We're silent. I put my hand on his knee. He rests his on mine. Throws his head back and closes his eyes.

'So full of rage,' he murmurs. 'So fucking angry.' He roughly takes my hand off him, pushes me away. 'Don't touch me. I don't want to . . . I don't want to act like I did the other day.'

I stay silent.

Then:

'Do you need to?' I ask.

'Fuck. Yes.'

I slide across the seat towards him, and his hand snakes around my head and neck and pushes me down. I unzip his pants quickly. And for the first time in our twelve years together, parked in front of his stepmother's driveway, Alex fucks my mouth. He thrusts, and he slams my head down on his cock. Tears fill my eyes and I gag.

It's what Matt does and what makes me drip, but right now, it is absolutely, absolutely horrible. I fucking hate it. There is no room or desire for fantasy. There is no sliver of pleasure. I don't even try to dissociate or fantasise. Tears streak out of my eyes.

I endure.

'Jesus, Jane, I'm so sorry,' he whispers into the back of my neck after he comes. 'I'm so sorry. Fucking hell. What the fuck is wrong with me?'

'Rage,' I whisper back. 'Rage.'

I don't know who's angry – the seven-year-old boy whose father left his mother, or the 33-year-old man whose father left his stepmother. And if it is the 40-year-old man sitting beside me who is this angry, is he angry because his father *left* his third wife – or *came back* to the second one?

I don't know.

But I have to tell him.

'Alex? Does it make it any easier . . . I don't know if it makes it easier. But I do know – it was Claire who left. Claire, not him.'

Silence.

He doesn't ask me how I know. He doesn't tell me it helped. He doesn't tell me it doesn't matter.

We sit.

'Do I have to go back in there?' he asks finally.

'He's your father,' I say. 'I don't know. I really don't know. But I should. Do you want me to just collect the kids?'

In the end, we go back in together. Alex's father looks up at us from his plate of eggs, bacon, waffles and mini-quiches – Jeanette truly did go all-out – and nods. Says nothing. Alex sits down. Says nothing.

'Did you know Grandpa was coming, Dad?' Eddie shouts. 'Did you?'

'No,' Alex says. 'Total surprise.' He spears a bacon rasher. Jeanette looks away.

Jeanette will tell me the whole story, such as it is, soon enough. She's still cooing and pirouetting. Despite Alex's exit and palatable anger, she's happiness incarnate. *He's* back. And she doesn't have to tell me what happened, not really. He's never been alone. He made sure of Jeanette before he left Alex's mom; he got Claire before he left Jeanette. And there he was. Alone. I wonder, did Claire leave him face-to-face? Did they have The Talk? Or did she do it through Skype? Or email?

Perhaps she was old-fashioned. A handwritten note, pinned to the ex-marital pillow.

And how long did he last by himself? A day? Two?

No fucking way he spent Christmas alone.

It briefly occurs to me that perhaps, if I had insisted we call him when we got the news, if I invited him for Christmas, this would not have happened. At least not this quickly, and *today* would not have happened. But would that have been a good thing or a bad thing?

I don't know. I know nothing.

Jeanette's keeping his coffee cup topped up and his plate loaded. And chattering to Cassandra and Eddie. Throwing me looks. Studiously not looking at Alex.

Alex's father is eating.

I violate all rules of etiquette and pull out my telephone. Start texting. To my dad, 'I love you. So very much.' To my mom, 'I love you. How are you holding up?' To Alex, 'Five minutes?'

He texts me back.

- Four.

We leave without father and son exchanging a word or making eye contact. Jeanette does not attempt to hug Alex goodbye. I don't evade her arms when they reach for me, but I struggle to reciprocate. The children, fortunately, are oblivious.

I drive to the airport.

Realise either Alex or I will have to tell his mother her ex-husband is back with the second wife. Before the kids do.

Fuck.

'I need to go to the gym tomorrow,' I tell Alex as I drop him off at the arrivals doors. 'Possibly for hours.'

He nods. 'I need to drink to excess today,' he says. 'Definitely for hours.'

I nod.

'How do Clint and Lacey do it?' I ask. 'In and out, in and out, drama and comedy and tragedy, and always, reunion? And she, always laughing, always trusting?'

Alex thinks for a minute. 'I don't know,' he says finally. 'Maybe she really is psychic and knows how it's all supposed to turn out. And maybe he trusts her. Completely.'

The drive home is full of Nana talking about Houston Christmas. None of the children mentions seeing Grandpa. And when we get to Okotoks, Alex fails to drink himself into a stupor in front of his mother, perhaps because she, again, seems quite unfazed by the news. Left this wife, back to that one. Does it matter? No longer hers, not with her. Perhaps it is irrelevant, really. It has been more than 30 years. Or, perhaps, she is a devoted mother putting on a good show for her son. The dinner is awkward, but not painful. Jeanette calls me. Six times. I let it go to voicemail.

After we put the kids to bed, I wrap my arms around Alex and hold him tight. He rests his head against my breasts.

'I really like your dad, you know,' he says suddenly.

'I know,' I say.

'I'm so sorry,' he says, again. What's he apologising for? His father's behaviour? His genetics? The awful mouth-fucking in the car?

It doesn't matter. What he needs to hear:

'I know,' I say. 'I love you.'

He's still awake, head on my chest, when I fall asleep.

Day 28 – Utilitarian Sex

Sunday, December 30

Are you still mine?
—Utterly.
Tell me.
—Always and in all ways.
Show me.

. . .

—Check your email.

. . .

Instantly hard. I envy your trainer.
—He won't get to see all of that.
Of course not. Better today?

I pause. Truthfully? Yes. Alex I'm not so sure about, although he's got game face on as he cajoles the children into snowsuits and out into the snow with sleds. And I know he's taking them sledding because he can't ever remember going sledding with his father.

—Yes. And I'll be better yet after I lift heavy things until I'm covered with sweat and too exhausted to even scream.
Now I envy every man in your gym.
—I have to go.
Go. Tease. Tantalise. Remember who owns you. xx
—xo

The gym is empty, as befits the last Sunday of the old year. It will be unbearably full next week. I ponder whether I should start with the hated pull-ups or work up to them.

'Jane?'

Jesse. Fuck.

'Why are you working on a Sunday?' I demand. Suddenly angry. Dealing with Jesse was not on today's agenda.

'I'm not,' he says. Defensive. 'I just needed to . . . you know. Lift heavy things. And not think.' I see him trying not to look at me. And I laugh. Disarmed.

'My fault?' I ask. He chews his lower lip.

'A little,' he says.

'I'm sorry,' I say. Genuine. 'I was . . . out of sorts on Thursday. It's been a rather intense week. Month.'

'I'm sorry too,' he says. 'You were – I know you were just thinking of ways to help your friend. Insane, stupid ways, yes. But . . . I was . . . I was . . . unfair.'

That's an interesting spin on it. Unfair?

'We're good?' I ask.

He nods. 'We're good.' Pauses. 'Do you want me to spot you?'

'No, babe, it's your day off. Go do your thing,' I say. 'I'm just going to do . . . pull-ups. And other shit that makes me want to vomit.'

'You'll never do more than two on your own,' he says. And boosts me up to the bar.

As his hands barely touch my still-tender hips, but linger on them for just a second too long, I realise we may not be OK after all. Fuck. And I keep my mouth shut all the rest of the workout. As does he.

I curse my bad judgement. And, for good measure, Nicola, although it's clearly not her fault.

He's waiting for me by the doors when I come out of the changing room.

'There's this New Year's Eve party I'm going to,' he says.

Eyes on the ground. 'Very casual. Lots of people. I could invite her to that. Would that help?'

'Oh, sweetheart,' I say. Disarmed totally. 'That would be above and beyond the call of duty.'

He stands there a second longer. Awkward. 'Well, see you in the New Year, Jane,' he says finally.

'Happy New Year,' I answer. Smile. Walk away.

Alex and the kids are home when I get back, watching *Muppet Christmas* and drinking hot chocolate. I slide on to the couch beside him.

'Better?' he asks. I nod. 'I called my father,' he offers, looking at the screen.

'Wow.'

'Well, I called Jeanette,' he corrects. 'I talked to my father.'

'And?'

'He's my father.' Alex shrugs. Which, I interpret, means they said 'How are you?' 'Fine' and 'See you in the New Year.' Perhaps an awkward 'I love you' – no, probably not.

Annie and Eddie start a fight over who gets to be in my lap; Alex scoops Annie into his. Eddie settles into my armpit. Annie sticks her bum up into Alex's face. He plops her down on top of Eddie who howls. We switch kids.

'Have you heard from Marie?' Alex asks. My hand involuntarily goes to my phone, even though I know there are no messages.

'No,' I say. 'I don't expect I will for a while. Although I think they're invited to Lacey's party tomorrow.'

'Well, that will be awkward,' Alex says.

'An appropriate continuation of the most awkward holiday season ever,' I agree. 'Marie and I will be OK, you know. Eventually.'

'I seriously pondered switching firms just so I wouldn't have to call him my partner any more,' Alex says. 'And I fucking swear, if he ever mentions your name to me again . . . all his teeth. Gone.'

'I'd rather enjoy seeing that,' I say.

'Did Mom just say she wants you to punch JP in the face?' Henry pipes up. 'That is so cool!'

'I keep on forgetting they have ears,' Alex says. I rest my head on his shoulder and, with Annie in my lap, and Eddie occasionally kicking my thighs, doze off until the movie's over.

The kids are all in bed and asleep. Alex disappears into the basement – 'I think I too need to lift heavy shit today to decompress,' he says – and it's late in Calgary, and very late in Montréal. But I'm his. So I check in.

—Lover.
Thank God. I have need of you.
—Anything.
I need you to get me hard and ready for utilitarian, reproductive sex.

  . . .
—Seriously? This, you ask of me?
What the fuck are you?
—Yours.
Continue.
—Your whore. Your fuckslave.
So yes. This I ask of you. Do I have to say it?
—Yes.
Do what you're fucking told.
—How much time do you have?
Enough. Make it good. Reproductive sex is fucking boring.

I understand him perfectly. I always did. I don't need to think for long; I know exactly what he needs to hear, right now.

356

—Do you remember . . . it must have been barely three days before my wedding.

Your and Alex's wedding. This is going to make me want to fuck my wife?

—Yes. You don't remember. You were already in Montreal. You flew back for our wedding, with Joy. You stayed at the fucking Ramada Inn.

We were still counting pennies. But I remember now. We met for coffee.

—Coffee? We met in the hotel room.

There was a coffeemaker. I made coffee. You said, 'Where's Joy?' She was shopping.

—Her suitcase was on one of the beds. You started pulling her lingerie out, showing me.

You were angry. I wanted to make you angry.

—I was sitting on the other bed. And I asked you how monogamy was going. You had been married, what, six months?

Something like that. I remember, I wanted to stuff her panties in your mouth.

—Instead, you asked me to tell you about my last pre-marital fling. How did you know?

I know you as well as you know me.

—And I told you.

Tell me again. Yesss. Just like you told me then. I sat down on the bed beside you.

—I said, it was a few weeks ago. Alex was – away. At some conference. And we had this big workshop – I was still coaching skiing then, remember, but not competing any more. They brought in some big shot from Quebec. So fucking hot. Mulatto. Six-foot-three. Blond corns. Ripped.

—Another guy from the team, from Edmonton, was billeting with me, for the workshop.

Mmmm. I liked that set up the first time, too. By

357

*this time, we were lying on the bed. I reached for your
legs.*

—I slapped you. I said, no fucking hands. Just listen.
Tease.

—So. Where were we? Fiancé away. House guest.
Workshop. Saturday afternoon. I have a work party
Saturday night after the seminar. The Edmonton guy –
he's got plans Saturday night *sans* me, but he's coming
back to my place, not necessarily with expectations, but
perhaps with hopes.

—We had, um, transgressed before.
Of course.

—Workshop is terrific. The Quebec guy spends a lot of
time on me, during the workshop.
I bet he did.

—That's what you said when I told you the story the
first time, too.
I'm consistent. Continue.

—As things are wrapping up, he comes up to me, asks
me what I was doing that night. I say, work party –
would he like to come? He says – too spent for the
party. Would I come see him after?

—And he gives me his motel room key.

—When I told you the story the first time, I pretended I
didn't know what he was saying.

—But of course I did.

—Although, in all honesty, I was not sure . . . how fully
I would transgress.

—There are gradations to this art, as you know.
Of course.

—(hard?)
(Very much so.)
Continue.

*Bold move, the hotel key. One of my favourite parts.
He gets bolder, if I remember right.*

—Yes.

—I call him from the party – it runs later than I had anticipated – to see if he was 'still up for something'. He 'is eagerly waiting'.

—So I go.

—I don't use the room key; I knock.

so shy

(so fucking hard)

—He opens the door wearing boxer shorts.

—'You made me get dressed,' he says.

—I say, 'Should you get dressed more, so we can go to the bar and get a drink or something?'

So innocent. When you told me that story the first time, at this point, I had you stroking my cock.

—No. You were fucking hard, and starting to fumble with your belt. Groaning a little. But every time you reached for me, I slapped you away.

That's not how I remember it. Your hands on my cock by this time. Yesss. Tell me more.

—So there I am, at the door. Demure. Honestly, not a hundred per cent sure yet. And he says, in that über-sexy French accent, something like 'The things I want to do with you, I can't do in a bar.'

—I totally freeze up. Possibly yelp.

—And he laughs, and says, 'English girls!'

Here comes my favourite part.

—You do remember.

—He shepherds me to a chair at the far end of the room, sits me down in it and then moves over to the bed. Sprawls there.

—And says, 'I will stay here. And you stay there. And we will talk, and you will tell me things about yourself. And as you feel more comfortable, move the chair closer. I won't come for you.'

Fuck, that is some serious skill.

—Yes.

—I think he had much practice.

Tell me, how long did you hold out. Now, when you're telling me the story the first time, my hands are definitely under your skirt, and yours are on my cock.

—Yes. I held out only a little while, for both of you.

—I move the chair closer, bit by bit, as we talk.

—Such a sexy voice.

a very erotic dance

—When I finally make it within arm's reach of the bed, he reaches for me and pulls me on to the bed.

And you fuck. And as I remember, the plot line – of the original event – goes downhill from here.

—Yes. The sex itself was anti-climactic. *He* had a good time. I was . . . underwhelmed.

—Terrible oral.

When you tell me the story, at this point, I put my face between your legs. I need to make that up to you.

—And I push you away. Hard.

Motel key in hand

slowly inching yourself towards him to get fucked

very sexy

I'm so fucking hard – then, now.

But yes, you push me away, and say, it's not quite over. I let you finish, but I stay down between your thighs. Caressing, licking, occasionally nibbling.

—And now?

Go on. Finish. She's not ready yet.

—So when it's all over (and I think 'Jeezus, finally, that was getting a little monotonous'), he lies on top of me and whispers what I suppose are all the right things (in French) into my ear. He starts trying to lull me to sleep, to stay the rest of the night . . . although there wasn't much left of that . . . with him.

This is the point at which you remember you have another man at your house. Possibly in your bed.
—That's your editorial. More importantly, there is another seminar session tomorrow, and the things I plan to wear for it are still wet in the washer.
—I leave with 'I have things I need to put in the dryer' as the genuine excuse.
—I don't think he believes me.
Of course not.
—I get home. My friend is asleep.
—In my bed, not in the guest room.
Nice.
—I lie down beside him.
—(I switched the laundry stuff to the dryer first, priorities in order.)
naturally
—. . . and sleep like the dead until the alarm rings.
—And in the morning, I am mean.
Hot. I like this part too.
—I slide out of bed, and give him a pat on the arm.
—'Too bad you were asleep when I came home.'
Cruel.
—Yes.
—I'm mildly sorry about that, now, you know.
—He was very fond of me. A good egg.
Tell me what happens next. In my hotel room. As you finish telling me the story the first time.
—Your belt's undone and your cock's out of your pants. My skirt is up around my waist and my panties down to my knees. I'm pushing you away, but you keep on climbing on me. Your fingers caress my pussy, then thrust in. You say . . .
'Are you done talking? Then you can suck my cock.'
—And I say, 'Fuck off.'
'Fuck you? I'm planning to.'

—I don't know when or how you get the condom on . . .

I'm talented.

—. . . but then you're splitting me in half. Fuck. I scream.

I tell you to keep on fighting me.

—It's the most violent sex we've ever had. Well, up to that point.

You're so angry.

—And you?

Perhaps. Yes, I expect I was angry back then. I wasn't as generous with my things yet. I liked the idea of sharing more than the reality.

—I thrust up against you with my hips as I push you away with my hands. I slam my forehead against your chest.

I fucking throw you against the bed, you hit the headboard. Fuck.

—That's when you cum.

You came as soon as I slid into you.

—Slide is not the right verb.

Thrust. Rammed.

—Yes.

—We're lying on the bed, my skirt still up around my waist, your pants undone, belt unbuckled, when we hear Joy fumbling with the door.

Continue. She is coming up the stairs right now.

—I pull up my panties and pull down my skirt. You just sit there, cock, with condom still half on it, hanging out.

—And not until you hear the door open do you slide it off – and into my panties – and do up your pants.

Oh, fuck yes. Thank you lover.

You are entrancing. Always.

—You're welcome. For you.

xx

—xo

Fumbling at my door too. Alex. Naked. Except for a towel wrapped around his waist. I did not hear him come up, or go into the shower. He searches for pyjamas, then glances at me, laptop on lap.

'What are you doing, love?' he asks. Smiles.

What am I doing.

How about: Facilitating reproductive sex for an old friend.

How about: Cyberfucking my forever lover.

Instead:

'Facebooking,' I say. Naked, pyjamas in hand, Alex slides into bed beside me.

'Anything new?' he asks. I look at the screen as I log off.

'Marie's still married. Lacey is yet to update her status to engaged – do you think that's intentional? My father's single and your father's in a relationship.' Alex swats me with a pillow. But laughs.

'And you and I?' he asks as I put the laptop away.

'Married,' I say. He spoons me and kisses the back of my neck. Then slides into me – no thrusting or ramming. The sex is short, but satisfying. My orgasm unfolds slowly and gently, and although part of me is in a hotel room in Calgary three days before my wedding, most of me is in the bed, here, in the present. Satisfied.

After he comes, he's asleep in seconds. I drift off a little more slowly. For the first time in several days, again mostly tranquil.

Mostly.

Because life, after all, is complicated.

Day 29 – For you

Cassandra is more excited about the New Year's Eve party than we are. It's her first time babysitting the troops – her brothers, Annie, Clayton and Marcello. My dad's coming too, but he's been cast in the role of assistant, passive over-watcher. 'Just make sure Gramps knows he's just here in case I need to send him to get you from Lacey's – *I'm* in charge,' she says about a dozen times. I nod. And then, another dozen, two dozen times throughout the day, 'Mom? Can I watch you dress and put on your makeup?' I frown. 'Maybe.'

I'm delivering the day's thirteenth 'Maybe' to her when the phone rings. It's Nicola.

And she's tittering.

I indulge in the thought that if I am ever master of the universe, I will outlaw all tittering. Trilling. Shrieking. Any and all high-pitched sounds.

'So what should I do?' she asks plaintively. Fuck. Apparently there was content in the tittering.

'About what?' I ask.

'Jane, why do you never listen?' she wails. I will also outlaw wailing. 'Jesse just texted me, asked me to go a New Year's Eve party with him! I really want to go. But I can't. The boys – it's supposed to be "Daddy" night, but the rat-fuck bastard assumed I'd have no plans and just dropped them off. He and the skank are going to some poly-dance . . . what the fuck is that? Anyway, God, *I* assumed I'd have no plans. Should I just say, "Oh, thank you, but I can't?" Or . . .'

Oh, Jesse. Sweetheart. Bless the boy's kind heart. I can do my part.

'Bring them over here,' I say. 'No, no argument. Do it. And have an awesome time.'

'I will,' Nicola says. 'I will. God, just to go *out*! Somewhere fun! With a man! Not that all you ladies haven't been great,' she adds. Also calling female friends ladies – against the law. Women. Fuck, girls. Chicks. Bitches. I hate the world ladies.

Apparently, I am in a mood.

But. I will be kind.

'Bring the boys,' I repeat. 'Lacey and Clint's boys will be here too. My dad's on hand to help Cass mind the kids. And we're just next door. Now, go. Get dressed. Look gorgeous.'

And then Nicola shocks me.

'If I sleep with him, I'll have to find another personal trainer,' she says.

Look at that. Perversely, I'm . . . yeah. I'm kind of proud of her. Impressed. Pleased.

Slightly, perhaps, jealous. He's my personal trainer too. Still. I am learning to be generous.

'Small price to pay,' I say.

Nicola squeals – yes, I will also outlaw squealing – and hangs off. I hold the phone in my hand. Text Jesse. 'Thank you.'

The response is immediate. 'For you.'

Well. Fuck. That might be a wee complication for the trainer-client dynamic in the New Year. Even if Nicola doesn't sleep with him, *I* might need to get a new personal trainer.

No good deed goes unpunished.

After the kids eat supper and take off for various corners of the house with their iPads (I am, suddenly, powerfully, grateful to my mother for her extravagance, and I text her a string of xoxoxo's), I take another long, slow shower. Shave, moisturise and generally indulge. Time seems infinite.

'Mom? Can I please watch you dress and put on your makeup?' Cassandra asks again.

I'm dressing, with no pretence that I am doing it for any other reason, to please Matt. Alex will enjoy it, of course. But. I'm not engaging in any self-deception as to who I'm really doing it for. So Cassandra does not get to watch me put on the underclothes. But when they are covered up with a slinky black dress, I invite her to watch me make up my face in the bathroom. I finish it off with sparkles, on my face and hair and on hers. Then, of course, on Annie's. And Henry's. And Eddie's.

'Daddy! You have to come see Mom, she looks like an evil princess!' Eddie yells as he thunders down the stairs.

Alex comes up from the basement, post-workout, for his shower. He's slick with sweat. I turn as he steps into the bathroom and smile.

His sweat pants hide nothing.

'Fucking hell, Jane, you are not wearing that to the party,' he says. 'Put on pants. And . . . a sweater.'

I laugh.

'Seriously,' he says. His erection grows. I bite my lips. 'Fucking hell.' He picks me up and manhandles me into the bedroom. Shuts the door. Dress around my waist.

'What's this?' He fingers the corset.

'A New Year's present,' I say.

'Jesus.' And, despite last night's languorous activities, he's on top of me, and inside me. Utterly selfish. I come in seconds anyway.

It is very, very good to be so desired.

Less good is this: 'And now, my love – pants.'

'A compromise,' I suggest. The dress is still bunched around my waist. 'Panties . . . and . . .' I pull out a petticoat-style skirt. 'This. To make it longer.'

'And sweater?' Alex says, eyeing the petticoat suspiciously.

'Shawl?' I counter, pulling out another lacy thing.

'Fucking hell,' Alex says. And I'm on the bed again.

It occurs to me he will probably freak again when he sees me in Matt's boots.

The doorbell rings. 'Gramps!' I hear screaming, and I hurry downstairs. Dad's already in the kitchen, getting a tour of the night's snacks from Henry. He hugs me, then holds me at arm's length. 'Alex is letting you leave the house like that?' he says.

'For fuck's sake, Dad,' I snap. And Henry giggles. 'Mom just swore at Gramps!' I hear him calling to his siblings as he runs down the hallway.

'I'm sorry,' Dad says. 'You look . . . sensational. But, you know, you will always be my little girl.'

He gives me a 'my little girl who's going to forgive me for leaving her mother, right?' look. I kiss his cheek.

'And you will always be my dad,' I say. 'Thanks for coming over; I know it's just next door, but I feel better having an adult other than Cassandra in the house. Oh, and you'll have a few other kids here.' I take him through the details. 'But Cassandra's in charge, and you're just backup.'

'Fine, fine,' my dad says. 'Glad to have something to do.'

He sits at the kitchen table.

'Your mom's at The Ball,' he says.

Of course. The Ball, hosted by my dad's lodge, is where my parents have spent New Year's Eve for the past . . . 30 years? More, I bet.

'You didn't want to go?' I ask.

'I wanted to go,' he says. 'I just thought it would be better not to. You know.'

I actually do.

'You didn't think of, um, going somewhere else, with, um,' I swallow, 'your friend? The widow?'

How's that for a fucking olive branch, dad?

My dad looks at me and blushes like a twelve-year-old boy. There's a flicker of gratitude in his eyes before he drops them to the table. And then he says . . .

'It wouldn't be right for me to ask her, for something like a New Year's Eve thing,' my father says. Shocked. 'Not now. Not when I just moved out.'

Anger rises in me again, sharp and sudden.

'Really? It wouldn't be right to ask her out on a date on New Year's Eve, but it's right to leave Mom alone in the house the day after Christmas,' I say. 'Really?'

'Janie!' My father says my name as if I am a little girl . . . and then covers his face with his hands. 'Janie . . . I just couldn't live a lie. Not any more. Not for an hour longer. Surely you of all people understand that.'

No. I don't understand that at all.

But that's me.

'Oh, Dad,' I say. Sigh. He turns redder, then white. I close my eyes and take a deep breath. Search for that feeling of 'all is right with the world' I woke up with this morning.

'Dad?' I say finally. 'I'm going to be pissed for a long, long time. But I love you.'

Alex comes down the stairs. He looks so good I think I lick my lips. Our eyes meet.

'Jerry.' He nods to my dad. 'Good of you to come. Ready, Jane?' I nod back. Smooch the kids. Reapply lipstick in the hallway. Put on my boots.

'Oh, my fucking God,' Alex says when I stand up. 'I think I have to take you upstairs again.'

It is very, very good to be desired.

We do make it out the door. Eventually.

Lacey kisses Alex, me. Then looks like she wants to kiss my boots. 'I am borrowing those boots the next time we go hiking in Banff. Oh, yes. But next time, we go without the kids, *and* we pick up the delicious Danish hitchhikers.' I laugh. She kisses me again. And whispers, 'Sofia's here. Be nice.' And there's Sofia, belly just a little swollen, her dress shorter than mine. And there's Clint.

'Is the other candidate-for-father here?' I ask Lacey. She's shocked.

'Goodness, no,' she says. 'How awkward would that be?' Alex bites his lips. Then my ear. I press up against him just as his phone announces a text message.

'Melanie,' I tell him. 'She's wishing you a Happy New Year, and telling you she's standing by for orders.'

'Do you want to text her back for me?' he asks.

'No,' I say. 'But if you need it, I give you permission to do so.' I brush my lips against his cheek and walk off.

I want to find Marie, reassure myself she's OK. But she's not there, and I do a complete round of the house – see Alex texting, Lacey rubbing Sofia's tummy, Clint looking profoundly uncomfortable – and am sitting in the kitchen, too close to the liquor table, when Marie and JP walk in. He takes a step back when he sees me. I look at him perhaps too intensely. I'm trying to see in him, in this moment, the man who is willing to do anything to keep Marie, to make her happy. And reconcile him with the jerk who wouldn't change diapers. Wanted her to get a boob job. Put her down at every possible occasion. Tried to implode my marriage with innuendo because his was falling apart.

I can't, and I feel my face assume a mask of distaste. And JP must see it.

He turns around. Faces Alex. Alex looks through him. Walks past him right to me.

'May I get you anything, love?' he says, his back pointedly turned on JP.

'A private moment with Marie?' I ask. He refills my wine, then his. Stays beside me, his back to Marie and JP, until I say, 'He's gone.'

'Fucking bastard,' Alex says. Nods to Marie. Leaves.

She doesn't want a private moment with me, that's clear in seconds. She pours herself a glass of wine quickly, jerkily, takes a couple of steps away.

'I'm fine,' she says before I ask. 'Well, I will be fine. And I don't want to talk about it. Any of it.'

'All right,' I say.

'Are you angry?' she asks. And I know she's asking me about what happened with Alex and JP, and afterwards, perhaps, with Alex and me.

'No, never,' I say. 'Never angry at you,' I say. Pause. 'Not even angry at him.' I shrug.

'I'm angry,' she says. 'And . . . I don't want to talk about it.'

'All right,' I say again.

'I'll be fine,' she says again. And walks away. Brushes past Lacey. Disappears into the other room, crowded with people.

Lacey sits beside me.

'You two will be fine,' she says.

'I know,' I tell her. 'And you?'

'Me?' she laughs. 'Always. Always.'

And that, today, I believe.

The house is quiet and dark when we get home. My dad's snoring in the boys' room. Alex staggers upstairs; is asleep before I undress.

It's very late in Montréal. But. I check.

Happy New Year, forever lover.
—So it is. Happy New Year.
Tell me. What did you wear tonight?
—All your favourite things.
Show me.
—I knew you would ask. Sent.
So hot. Dress a little longer than I like. The boots are making me hard, and I'm a little drunk and thoroughly exhausted.

370

You healed quickly.

—My arms, the evidence of you? Yes.

—Good party on your end?

Fine. There was karaoke. But I survived.

You're resilient. That's good.

—I have a story for you.

Oh, yes? From your party?

—Yes. Well. Not the party that was. The party that could have been.

Intrigued.

—Shall I tell it? I can save it for another time. If you're too exhausted.

Tell me.

—The real party – it was at my neighbour's house. This party – it was just the same, but at my house. And it was all right. Friends old, friends new. Wine and beer flowing.

Jäger shots?

—Always.

And you're dressed . . .

—Like in the picture. Shorter dress, if you like.

—It's about 10, 10.30. The doorbell rings, and I go to answer it.

—You're standing in the doorway.

—I stare at you, totally and completely frozen. House full of guests. Including mutual friends of ours. And of course, my husband.

Of course. Type faster. The anticipation is killing me. What do I do?

—You smile. And you say . . .

'Happy New Year, fuckslave.'

—Um, no. 'Aren't you going to let me in?'

I say 'Happy New Year, fuckslave.' Of course you're going to let me in.

—I open the door wider, and you step in. God, you

look good. There's a sprinkling of snow on your hair and your jacket. The cab's pulling away. You tell me something innocuous like 'I've come straight from the airport' but I don't really hear you. The nearness and reality of you are overwhelming.

You don't take me in, to the party. Where do you take me?

—I'm just standing there, in shock. And you look around – we live in this sort of split-level house, where the front door is on the landing – half a staircase goes up to the main living and dining and kitchen area, and the other half down, into the basement.

The basement? With the workout bench? Where you came for me on the telephone the first time?

—Yes. So you look up and down, and down again, and you say, 'What's down there?' And I say – the basement. Gym stuff. Laundry room.

And I say, 'Laundry room.'

—Yes. Were you there?

I am now. Go on. I'm already so hard.

—You push me towards the stairs, and I stumble – my present (I thank you) is hard to walk in. You put an arm around my waist and half-carry me down the stairs. The laundry room is just at the bottom – there's no door on it, just a curtain.

Privacy enough (you're welcome; it is as much a present for me as for you). I push you through the curtain, or do you draw it back?

—I draw it back. It's very small – washer and dryer, a couple of shelves. A lightbulb hanging from the ceiling; just a naked bulb with one of those string-pull things, you know?

—You pull on the light.

I want to see you. Are the washer and dryer stacked or side by side?

—Side by side. I pull off the light.

—'People have been coming down here to get out onto the patio and smoke,' I say.

I don't care.

—It's dark. I reach for you – or you reach for me – and for a while there's just hands and breathing. A little frenetic, as if we each want to make sure the other is really there. It's been a long time.

Five days.

—Five days, five months, five years. An eternity.

Yes. Go on. When do I shove you onto your knees?

—Right away. You say,

'Now.' Or maybe, 'Go to work.'

—'Go to work.' As you undo your belt. I slide down onto my knees, onto the floor. Maybe there are some towels on the floor. I kneel on those. You don't need to shove. But you guide me down with your hands. Keep them in my hair as I fumble with your button and zipper and take you out.

I won't face-fuck you, I want you to work me.

—Yes. I lick and suck – use my teeth, just a little.

You take me deep, it's fucking unbelievable what you can do with your mouth.

—And I'm greedy, and I'm conscious of the time, and worried that I'll be missed upstairs, so I work fast, taking you to the edge.

No fucking way did I just fly across the country to come in your mouth five minutes after I arrived.

—Yes. You pull out and yank me up. Flip me over; lean me against the dryer. Push my dress up.

There better be nothing under that dress.

—There isn't.

There wasn't anything under that dress tonight in real life, was there?

—There was. Short dress. Some sitting required.

Disobedient fucktoy. I will need to punish you later.
—I'm trying to make it up to you now – may I go on with the story?
Of course. Type. Against the dryer.
—You slide into me quickly, I'm so wet, and I've made you so slick. You're bent over me, your torso pressing me into the top of the dryer, your breath on my neck. You kiss my neck, my shoulders. Mark them.
So hard . . .
—So fast. And I bite my lips, and then, I grab a hold of reality, and I say, 'Condom! Ridiculously fertile!'
My fecund lover. I don't want to use a condom. There is no fucking way I'll be able to find one much less get one on in this dark little closet. In the mood I'm in.
—I know. You lean into my ear, and you whisper, 'I'm not planning to come in your fucking pussy.'
So fucking hard. I thank you in advance, fuckslave.
—You pull out, and put your hands over my slit, then inside me. Move your wet fingers to my asshole.
You tense up. You always do.
—Yes. I close my eyes. Make myself relax. Think of this as a gift for you.
It won't hurt as much this time. Maybe I'm lying. But you're so wet, I spread your pussy's wetness all over your ass, inside it. And I'm so slick from your mouth. I thrust into you easily.
—It hurts. I grab onto the sides of the dryer and bury my face in some towels on top of it to keep myself from crying out. Your hands are on my hips, and you're moving quickly, not as frenetic as before, but you do not want to take your time.
Selfish.
—Focused.
Do you relax into me?

—A little. The idea of you – and that you are here – and that I am yours. That gives me so much pleasure, so much ridiculous, excessive joy, the pleasure invades the physical sensation.

Type 'the physical sensation of your cock in my ass.' Don't engage in literary euphemisms.

—The physical sensation of your cock in my ass.

—Your hands move to my clit and my pussy.

—I flail my hands, accidentally turn on the dryer.

Your attention to detail in fantasy is fucking hot. Typing with one hand . . .

—Do you ever type with two hands to me, my lover?

—The dryer whooshes. Footsteps on stairs. And that's when you cum.

In your ass.

—Yes.

Type it.

—In my ass. Jeezus. And then you say,

'And now you can cum.'

—Yes. And you stroke me a little, but you don't really have to do much, I orgasm on your command.

One of my favourite things about you. Tell me about the footsteps.

—Past the curtain, through the basement, to the patio door. We hear the door slam.

I turn on the light; I want to look at you.

—Yes. We're both a little dishevelled.

I rather think I pick you up and sit you on the dryer.

—You do. You spread my legs and look at me.

At your pussy.

—Yes.

Fucking type it.

—At my pussy. I'm shaking. You look at my wetness, my juices mixed with yours, seeping out of my ass, and I

375

know you're trying to decide whether to clean me up or not.

I don't.

—But you're considerate enough to know that if I walk upstairs with cum streaking down my legs, questions may arise that will compromise our enjoyment of the rest of the evening.

I suppose. Fucking reality. Seeping even into the most perfect of fantasies . . .

—You take one of the towels I was kneeling on and press it against my thighs, just a little. I stay wet, but not dripping.

—Then you fix my stockings and garters.

—Your jeans still unzipped, belt hanging. Shirt out.

Fix me.

—In a moment. You're not finished yet. You readjust my dress. And put your hands in my hair, smooth it down a bit. Use your sleeve to wipe the saliva and spit from my chin and the corners of my mouth.

'Your eyes are smudged.'

—'There's a mirror in the front entryway, I'll fix them before we go up.'

—Now, when I was thinking of this story, you button yourself up while I watch. Do you want me to fix you instead?

You're doing a fine job with the story. As you scripted it.

—You do up your jeans, the belt, while I watch from atop the dryer. And then we just look at each other for a while.

Seeing ourselves in the other.

—Yes. And then, I take you up to the party. Checking my eye makeup in the mirror on the way up. You right behind me, your pelvis pressed against my ass, reminding me.

Is it hard to walk up the stairs, in those boots, after being fucked in the ass?

—It's awkward.

—I take you up. The people who know you, they're so excited to see you. It's been years. You lie. You say you were passing through town on something – whatever – you saw the chatter about the party on Facebook – and you couldn't resist dropping in.

Does anyone notice there was an interval between my arrival upstairs and the last doorbell?

—Perhaps they do. Perhaps they exchange looks or raise eyebrows. We don't care.

No. And then what happens, my story-spinning whore?

—Well. Several different endings. In the least plausible one, you close down the party, and as you're helping clean up, and Alex thanks you, you say, 'Don't thank me. I'm only here to fuck your wife. Are you going to watch?'

I think this is the image I will be cumming to when I release you. Fuck. But implausible.

—Never going to happen. And the thing about effective fantasy, is it has to seem like it might happen.

Next scenario?

—Alex has too much to drink and goes upstairs to sleep. Everyone else leaves. And you take me to the basement and tie me to the exercise equipment and fuck me all night.

This one has potential too. Although I like the humiliated husband scenario better.

—You would.

—Or – you don't even go upstairs. Leave right after you fuck me. To catch a flight that gets you home for morning.

Crass.

—You did what you came for.

Hot.
—Well. I can barely keep my eyes open, my lover. And the little people will be up in a couple of hours, I bet.
I release you.
But first – what are you?
—Yours.
—Utterly.
Mine. My what?
—Your whore, your fuckslave. Just – yours. And what are you?
Your owner. Your forever lover. Your counterpart.
—xx
xo

Day 30 – Unresolutions

New Year's Day , Tuesday, January 1

It's a beautiful sunny winter's day, a perfect day for new beginnings and new resolutions and remaking and re-imagining everything, but as I lie stretched out in bed, Alex's tousled head on one side of me, Annie's tiny forehead pressed into my armpit on the other side – when the heck did she crawl into our bed? I don't even remember – and I hear the noise of Henry and Eddie and all the other kids downstairs, and smell – bacon? Is my dad making bacon? Oh, yes – I don't want anything to change. I want all this. I want all this, to be all this: wife, mother, daughter, friend.

Lover.

I caress Annie's baby-not-so-baby-any-more cheeks. Then kiss the nape of Alex's neck. I love him. I want him. Just as he is. Just as we are.

But I want the other too. The lover. The demon. The madness.

Unsustainable. Will I be able to keep it? Keep this, and the other?

I walk down the stairs quietly, and stand in the entryway to the kitchen. The kids are all crowded around the table. My dad's frying bacon and pancakes. He looks . . . very, very happy. He gives me a peck on the cheek and another 'Look what a good grandfather I am' look.

By the time he goes home, I know he is resolved to call the widow and ask her out for . . . something or other. And also that he thinks he has my permission, if not precisely approval, to do so. Did I give it? I'm not sure.

I did not withhold it, anyway.

I get a text from Marie: 'I love you. I'm sorry about last night. And I apologise in advance for today and tomorrow. And the days after.' I don't write back: that's Marie asking for space and permission to not talk to me for a while, and that I can give her best with silence.

A text from Nicola, 'Yes!' And then, 'Will come get the boys by noon, promise. Yes! Yes!' And, oh, fuck, from Jesse, again: 'For you.' And another: 'I'm not suggesting you owe me. Just that – this is for you. Not her.' I think he's probably being sweet. I think. Possibly manipulative. I will evaluate next time I see him at the gym. I really do not want to have to get another trainer. I like him. All the more for making Nicola happy, whatever his reasons, however briefly.

Another text from my mom: 'Had a great time at the BALL last night. Danced until 5 a.m. May the next year be full of WONDERFUL new beginnings for us all. Love, Mom.'

New beginnings?

I really don't want any new beginnings. I don't want anything to change. I just want a series of continuations.

Unsustainable.

I know this.

But.

For now, for today, I make no resolutions.

After

I'm waiting for Marie, and, as I stir my latte, I realise I'm waiting for her in the café in which I encountered Craig. Still her current lover – more accurately, *one* of her current lovers. But then, she doesn't know that this is where I met him, so it's OK.

She's late, and for a few minutes I worry she won't come. I haven't seen her much lately. I miss her.

But there she is. And she almost runs to the table and wraps her arms around me before I get up.

I guess she missed me too.

'Why aren't you drinking a mocha?' she demands, looking at the milk and cinnamon in my drink. 'Our drinks! Mochas and Caesars! And wine! What is this shit? Jane, I swear to fucking God, if you are drinking a non-fat green chai soy-milk latte, we are done!'

'You may order me a mocha,' I say, and then she's back at our table with two mochas, smothered with whipped cream. And she smiles at me.

'I'm good,' she says before I ask. 'I really am.'

I nod. She looks good. And I've been hearing that she's good. From Nicola. Colleen. The other divorced women. Who've extended their unconditional love and support to her even though it was she, and not her cheating rat-fuck bastard of a husband, who did the cheating and leaving. Or, to be strictly accurate, it was she who had the *intention* to cheat. Confessed the intention. Dealt with the fall-out. And left. She didn't *lie* to him, at least in the end. Is that why the other wronged wives have forgiven her, embraced her? I don't know. The secrets of the Sisterhood of the Divorcées are not mine to know.

Marie and JP's divorce – 'It's all official now?' I ask, and she nods – was, to everyone's shock and surprise, *not* a gongshow. It was JP's second, and how he treated Marie and his children throughout the process did more to impress me with his value as a human being than anything he did for them while the marriage was intact.

'He learned the price of acrimony the first time,' Alex said sceptically when I mentioned this.

Perhaps. Still. He learned.

'I'm sorry I've been so distant,' Marie says suddenly, interrupting an irrelevant, but amusing, story of her latest Lavalife hook-up.

'It's all right,' I say.

'You say that to me a lot,' Marie says. Laughs. I shrug.

She doesn't say I shrug a lot. I know I do. We smile at each other. She gives herself a whipped-cream moustache, and then starts to talk again. Some of it I already know, because we have not been totally estranged – just not as close as before. She wants to make sure I don't resent her drifting closer to Nicola, Colleen and the 'other divorced wives'. I don't. I understand. What do I know about the competence of family lawyers, fiscal disclosure, Canadian child-support guidelines, co-parenting plans or the challenges of being always the only parent in the house? Or why, when he wants to switch a Tuesday night for a Wednesday night, it's a massively big deal that, three out of four times, ends in a shouting match or another appointment with the mediator? Nothing.

I am not what she needs at this stage of her life.

She lauds JP's performance as a divorcing husband. 'I don't think I've ever loved him more than the day we actually signed the papers,' she says. 'Isn't that terrible? But also telling?'

382

I laud her performance as a divorcing wife. She complained and railed against the man for years. But there isn't much bitterness or anger in her right now.

Of course, she is the one who left.

But then, Nicola's the one who left too.

But then, first, Paul cheated.

But then . . . I interrupt that train of thought. It has no purpose.

Neither does this thought, but still it comes, and I let it: I wonder whether, between the spirit of openness and total honesty polyamorous Paul espouses, and the newly found camaraderie Marie and Nicola now share, one or the other of them has felt compelled to tell Nicola about their briefest-of-sexting-flings.

'Jane? Where have you gone?' Marie demands. 'You always do this. You float off.'

I apologise. Focus.

'Nicola's gone a bit pudgy and flabby since she's stopped seeing Jesse,' Marie says with more than a tinge of bite, and I decide that *if* Nicola knows about Paul and Marie, it wasn't Marie who told her. And if Nicola does know, she did not take the revelation well. 'How about you? Are you back with him?'

'Yes,' I tell her. 'I lasted for, what, two months? I tried other trainers. It just wasn't the same. I really missed him. So one day, after a really terrible session with Ilsa, Queen of the Nazi Love Camp, I texted him . . . oh, what did I say? "I hate my new trainer. I miss you. Can I please come back?"'

'Short and to the point,' Marie approves. 'And he? Opened his arms?'

'Well . . .' I pause. 'He said . . . "Only if you promise to never ask me to mercyfuck one of your friends again."'

I don't tell her this part of the message: 'And the next time there's something I shouldn't see, fucking wear long sleeves.' Or the tight, blanched look on his face on the occasions when

I've kept a long-sleeved, high-necked shirt or hoodie on throughout a workout.

Sometimes, the cover-up communicates as much as the disclosure.

But even though I don't tell her everything, I've told her enough, and Marie howls with as much abandon as she did when I told her what happened with Nicola and Jesse and why. No, she definitely did not tell Nicola about her brief interlude with Paul. The bonds in the Sisterhood of Divorcées are not, I think, that strong.

Our bond? I'm not sure it will ever be the same either.

Marie's telling me about Craig and his freak-out and pull-back when she told him she was leaving JP.

'I've never seen a man more terrified,' she says, laughing, and I wonder how long it was before she was able to laugh. And if, in the moment it happened, she laughed, or if she felt betrayed, abandoned – the same vulnerable, mad Marie who sobbed over the Zoltans, the Pauls. 'He was *terrified* I was leaving JP for him. He didn't understand at all that I just wanted to be, well, not alone, exactly, but . . .'

'Unfettered,' I supply.

'Yes!' she shouts. 'Unfettered. That's the word. Anyway. It's all good now. Although it's quite funny, you know. He doesn't want to leave his wife for me or for anyone else. He doesn't want to be the love of my life. But anytime the conversation skirts the idea that there are other men in my life – he does not like that. At all.'

'Few men do,' I say. Don't think of Matt. Fail.

Of course you do. She is unfettered. And you?
—Tethered. Always.
The image of you tethered. Appeals. In so many ways.
—And you? You're free?
It takes two.
—Two.

'But we're talking just about me, as we always do,' Marie says. 'What's been happening with you? How are things?'

So I tell her – about Clint and Lacey. Their amazing fairy-tale wedding. Lacey's red dress – 'Yeah, it was gorgeous, I saw it on Facebook,' Marie says – and Clayton and Marcello being co-ring-boys and co-flower-boys. Sofia sitting at the head table. ('They know for sure the baby's his, then?' 'No, actually, it's not his – it's the other guy's. But he's gone . . . so Clint will effectively be the daddy for Marcello's little brother anyway . . .' 'And Lacey the stepmom?' 'Yup.') And the most important part of the story, for me anyway, the denouement. It's still vivid in my memory: Lacey sliding in between me and Alex. 'Isn't it a perfect day?' 'Oh, yes, absolutely.' 'I just wanted to tell you two, in case you were worried, Jane, that you'd have to get used to having new neighbours to ignore or something, that nothing else is going to change.' And my immediate horror – until that moment, it hadn't occurred to me that Lacey would sell the house and move, of course Clint was going to move in . . . but oh-my-God, of course, they will want to buy a new house together, this is what people do when they get married, what the fuck am I going to do without Lacey next door to me?

But before the panic manages to totally consume me, Lacey saves me, says, 'Clint's keeping his apartment, and I'm keeping the house. We're going to spend even more time together, I'm sure, but we've decided we each need to maintain our own space.'

'Oh-my-fucking-God,' Marie says. 'So – married, but living separately? Jesus. Only Lacey.'

'Well, it's been like that for – it's got to be close to a year now,' I say. 'Or eleven years, if you count back from when they first hooked up. Seems to be working. They seem happy – as together as ever.'

'And she has her wedding band,' Marie says.

'She has her wedding band,' I echo. Finger mine.

And then I tell her about my mother, married to her high-school sweetheart at twenty, and now rediscovering dating at 64. 'And it's crazy, Marie. She loves it. She's on all the websites – Match.com is her favourite, I think. She's got three or four different coffee dates a week. Two "gentlemen friends" – seriously, that's what she calls them, how much more Victorian can you get? – she's very fond of and sees regularly.' I don't add that I'm pretty sure she's sexting. Or doing her 'ladylike' version of that. I see her with her phone in her hands often. Very often.

'Good for her,' Marie says. And then: 'And is it hard for you to watch?'

'A little,' I confess. 'Well, a lot. But, you know. It is what it is.'

'And your dad?'

My dad. That's actually harder to watch. My dad is shacked up with the little widow. He's used the word 'soulmate' in front of me once and, as blood drained not just from my face but possibly my heart, never again. I haven't been to their new place. Nor have the children. He understands, he says. I'll probably get over it. But maybe not.

He comes over and spends lots of time with the kids. He and Alex go out for the occasional beer. He and I still do our first-Thursday-of-the-month lunch. But. I'm still struggling.

I tell this to Marie, and then I tell her about this past Christmas, which made the previous year's worst-Christmas-ever look like a Hallmark family get-together. My father back in what is now my mother's house. Alone, of course, because it 'wouldn't do' to bring the widow to such an event. And then, my mother's 'gentleman friend' dropping in to wish her a Merry Christmas. My father's reaction.

'They were still screaming at each other as Alex and I ran the kids to the car,' I say. 'Annie and Eddie crying, because we didn't open presents. Cassandra crying because Gran and Gramps were fighting. She'd never seen them fight, you know

– it was always her sniping and him giving way. And now . . . wow. Alex was laughing – he denies it, but I swear he was laughing. Me, I was feeling I was living in a really, really bad soap opera.'

'Is it wrong that I sort of love it?' Marie asks, and we both laugh. 'And Alex's father?' she asks.

'Still with Jeanette,' I say. And choose to say no more. Alex's relationship with him is, really, no better. What it was, I imagine, when he had first left Alex's mother for Jeanette. So perhaps a little better than when he left Jeanette for Claire.

'And Claire's remarried. Pregnant,' I add. Marie makes the appropriate exclamations of congratulations and interest, but Claire is very tangential to both of our lives, so she does not really care. Falls silent, and so do I.

I look up from my coffee cup to find her eyes boring into me.

'But what's happening with you?' she demands. 'With *you*. Not Clint and Lacey, not your parents, not Alex's dad. With *you*.'

I know what she wants to hear. But, instead:

'The life ride continues,' I say with a smile. 'Another year, another anniversary. Each kid a year older. Comfortable. Sometimes boring, sometimes annoying. Quotidian life interspersed with bouts of hot sex. Ennui punctured with passion. Fights, making up. Laundry, dishes, dinner, interlude for a date. You know.'

No. She isn't satisfied. This is not what she wants to know, and what she wants to know, I won't tell her. But. I can tell her this.

'Do you remember Shelley-Susan-Melanie?' I ask. And Marie laughs.

'The latest office wife,' she says. 'Whose name is Melanie, as you fucking well know.'

'Melanie,' I concede. 'Anyway. In an overture of grand marital co-operation, we invited her and her fiancé over for dinner.'

'Oh, Jesus,' Marie loves it. 'Was it awful?'

'Not totally awful. But, yeah – awkward. She spent the whole evening talking only to Alex about work. Ignoring me and the fiancé with equal abandon. The fiancé spent the whole evening seething with resentment, feeling left out. Slighted.'

'And what did Jane do? Did you space out as you always do?'

I'm mildly offended. I don't space out – OK, whatever. I do. But not that time.

'No, actually, I stayed fairly engaged,' I tell her. 'I watched the interplay with . . .'

'Amused contempt,' Marie supplies. I shrug. Hard not to agree.

'That about describes it. I heard them fighting in our driveway as they were leaving. They're still engaged, though.'

'And you never have to have them over for dinner again,' Marie says. Then, abruptly: 'Do you think Alex is fucking her?'

'Her? No.' I shake my head. 'I don't think he even particularly wants to. He likes the attention, though.'

'And you'd just let him, if he wanted to,' Marie says. 'Like JP said he'd let me.'

We are nearing dangerous ground here, and I want to pull away. But I'm shrugged out.

'Not a fan of the emotional striptease,' I tell Marie. 'And, you know. Not insecure. Alex and I, we're good. Solid. It's about the long play. The endgame.'

'Fine,' Marie says. 'But you know what I want to know. Come on, Jane. This is me. Tell me. Tell me about . . .' Her voice trails off.

She doesn't know exactly what it is she is asking for. But, of course, I know what it is she wants to hear.

She wants to hear you're my whore.
—She wants to hear that we fuck.

388

*Do you think she could still look at you if she knew
how?*
—I expect so. That's not why I don't tell.
If you were going to tell her – what would you say?

What would I say?

I could tell her about . . . events. My extremely indirect
flight to Toronto – via Montréal. Or his last client visit to
YYC. The memory still makes my skin tingle, my cheeks burn.
My clit tingle . . .

I could tell her about the brutality and intense eroticism of
cramming twenty years of intimacy, ten years of estrangement,
six months of passion and mindfucking into one night, one
hour.

I could tell her about the ecstasy and bliss and . . . fuck,
tranquillity and release that come when this other, this mindfuck, augments and fits reality so perfectly and so well – when
the rhythms of real life and this secret mind-life are in perfect
sync, and in as near a perfect balance as anything involving
sex and lust and madness and life can be.

But then I would have to tell her about the times when the
mindfuck reaches such a pitch that it all seems more real than
the grittiest, grimiest reality. When it's clear, painfully clear,
that the consequences aren't just in our heads. But affect our
reality. Our other loves.

And that, I could tell her, that is when it ends. And oh,
fuck, it is so hard, could I tell her that? How fucking hard
it is to stop, to not – reach out. Respond. So hard. Walking
on the verge of tears for a week. A month. And then – the
discipline breaks down. 'More difficult than I would have
imagined. Like I'm missing an arm.' Such pain. And what
next? Three words: 'Always thinking. Always.' Two words:
'Tell me.' And . . . what next? Has there been enough space?
Are we sufficiently anchored in what is real again? Is it, again,
just about us, release, lust? 'Yours. Always.' Or, 'Lover. Do

not come to me if you need to disappear again. This kills me.'

And then, 'Good. I do not want to suffer alone.'

And silence.

So much silence, restraint. Recognition of the unsustainable. Submission to . . . reality.

And then, an eruption. Like a volcano, oh, fuck, at the most inappropriate time . . .

Are you there?

—Yes.

I want you to cum for me. On command. Right now.

—I'm on the verge of cumming every time I write with you.

I know. So fucking cum now.

—I can't touch myself where I am.

—Want me to perform? Mindfuck me over the edge.

Ask properly.

—Your whore says, mindfuck me over the edge, master.

Just do what you're fucking told; I'm not your cunt's babysitter; I'm its owner.

Give it to me.

I own it.

—yours

Now show me it's a well-trained pussy you've given me.

—Well – fucking hell

My shameless whore. Is that all it took?

—Hiding my face so what just happened isn't writ large on it

Tell me your surroundings, whore

—In the library at fucking story time Matt. I'm sitting up against the wall fucking you while my kids watch a puppet play. I'm so clearly in-fucking-sane.

More proof of ownership. I like it. Do you want to know where I am?

—No. Will knowing make me feel better?
No. Worse. Shamed. Degraded.
Aware of your true place.
—At your fucking feet.
At my feet. Yes.
We are destined for this.
Made for this.
—Terrifying.
Yes.
—Go. xx
Gone. xo

And then, again, the silence, suffering, shame. Because we are entwined . . . made for this . . . but unsustainable. Wrong. Always.

I could tell her a lot about how unsustainable doesn't really mean what she thinks it means. Or how you can hope for things to burn out and long for the return of sanity – and then, when it looks like it's all ebbed and burned out, at least for now, how you . . . how *I* suffer. I could tell her a lot about suffering. And how it's worth it, every moment of angst, every tear, because of the ecstasy when it fires up again. And I could tell her about the inevitability of the cycle. The compulsion of it.

But maybe she's learning all that through her Lavalife affairs.

Probably not.

Would she understand? I don't know. I do not know what of this story is life's archetype and what is our own personal chemistry, our own unique insanity.

Does it matter?
—Maybe not. What does matter?
Perfect trust, perfect understanding. The purity of our lust.
—Sophist.
Whore.

—Harlot.
Two of a kind.

And I could tell her that right now, in this moment, I do not know if we are suspended or spent, burned out or still burning. I do not know if we are in a period of silence that will last weeks, months or another decade or if there will be a message waiting for me the next time I check my phone. And I could tell her how sometimes that uncertainty doesn't matter – how I feel such complete surrender and trust that it doesn't matter. Or such anger, resentment, fury at my tethers that I don't want it to matter, and expend all my energy in forcing myself to live as if it does not matter. And sometimes it's all that matters, and when I think of what he is, what I am, what we are, I can barely breathe and I long for only one thing.

And that is?
—To kneel down at your feet.

But. I won't tell; I do not tell. It is not that I fear judgement, not from my Marie. Or even betrayal, although I remember that in the depth of her angst and anguish, even with no knowledge, she acted as though she had power of disclosure over me, and she wielded it, clumsily and bluntly, against her husband, who, in his pain, tried to wield it against me.

But that doesn't matter.

I don't tell, because . . . I do not want her to try to understand.

This story, this part of me belongs only to him. To no one else. No one else sees it; no one else needs to understand.

I do not want anyone to try to understand what I barely understand myself.

It just is.

I just am.

His.

So, instead:

'Are you happy?' I ask. And Marie thrusts her eyes at me and thinks, really thinks about the answer.

'Yes,' she says finally. 'Yes, I am. Mostly.'

'Good,' I say. 'So am I. Mostly.'

And that's enough. For now.

Tell me.
—Yours.
Good.

Life continues.